FEB 1 5

The SECRETS
of
LIFE *and* DEATH

The SECRETS

of

LIFE *and* DEATH

Rebecca Alexander

B\D\W\Y
BROADWAY BOOKS
NEW YORK

Copyright © 2013 by Rebecca Alexander
Reader's Guide copyright © 2014 by Random House LLC

All rights reserved.
Published in the United States by Broadway Books, an imprint of the
Crown Publishing Group, a division of Random House LLC,
a Penguin Random House Company, New York.
www.crownpublishing.com

Broadway Books and its logo, B\D\W\Y,
are trademarks of Random House LLC.

Originally published in the United Kingdom by Del Rey, an imprint
of Ebury Publishing, a Random House Group Company, in 2013.

Library of Congress Cataloging-in-Publication Data
is available upon request.

ISBN 978-0-8041-4068-3
eBook ISBN 978-0-8041-4069-0

Printed in the United States of America

Book design by Lauren Dong
Cover photographs: (street) Gallery Stock;
(girl) Christian Cueni/Flickr Open/Getty Images

10 9 8 7 6 5 4 3 2 1

First U.S. Edition

To the seven special people I have had
the privilege of helping to bring up:
Léonie, Jennie, Sophie, Carey, Sam, Isaac and Rosie.

PROLOGUE

When I was a boy, on one frosted morning, my father bade me dig out a pile of rotting straw that was obstructing the stable. I took a shovel and plunged it into the heap. Within, a knot of serpents in their winter sleep had been injured by my blade. One had been cut almost in two, and their bodies writhed together even in the depths of their hibernation, the severed bodies pumping blood upon their brethren. That night, I was reminded, as the bodies of the count and his lady writhed together over the bloodied limbs of Zsófia, the witch. The countess, no longer with the grayness of death upon her skin, looked young again. Her teeth were stained with the witch's blood, and her body scarred with the symbols I had seen burned and carved into her living flesh. I knew then that I was damned, and the sorcery we had completed would haunt the world.

But at the beginning of our journey, I knew nothing but the flattering invitation of King Istvan Báthory to travel through his beautiful but barbarous country to aid his dying niece, the Countess Elizabeth Báthory.

—EDWARD KELLEY
St. Clément's Eve, 1585

On paper owned by Ms. Jackdaw Hammond, translated from the Latin original by Professor Felix Guichard, retained in evidence in the case of the death of SADIE BETHANY WILLIAMS, coroner case no. 238956-3-12

Chapter 1

ANOTHER CRIME SCENE, A DEAD BODY AND POSSIBLE EVI-dence of sorcery. Felix stood in the car park, and watched the activity in the railway station in Exeter. His gut squirmed at the thought of what he would see. He assumed the police became accustomed to seeing bodies, but he never had, despite spending time in Liberia and the Ivory Coast, where human life had become disposable. He pulled his collar up against the rain.

The station was lit by temporary lights on stands, illuminating one of the carriages of a static train. Felix paused at the entrance. The last crime scene he had attended involved an elderly woman stabbed to death, and her yawning wounds had haunted him for weeks. The police had consulted him on some "black magic" graffiti, which had turned out to be the logo of a death metal band. He took a deep breath, blew it out. Hopefully, his involvement in this case would be unnecessary as well.

A movement caught his attention as he walked across the car park. There was a woman standing in the rain a dozen yards from the ticket office, looking through the railings toward the train. She appeared to be watching the police as they worked, but her posture was odd and she didn't look like a chance spectator observing a tragedy. The rain poured off a hat, the brim sheltering her face, which was whitened by flashes from the scene. She wore a long coat, with water streaming down it, and what looked like boots. She was definitely female; her features looked delicate in a long face, framed by short fair hair that was haloed against the arc lights. She was young, he thought, younger than him, anyway. Her attention to the scene was intense.

He turned away and approached the officer at the gate.

"Sorry, sir, the station is closed. There's a bus to take passengers to the next station." The policeman had water running from the edge of a cap, dropping in silver lines down the wide shoulders of his coat.

"I was asked to attend. I'm supposed to ask for Detective Inspector Soames."

"I see. Can I have your name, sir?"

"Felix Guichard. Professor Guichard, from the university."

The man nodded to another officer, a woman who stared straight through Felix, then looked away.

Felix's eyes began to adjust to the glare. Through the gate, he could see cast-iron columns supporting the roof of the station, the grandeur somewhat marred by billboards and modern wooden benches. A police barrier obscured the view of the window of one of the carriages. A number of people were walking about in white suits. Flashes lit up one carriage, greening the scene with afterimages.

A bleached figure beckoned to him. "Professor? Professor Gwitchard? Is that how you pronounce it?"

"Well, it's Gwee-shar. It's a French name." A gap appeared in the ranks and he walked through to the white-suited officer.

"DI Dan Soames." The man's hand was warm and solid in the drafty, wet station. "We were hoping you could have a look at this scene for us. You're a professor of what, exactly?"

"My subject is the culture of belief systems, religions and superstitions. I've worked with your chief constable before, on a case of a witchcraft killing in London." Inside he was shivering. Soames was maybe five foot eight or nine, inches shorter than Felix, but had a restrained energy that made him seem like a larger man.

"Well, these markings have us stumped. Any ideas why someone would draw all over a dead kid are welcome. You'll have to suit up."

Felix followed him into a tented area, where a young man helped him into a one-piece coverall and booties.

"Tuck your hair in, sir," the young officer said. "We're still looking for DNA and trace evidence."

Felix pushed his curly fringe back. A single flash from a camera illuminated an image, which glowed for a moment in his brain.

It was the face of a girl, just a teenager, blond hair stuck to damp glass, over pearl-colored skin. She must have slid down the window, her eyebrow dragged into a curve, and her open eye stared, it seemed, straight at Felix.

Soames's voice scratched into Felix's awareness.

"Professor of superstitions and religions?"

"My subject is social anthropology, but I specialize in esoteric belief systems."

"Esoteric what?"

Felix tore his attention away from the fading image of the girl. "Beliefs outside of a culture's mainstream. My PhD was in West African beliefs. Witchcraft, sorcery, magic."

Soames shrugged his shoulders and tucked the hood of his coverall closer around his face. "We're investigating the disappearance of several young girls from the town."

"Oh, I see. Is this one of them?"

"Possibly. The thing is, there are symbols—come and have a look. We were told you've done this sort of consulting before and attended crime scenes."

Felix followed him along the platform and into the doorway of the carriage. "A few times. Do you know what happened? How she died?"

"We're not sure. It looks like an overdose, but it's too early to tell."

He led the way toward the end of the carriage, where a scrum of white figures was strobed with camera flashes.

"Can we have a look at the body, Jim?" At Soames's approach, people fell back a little, some to the other side of the aisle, some to the corridor between the two carriages. The faint sour odor of the toilet was signposted with a glowing "Vacant" sign.

Felix squeezed between two officers to look down on the body.

At first, tiny details hit him. Her hand, lying on its back, her fingers curved like a dead crab on the beach. Her lips were distorted by the glass into a half smile, their lavender skin parted to show a few gleaming teeth. The space in front of her was covered with litter left for the train cleaner at the end of the journey. Felix wondered how many people had discarded used paper cups and newspapers on her table, walking past the slumped girl without realizing she was dead.

Soames gripped his shoulder. "You OK, Professor?"

"Yes." He cleared his throat. "Yes. You said there were symbols?"

Soames nodded to the man sitting beside the body, and he lifted the bottom of her T-shirt with gloved hands.

Felix flinched as her pale skin was revealed. Red marks crisscrossed her body, and for a moment he thought they were injuries. Then he realized she had been marked with red pen.

"That's an Enochian symbol." As the shirt was lifted higher and the slack skin on her belly was revealed, more symbols appeared in two concentric curves. "And that one, too. I don't recognize all of them. Two circles of what look like sigils." He bent forward, to get a better look, and caught the flowery scent of clean laundry and the acrid smell of voided urine from the body. Sadness rolled over him, and he looked at her face for a moment. So young. The surface of her eye was just touching the glass, starting to lose its gloss as it dried.

"We'll photograph them at the postmortem." Soames stepped back into the aisle, away from the actual scene. "So, what are these drawings?"

"Enochian symbols. They're supposed to be an alphabet given to John Dee, an Elizabethan scholar. He got them through a man named Edward Kelley, who channeled angels for him."

"Channeled?"

"Like a psychic speaking for the dead." Felix's mind was flying through memories. The arrangement of the characters in a circle seemed familiar.

"You believe all this?" Soames was staring at him.

"Of course not, but some people do. These symbols are used in ritual magic."

"Like black magic, Satanism?"

"Colloquially, yes, I suppose so." Felix leaned in for a closer look. "But black magic wouldn't necessarily use Enochian sigils, and I can't see any pseudo-Christian shapes. I think you can rule out Satanism."

"Sigils?"

"Designs that are supposed to construct magical intent. Magic talismans and lucky charms sometimes have them." Felix stepped back, his legs shaky, whether with tiredness or adrenaline he couldn't tell. "I've never heard of them being used in this way."

"After we photograph them at the postmortem, we'll let you have a better look. The pathologist says there appear to be more on her back."

Felix took a deep breath, and stepped out of the circle of genderless suits gathered around the girl. She glowed in the light of arc lamps, propped over the backs of surrounding seats. Soames followed him.

"You OK?" Soames brushed the hood back from his face.

"Yes, fine. It just seems sad—she's so young."

"First thoughts?"

"I'll wait for the photographs and then do a bit of research. Inspector, are the symbols in complete circles?"

Soames nodded. "We think so; we'll know more at the postmortem. It looks like two concentric rings of maybe a dozen or so shapes in each, drawn in some kind of pen. Why do you ask?"

"I'm not sure . . . I think I've seen something like it before, that's all."

Soames ushered him off the train and started stripping off the white suit. "I'm sure I don't need to remind you to keep this confidential, Professor."

"No, of course."

Soames smiled. "We don't want a big 'black-magic sacrifice' headline in the local press."

"I understand. But there is no evidence, in the UK anyway, of Satanist sacrifices of any kind."

Soames's smile faded. "What about that boy, hacked up in London? I hear you were consulted on that one."

"That was a different kind of case altogether. A Muti killing, taking body parts to make magical charms. Terrible, but from a different belief system completely." Felix dropped the suit and booties into a bin. "Anyway, you said this case is probably an overdose?"

"Maybe. She was a known drug user and prostitute. But we have three other young women who have gone missing over the last few months. Normally, we trace them to London or they've run off with boyfriends, but we haven't had even a whisper about these girls. No texts, e-mails, no social networking, nothing. Then one turns up dead."

"Well, get the pictures to me and I'll do the research. I noticed someone in the car park. A woman, she looked distressed, like she might have known the girl . . ."

"What did she look like?" Soames scanned the station.

"I suppose, medium height, slim, attractive, shortish hair . . . blond. Striking. Thirties, maybe, it was hard to tell." He looked across the tarmac, the rain drifting through cones of light onto parked vehicles.

The woman had vanished.

Chapter 2

It is said that the wolves of the Klaj, or the royal hunting forest of Niepolomice, are the largest in the world, fed as they are upon the great aurochs and bison that dwell there. Also the bodies of peasants, thrown out by cruel masters onto the frozen ground when graves cannot be dug, which has given them a taste for human flesh.

—EDWARD KELLEY
   Journal entry, 11 November 1585
   The Royal Road from Krakow

THE DARKNESS WAS FILLING THE SPACES BETWEEN THE trees when the first howl rang out. My horse flinched and tossed her head, I had to cling to the high-pommeled Magyar saddle. The mare stumbled behind the main party, flinching at the echo of the strange sound, neither hound nor man. I looked about me, the cry hung around the black trunks lining the forest road. The horse flared her nostrils, huffing in the cold air, rolling her eyes back at me. Whatever she scented put a judder in her trot. Veils of mist dropped through the canopy. Dew beaded on my cloak and ran off the brim of my hat. I turned in the saddle to look behind me, but the silent trees seemed empty.

Doctor John Dee, my master, sat tall atop a great horse. He was draped about in the cloak given to him by Her Maj-

esty Queen Elizabeth herself, at Greenwich palace after Dee
had demonstrated necromancy. Another howl, this one more of
a shriek, was cut short by a deep rumbling. I jumped, and the
nag's ears flattened onto its sweaty neck.

"God preserve us," I prayed, clutching the pommel. I resisted the urge to cross myself, clinging instead to the greasy
leather. Our rented house in Krakow, my mentor's wife cooking, the sound of Dee's children playing—all of it felt very far
away. I longed for Richmond and the library at Mortlake.

Once out of the city, this country closed in on all travelers.
No one dawdled on these roads, or ventured off the track into
miles of dense forest. I had long since lost all sense of where
we were. Dee was the navigator, keen to add to his collection
of maps and charts. We met few people on the road, and they
treated us with equal suspicion. The Hungarian Magyars galloped everywhere on shaggy ponies, often with swords in their
hands. The Poles traveled in armed caravans, guarding themselves against the Hungarians, the Lithuanians, the gypsies
and, most of all, the forest. I caught a drop of the mist on my
tongue. Winter came early in the mountains of Poland; the rain
had the taste of melted snow.

A flicker of movement in the edge of my vision made me lean
back in the saddle. In the scrub that separated the forest from
the road, blackened brambles shivered and cast silver droplets
to the ground. The lead escort shouted to his countrymen with
urgency in his tone. They kicked their horses into a canter,
Dee's horse swept along with them as the party rode away from
me. I shouted at my steed in good English, then in poor German, but all the rangy mare could manage was a jaw-jarring
trot. Then I saw it, a gray pelt sliding between decaying brack-
ens. The wolf—for it was certainly no dog—threw back a long
snout over the leaves, and howled with an eerie, halting voice.

The sound echoed between the trees. I could see, in the
fading light, Dee's horse being dragged by one of the bear-

skinned escorts toward a bend in the track. Dee was looking back, his face and long beard pale against his scarlet cloak, as the wolf loped onto the road. My mount stopped abruptly and only the saddlebow stopped me from sliding over its neck. The horse squealed, backing, hooves catching on the road. I saw other shadow shapes oiling out of the undergrowth, hesitant at first, then bolder. They were thin, their bellies arched like siege mongrels, open mouths bloodred in the grays of dusk. I kicked the horse with renewed energy and it was startled into a canter past the wolf before us. Another leapt at the horse's throat but a cut from my whip made it cringe away. It was then that I felt my seat slide loose on the horse's back, the girth slack. Perhaps when she had stopped, it had loosened or snapped. The saddle, with both packs tied to it and I perched between them, fell into the road. I managed to land on one foot and to stagger into the crowding creatures, waving the whip. One of the beasts had stopped the mare again, who was now screaming in panic, backing step by step toward me and my protection. She lurched into me, so I lost my footing for a moment. The stumble to one knee brought the gleam of white teeth all around me as they closed in. I lashed out with the whip, and shouted at them in English. A few wolves scattered but then re-formed into a loose circle of gleaming fangs and scarlet tongues.

The gurgle of the horse made me turn. She was caught by the throat, and fell to her knees even as she tried to pull away, her gaping mouth and whitened eyes a horrible sight. I used the distraction to grab at my leather pack, wrestling with the straps that held it onto the saddle, in an effort to reach a weapon.

"Edward!" Dee, his voice very far away, began shouting in a mixture of English, Latin and German. I feared any rescue would be too late as another wolf leapt at me, only to be repelled as I swung the bag in panic.

Hooves pounded in the distance and two of the Magyar escort approached, Dee cantering in their wake. The men drew up short of the circle of wolves and the now dying horse. One man, heavily bearded, called to me in his barbaric language and gestured for me to run through the circle toward them. They had drawn their heavy swords and were using the flats to urge their ponies on.

A shout from one of the men made me spin around to see the open jaws and flattened ears of a wolf bounding toward me. I swung the pack again, knocking the beast sideways, its teeth caught in the hide. As I grappled with the bag, now in a tug of war with the animal, it yelped and cringed back. The smell of burnt fur rose in the air. The wolves fell back into a wider circle, even the ones that had started to open the horse's belly, which sprayed red mist with each of the moribund mare's labored gasps. I could now see, in the half darkness, the glint of pink flames around me, a narrow circle of foxfire, even as I heard Dee's deep voice chanting. I could see his hands inscribing the symbols in the air as he strode toward the pack, his cape flowing out from his shoulders, making him look twice his usual size.

The guards had retreated, looking as feral and wild in the gloom as the wolves. The beasts were circling maybe a dozen yards away, salivating at the stench of the mare's entrails spilling into the mud.

I hefted both packs, one with its precious books, the other with my clothes, and ran toward Dee. I staggered around the dying mare, my boots splashing in the blood, and jumped over the flames between the two Magyars. Dee had one of the pack mules reined to his saddle, and I clambered onto its bare back, careless of my comfort, lodging the packs in front of me.

As soon as Dee stopped chanting the fires started to fade. "Edward! Are you injured?"

"I—I am well. Thank you, Master Dee."

My master hauled on the reins and the mule was forced into a gait somewhere between a trot and a canter, rattling every tooth in my head. The Magyars rode their ponies tight around us, waving swords and shouting strange battle cries. I fought the urge to burst into tears with gratitude or relief and concentrated my efforts on staying on the rough-coated beast. I grasped a handful of bristly mane and urged it forward.

"The castle is ahead. Barely half a mile." Dee's bridle was grasped by one of the men, who spoke in a guttural dialect to Dee, who nodded his head. "Come, Edward, not much farther now. The king's castle will offer us refuge," he shouted, as if exhilarated. I shivered inside at the memory of the circle of red mouths, and the stink of the mare's death.

As we rounded the corner, I could see the curve of a hill silhouetted against an ultramarine sky, jutting above a layer of mist. Perched on the side of the peak were the shapes of defensive walls, surrounded by smaller hovels. The remaining guards had raised the alarm, and an escort of fur-clad men rode out, bearing torches that hissed and spat in coils of smoke. The men's faces were impersonal, their sharp eyes darting everywhere, their teeth flashing white in dark faces. Surrounded by the stink of burnt tallow and horse sweat, I had the strange sense of being trapped. Behind me, the feasting wolves raised their voices in the song of the forest.

Chapter 3

STANDING AT THE STATION HAD LEFT A CHILL THAT JACK-daw Hammond couldn't shake. Two days later, she wondered why she was putting herself through it again. Another girl . . . but first, she had some business to transact.

She let the rain trickle over her collar and her eyes adjust to the low light. One hand rested against the coat touching her thigh, and against her fingers she felt the outline of the dagger sewn into the lining. Streetlights lit the underside of low clouds, glowing to infuse the passageway in front of her with a faint orange.

She crept along the side of the alley, remembering every cobble, the raised drain, tussocks of weeds. She allowed a fingertip to trail along the brickwork wall, counting steps in her head. Three—four—five—six—seven. She could see the archway onto Thistle Street, the light reflected off water on the pavement. As she approached the entrance she stopped, letting the sounds and sights sink in. There were voices from a few directions; a dog barking somewhere, quickly shushed; traffic humming into the city on the A road. She sniffed the air, getting wet stone, the trails of car exhaust, the waxy scent of her own coat. Colors flickered over a bedroom ceiling, perhaps from a television. She pulled her leather hat lower on her forehead against the rain.

Yellow light spilled out of a pub doorway. The Seven Magpies, George Pierce's preferred rendezvous. She walked past the Tudor building to the narrow yard that led down its sagging flank. The darkness was grayed by the flicker of a fluorescent light in a back kitchen. Jack glanced around the street, then slipped into the alley. She switched on a pencil flashlight, found a blank piece of wall and started chalking. The rain came down harder, inching down her neck and smudging some of her handiwork. She let her mind settle, alert to any change, switched off the light, and waited. She checked her phone again, for the clock. *Don't be late, not tonight . . .*

"Jack." He surprised her, his voice reaching her at the same time as the smell of stale cigarettes and sweat. His outline must have melted into the shadows along the wall.

"Pierce," she said. He was there somewhere. She slid one hand to the hilt of the knife.

"You got my merchandise?" He coughed, and spat, close to her boots by the splat of it.

"I have. You got the money?"

"Two grand for five grams, as agreed." He stepped out, silhouetted against the end of the alley and the lit street beyond. He was a small, thin man, somewhere between fifty and seventy, barely taller than Jack. The glow from the kitchen window dropped spots of light onto his eyes and illuminated a shock of white hair, yellowed at the front.

"Two thousand for *four* grams of pure merchandise." She reached into an inside pocket, past the hilt of the dagger, for the folded bag of powder. It shimmered as she lifted it out. He shuffled forward in anticipation and she stepped back, closer to the wall and the symbols. Adrenaline rushed through her, warming her.

"Back, ratman," she warned.

"Hostile, Jack." His voice was full of hissing sounds, and he leaned forward into the faint light, squinting at her. "That's no way to treat a business associate." He reached for the bag but she stepped back, one hand reaching out for the symbols she had sketched on the bricks.

"I mean it. Remember last time?"

He choked a cracked laugh, the dog-fox reek of him hitting her. "We could conduct our transaction in the pub like proper partners. Then I could have a good look at my merchandise."

"In there, with you?" She laughed at the thought of taking the raggedy man into the pub. "Just throw me the money."

He bent over one pocket, drew something out. "You and I are two of a kind, *Jackdaw*." He waved the packet at her. "The money's good. Give me the stuff."

She hesitated, four grams of prepared bone dust grinding like sand in the plastic between her fingers.

"What's it going to be used for? Is this more weird voodoo shit?"

He shuffled half a pace closer, almost within reach. She kept an eye on him, even as her hand hovered over the chalked sigils behind her.

"What do you care?" He snorted. "Think of it as lucky charms for the modern executive. There's a stockbroker staying on the coast, just needs to knock up a few talismans." He tossed the packet over with a quick movement, making her jump.

"Get back," she growled at him, every muscle braced against attack. She was aware of a movement in the road ahead. "You better not have brought your human Rottweilers with you." She weighed the package, a battered envelope, in her hand. It was heavy enough to be two thousand and he hadn't short-changed her yet. Good suppliers were hard to find, and Jack was one of the best. Having said that, if he could take the bone powder and get his money back . . .

"I don't need help to deal with one skinny little bitch." He pointed at the powder. "Give it to me."

She tossed it to him and he caught it with a snap, holding it up against his face, and then opened the bag, careless of the rain, and sniffed deeply.

"Long dead," he commented. "What is this, Roman shit?"

"It's good. A suicide."

"It'll do." He sneered at her, now close enough to see in the soft gray light. "I heard you got yourself a girl. Blood to sell."

"You heard wrong." Her heart speeded up, as she tried to shrug it off.

"Then I heard about this girl, dead on the London train, Monday night." He licked his lips. "I thinks to myself, that could be one of yours. Then I heard about the sigils, and I knew for sure."

"I don't know what you're talking about." *Shit, where does he get his information from?*

"Oh, you do." He spun on one foot toward the road. "You need a girl, or that healer on Exmoor's going to run out of her supplies. I'm not judging, Jack, doing the work of the angels, you two, healing them little kids." She saw his tongue slide out and lick his lips again in the dim light. "Thing is, I got a healer too. If you gets another girl, and I'm sure you will, then I can get you very good money. You hear what I'm saying?"

"I'm just a dealer in occult ingredients, for whackos and weirdoes." She tucked the money away, drew out the knife, held it loosely in the folds of her coat. "Time's up, Pierce. Now fuck off." A scrape of a shoe somewhere distracted her for a moment.

He bounded forward, arms swinging in her direction. She slid her hand onto the chalk marks she had drawn on the rough bricks behind her, and let the adrenaline charge her up. Maybe the rain helped conduct the energy through the knife, because at the lightest contact a blue discharge crackled between them. He fell, arched into a bow shape, his face distorted with the shock. His eyes were rolled back in his head, and for a moment, she thought she had killed him. After a long moment, he started to wheeze, chest heaving like an old set of bellows.

"You . . . you . . ." he managed, but Jack leapt over his twitching feet and into the street. She surprised two of Pierce's minions, who loomed either side of the alleyway, by racing between them toward the sanctuary of her car.

With shouts and heavy footfalls echoing behind her, she turned into the next alley, pulling the bin into the middle of the shadow of the high walls, then ran to the car. She had left the driver's door unlocked, keys in the ignition, and by the time she had started the engine the first bear was in the road, looking toward her. She snapped on the headlights—full beam—and watched as he staggered back, arms over his eyes. She hit the accelerator, steering around him as he spun in the road, and the car fishtailed on the wet tarmac. She accelerated down toward the town center, and raced through red lights on the empty street. She glanced at the dashboard clock. Shit, ten-oh-five. It might already be too late.

Rain clattered on the roof of Jack's car as she peered at street names. The seer had predicted the death would occur at around eleven. But seers' prophecies were always a bit hazy. Their directions were worse—*along the river, by the spring, the crossroads southeast of the oak-topped hill* . . . The city center was winding down. The directions had been based on an ancient geography, now smothered under a sheet of roads and houses in the eastern end of the city.

Nelson Road, Trafalgar Avenue, Oak Hill—that might be it. She could feel the muscles in her neck tighten as she thought of the teenager. Ten-twenty-three. Maybe the girl was already dead. She slowed to a crawl, wiping a mist of condensation off the inside of the window, scanning both sides of the road.

A small figure under the bus stop bench might not have been obvious to someone walking by, but Jack's headlights swept around and picked out a bundle of clothes. She drove the car onto the pavement and leapt out, the engine still growling. She dropped onto her knees and reached for the figure, cold water seeping into her jeans. She grabbed an arm, and dragged the teenager across the ground. The seer had said it would be a long shot.

"Come on, kid, a little help would be good," she muttered. Jack pressed her finger to the girl's throat, feeling a weak flicker of a pulse. Long shot or not, she couldn't just leave her to die. Jack grabbed two good handfuls of the teenager and lifted her. She staggered under the awkward burden to the car, and managed to get a thumb onto the lock to open the tailgate. Jack half dropped, half rolled the body onto the dog blanket. The interior light revealed two short boots, slim ankles, pink tights and a leather band that could charitably be called a skirt. Her top half was wrapped in her coat, and as Jack uncovered her head she revealed vomit stuck to the white face and spiky black hair. She stank of cider.

"Just hang on, OK?" The girl moaned wordlessly in response. Thirty-three minutes to go. Jack slammed the tailgate closed and jumped into the battered station wagon. This was going to be *really* close.

Driving as fast as she dared, she fumbled for her phone and dialed Maggie's number. Please be ready, please . . .

"Hello? Jack?" The soft voice on the other end of the line was sharpened with alarm.

"I've got her! The girl, she's still alive. Shit, Maggie, what are we doing?"

"Saving a life. Just focus on that. I've got the room ready, just get back in time." She hung up and Jack dropped the mobile onto the passenger seat, praying the police didn't notice her doing fifty in the city.

She powered through red lights, and was out of the town in eighteen minutes, down the main road to the turnoff in another eight, into the village in six. She no longer had time to count, so she rattled over the cattle grid, and skidded into the yard behind the cottage. She had barely opened the tailgate before the girl started vomiting again, her lips going blue in the interior light. Jack wrestled her over one shoulder, and lurched toward the back door, held open by Maggie.

The older woman restrained the dog with both arms. "Quick, Jack!"

Jack staggered in and clipped the kid's head on the door frame. That would be the least of her problems if she didn't get her between the circles of sigils.

The girl stopped choking and fell against Jack's back, her breath rattling. The concealed door in the paneling that led down to the priest hole was propped open with a pile of books. With the last seconds ticking away, Jack threw the girl down the stone steps into the sanctuary of the cellar.

Chapter 4

THE PACKAGE WAS HEAVY, SEALED WITH "CONFIDENTIAL—POLICE" tape, and marked "FAO FELIX GUICHARD ONLY."

"Professor? A police officer brought it in for you." The admin assistant was looking curious. "Rose had to sign for it."

"Thanks." He tucked the parcel under one arm, and kept his head down through the group of students, hoping none of them were in any of his classes. He'd only seen them a few times, and he never seemed to remember faces . . .

A girl stepped in front of him. "Professor Guichard?"

Damn. "Um . . . yes? Alice, isn't it?"

"Alix. Hi. I was wondering if I could talk to you about the assignments this semester."

He searched in his pocket for his office key, juggling the package, a briefcase full of papers and a laptop in a rucksack. The Georgian door had an original lock, with a key like a church door's, and he fumbled it into the hole.

"Sorry, I don't have much time this morning. If you could come back after lunch . . ."

"I have lectures this afternoon. Can I help?" She leaned disturbingly close and smiled up at him. She was a leggy, auburn-haired girl, with a healthy tan. He shook off the momentary attraction and smiled.

"Thank you, I'm fine. Or I will be—when I unlock this." The mechanism thumped internally and the door swung open.

"Professor Guichard?" His assistant Rose's stern tone came

from behind him. It got rid of the girl, who mumbled something about coming back later in the week.

"To the rescue, as always."

"It's just transference, you know," she said. "Indiana Jones has a lot to answer for."

"He's archaeology, I'm anthropology," he said. "He's also completely fictional."

She took the parcel from him. "Well, she's eighteen; she can't help herself. Don't encourage them, that's all. You aren't exactly unattractive, and you have that fatherly thing going on . . ."

Before he could form a cutting retort, he saw her standing by the desk, looking down at the bulky package. Her round, middle-aged face looked pensive.

"That contains the postmortem photographs from the police," he said. "I was hoping you would be able to help me with them."

"I thought so. Is this case going to cut into your time?"

Felix dropped his briefcase on the desk and slid the laptop onto his chair. "Maybe. How many departmental meetings are there this semester?"

She handed him the envelope. "You never go to them anyway. Is this to do with that poor girl on the train? I saw it on the evening news."

He hesitated, feeling the weight of the package in his hand. He could feel a flutter of adrenaline just by holding it. "She was covered with symbols, some of them Enochian letters."

"Well, let's have a look at them. At least they didn't make you attend the autopsy."

"They called me to the scene to view the body." He fumbled with the seal. He slid the pictures onto the desk, large glossy prints that catalogued every inch of the dead girl's inscribed skin.

"Good God." Rose picked up a picture showing the girl's torso, with two concentric circles drawn over her hollow belly and flattened breasts. "That poor girl." She reached for another picture, peering at a symbol at the top of her chest. "These look Enochian. But these others, what are they?"

"They look cuneiform, but unlike anything I've seen before. Is the layout familiar? I keep thinking I've seen something similar."

Rose started laying out photographs on the desk as Felix cleared piles of paperwork and academic journals onto his chair. There was a stack of eight-by-tens of both sides of the body. The circles on her back were smaller and were composed of fewer figures.

"Do the letters spell anything?" she asked, looking up at Felix with a frown.

He reached for a pen and started jotting on the back of a memo he hadn't read and had even less chance of responding to. "T . . . G . . . C . . . E . . . is that an O?" In between were other shapes, more elaborate.

She traced one, her finger almost touching the paper. "It's so sad. She doesn't look much older than my daughter."

He glanced across at the pictures that included the dead face. Blond hair, almost white, had fallen back away from her pale forehead. Her half-open eyes were shadowed with a soft gray. "I don't know how old she was. Young."

"The shapes do look familiar." She stepped back, head cocked to one side.

Felix felt a surge of excitement as memory flickered in his mind, just out of reach. "That's what I felt, at the station. Only, on something metal. Coin, maybe?"

She started. "A medal, perhaps? Do you remember . . . ?"

He crouched down and pulled open the bottom drawer of one of the filing cabinets. "There were two medals, the ones

Dee was awarded by the king of Poland. I did an authentication for an auction house, around 2009, I think."

"I remember. There were some letters with them, and some notes. I photocopied them for you."

He paused, looking at her round face. "We weren't supposed to keep duplicates. They were bought up by an American museum, they probably have some sort of copyright."

She shrugged. "The photocopies were in a big blue folder, if it helps. I just hope you kept them."

He paused, smiled at her. "You know I keep everything you ever give me."

She snorted with disbelief. "So you've got all those grant applications you're supposed to keep for seven years?"

The back of the drawer was stuffed with outside consultation records. "Here we go. British Museum." He pulled the folder out and lifted it onto the edge of the desk. "Put those photographs away, for the moment, will you? Just leave the ones that show the whole circles."

He rummaged through the folder, until he found the photocopies. The documents were mostly written in Dee's precise hand. Many were household accounts and notes on vellum, but a smaller packet had been inscribed in a rough hand, on water-stained and pest-damaged paper. The medals, two large bronze disks, were the size of his palm, and she had copied each side. One had the face of King Istvan Báthory of Poland, the other had a curled dragon surrounded by two circles of inscribed shapes. There appeared to be a date, and he felt in his pocket for his glasses.

"These must have been awarded during the fifteen eighties, when Dee was in Europe." He leaned over the grayscale image. "Hand me that magnifying glass, would you?"

"The letters are very similar," she said, as she passed him a hand lens. "That spiral one looks like the one on the back of her neck."

He lined up the postmortem photograph of the girl's torso with the photocopy. "Did the medals sell?"

"The British Museum bought them for a couple of hundred pounds. The letters were more interesting, they sold for thousands."

He picked up the pictures and slid them back in the envelope. "I'll follow up with the BM."

"Because you have so much free time at the moment." Rose's voice was dry. "You do remember you have a meeting with your solicitor this afternoon?"

"Oh, well, maybe I'll just phone the museum, see if they can send me better images." He flipped through the copies of the papers Rose had done for him at the time. "These are obviously Dee's hand. There were some notes with them, by Kelley."

"So you thought at the time."

He found the image of the stained and folded booklet that Rose had recorded by teasing the sheets apart. The writing was cramped and faded. "This was on paper?"

"So you said. It didn't last as well as the vellum Dee used."

"Well, paper was a fairly new technology at this date." He squinted at the pale impression of the lettering. "Cheap ink, too, organic. And he's crossed his lines."

The pages had been closely packed with script, then turned ninety degrees and more writing added, making it even less legible. The author had written close to the margins, and time and damp had frayed the edges, losing a few words.

"Well, I'll leave you with your research." She patted his shoulder. "And don't forget your appointment."

"Oh, yes. The custody battle over who gets the Lucian Freud print and whether the cat can come over every other weekend." He hated the waspish note that crept into his voice when he mentioned the divorce. Rose shut the door behind her. He turned his attention back to the first faded scribble. Something, something . . . account . . . *Secryts of Lyfe and Death* . . .

Chapter 5

The people of Niepolomice are mixed, fair Saxons,
tall Poles, and among them, the dark Magyars
and Székelys. I noticed, for I am observant as any
scientist shall be, that one party came with soldiers,
menservants and then a group of six or seven young
children, all girls as I could divine, shepherded by
an older woman. I wondered what household would
bring so many young attendants. I also noticed their
abnormal pallor and weakness, and disapproved of
such sickly creatures being introduced to the castle
where contagion could spread. For they were very
white, dark eyes sunken in their faces, lips pale, and
some had to support the others. Fever, I thought.

—EDWARD KELLEY
    14 November 1585
    Niepolomice

THE CASTLE AT NIEPOLOMICE WAS DARK, AND THE GREAT
oak doorway seemed to swallow us whole. King Istvan
Báthory's banners hung over each doorway: a dragon
curled around a shield, with three teeth inscribed upon it. The
outer courtyard was a combination of an army marshaling yard
and a country market. Women sold everything, from chick-
ens swinging unhappily by their feet, to sausages the size of
a man's arm, carried aloft in great bunches. Soldiers stood in

clusters, hands on weapons, hostility on every face. I soon realized it was not aimed at two weary travelers from England, but at one another. Bearskin-clad Magyars strutted in groups, the blue-uniformed Polish soldiers watching their every move, and polishing their weapons was a company of the emperor's black-coated soldiers.

The captain of our escort beckoned to us as the last of our luggage was tossed onto the ground from the mules.

"I suspect we shall carry our own bags," murmured Dee, still in a good humor.

That meant I carried most of them, my master leaning over for the book bag and the leather packet containing our charts and maps. I followed Dee and the captain through the outer courtyard to an inner one, and along a corridor, which lifted my nose to the smell of roasting meat. We skirted a gallery full of portraits, then a feasting hall with raised dais and tables, and went into a warren of smaller rooms and antechambers filled with courtiers and servants.

I dragged the packs up a curving stair, and into a hall lined with doors. One was opened, and we were ushered into a larger and more brightly lit chamber than I had expected. A new fire spluttered in the hearth, glowing yellow. There was no chimney, but a smoke stain up the wall led to several openings at the top, the arrangement of which must have been unruly in windy weather.

A manservant, as black-eyed and brown-skinned as a Turk, bowed low to Dee and then clamped the shutters against the night air. I saw a tallow candle upon the table, lit against the darkness, and fine lamps ready for a flame. A bed, as high as my waist, was stretched against the wall, leather straps across a frame, and as I watched, two women bustled in carrying a mattress. They lifted it onto the bed, and the manservant opened a coffer, handing them a thick, felted blanket.

I slipped off my cloak, stretching it in front of the fire. One of the serving women started unpacking our clothes. I noticed she seemed afraid of Dee, who was already sharpening his pen. My sleeves were damp and stained, and she beckoned for me to give up my shirt. I changed it for a clean one, sewn with exquisite tiny stitches by Mistress Jane Dee herself. I had often seen her bent over her needlework, drawing on her experience as an embroiderer in her youth. Strange to think she was but thirty, the same age as myself. I fancied I could smell her perfume, and felt a momentary pang. I chastised myself for the sin of covetousness, for breaking the tenth commandment.

The door creaked open, and a maidservant carried in a rush bag of logs. I stroked my beard, trimmed in the style of Drake, and she dimpled. Her smile faded at Dee's voice, and she turned, crossing herself as she fled the room.

"Why don't you ask for some wine?" Dee suggested, already looping his letters, chronicling the thoughts and observations he had memorized during the day's travel. What he meant was, "Go away so I can write," but I was thirsty myself. I opened the door and walked into the armored chest of a guard.

I staggered back, and mimed holding a goblet up to my lips and drinking.

"*Crapula*, wine, understand?" The bearded man looked blank. I tried again. "*Vinum?*" The guard extended a long arm and pointed down the corridor whence we had come. He looked into the room, as if to check that Dee was safe, or perhaps to confirm he was confined, and then shut the door behind me.

The perfume of seared meat drew me by my nose down worn stairs and along dark hallways, and my belly growled. The vast kitchens were hellishly hot. The tongue-twisting language faded as a dozen or so men and women appeared to notice my shadow in the doorway.

"Good evening," I managed, in passable Latin. One of the men spat on the blackened rushes at my feet. I tried again, in German, then in French.

"They don't understand you." A voice, in impeccable Latin, came from a corner I hadn't noticed. A man that I had mistaken for a heap of rags tottered to his feet, and pulled back a hood. The bald head of an old man was revealed, his beard white where it wasn't stained by food. "And if they did, they wouldn't speak to you. They are *his* Carpathians, Transylvanians."

"Can you tell them I mean them no harm? I simply want wine and food for myself and my master."

The man shrugged, limping closer to the light of the fire. "They fear you, just the same. They know you are here with the sorcerer."

He jabbered something in the language of the Magyars. A woman, no more than a girl, cut off a slab of bread and topped it with a slice of the roast meat in the fireplace. Stepping around me, she handed it to the old man, then ran back. The smell of meat hit me, and my mouth filled with sweet water.

The man tore the offering in half. "Here."

I hadn't eaten since we left Krakow at dawn, and nodded my thanks to the fearful girl. The meat was good venison, but I struggled to swallow the dry bread. The man handed me a horn cup and I drank deep of half-fermented ale.

"My thanks, good sir. You speak Latin like a scholar."

"Or a priest?" The man grinned, revealing half a dozen rotten teeth. "Are you as wary of ecclesiastics as your master?"

I took another bite, feeling my stomach cramp around the food and the yeasty brew. "In our land, our queen has some tolerance for those who follow Rome."

The man settled back on the stool in the corner, chewing the meat with his good teeth. "You are fortunate. The king invites the Pope to purify his Catholic court, while his own family and noble allies follow the Protestant heresy. Voivode of Transylvania, king of Lithuania and Poland—hah!" He spat into the fire. "Istvan rules over three barrels of gunpowder, and spends his days putting out sparks."

I hesitated to speak anything but glowingly of their king. "The people at least live in peace."

The man spoke around a mouthful of the meat. "At present, they are united against the bastard Turks." He washed the mouthful down and belched. "Whenever we drive them back, the people turn on each other like hungry dogs."

I shrugged. "He seems to have the respect of the nobles."

"Hah!" The man spat a laugh at me, with the stench from his rotten mouth. "Them! They either owe him money, and seek his indulgence against repayment, or he owes them money, in which case they need him to live long enough to pay it back. The court is bankrupt. The soldiers on the Turkish front get paid, everyone else waits."

I finished the food, and licked my greasy fingers. "My master is invited here to talk of theology and science. Then we are back to Krakow and on to Prague."

The man started making a choking noise and for a moment I thought he was ill. Then I realized the coughing was laughter. "You are here to help the witch save the lady countess."

"I assure you, I know of no witches . . ."

He stepped forward into the flickering light of the torches and the roasting fire.

"He may try to wrap himself in the blessings of Rome," he whispered, "but the Báthorys are cursed. Why else would he need a sorcerer's spells and talismans? You know the devil's own magical letters, that is why you were invited here."

I stepped back from the reach of the man's stink. "We have been blessed by angels who have spoken wisdoms to us," I said, with some anger. "Those angels affirmed that Jesus was the son of God."

"And demons cannot lie?" He chuckled, then coughed, his whole body shaking with each racking paroxysm. I stepped back, and he splattered the stones and rushes at my feet with spots of blood. "Stupid child," he gasped, his lips speckled. "The witches will take your magical letters, and build abominations and monsters from the bodies of innocents."

"The king is a devout man. A true Catholic."

He cackled for a moment. "Devout, yes. But for Istvan, family comes first, and with family, money. Always money."

I stepped away from the man, from his malice.

"We are serious men of science." I drained the last of the flagon.

"You raise the dead."

I knew speaking to a spirit beyond the grave was a glimpse of heaven, or, at least, purgatory, worthy of scientific inquiry. "I have been a mouthpiece for angels, old man."

"You are a deluded child, manipulated by demons." The man shuffled closer until I could see the crucifix against his ragged robes. "Istvan will have you keep the dying from the grave with your demonic magics." He crossed himself, and despite myself I followed suit. "Leave the heretic sorcerer. Go, before—"

A man entered, in the embroidered robes and red boots of a noble, and raised a fist at the priest. The old man returned to his humble stool, babbling what I took to be apologies.

The newcomer turned to me. He tipped his head toward the door. I followed him, but cast a final look at the old man, his eyes bright with something that looked like malice. He was mumbling something familiar, crossing himself.

". . . *et Judicis nostri, et in virtute Spiritus Sancti, ut descedas ab hoc plasmate Dei* . . ."

My throat tightened as I recognized the rite of exorcism.

Chapter 6

JACK'S COTTAGE WAS MORE THAN FOUR HUNDRED YEARS old, hunkered into the landscape like a tortoise under a thatched shell. Built with two rooms downstairs, two upstairs, it had had a small bathroom squeezed between the two bedrooms at some time during the last century. The kitchen, added in the sixties and looking over the back of the plot, caught whatever morning sun was available. It was warmed by a chipped wood stove. Jack huddled by the open firebox, occasionally poking the logs as they started to catch off the embers.

"You'll put that fire out," Maggie said. She was drying up, the familiar movements graceful and reassuring. Jack stretched her hands toward the warmth.

"It's cold in here."

"Still cold?" She touched Jack's forehead. "You can't afford to get chilled like that. It's been two days, and you're still icy to the touch."

"There's a terrible draft coming in the bedroom window. I'll get some newspaper to stuff in the cracks when I've got time."

"Make time. I'm serious, you look blue." Maggie tutted. "You could just mend the windows."

"How about the kid?"

Maggie put the mug down with a thump. "She has a name, you know. How would you have felt if I'd called you 'the kid' when we rescued you?"

"OK, how's *Sadie*?"

Maggie shut the firebox door down to a crack. "Still alive. She's got a terrible bruise on her back from the fall, but I think she's breathing better."

Jack leaned against the back of the rocking chair, feeling the warmth of the dog against her leg. "At least she is still breathing." *Breathing, yes, but for how long?* The sadness at Carla's death crept into Jack. She wondered if they would be able to save this one.

Maggie hung the tea towel on the front of the stove. "Are you ready to talk about Carla?"

Jack shut her eyes again. Carla's last triumphant wave through the window of the train as it pulled out of the station flashed into her mind. "What do you want me to say? She got out, legged it over the fields to Hambolt Halt and onto the train. She was doomed the second she left the house."

"You looked after her, nursed her back to health for four months. You got to know her."

"We never bonded." A memory intruded, of the morning sunlight gleaming across Carla's blond hair, a shade lighter than Jack's but straight, as she crooned to something she'd made up on an old guitar. "She never trusted me. And she used to feel high if she even left the middle of the circle. She fought me when I drew the sigils on her, even when she felt better."

"You can't live with someone—"

Jack jumped up, startling the dog. "I don't want to talk about it. I warned her, she escaped, she died. That's it."

Maggie stopped her, and for a moment Jack looked at her face, seeing the lines, the sagging skin under her chin, the gray hair that had somehow become white. Maggie was getting old, shit, she must be over sixty already.

"Jack, I'm worried about you. You've grown . . . hard. You have a child to look after now, you can't bottle up your feelings all the time."

"She was an addict. She whored her body to buy heroin."

Carla's casual stories of what she had done to get drugs had shocked Jack. "I warned her every day: if she left the circles she would die in minutes. I was amazed she managed to get across two fields and onto the train. All to get back to her addict friends. Even her own mother took three weeks to report her missing. Couldn't give a shit."

Maggie sighed. "Well, Sadie's mother reported her missing the night you took her, and has been on television appealing for her daughter to come home ever since."

"And now she's what? Barely alive for a few months or years, at best."

Maggie snorted. "You think dead is better?"

Jack stepped into the living room. She looked through the doorway in the paneling that led down to the underground cell. It had been designed as a sanctuary for Catholic priests, and the sigils provided a haven for the girl. The orange light from the controls of an electric radiator cast a glow over the girl's features, graying her sunken eyelids with shadows.

"She looks dead now."

"Think positive. There's a casserole for you in the bottom of the oven. Don't forget the decoction mixture, it's keeping warm by the stove, strain it in a minute. You can sweeten it with some honey. She needs at least four doses a day. You could do with a cupful yourself."

Jack made a face, and settled on one of the two sagging sofas that decorated the room, otherwise lined with bookshelves in front of two of the paneled walls. A wood burner heated the room, flames glowing through the sooted-up window, and eased the draft coming under the door that led to the stairs. Life in the cottage suited her, raised out of the modern world as she had been, but she was beginning to see the appeal of modern heating systems. The dog leaned against her. His Arctic pelt was warm, and eight stone of bone and muscle felt like protection against everything but the nightmares. His head was turned toward the fire, an ineffable sense of wolf coming through the husky skull. *You can't save them all* . . . Ches picked up on her sadness and whined, a soft graze of a sound.

The click of Maggie shutting the door in the paneling brought her back to the present.

"She's improving," said Maggie. "I'm leaving you with enough herbs to keep her going for a week. She's already doing better than Carla did. Maybe this one will understand and be more cooperative."

"She's a valuable asset. Don't forget the little detail that I'm going to make thousands selling her blood." Jack looked out at the pale blue sky. "Like you did from me."

"Would you rather I'd left you to die?" Maggie bent to kiss Jack on the forehead. "Warm up, look after Sadie. I'll be back in a few days. I've got to help Charley move into her new student house."

Jack pulled her sleeves down over her hands in an attempt to keep them warm. The back door clicked, Maggie's car started up and pulled out over the gravel and cattle grid. She rested against familiar, baggy cushions, listening to the birds cawing in the centuries-old rookery. They nagged and squabbled outside, in the boundary beyond the cottage. The trees stooped and leaned against one another along the remnants of the hedge, half a dozen oaks that first reached for the light in Tudor times. She shut her eyes for a moment.

Ches took her fingers between his teeth and pressed lightly, before sweeping her palm with his tongue. She rubbed his head with the other hand, not sure who was comforting whom.

The croaking of the birds stopped as the clapping of their wings signaled that the rookery had lifted. She looked through the curtains, but couldn't see anyone outside. She waited, almost holding her breath, until the rookery settled again.

Chapter 7

SADIE WOKE, WITH A RECOLLECTION OF ALMOST MAKING IT to the surface a few times before, memories of choking, then sobbing in gasps that trailed back into sleep. Her stomach was cramping, her mouth full of the taste of vomited cider and burger. *Shit, I am never going out with Tash and Claire again*. Her ribs ached, her body hurt, her head . . . *What a hangover. Mum will go mad.*

She unglued her eyes in the dim light, realizing that she was not at home, or in her own bed. She retched, but her mouth was dry, her lips cracked when she tried to move them. Her tongue was spongy and heavy and she gagged on it. She trembled a hand to her face to brush her hair back. One wrist clinked, and she stared at a metal bracelet, padded with something.

The dark little room was like a prison cell. Stone walls glistened with damp and a lantern glowed from a rusty hook. Tales of kidnap, rape and murder crept into her mind, and filled her mouth with bile. She looked around, found a bowl on an upturned box beside her, and heaved into it. Tears erupted from her, spewing sobs and vomit into the old plastic bowl, her ribs aching with the effort. She couldn't breathe, she couldn't—

When she next came to, she realized someone was standing over her, and she flinched away. There was a woman, slim and boyish with feathery, shortish blond hair. Her green eyes glinted in the low light as she leaned toward Sadie. Her features, even her lips, were bone white.

Sadie whimpered and put up the shackled hand to hold her off.

The woman ignored her, knelt on the floor and put her arm behind Sadie to lift her against one shoulder. Sadie tried to wriggle free, but was too weak.

The plastic cup was half filled with what looked like flat beer, but as soon as Sadie's nose got near it, it stank like moldy compost.

"No!" she screamed, nausea and terror rising inside her. She leaned back, tried to push the woman's hands away, but her arms shook. Her fingers felt numb, as if they were swollen, and Sadie clenched them into loose fists. The cup was pressed against her lips, not gently, and the stuff poured into her mouth. She swallowed the first mouthful on reflex, the second because it didn't taste as bad as it smelled and she was so thirsty. Then one hand wavered up, heavy, to knock the cup away, the liquid spilling over her clothes. The cold seeped into her.

The woman eased her back against the pillow. The mattress twanged like the folding bed Sadie remembered from family holidays in the camper by the sea. Showering off the sand in the plastic bathroom, meals around a table overlooking the beach, fish and chips vinegary in paper, followed by individual trifles from the site shop. The days before Dad had left them. Sadie cried, cramped with longing for home, her mother, for the old days. She hadn't seen her father for years; her mother had become her whole family.

She tried to push herself up the bed, away from the woman, but one arm was held back. She turned her head to look at her wrist. The bracelet was trailing a chain. The woman waved the cup at her.

"I'll get you some more. When you've drunk it, you can have as much water as you like."

Her soft footfalls padded up a few steps, retreated into another room, revealing a glimpse of books crooked on a shelf, and sunlight on a wall.

It's daytime? How long have I been here? I have to get out.

The door squeaked to half shut, shadows gathering and deepening around Sadie. She lifted her head to look at the small room. The walls seemed to be real stone; a tentative hand felt clammy roughness. It—the dungeon—was just big enough for the bed and a space beside it. A wooden box served as a bedside table, and a scrap of flowery carpet covered the floor. She pulled at the chain, but her muscles were weak, and her arm heavy. Nausea, and the taste of meat and cider, surged back into her throat with every movement. She swallowed hard, feeling dizzy.

Lying back, the world revolving and buzzing, she tried to remember what had happened. She remembered the girls staggering in the road, both laughing, even when Tash broke the heel of her shoe, Claire trying not to cough when she inhaled her first cigarette.

The woman returned with the cup and a bottle of water. Sadie opened her mouth again, her lips numb, tongue uncooperative. The first word came out as a husky moan.

"Please . . ." She coughed, and once she had started, she couldn't stop. She started gasping for air, fighting to sit up. The woman lifted her easily, and tucked a couple of cushions behind her as Sadie was bowed forward. She labored to get her breath back, for the spots in front of her eyes to go. Her ribs and stomach muscles stabbed with each spasm.

"Easy. It will pass. Just relax."

The attack receded, and Sadie remembered snatches of similar episodes, and vomiting, her breath dying away until she felt like she was drowning.

"I know this is confusing," the woman said. "You've been ill, really ill."

"I won't tell anyone . . . please, just let me go." Her voice came out like a wheeze. She took another raggedy breath in, panted out. In . . . out. She realized her heartbeat was slowly thudding in her ears. As she relaxed, it started to slow. "Why," she started, and then needed another breath. *Are you going to hurt me, kill me?*

The woman seemed to understand. "You need to be here. You'd die if you left this room. It will take time to get better."

"I'm . . . chained up." Tears tickled down her face to her chin. The woman handed her a fistful of tissues.

"Cry it out. It's all you can do. I can't explain it yet but you have to stay here. You wouldn't last five minutes out there. My name is Jack. Go on, drink some more. It will help."

"Help?" Sadie choked.

"Just drink." Jack held out half a beaker of the foul liquid.

"Then will you let me out of this . . . dungeon?"

"It's not a dungeon, it's a priest hole," Jack said. "They used to hide Catholic priests in here. It's a sanctuary."

After the last earthy mouthful, Sadie could feel herself slumping back on the cushions, relaxing. "The police must be looking . . ."

"I thought that," Jack's eyes met hers, calm, "when I was kept here. Now, sleep."

Sadie willed her eyelids to stay open.

She awoke with the words "Let me go home" echoing in her mind. The light was different now, darker. The box beside the narrow bed had a bottle of mineral water on top of it, unopened. Sadie struggled to crack open the top, and drank deeply. A twinge reminded her of her full bladder.

Wiping the water from sticky lips, which split as she touched them, she leaned forward to see through the doorway. There was a light spilling through the gap onto the stone walls, which seemed to be covered in some weird symbols, like graffiti. Her hands looked strange in the gloom, her fingers thin, and the skin dry and crazed like old paint. She started to examine her clothes. Old, soft pajamas, several sizes too big.

Someone must have undressed her and redressed her in these old clothes. *Oh, God.*

Somewhere, a phone rang. Sadie could hear the distant voice answer.

"Hi, Maggie . . ." The woman must have turned away because Sadie couldn't make out the words. Then: "No, she's come round again, but she won't be ready for weeks, maybe months . . ." *Months?* Terror gripped her bladder again.

The voice faded away to a murmur. Sadie's bladder spasmed painfully. Maybe they would let her out to use the bathroom.

"Excuse me?" she tried. She started coughing again, but this time it passed by itself. Holding ribs that ached with every breath, she shouted again. "Hello? I . . . I need to pee."

Footsteps approached, this time the padding of smaller feet, followed by the snout of a dog in the doorway, nudging it open with a creak. Maybe it was the light, or the steps up to the threshold, but Sadie's first thought was that it was the size of a pony. It seemed to fill most of the opening. Its eyes were pale, light fur sooty along its snout, around its eyes, like a giant husky. It gazed at her, sniffing the air, but it didn't seem hostile, and she relaxed a little.

Jack appeared, and hauled it back by its collar.

"Out of the way, Ches." She seemed to be carrying a plastic bucket and, with complete horror, Sadie noticed the toilet roll under one arm.

"No." She slid back up the bed, an exposed bit of shoulder touching the dank stone. Jack just put the bucket between the box and the bed, and took the lid off.

"Just get on with it."

"You must have a toilet!" Sadie slapped Jack's outstretched hand away, panicking. "No!"

Jack sat back on her haunches, observing Sadie with those light green eyes. Ches gazed over her shoulder, his gray eyes even lighter.

"No one's trying to hurt you. I told you, you can't leave the priest hole yet. I can wait until you pee yourself again, but that would be a lot worse for both of us."

Sadie dashed a hand over her face, smearing tears across her cheeks. *Again?* "Please, let me go home."

Jack looked at her and it seemed like her stern expression was a bit softer. "Look. Think of me as a nurse. You'd let a nurse help, wouldn't you?"

"No," she said, but her bladder was agony now.

"You're too weak. You'll fall."

"I won't!" Sadie found enough energy to shout back, and flapped a hand at Jack. "I can do it myself. Please!"

Jack shrugged, stood, and walked up the steps.

The door swung shut behind her, the light fading to a pool over the bucket. Sadie moved her body to the edge of the bed, struggling to find some tension in her arms. She swung her bare feet onto the bit of damp carpet, the shackle knocking against her thigh. She could see the chain ran down to a ring in the floor. Her legs, always slim, were like sticks. They shook, and she had to cling to the side of the metal bed, ease the loose trousers down, and balance on the bucket. For a moment, she felt like she would burst, her bladder squeezed by the position but unable to let go. Then, with a pouring sound that filled the room, along with the acrid smell of urine, she put several inches of liquid in the bucket.

It took her a few moments to catch her breath enough to nudge one hip onto the edge of the bed and crawl in. The pajama bottoms had fallen to the floor. She tugged at the chain, but it didn't budge.

Jack came back a few minutes later and covered the bucket without comment.

"Would you like some soup?" She placed the pajama trousers on the bed.

"No," Sadie muttered, as Jack lifted the pail.

"You need to keep your strength up."

Sadie lifted her arm into the light spilling through the door. It was thin, the bones rolling under the skin, the fingers more like claws.

"How long have I been here?"

"A few days."

"My mum. She'll be worried sick." Sadie tightened her lips, staring back at the woman, seeing some emotion flashing across her features. After a long pause, Jack shook her head, once.

"I'm sorry. I really am, Sadie."

Sadie looked up, the words stalled in her throat. *How do you know my name?*

Jack's voice was soft. "I will explain everything to you, when you are a bit better. I was the same as you, twenty years ago. I had the same illness."

Sadie looked at the shackle on her wrist. Hot tears fell onto the dry skin on her hands.

"Illness . . . what was wrong with you?" Her voice came out cracked, like an old woman's.

"Same as you." Jack turned to look down from the top of the steps. "I was dead."

Chapter 8

*It is said, in the court of the emperor, that when the
Great Palatine of Hungary besought a bride for his
only child, Ferenc Nádasdy, he secured an heiress of
great wealth and influence. But the young man had
no interest in her, but flirted with the most beautiful,
the most charming ladies. It was only when the young
Erzsébet Báthory grew into womanhood that Nádasdy
claimed his bride. But Erzsébet was from a line tainted,
it was said, by dragons, witchcraft and by death.*

—EDWARD KELLEY
  15 November 1585
  The King's Castle at Niepolomice

THE ARRIVAL OF A COVERED CARRIAGE DRAWN BY FOUR
black horses and attended by two dozen outriders and
a score of hounds was a spectacle I amused myself with
as we waited for the king to grant us an audience. The leader,
surely a great man, was wrapped in a bearskin cloak that fell to
his boots, and covered his head from the light rain. When he
drew it back, I saw that his black beard half covered his brown
face, and a hooked nose curved toward his mouth. He glanced
up at the battlements, but I doubt he noticed me among the
many spectators. A lord—a Lithuanian, much refined—named
him for me. Count Ferenc Nádasdy, son of the Great Palatine

of Hungary, like our own Lord High Steward, a high position. Nádasdy was the commander of the king's forces and, the Lithuanian whispered to me, known as the Black Bear.

When the servants let down the steps of the carriage, the giant swung himself off his charger, and strode forward. A manservant left the coach first, carrying various bags. Then the count reached in, and lifted a pale figure wrapped in an embroidered cloth, its head falling onto his arm, no bigger than a child. The white skin, a shade not seen in the living, spoke of death, yet the head turned upon his arm, and the bear bent his head to hear what it said. As he carried his burden—surely sick unto death—across the yard to the great doors beneath us, a linen cap fell into the mud, and a sheet of hair tumbled across his cradling arm and almost to his knees. It was a woman.

When I returned to our room, Dee had news for me.

"Edward. We are summoned to dine. I am to entertain many noble visitors from Poland and Saxony with some 'magical' tricks." The tone of his voice was acid, I knew how much he hated performing, although he was a good stage trickster. Almost as good as myself.

I sat on the bench and looked at the meticulous map he was annotating. "Master Dee, shall you wear the black doublet?"

He looked up, and stood, stretching his back. "The red, I think. Then you may wear my black and we shall both look like gentlemen of Her Majesty's court, and less like vagabonds."

I opened the press, and began unpacking his clothes, shaking out hose and shirts. The queen had made him a gift of a number of courtly dresses, and he had chosen a doublet in the latest fashion and hose from Italy. The scarlet doublet was tailored to make him look bigger, and fell onto his lean thighs. It would have dwarfed me, and I was glad to tie on the sleeves and ease the shorter jacket about me. I brushed the fine brocade, smoothing off the creases from my packing.

Dee froze at another creak outside our door. "Are they there to confine us, or guard us, do you think?" He blew upon his notebook to dry the ink and replaced it in its calfskin satchel. He looked around for the leather bucket provided instead of a night stool. "This isn't the king's principal residence," he said, over his shoulder, as he pissed. "But it is big enough to confer with many of his soldiers and nobles. He has two regiments here on leave from the Turkish front." The sultan's troops, never far away, were capturing territory in Istvan's homeland of Transylvania.

I laced the doublet, in sober black but with some good-quality embroidery, as the door opened. I smoothed my cap over my ears, as was my custom, to hide the notches there. A moment's incaution in my youth found me accused of coining. I grew my curly hair long to reduce comment, for it was a cruel injustice.

An armed man, taller even than Dee and filling the door-way, barked a command in Polish. Dee bowed his head, but did not hurry. I held out the coat and fussed about the buttons. He picked up his cane and placed his round hat upon his bushy hair. I ran a comb through his long beard and looked up at him, as he spoke softly.

"Edward. You know I have eschewed all sorcery."

"Indeed, sir."

"But seeing you in such danger today, I called upon forces of magic, endangering our immortal souls. We must guard against such necessity. Better that we were both dead than condemned forever."

I was still heartily glad not to be resting in the bellies of a dozen wolves, and my face must have shown it.

He smiled. "But I am glad you survived, all the same. Come, dear friend." His eyes twinkled in the light of the fire. "Let us see how the court of King Istvan Báthory compares with that of Her Majesty Queen Elizabeth."

The feasting hall was a long room with a vaulted, smoke-darkened ceiling. It rang with voices and few of the noblemen gave us more than a covert glance. German and Latin were spoken freely, as well as Polish. A huddle of brown-skinned men—Istvan's vassals from Transylvania, I imagined—spoke in a dialect as full of hissing and spitting as kettles over a fire. They were seated behind the king, and along his left flank. They seemed to dress as if for riding even here, at table, but the Polish noblemen wore trimmed beards, velvets and embroideries, much as in England. Beside the king sprawled the Black Bear, Lord Nádasdy, in courtly attire.

King Istvan, in green velvet dress and a collar of rubies, rose and nodded to us.

"Doctor Dee," he said, in Latin. "The court bids you welcome. Please: sit, eat, drink."

A space appeared on the nobles' bench and Dee climbed into it. I looked around and saw an area full of soldiers, and insinuated myself onto the end of the seat.

The meal was much as you would have at a hunting lodge in England. There was beef and venison and wine. The bread was almost black, and inedible until soaked in either the meat juices or in drink. Spiced sweetmeats followed the viands, and good cheeses rolled in herbs were brought with dried apples and little cakes.

Finally, the king stood again. The conversations fell away, to leave the sound of the crackling of the fire and the splintering of bones by half a dozen wolfhounds.

The king started speaking in Latin, and dropped in a few words of German and Polish. I got the meaning. The renowned scholar from the court of Queen Erzsébet of England would now demonstrate something. I didn't catch quite what, but Dee stood up, and walked to the middle of the room.

"Your Gracious Majesty, my lords." He spoke in what we called his theater voice, in precise Latin. "That nature of the universe that we think of as commonplace is far richer and full of mysteries than we see. Take, for example, this cup of wine."

He held up the horn goblet he had been using, and turned in a flash and threw the contents in the fire. He had moved too fast for some of the Magyars, who jumped to their feet, their weapons half out of their scabbards. The wine hissed like the belly of a dragon, and two of the dogs shrank back, teeth bared. I held my breath, but Dee turned around with a flourish.

He held the goblet at an angle to show the inner surface. It glowed with the brightness of pure gold. The nobles started whispering to one another, leaning forward to see the gilded interior.

"Some might think: magic, sorcery, witchcraft," he intoned.

With each word, the atmosphere in the room stilled further.

Dee continued. "But this, Your Majesty, my lords, is natural science. A few drops of a rare alchemical, shared with me by the goldsmiths of Venice, is placed in water, and a pinch of salt is added. The gold, hidden in the liquor, is forced out by the purifying action of the salt and gilds any surface it touches."

Dee offered the cup to the king, who, after a moment, took it. Few others would hold the cup. Clearly, the idea of sorcery was still in their heads.

Some sense of self-preservation made me look around, perhaps a draft was coming from the doorway. A man stood there, leaning against the wall, his dark eyes intent on Dee. His cloak was wet, and covered his dress down to his Italian-style leather boots.

The king leaned back in his chair and smiled. He had a long face, with a strong nose and a weak chin, partly concealed behind his beard. "My men tell me that you summoned a circle of flame on the road, which burned without wood. Was that science also?"

Dee bowed. "That, Your Majesty, is a trick I learned from an Arab on the southern coast of France, an expert in natural science." The lies rolled off his tongue.

The man against the wall stepped forward, pushed back his hood and reached for the cup.

"Natural science?" His black beard was close-cropped and framed his mouth, which flashed with even teeth when he grinned. "When I hear of flames with no wood, I think of the inferno of hell, and the trickery of demons."

He placed the cup back on the table. I noticed the Magyars had closed ranks even more, and were staring at the man with a mixture of contempt and fear.

Dee's voice was serene. "No demons, sir, but a secret formula known to the Arabs since Emperor Leo the Wise."

"As described in the *Tactica*?" The man bowed to the king, placing his hands inside the sleeves of his cloak. "A book of military strategies, Your Majesty. I believe the doctor refers to some formula for Greek fire, much used in the Byzantine era."

Dee smiled at the man, and bowed. "You have the advantage of me, sir."

The man bowed back like a courtier. "The name of the great scholar and alchemist Doctor Dee has reached all the courts of Europe." He held his hands aloft, and turned in my direction. "And young Master Kelley, who speaks with angels." This time his voice had an edge of irony. I stood, nevertheless, and bowed low.

"Your servant, sir," I ventured, in my best Latin. "How may we address you, my lord?"

He turned to Dee, again flashing that mouthful of white teeth.

"I am Reichsritter Johann Konrad von Schönborn."

A knight of the Holy Roman Empire, in this mongrel court

of Lutherans, Catholics and pagan gypsies. He swung his cloak off his shoulders in a flourish, revealing scarlet robes underneath, and a crucifix swinging against his embroidered breast.

"But you may call me Father Konrad, His Holiness's representative from the Vatican."

I felt a shudder run across my shoulders. Istvan had invited the Inquisition.

Chapter 9

"WHAT DO YOU MEAN, YOU WERE DEAD?"
Jack had been able to drag a struggling Sadie into the warmth of the living room. The teenager had woken more alert this morning, and was installed on one of the two sofas. She seemed less afraid and more defiant now that she had a little energy. Jack had no doubt she was looking for an opportunity to escape. Sadie had passed out briefly as she was carried between the circles of the priest hole and the lounge, but was now glowering over a tumbler of herbal decoction. Jack had made buttered toast, the bribe she had offered for choking down the malodorous brew.

"Dead. Defunct. Expired." She lifted the plate of toast over to Sadie. "If you drink all the potion you won't be sick when you eat."

The girl sipped the drink, her nose wrinkled and her eyes shut.

"That's disgusting." She put the empty glass down and balanced the plate on her lap. "You can't have been dead."

Jack hesitated, trying to find the words to explain it to Sadie. "I was destined to die nearly twenty years ago. Maggie saved me using this special treatment. The same treatment we are giving you."

"What do you mean, destined?" The girl was looking around the room, her gaze returning again and again to the shackle on the floor where the chain was anchored.

Jack picked a couple of dog hairs off her buttery toast and

took a bite while she tried to find the words to explain. "I don't completely understand it," she said, "but most people just die when their time is up. A few people are special. Their death is *almost* certain but they can, in some circumstances, be saved."

Sadie scowled. "I don't get it." She was like a robin, gaze flitting around the room, looking for a way out, perhaps. Her hand pulled at the metal cuff on her wrist, which had already rubbed a sore patch on the skin, despite the padding of an old sock.

Jack pulled her feet up on the other sofa. The November wind was finding ways through the thin carpet, stretched over gaps between the boards. Each winter was harder to deal with.

"Touch your pulse, like this," Jack said, pressing her wrist with a finger. "What does it feel like?"

Sadie put her plate down and curled up into a ball, her knees tight against her chest. But her fingers pressed her wrist, moving, looking for a pulse.

"It's really slow." The girl's face was surprised.

"Your body temperature's lower, too. Feel my hand." She stretched her arm within reach of the teenager.

Sadie frowned, but reached out her fingers to touch Jack's skin lightly for a second, then withdrew. "You're cold."

"So are you. Your body temperature has dropped about two degrees. Mine is even lower."

Sadie felt her other wrist. "So, something's wrong with me. Why aren't I in the hospital? They must have medicines . . ."

"Not for what's wrong with you. You need to be inside the sigils."

"What?"

Jack leaned forward and caught the edge of the old carpet. Pulling it back she revealed the arc of symbols burned into the old wooden boards. Maggie had done it with a soldering iron when Jack was a child. "There's a circle on the floor and another up there."

The girl looked up, squinting to make out the cream symbols painted on the yellowing white of the ceiling. "So these are what . . . magical? You believe they are some sort of . . . super-natural cure?" She jingled the manacle on her wrist, the chain reaching through a hole in the center of the carpet. Her voice was skeptical. "O . . . K."

Jack stroked the dog's head. "You passed out between the priest hole and the middle of the circle, don't you remember? Even a few seconds and your heart slows down. We had to draw the sigils all over your body just to keep you alive. We call it 'borrowed time.' "

Sadie pulled the jumper from around her neck, squinting inside the T-shirt underneath. "What . . . ? Who drew all over me?"

"Maggie did. She's the person who really saved you. She knows all about this stuff."

Sadie pulled her clothes back around her shoulders, crossing her arms over her chest. "So, why?"

Jack rolled dog hair off her hands and onto the floor. "People like you and me, saved from death, we're valuable. We are worth thousands to the right dealer."

The girl's face paled and she froze, hands tight on the blanket. "Dealer? Like . . . selling me?"

Jack shook her head. "Don't be an idiot. Roisin—you don't remember her, but she was here when you were really bad, she helped look after you—Roisin is a seer, she gets visions. She saw you, dying, in the city center and told me to find you. To try to save you."

"But I didn't die . . ." Sadie's voice was hard. She leaned back on her cushions, and looked around the room, gaze darting over the wall of bookcases, and the doors into the hall and kitchen. "When will I get better, then? When can I go home?"

Jack stood up, opened a door on a cupboard, the top piled with papers. She took out a dog brush. "I never went home." She started grooming the dog's thick pelt.

The words seemed to hang in the air, over the sound of the crackling of the fire and the bristles sweeping through the dog's coat.

"You can't keep me here forever. I'll get out."

"You'll understand, with time." Jack turned back to the girl, seeing her blue eyes staring at her, but brimming with tears.

Sadie dashed her sleeve over her face and sniffed. "You have to let me go. If you don't, I'll get out, I'll tell the police."

Jack felt a lurch in her chest at the memory of Carla saying much the same thing.

"I can't let that happen again."

"Again?" The girl was sharp, jumping on every snippet of information.

"The last girl here, was like you and me. The same sickness. She . . . bolted, she escaped. She didn't understand, she wouldn't listen. She died a few minutes after leaving the cottage." Her throat tightened, roughening her voice. "That was after months here. All you would have to do is step into the kitchen and your lungs will fill up and your heart will stop. It's the way you were supposed to have died. Choking on your own vomit."

There was a long silence, then the girl broke it. "I've never even been drunk before."

"It doesn't matter now, that was your old life. Now you have a new one. You're on 'borrowed time.' If we get one herb wrong, leave one sigil out or let you go out of the circle, you will choke to death."

Chapter 10

*The lands of Europe are scourged by the Inquisition,
at the expense of many a fine English or Dutch sailor
or anyone who espouses the Protestant creed. Konrad
von Schönborn, a knight of the Holy Roman Empire,
is an inquisitor with the ear of cardinals. Yet no one
who has met him could doubt that he wields a sword
with as much force as his crucifix, and carries the
authority of the Pope himself.*

—EDWARD KELLEY
16 November 1585
Niepolomice

IN THESE BARBARIC LANDS, IT WAS CUSTOMARY FOR TRAVEL-
ers to share beds. Climbing between coarse sheets, next to
my mentor, I had not expected to sleep well. I was grateful
to be given a bed at all. My head was full of tales of English
sailors tortured by the Inquisition. But the mattress was well
stuffed with bracken and soon Dee's soft breaths soothed me
into sleep.

I awoke to the scraping of the door over dry rushes. The
fire's embers still smoldered, the light glowing on a yard of steel
advancing toward my nose. It is these moments when your body
freezes, even as your mind races for your dagger. Another man
followed the first, carrying a shuttered lantern.

The form behind the broadsword was stocky and concealed

within a cloak, and he stepped toward me on quiet soles. My horrified eyes were drawn to them, mud-stained calfskin riding boots, laced up the front. I was about to die as I had lived, the son of a shoemaker.

I then realized that Dee too had woken. I pushed myself to sitting and flattened myself against the wall, away from the tip of the advancing blade. My fingers fumbled beneath the blanket for my stiletto.

"How may we help you?" Dee said, in courteous Latin.

"*Exsisto silens.*" Be silent. Something in the words froze any movement and the sound in my throat. It was the tone of command, coupled with the touch of the sword tip nudging my throat under my chin. It gleamed, the cold burning my skin like ice.

"Put the dagger away." The other man spoke in a soft voice. Even as my trembling hand dropped the few inches of blade I had started to hold up against the apparition, I recognized the tone. It filled me with a mixture of relief and indignation. The man swept the hood off his head and turned toward the light.

"Do you not recognize me, Master Edward Kelley?" he said, in perfect Latin.

"Your Majesty." I bowed as best I could, huddled against the wall.

He swept off his cloak, making the small fire waver and smoke drift around the room. He spoke in a low growl to his companion, who lowered his sword and walked over to the fire. He pushed another log on with his foot, then set the lantern upon the table. In the light, I recognized the man seated beside the king at dinner.

Dee gestured the king to the chair. "Your Majesty, if you will sit and tell us how we may serve you?" He sat up in bed as if he were accustomed to armed men waking us in the middle of the night.

The king sat in the chair. The big man leaned one shoulder against the door as if he would stop an invasion.

"My half brother, Count Miklós Báthory." The king set his own sword, point down, against the arm of the chair, always within reach. "You may speak freely before him. He has my absolute trust." He spoke in another tongue, and the big man nodded, once.

Dee nodded to the count, and I managed another bow as I scrambled out of bed and onto the low stool.

"I need your help, and the utmost discretion. I have a niece, and she suffers from the most serious disease." The king's face creased into wrinkles, as if careworn. "No physician can help her."

Dee held out his hands. "If my studies in natural science can help in any way . . ."

The king ran his hand through dark hair, speckled with age, and glanced at me. "What ails Countess Erzsébet is not something a doctor can heal. Have you heard the story of Anna, my sister?"

"I am sorry—we have been here so little a time," Dee said.

The king cut him off with a wave of his hand. "It is better that you hear the truth from me, rather than the lies people spread. All you need to know is that my youngest sister, Anna, was born in the most strange and . . . demonic of circumstances."

Dee pulled at his beard, as he did when he was lost for words. "I am no expert on demonic forces, Your Majesty. Can you explain further?"

I watched the other man, his eyes darting from Dee to Istvan.

The king spoke, his voice a rumble. "My sister Anna quickened inside the body of my mother . . . when she had been dead five years."

Chapter 11

FELIX WAS SUPPOSED TO BE GRADING ASSIGNMENTS IN HIS study at home. Rectangles on the wallpaper suggested where pictures had hung, dents in the old carpet remembered where furniture had stood. He had also conceded the cat, and exactly half their savings. The divorce was leaving him the house but had taken almost everything else. The desk had belonged to his father, when he worked for the War Office, so he had kept it.

He was relieving the tedium of reading essays by researching the markings on the dead girl's body. He had scanned in each of the individual symbols from the postmortem photographs, and could examine them separately. It helped to remove the distraction of the face, with its blank gaze. The shapes were separate, and those on the girl's back, one circle inside another, were different from the ones on the front. About one-third of the symbols appeared to be based on the Enochian alphabet, but he couldn't make them form recognizable words in any language he knew. The differences were subtle, sixty-six distinct characters. He catalogued them into Enochian; degraded Enochian; unknown, possibly cuneiform; and what looked like an early Indian script, maybe Vedic Sanskrit of some sort. Three pictographs—what looked like a sun, a crescent moon and a spiky seven-pointed star—occurred several times. The images were laid out over his desk, some spilling onto the carpet. The house was so quiet, the radiators humming and bubbling into life were distracting. Images of Marianne intruded. Curled up in the armchair beside him, discussing work, falling asleep over a book, playing the baby grand . . .

Shaking off the memory, he searched through his diary for contacts at the British Museum. He'd last visited in January—or was it February?—to give a lecture on superstition on the Internet. He dialed the number.

"Can I speak to Dr. Martin Mackenzie, please?"

"Speaking." The voice, as un-Scottish as you could imagine, was pure East London.

"Hello, it's Felix Guichard here, from Exeter. We met in the spring—"

"Felix! The modern witchcraft guy, right? What can I do for you?"

Felix leaned back in his chair, looking out of the window at the darkening sky, and the overgrown shrubs. What do people *do* with gardens? Beyond mowing the grass, Felix had left all that to Marianne.

"I'm helping the police with a case and there are some symbols involved. I believe you have something in the museum that may be similar. A medal."

"Ah. We have thousands of medals here. Can you narrow it down?"

"It was bought by the museum about two years ago, from an auction." Felix turned over his notes and the pictures. "It was given to John Dee by King Istvan Báthory of Poland, around 1585. My photocopies are very basic; I really need a high-quality, magnified scan."

He could hear the clicking of fingers on a keyboard. "It says here, two medals, bronze, report attached by one Felix Guichard. You authenticated them?"

"I looked at a batch of papers, mostly notes written by Dee and his assistant, Kelley. I believe they went to a university in the States, but the museum got the medals."

"No one else wanted them, probably. The papers will be

good for a bit of research money, maybe a couple of doctoral theses. So, how can I help? I can e-mail you our scanned records, they're pretty good."

"That would be great. The other thing is, I need to know the name of the person who sold them."

There was a long pause at the end of the phone. "Strictly speaking, that's confidential."

"I know. But this is an official investigation into a suspicious death. I'm sure the police could get paperwork in order—eventually. Between you and me," he paused for effect, "the symbols were drawn on the body of a dead teenager. You could be helping in what may turn out to be a murder."

"Well, obviously I want to help." There was some tapping of keys at Mackenzie's end. "And I suppose you may have had this information, when you did the authentication."

"I may well have done. You would only be jogging my memory, I'm sure no one could blame you."

There was more tapping and clicking. "The name of the vendor was Mrs. Margaret Slee, and the check was made out to J. Hammond. No address recorded but I have a phone number. Got a pen?"

Felix rang off, and sipped his cooling coffee. He ought to finish marking the essays first. Instead, he dialed the mobile number. After a few rings a woman answered.

"Yes? What?" He could hear her shut a door.

"I believe you may be able to help the police with their investigation. My name is Professor Felix Guichard."

"How did you get this number?"

"It is on the record of some artifacts auctioned two years ago. I'm looking for Mrs. Slee or Ms. Hammond."

"Mrs. Slee moved out years ago." Her voice was husky, soft.

"Ms. Hammond, then?"

The voice hesitated. "What's this about?"

"I'm phoning about some medals you and Mrs. Slee sold to the British Museum."

"What about them? Look, I'm really busy . . ." He could hear thumping in the background.

"I'm investigating the symbols that are inscribed on the medals."

There was no response from the woman on the end of the phone, but he thought she took a deep breath.

Felix continued. "I was hoping we could discuss where you got the items from, and any background information you might have."

"Look, I don't want to be rude, but we don't want to get involved." Her voice was firm. "I don't know anything about them, just a few old things in a box in the attic. I'm sorry, but I have to go . . ."

Felix started to get annoyed. "Ms. Hammond, I'm helping with a police investigation into the death of a young girl. I would rather not pass your details on to the officers working the case. I thought if you answered my questions, they wouldn't need to follow up in person."

"Well, OK," she responded, eventually. "I just can't see how I can help."

"Would you prefer me to visit you at home, or perhaps you could come to the university?" He tapped his pen on the paper with her number on it.

"I'm, uh, working in town this week. Perhaps we could meet at a pub? Do you know Princesshay at all?"

"Fairly well." It was an area of shops near the cathedral.

"There's a pub, the Keg and Apple. Could you meet me there?"

"How about tomorrow? I'm teaching until six, I could make it by six-thirty. It should be quiet."

Another silence. He started counting. She seemed strangely

hesitant. He had just got to seventeen when she replied. "I'll be there." Then her voice lightened a little. "I'm five foot six, blond and will be wearing a green jacket."

He smiled. "Thank you, Ms. Hammond."

"Jack. My name is Jack."

"Felix. So—six-thirty tomorrow."

Felix turned to write the time of the meeting on the calendar, before he remembered Marianne had taken that, too. He made a note of it on his mobile phone instead.

He walked around the kitchen for something—anything—for dinner. The fridge was almost empty. He had no idea how much of his life had been organized by Marianne. Food, laundry, messages, somehow all accomplished while she worked teaching music full-time. As he stood in the kitchen he glanced out toward the street. It was empty, but he felt a strange uneasiness. The face of the girl against the glass was haunting him.

A sound behind his back made him jump. He swung around to see Tycho, Marianne's fat tabby, pushing the cat flap open with his nose.

"Why are you back again? Don't like Heinrich, eh?" At least Marianne had left the kitchen phone. He sat on one of the remaining chairs.

He keyed in Marianne's new number as Tycho, rasping a purr, settled on his lap.

"The cat's back," he said, the second she picked up.

"Well, he's used to living there. I don't think that's surprising after twelve years. I'll pick him up tomorrow." Marianne's low voice was still sexy.

"I haven't got any cat food."

She sighed. "Felix, don't be childish. I'm not coming over, and it wouldn't do any good if I did."

"Don't flatter yourself." It was cheap, and he knew it. He did want her to come over. "I've been working, that's all. I'm consulting on a case for the police. I don't have time to cat-sit."

"Oh, God, not like that child in the Thames?" Her voice got more husky.

"Not that bad, no." The cat rubbed its face over Felix's hand.

"Look, there are a few tins of tuna in the cupboard. Just drain off the brine for him, and I'll pick him up tomorrow." He could almost see her, curled up in her favorite wing chair, running her hand through her long hair.

"I really miss you, you know?" His voice was a growl, and he regretted saying it almost immediately.

He could hear her sigh down the phone.

"I miss you too, Felix. But I'm in love with Heinrich, and that's where my future is." There was a long gap, which she might once have filled with some comment like "Love you" or "Bye darling," in her slight Swedish accent. Instead, she said, "Goodbye, Felix." Before he could answer, the phone clicked in his ear.

He sat for a long moment, letting the sadness settle on him as he remembered the easy affection they had had, the passion of the early years. It all seemed a long time ago, yet until Heinrich came along, he would have said they were just as happy. Just more . . . separate, as their careers took them to different places. When she left she said her love had just faded away, which was fine for her, but he didn't feel any different. He shook off the melancholy and put some music on in the study. He checked his university e-mail account. Two excuses why assignments would be late, one reminder about a budget meeting, and an e-mail from Mackenzie at the British Museum. He opened it.

Hi Felix,

I've done a detailed pic for you of each side of the medals. The curator of the collection said someone else was looking at them a few weeks ago. She wanted to know the vendor too; I'm not sure if they gave the information to her. Then, last week, a man from some police task force asked who sold them and they gave the info out. Let me know when you solve the murder and catch the bad guy.

All the best,
MM

He looked at the images Mackenzie had attached to the e-mail. They were much better quality than the quick scans Rose had done. Mackenzie had also included files of every one of the sixty or so sheets of paper and vellum that had been auctioned. The folded and damaged paper, hatched with Kelley's illegible script, was much clearer in the museum's scans. He opened them, one at a time, on the screen. Kelley's spellings were inconsistent as well as archaic, and he switched into Latin frequently. Felix started to see whole phrases. Far from being notes of experiments or alchemical formulae, the pages seemed to be in journal form. A sentence unraveled itself from loops and blotches.

Her mother gave byrthe to a chyld—when she had been ded fulle five yeares . . .

Chapter 12

It is said in Poland that nowhere is the line between alive and dead finer, than in Transylvania. Only when a corpse is bloated and festering, or entirely beheaded, is it believed dead.

—Edward Kelley
  17 November 1585
  Niepolomice

Her mother gave birth to a child—when she had been dead fully five years? It filled my mind with horrid possibilities.

I looked at Dee, whose hair was already standing on end from being asleep, and back to the long face of the king.

"You do not believe me. What rational being could? I was just a small child when my parents were ambushed on the road to Buda." Istvan looked troubled, his face reddened by the glow from the fire as it brightened. A tendril of smoke stretched out and caught in my throat.

"We have seen many things that have defied belief, Your Majesty," Dee conceded. "Yet they were found to be true."

The king stretched back in his chair, looking first at me, then at Dee, as if looking for signs of disbelief or deception. I gathered myself in my cloak, which I had hung upon the end of the bed to dry. I shall tell you the story in his words, for to relate it makes me shiver.

"My father, the Voivode of Transylvania, was attacked by rebels. He managed to get my mother, Katalin, safely to the citadel at Poenari before he died of his wounds. But she had been gored in the side by a pike, and her women could not stanch the bleeding. They feared, not just for her life but for that of her unborn child. They called upon a woman, known to the local peasants as Zsuzsanna, who was reputed to be skilled in herbs and midwifery, to save their mistress.

"She sent my mother's servants away, then demanded faggots of firewood, as many as the castle held. She barricaded the door to the tower where my mother lay, close to death. All night the people of the castle heard the terrible screams and moans of my mother, as if she were being tortured by the Turks, and smoke hung over the stronghold.

"My mother's servants tried to break into the tower, but the soldiers were afraid and stopped them. The castle guards confessed that Zsuzsanna was a notorious sorceress. After a night of terrible suffering, the door was unlocked and my mother's retainers rushed to her aid.

"Their lady, though deathly pale and weak, still breathed. She commanded that the witch Zsuzsanna be placed in charge, as only she could keep my mother alive with her herbs and potions.

"They had to defer to the witch in all matters concerning the countess, including her virtual imprisonment within that one chamber. She could not step outside the room for a whole year, during which her belly swelled with her living child, but very slowly. At the end of that time I and my brothers and sisters were taken to see her, but although she knew us, all affection seemed gone. Instead, her love was focused on the child inside her.

"By the following year, the Lady Katalin could walk slowly within the confines of the tower. Her strength grew, but she was attended only by Zsuzsanna, who held her own peasants' court in the castle's yard, doing her devilish work. Although the palace servants loathed her and distrusted her entirely, the local people revered her and claimed she had saved many of their lives with her medicines and spells. The story of the lady with the baby forever trapped inside her womb spread, and there were those in the church who even said my mother—my own, gentle mother—was a witch, or else some dead creature, kept alive by evil spirits and carrying a dragon inside her.

"She lived for five years inside the castle, getting stronger each year, until the time when the pains came to birth her child. The labor was cruel and lasted two nights, and it was said that the servants took out sheet after sheet soaked in Katalin's blood, before a huge scream shook the castle and the baby was born. It was a girl—not a monster, not a dragon—and except for being born with a full head of curls and a few teeth, the baby was as other babies.

"My mother did not survive, slipping away after her child was shown to her, but blessed her and named her Anna. The child weakened over the day and many prayed that it would also die. At Zsuzsanna's insistence the baby was put to the breast of a fearful peasant woman, who had been chosen to nurse the child, but when suckling, the innocent babe bit the woman and blood mingled with the milk. She seemed to strengthen, and suckled fiercely while the woman cried for help, but Zsuzsanna made her feed the baby until she was strong and pink.

"This was the beginning of the legend of Anna, which haunted my family for many years. It was only as they prepared the body of my mother that her servants saw the scars upon her skin, and realized why she had screamed on that first night. There were burns, strange shapes and letters branded into her skin, a little like your angelic alphabets, Master Dee.

"Anna grew up attended, as her mother had been, by Zsuzsanna. And in her time, she married my Ecsed cousin, György Báthory, and had children. She was, in many ways, like other women, though weakened by her unusual birth."

The king leaned back in the chair, as if exhausted.

"Now Anna's daughter Erzsébet is ill, close to death, in the way her mother and grandmother were. Zsuzsanna died last year. Her daughter Zsófia does what she can, but if you . . . if you understand these magics, then you must help her."

"When did this illness start, Your Majesty?" Dee's eyes glittered in the low light, and I knew his interest was caught.

"My niece was a wild girl in her youth. She was betrothed at the age of eleven to one of my most trusted lieutenants, Count Ferenc Nádasdy, although they barely knew each other. Three years later she disgraced her name when she bore a daughter to a groom. The pregnancy weakened her, and after her marriage she could not conceive again. She is now five-and-twenty and suffers bouts of weakness that only the witch seems able to treat. But she is worsening and, as her uncle, I have sworn to try to help her."

Dee looked at me, and I saw a strange expression in his eyes. "I would need to consult the witch's daughter about the symbols. But, Your Majesty, if these are demonic interventions, I cannot in any conscience interfere with God's purpose."

Istvan's hand was like his face: big, square and battle-scarred. He ran his fingers through his bushy hair.

"My niece is now as devout a young woman as you could hope to meet, Master Dee, even though she is Protestant. As my sister Anna was." He reached into his clothes and brought out a folded parchment square. "These were drawn by my mother's priest, after her death. They are some of the brands she suffered." His hand was shaking when he passed the paper to Dee.

Dee got off the bed, opened the note and spread it on the table. "Edward. Get me Bacon's *Demonica*." He rummaged through the pack for vellum and pens. "Do you know what the other symbols look like? Does anyone know what any of them mean?"

The king spoke. "There is one who does. Zsuzsanna's daughter, Zsófia Draskovich. She knows them."

Dee pulled out half the books in the pack. "And more lamps. I need light. Edward, clear the table."

King Istvan stood up, easing his back. Even in the light of the lantern I could see that he wore his years heavily. "I will send her to you." He paused for a moment, a frown creasing his heavy forehead. "Zsófia is one of the gypsies from the mountains of my homeland, Transylvania. Beware her trickeries."

I wondered what misfortune and wickedness this hag would bring to us.

Chapter 13

Between spasms of dry heaves, Sadie hunched over a bowl. She no longer fought Jack's help to leave the dungeon, although she hated the feel of the woman touching her. Jack's hands were cold and dry, cracked like an old woman's, even though she seemed quite young. She was strong, though, and not unkind. Sadie looked across at the woman, bent over what looked like an accounts book.

Sadie looked around. The room reminded her of old people's houses. Saggy sofas, patterned carpets, books everywhere. The walls were covered with wood, painted some dingy white.

Jack looked up, rubbing one temple in gentle circles. "God, I hate numbers."

Sadie stared at her, trying to understand how Jack could kidnap people and chain them up, but then chat to them like they were friends. Sadie choked on a mouthful of sick. It was happening less often, and wasn't so bad now, but it was still a problem. She sipped some water. She brushed her long bangs out of her eyes. She had dyed it jet black from its natural chestnut, and got it cut short before . . . Mum had been furious.

"Do you think you can have dyslexia just for numbers?" Jack crossed something out, and wrote above it carefully.

Sadie pushed the bowl away and picked up her drink. "I'm missing school."

Jack shrugged, keeping one finger on her page and closing the book around it. "School won't be much use to you if you're dead."

"You can't believe that!" It burst out of Sadie, and she flung the empty cup across the room, where it bounced off one of the bookcases and thudded to the floor. The dog started growling, lifting himself off the ground, his lips pulled back away from his long teeth and red tongue.

"Ches!" Jack turned to Sadie. "Stay still, you idiot. He's not used to you, he's not . . . tame."

For a long moment, the only sound was the panting of the dog. He sidled closer to Sadie, and she slowly extended an open hand to him. He sniffed it from a distance, then took one step closer, and scented her more thoroughly. Finally, his tail began a slow beat, and he stepped close enough for her to touch his head. His fur was so dense her fingers bounced off it.

Jack seemed to relax. "It seems he likes you. But be careful with him, he's not very sociable."

Sadie stroked the top of his head. "I'm good with dogs. I want to be a vet."

Ches sat down, then slumped onto the carpet between the sofas.

Jack opened her notebook again. "Sometimes, people bring me injured birds and animals," she said. "I rescued a pair of magpies last year, they're nesting in one of the trees out the back."

People come to the house. Maybe I can get help.

Jack closed the book, and stretched out on the sofa. "We get a few hedgehogs, too."

Despite herself, Sadie was interested. *Maybe if she'll take me outside, I can make a run for it.*

"In fact, Maggie is coming here, later." Jack continued. "She's going to keep an eye on you while I go out, but she's also looking after a hedgehog for me. She helped nurse you when you were very ill."

Sadie looked around the room. "Where's the telly?"

"What?"

"Well, I can't do anything else, so I thought I could at least watch television."

"I don't have one."

The concept seemed so strange, Sadie realized her mouth had dropped open. So, there was no telly, no computer, just the quiet crackling of the fire and conversation with Jack.

She folded back the blankets and quilt she had made into a nest, and put her feet on the floor. She stood up, shaking with the effort.

"What are you doing?" Jack said.

Sadie put her hand up, to brush her bangs out of her eyes. The shackle chinked against the chain.

"I just want to see what I can do. You said I have to stay in the circle?" She rubbed the skin where it was reddened by the handcuff. "So, the middle must be the best place." She stepped into the center of the room, where the chain was fastened to a plate in the floor, with a steel ring poking through a hole in the rug. She took a deep breath. The shaking had stopped. She tugged the neck of her T-shirt down a little, revealing the drawn sigils across her exposed collarbones. "Do I really need these?" She rubbed one with her thumb, but it didn't smudge.

Jack closed her accounts book. Ches waved his tail gently, as if hoping Sadie would play with him.

"You'll always need them. We all do. There's a load on your back, too."

Sadie's lips tightened into a humorless smile. "You really believe that a few shapes are some sort of magic charm?"

Jack stared at her. "Go on, then. Try it. Go to the edge of the circle. Then tell me what you believe."

Sadie took a step away from the center of the circle, between the sofas, toward the open kitchen door.

"Still OK." She took another step, the chain uncurling along the floor, then half a pace more.

The feeling, at first, was just cold, as if the middle of the cir-

cle was warmer, but was followed by a surge of bitterness filling
Sadie's mouth. She was aware of her heart thumping slowly in
her chest, and a rising dread. She closed her eyes, fighting the
terror that rose inside her. It was hard to breathe, her throat was
squeezing shut and it felt like her tongue was swelling.

"I didn't do that to you." Jack sounded close, and Sadie
opened her eyes to find the woman beside her, arms ready to
catch her if she collapsed. "I just saved you. Careful, Sadie. Just
a little at a time."

Another shuffle, and this time the response was immediate.
Sadie retched, and the floor pitched under her feet. Sadie tottered, but held one trembling hand out to push Jack away.

"No!"

"I'm telling the truth, Sadie. The farther you go, the closer
to death you get. Be careful. I don't want to have to resuscitate
you again."

Sadie glared at her, the other hand pressed to her mouth, her
body shaking. But she took a tiny step back, and breathed deep.
Then another, tears building in her eyes as she capitulated.

Jack sighed, and retreated. Sadie curled into a ball and covered her face with her arms, sobbing, letting the anguish out. *I
want to go home. Mum . . .*

The dog walked over, sniffing the top of her bent head, and
after a moment, her hand buried itself in the thick fur on his
head. Ches bumped her with his snout, and finally licked her
fingers.

Sadie wiped her face on her sleeve, then looked at her hand.

Jack held out a wad of tissues. "I didn't believe it, either. I
made myself worse for months, trying to get out. Then I understood. We can never go back."

Chapter 14

*Rich meats and heavy wines made me sleep heavily,
but my dreams were haunted by strange images:
women who lay with wolves, ghosts that spoke from
the lips of corpses, and men who served dishes of
human flesh.*

—Edward Kelley
  19 November 1585
  Niepolomice

I SLEPT A LITTLE BEFORE THE DAY DAWNED GRAY, THE CLOUDS glowering over the castle, and I covered myself in extra layers as I huddled next to the burned-out fire. Dee had worked through the remaining night, muttering to himself, making notes. The door opened and a dark-skinned servant woman brought a tray with bowls of thick porridge and some sort of bread. I misliked the look of the greasy tray, and instead refreshed myself from the jug of thin ale. Dee started spooning the yellow porridge into himself—but he had little discrimination in his tastes.

"I believe the shapes the woman suffered, branded into her skin, were magical talismans that call upon the angels Uriel, Raphael and Michael," he said. "The symbols are somewhat like our 'u,' 'r' and 'm' in the angelic alphabet." He took another spoonful of the porridge, and swallowed it with apparent enjoyment. "We should at least try to help this poor young woman.

Whatever the sins of her mother and grandmother, we cannot blame the child."

I stood looking at the drawings, faded on stained and creased parchment.

He turned the sketches around. "This one, for example, is a crude imitation of the symbols we use for *Deo*, God." He took his pen and dipped it in the ink, making a better, clearer shape in his notebook. "Perhaps the burns scarred into different shapes over time."

"But, master, how could a child grow within a woman who was barely alive—or, as the king says, already dead?"

Dee shrugged, reached behind him and lifted his jacket over his shoulders. "The king overstates the case. Nature cannot defeat death itself, only prolong a weak life. Perhaps if this woman was treated by healing herbs and rituals, and blessed by these symbols—however cruelly applied—she was able to spare enough life force to infuse her child. We should get more information about the herbs they use."

"Witchcraft?" I was appalled at the idea. While, as a man, I might dabble in powerful natural forces such as alchemy, everyone knows witches attract the devil himself with the sinfulness of the female nature.

Dee finished writing his note, scored the edge with his penknife and tore out the page. He folded it, and wrote the king's name on the outside with a flourish. "There is a great mystery here, Edward. We must meet this young woman. Is she here, at the castle?"

I remembered the pale creature in the coach. "I believe she arrived after us."

"Excellent. And, if you would be so good, pass this to our guards."

I pulled on the heavy door and offered the letter to the one I judged to be the captain.

"*Is nuntius est pro rex*," I tried. "For His Majesty, King Istvan

Báthory." The man eventually held out a callous hand and took the folded parchment.

I tried to step by him but his arm shot before me, and I cannoned into it. He rumbled something but I shook my head.

"*Volo ambula.* I need to walk." I stretched my arms up and feigned a yawn. When the man was unmoved, I crossed myself. "*Ut saluto abbas.* The priest." After a gruff exchange over my head, the guards let me pass.

The bundle of rags had gone from the kitchen, but a maidservant pointed toward the marshaling yard within the outer wall. I found him there, sitting on an upturned barrel, giving spiritual comfort, or perhaps taking the confession of a man hardly less ragged than himself. I awaited my turn and approached him when he became free. In daylight, I realized his eyes were milky. He squinted up at me for a long moment before he greeted me with a malicious grin.

"The English wizard. Or, I should say, the wizard's servant." He seemed in a better humor.

"I must ask you some questions."

He cackled a laugh. A group of armed men looked at us.

"You may ask, but keep your voice down." He spread out his hands, the fingers reddened and swollen with cold. "You should have stayed in your England, young heretic."

"Tell me of the Lady Erzsébet."

"She lies within, sick unto death," he said, "thank the Lord. Did the king tell you why he risks his immortal soul, and treats with witches and sorcerers?"

I stepped back from the odor that clung to him like his rags. "He seeks to use natural sciences and angelic intervention to save his niece, the child of his sister."

"You think he doesn't have a dozen other nieces? I doubt Istvan would risk his eternal soul for his own wife or daughters." A laugh turned into a cough, and he spat red onto the stone courtyard. "He owes her money, maybe more money than anyone else. He can't offend her husband, Nádasdy, the Black Bear. Without Nádasdy and his niece, Istvan would have been bankrupted years ago."

"And now he is trying to help her." I tucked the neck of my jacket around my ears against the wind.

"She was cursed at birth." He spat, and crossed himself, murmuring a blessing, and raising his milky eyes to heaven for a moment.

"Amen," I added, almost without thinking.

"You know the tale of Katalin? Her dead body shambling around for years, bloated with the devil's child." His mouth tightened into a thin line. "A child who lived on blood and witches' brews. No matter how much time Lady Anna spent on her knees in prayer, that one was spewed out of hell."

"Did you ever meet her?"

He shrugged. "I was a priest in her brother's house. She was small, pretty and always pale. A Somlyó Báthory heiress."

His eyes slid over me and I glanced over my shoulder. A woman stood in the doorway to the keep. She was tall, but unlike the servant women who all covered their hair, hers was thick about her shoulders. It was dark red, the color of a fox. I was much struck by her beauty, her eyes looking shamelessly at me, her hands carrying a basket of leaves.

The priest hissed. "That is the witch. Zsófia Draskovich. I recognize the devil's hair." I looked with interest at the woman Istvan had described the night before, but the priest caught my arm. He led me around the corner, into a fetid stable.

The strange woman still seemed before my eyes like the ghost of the sun when you gaze at it. "Tell me about her."

"The witch? Promise me, stranger, that you will not help her. She and her kind, *czarownica*, hags. Do not look at her; do not listen to her. She is the devil's own whore." He was rambling, clutching at my sleeve.

I pried his fingers off my arm and stepped back.

"Tell me of Anna."

"Anna married György, of the Ecsed Báthory family, and so kept the name Báthory. Countess Erzsébet was born an heiress, a rich woman before she married."

"And now she is sick?"

"Zsuzsanna, the witch's mother, is dead, thanks be to God. No one alive knows how to bring one of that cursed line into the world. The countess weakens." He looked up at the sky. "And may God bring us deliverance from evil."

He shuffled to the corner of the stable to peer around the wall. The memory of the witch's searing glance filled my thoughts again, even when I closed my eyes. I sought to bring my own wife's face to my memory, sour little Jane Cooper, at home in Krakow. Instead, Mistress Jane Dee's smile was the best I could summon.

The priest leaned against a handcart. "Now Istvan has brought an inquisitor from Rome to convert his court, even while he convenes warlocks and witches. It matters little to me, I will be dead soon enough. But you, sorcerer, I sense a good Catholic lurking under that English heresy. Maybe Konrad will permit you to confess your sins and denounce your master. At least you will die in the forgiveness and mercy of the Lord."

"I don't intend to die at all, old man."

He looked at me through clouded eyes, grimaced and spat. "You were dead the day you set out for Niepolomice."

Chapter 15

ONCE MAGGIE ARRIVED, JACK COULD GET OUT OF THE house to meet with the professor. Sadie had met the older woman with suspicion, but Maggie had brought warm cookies from home and a box of books and magazines for Sadie. By the time Jack left, the girl was feeding the crumbs to the cautious dog, and Maggie was cooking pasta.

Jack drove her old station wagon into town as the day faded and streetlights flickered on. She parked a hundred yards down from the pub.

A short man by the bar, in ill-fitting corduroy trousers and a tweed jacket, looked like Jack's idea of an academic. She ordered a sparkling water and sat in the corner of the bar, near the log fire, to watch him. A quick look around found a couple of girls chatting, a young man who seemed known to the proprietor, and a thin man in a suit with a briefcase. She dismissed him as a salesman.

She focused her attentions on the shorter man. He looked around a few times but without interest. She settled into her wing chair and reached her cold feet toward the fire. Each winter was becoming harder to endure. Perhaps the diminished life force, or energy, or whatever it was, was running out. She'd never heard of a borrowed timer over forty. For a moment sadness crept into her along with the cold, and she leaned toward the fire.

"Ms. Hammond?" A man she hadn't seen was leaning over her, one hand extended. She took it with some surprise, the skin feeling warm and strong as he gripped her fingers. "I'm Felix Guichard."

"Jackdaw Hammond."

He was tall, over six feet, she guessed, and lean, dressed in a navy suit and a blue shirt but no tie. His eyes were deep set and dark green, and for a moment she couldn't look away. She watched him pull up a chair and sit opposite her. He didn't look like a professor of esoteric religions, he looked like a country solicitor.

He opened his mouth as if he was going to say something, but then narrowed his eyes, looking her over. "You were at the station last Monday night."

"Sorry?"

"I was there. The police called me in."

"Oh." She shrugged, trying to look unconcerned. "I was going to see a friend but the trains were canceled. I didn't fancy the bus. It's a strange coincidence, isn't it?"

He turned his head a little, as if looking at her from a different angle would tell him more. Jack could feel warmth creeping into her face.

"I don't believe in coincidences." His voice was a soft baritone, but it had a harder edge now. "What's the chance that someone who once owned a medal covered in symbols would be at the scene of a dead girl covered in the same shapes?"

She stared down at her drink, watching bubbles shiver against the glass until they lost their hold, and wavered to the surface. Gathering herself, she looked up, meeting his eyes. "You asked me to help you, Professor. What do you want?"

He stared at her for a few seconds, and then nodded. He reached down, and lifted a case onto the table. Locks clicked over a background of hissing and crackling in the grate and muted conversations at the bar. While he was looking down she had a chance to examine him. His hair was dark and wavy, sprinkled with gray, framing a tanned face. Lines around his eyes, and a little slackness on his neck, put him in his forties or so. He wore a wedding ring on long, brown hands. He glanced up and she looked away.

"The symbols were drawn on the body of a young girl," he said. "Did you see her?"

"No. I got to the station just as the police were covering up the train." That at least was true. "And she had things drawn on her that were a bit like the ones on the medals we sold?" She looked up, trying to keep her eyes level and straight, acting innocent. The laser stare was too intense and she dropped her gaze and picked up her drink.

"How did you come by the medals in the first place?"

"They belonged to a friend, Mrs. Slee, Maggie. Her grandmother inherited them." She shrugged. "She was a bit of a collector of historical items. There was a whole box of stuff, papers, medals, even a couple of swords and a pewter plate."

He drew out some scanned pictures of the medals, blown up to A4 size.

"These were struck in Poland, by order of King Istvan, in honor of John Dee." He showed her the four sheets, each medal, back and front, spreading them on the table in front of her. "What do you know about them?"

"Not much. Maggie kept them in a box in the attic; I used to play with them as a kid. I can't see that they have anything to do with a dead girl." She shifted in her chair, uncomfortable with the lies.

His hand stalled over the briefcase, then drew out a sheet of paper covered in sketches of the symbols. *Shit. They must have taken the drawings from Carla's body.* She stared at the sigils, although she could draw all of them from memory.

He continued. "It would be a very strange coincidence that those exact symbols, which until three years ago only you and your friend knew about, ended up in the same sequence on a dead body." His voice deepened as he lowered it, like a growl from a dog that might not be friendly. "They are unique in the textual record."

She pushed the paper back toward him. "We sold those medals two and a half years ago. I don't know how many people have seen them since. The auction house, the museum . . ." She looked up to find him focusing on her. "There was some expert who saw them for the auction, for example."

The corners of his mouth turned up. "Actually, that was me. I was asked to authenticate them."

She smiled in return, although she was shaking inside with cold or anxiety or just the attention of this strange man. He pulled out some more sketches, the circle of symbols she had copied onto Carla's bony back.

"They look like made-up letters to me," she lied, and finished her drink. "Sorry I can't be more help. I do have to get back." The shivery feeling condensed into a sensation of being watched. She turned slightly to one side, as if looking for her bag, while sweeping the bar with a glance under her lashes, then turned back to the professor.

He dropped his voice to a murmur. "I don't know what's going on, but a young woman has died. Another is missing. You or your friend might have a piece of information that would lead the police to solve the case."

"I suppose I could look around the loft, see if there are any more old items," she said, shrugging. "And I could ask Maggie if she knows something. But . . . is this a murder investigation?" She pushed the drawing back toward him.

"Maybe." A sad smile touched his lips, and he suddenly looked younger, and rather more attractive. He took the paper, his warm fingers brushing hers with a tiny, electrical contact. Jack pulled her hands back into her lap.

She glanced at the bar. The thin man in gray sat immobile on a stool, staring at the specials' board, their table in his peripheral vision.

She leaned forward. "I have to go, Professor."

"Felix, please." He sounded tired. "Well, I won't waste any more of your time. Let me know if you find anything else, or remember more details."

She stood, and he unfolded himself from the chair and reached out a hand. She hesitated before his warm skin pressed hers, and for a moment she felt the urge to stop time and let his warmth spread through her. For a long moment she waited for him to speak, then pulled her fingers away and turned to go.

"Goodbye, Felix."

"One last thing. At the station, you looked . . . sad, really upset. Why?"

She was still for a moment, aware that the man at the bar was now watching both of them, and within earshot. She stepped closer, surprised to find how tall he was, and murmured up at him.

"Don't look round. A man at the bar is watching us, I think he's listening too."

Standing so close to him, she staggered a little, and he put one hand on her waist to steady her. The heat from his hand radiated through her clothes.

"What?" Despite her warning he started to turn his head.

"No! Just pretend you are saying goodbye. Look . . . I don't think the medals, or any of it, had anything to do with that girl's death. Can't you just let it go?"

"I can't. Not just because of the police—but also because something happened to that girl, something to do with belief in magical systems connected with Dee. I can't see the association yet, but this could further my research. Maybe it will help solve the mystery about her death, too."

She stepped away from him, and forced a smile for the benefit of their observer. "I'll call you, we can talk more. OK?"

"Just make sure you do call. I have to give a full and comprehensive report to the police."

"Can you keep my name out of it?"

"If you tell me everything you know. Hopefully, that would be enough."

Avoiding looking in the direction of the bar, she wrapped her coat around herself and slipped out of the pub. She waited in the shadow of a wall for a few moments.

Felix walked out of the doorway into a wedge of light from the porch, and crossed the car park. He opened the door of an old Jag.

As Felix was momentarily lit up by the interior light, the gray man slid out of the pub doorway and into a waiting vehicle. When Felix's car pulled out, the man's rumbled into action, and slid after it.

Jack turned up the hill toward her own vehicle, unlocked it and threw her bag onto the passenger seat. She started the engine, turned on lights and windscreen wipers, and glanced in her mirrors. As the car pulled away from the curb, the rear window was backlit by a streetlight. Jack's breath stuck in her throat.

There was someone in the backseat of her car.

Jack stiffened. She could see a narrow head with wispy curls. She braked in the middle of the road, and a driver behind her had to brake as well. His headlights reflected enough light around the car to see that the uninvited passenger was an older woman. Before Jack could react, she heard a soft voice.

"Stop."

The tension fell away.

Jack sagged, eyes locked on the mirror, her muscles softening. The woman's voice was gentle, and she felt a wave of warmth and well-being creep over her. A distant voice in the back of her mind screamed for action, but the rest of her relaxed. A car beeped its horn, but it sounded far away.

"Who . . . who are you?" Her slow tongue formed words that rolled out, one by one.

"You don't need to know." The words filled Jack's head with cotton wool, stifling the beginnings of questions or thoughts. "Drive me to your home."

Jack's body drove the car slowly along the road, as the remaining kernel of consciousness screamed at her to stop. Out of habit, Jack looked in the mirror again, but the woman's gaze seemed to fill the view of the back of the car. The eyes were the lightest of blues, and so full of understanding and compassion that Jack started to well up with tears. The woman's face was beautiful, but unreal. *Like a fairy queen.*

Jack's hands and feet, independent of her mind, changed gear. Some part of her, some small homunculus lost in her brain, started shrieking with protests, but her numbed body drove efficiently out of the town. Minutes passed as she dazedly followed the road and responded to traffic. With horror, she realized she was approaching the turn toward the road to the village.

"Drive home." The woman's words lanced her tiny resistance and she felt her own face crease into a smile at the pleasure of being able to comply. The rain came down harder, and her shriveled consciousness was mesmerized again by the quiet sweep, sweep of wipers. The next time she was aware of her surroundings, she was turning the car into Hambolt village, about a mile from the cottage. The council had installed traffic-calming measures, and she had to wait for a car approaching. On either side of the road stood two massive limestone blocks, once part of a megalithic tomb. She could feel, under the blanket of sedation and obedience the woman was weaving, the dark energy seeping from the stones. As she moved the car forward she mentally reached for it, feeling energy like icy water washing through her. She gripped the steering wheel tightly with hands that felt numbed with cold. Gathering her will in the moment when the enchantment was weakest, between the stones, she stamped on the accelerator. The car jerked forward as she slammed into another gear and concentrated on the moment of clarity. The woman was jolted back into her seat, breaking the spell further. Jack tore through the village and wrenched the wheel at the first corner, into the church car park. Floodlights picked up the motion and snapped on, almost blinding her. Every nerve burned as her limbs throbbed back to life, and she smashed the car into the wall of the churchyard.

Chapter 16

They say that wealth lays beauty upon a woman,
but I believe it is rather power that does so. She
could have had, at a whispered command to any of a
hundred nobles and servants, my death. It was this
that impressed me when I met the Lady Erzsébet
Báthory, despite her mortal weakness, because I
could not take my eyes off her.

—EDWARD KELLEY
  20 November 1585
  Niepolomice

FTER THE NOON BELL, WE WERE SUMMONED TO OUR audience with King Istvan in his own quarters. These were a set of large rooms in the new wing of the castle, and the paneling, tapestries and generous glass windows were akin to one of Her Majesty Queen Elizabeth's minor palaces. A polished black table ran down the middle of the room, big enough for a score of people. Only four high-backed chairs were occupied, and I bowed to the king and Lord Miklós. My master was shown to a padded stool and offered wine by a silent servant. I was gestured to a bench beside him, and also given a cup. A dozen guards stood around the doorways, out of earshot.

"Doctor Dee." The king inclined his head with slow courtesy. He indicated the powerful man beside him. "Count Nádasdy, commander in chief of my armies."

Up close, the man was in his late twenties or so, and dressed more regally than the king. His eyes flickered over Dee and focused on me, sneering at us both. My attention was then drawn to the remaining person on the left side of the king.

She sat straight in her chair, and at first I thought she was a child. I had never seen that color on a living person, her skin as bloodless as a corpse. Her blue eyes, deep set into the emaciated face, burned with an unnatural light and seemed to scorch as her gaze swept over me on the way to Dee. She stared at him with the rudeness of royalty. Her dress was embroidered and so stiff with metal thread and jewels that it seemed to hold up the shriveled body within.

The king waved a hand at her. "And this is Count Nádasdy's wife, my niece. Countess Erzsébet Báthory Nádasdy. As you would say, the Countess Elizabeth Báthory."

She nodded to Dee, and then to me, dropping her eyes for a moment.

Dee stood and swept a courtier's bow. "My lady. Are you comfortable in Latin?"

"In Latin, German, French . . . but not in English, I regret." Her voice was low, and I leaned forward to hear. Despite her frailty, her blue eyes were keen and flicked over us. Her voice had more power than her weak body would suggest, even as she steadied herself against the table. Despite the early hour, the room was dark and the servant set a branch of candles on the table. She wavered her other hand to her eyes and the servant moved the candelabra farther away.

The king waved and the door closed with a soft clunk. Barring the servitor with the candles, we were alone with the king and his noble relatives.

"You may speak freely. Gábor is mute. He is also one of my most loyal servants." King Istvan put out a hand, and a golden goblet was placed in it.

Dee nodded thanks for his goblet—more ornate than mine, I noticed—and took a sip. Then he placed it on the table, all the time scrutinizing the lady.

"Countess, may I ask what ails you?" he said.

"You know my mother's story?" She waved away the servant. "Lady Anna was a good and devout woman who deserved a longer life. But she suffered from a weakness, a sickness that can only be treated by certain herbs and remedies. Feel the pulse in my wrist." She reached out one hand, the fingers skeletal, the knuckles prominent. Her skin was very white and soft, her nails long and oval. A ring, loose on her emaciated thumb, had a dragon coiled about a ruby the size of a robin's egg. It was so red it was almost black.

Dee hesitated for a second, and then took her hand. I could see the shock on his face in the candlelight.

"My lady . . . you are very cold." He pressed two fingers to the pulse in her arm, searching for it gently, failing to find it for a long moment. No one moved or spoke, and when he breathed out it was a shocking sigh in the silent room, as if we had all been holding our breath.

"I am no doctor," he said, releasing her hand, "but your heart beats very slow."

"Since my marriage, the treatments my healing woman gives me have become less effective. I am not normally as weak as you see me now."

Dee spread out his hands. "My lady, I am a scholar and, I hope, a good Christian. If I can help—"

The king leaned back in his chair and rested one hand on his spreading belly. "We have heard about the speech you have had with angels."

"Indeed." Dee bowed his head for a moment.

"How can you be certain that any such communication is with angels, and not demons or evil spirits?"

"The messages have been for the benefit of mankind. Of that I am sure. There is a . . . an odor, an atmosphere, when they reveal their wisdoms to me, their servant."

King Istvan crossed himself and murmured a blessing. I noticed the woman did not.

"And you saw these beings," the countess pressed, like a child.

"They spoke to me when they inhabited my colleague, Master Kelley. He has seen them."

All turned to me, and I felt unpleasantly hot.

The king rested his hands on the table and leaned forward. "What did you see?"

I could not lie to either and mumbled the truth. "I have seen a great radiance, and a sword, and great giants made of blinding light that burned my eyes."

"And these beings . . . possessed you?" The young woman's eyes, blue as a summer sky, stared at me. I found myself speaking directly to her.

"When he appears to me it is like a dream, in which my mouth speaks and Doctor Dee listens." I took a deep draft of the strong wine. "He—Saraquel—fills me with such hope, but such fear."

The king put a hand on his niece's shoulder, as if to prevent her from touching me as she leaned forward. "I must consult my priests," he said in his gruff Latin.

"We welcome it," said Dee, as calm as ever. "We have discussed our findings with many bishops and clerics, as well as scholars and philosophers."

"Father Konrad will also wish to examine your story." The king beckoned to the servitor, who took the goblet from my hand, and when I did not move, twitched his fingers to make me stand. "And your piety."

Chapter 17

JACK SHUDDERED BACK INTO CONSCIOUSNESS. AS SHE LOOKED around the inside of the car and the crazed windscreen, the noise of the engine intruded, and the memories re-formed in her head. She turned the key, and silence flooded back in. Pushing on the door didn't even budge it, so she fumbled with the seat belt and dragged herself to the passenger side. That door creaked and groaned open, and she reeled onto the gravel. The memory of the car hitting the graveyard wall crept back.

A few blocks were knocked askew, but the car had come off worse. The hood was crumpled, and steam rose. As she watched, the motion-activated floodlight went out.

The woman. Damn it, where was she? Jack pulled at the passenger door, and it opened, the interior light glowing yellow. The woman was silent, crumpled half on the seat and half in the footwell. Apparently, she hadn't used her seat belt. For a moment, Jack thought she was dead, but then the woman raised her head and stared back at her.

Jack's instincts hauled her backward over the loose gravel, out of reach of the woman's strange gaze. The car park light snapped back on, and Jack jogged to the wall, her feet slipping in painful slow motion in the shingle.

When they had built the church, they had used any available stone to build the graveyard wall. At the site of a stone horseshoe, the locals had cut up what was lying around. Jack pressed her hands to an ancient block of limestone, and felt her will asserting itself in the dark energy. Behind her, the woman stepped—or fell—onto the stones. Jack took a breath, and turned to face her.

She fumbled in her pockets for a talisman, anything that might boost her flagging energies. She realized pain was grinding into her shoulder, and burning across the center of her chest. She focused on the ache, anchoring herself in her body.

She carried a handful of Maggie's charms. Talismans to ward off illness, robbery, bad luck, but she couldn't think of one that would ward off mind control. She looked up at the woman, who leaned against the car, dabbing away blood from her forehead with a tissue.

"How resourceful of you." She grimaced, and brushed her coat down. She was wearing high heels, which should impede a chase, at least. Jack wasn't sure she could keep her own will.

"I suppose that answers the question of what you are. Some sort of witch." Jack tried to keep her voice steady, but her breath was coming in little sobs, and her voice stumbled through the words.

"No more than you. You created a *morturi masticantes*. So few can raise the dead." The woman took a step, then caught herself against the car and lifted her foot to inspect the heel, which looked like it was loose. "I have to admire your skills. The sigils came from Dee's notes, I assume, or the medals?" The light flickered off, and a second later, snapped back on. The woman had somehow narrowed the gap between them by half the distance. "But you lost that girl, yes? Now you will take me to your new one."

One of the carved stones in Jack's hand was heating up, and she dropped the others back in her pocket.

"No." In her own ears, the denial sounded weak. "No, I won't" came out stronger. She traced a line in the gravel with her foot and stepped away, pressing her back against the fractured wall. She began to chant the protection spell Maggie had taught her from childhood.

When the light flickered off again she braced herself for an assault, and waved her arm to set off the sensor. Nothing happened. *Must be out of range.* But the faint grind of stone on stone suggested the woman was moving. When the light came back on it caught her face, frozen in a grotesque game of "statues." Stalled at the line in the gravel, her mouth was distorted into a grimace, her lips drawn back from her teeth. She hissed like water hitting a hot iron. She shrank back, her features composing themselves. Jack realized her first impression had been of a woman her own age, with fair hair, and a slim figure. The momentary flash had revealed a different woman, gaunt rather than slim, with wispy hair tinted an unlikely shade. Her neck was creped with loose skin, teeth lengthened by time shrinking her gums.

"I will find her." The woman spat the words at her in a shrill voice. "And then I will brush you aside like an insect."

The sensation of standing in rushing water pulled at Jack's thighs and back, and she found herself fighting to keep her feet. The air around her seemed to have thickened and was moving along the wall, sweeping Jack with it. The talisman was burning her palm with the energy of resisting the woman, but clutching it gave Jack strength to battle the force dragging her toward the churchyard gate. The car-park light flickered out, and with it the sweep of air vanished, and Jack staggered, and fell to her knees. The motion set off the sensor, and a pool of fluorescent white saturated the front of the church and the gravel drive. The woman had gone.

Jack wrote a note to the effect that her brakes had failed, propped it in the shattered windshield of her car, retrieved her bag and started walking along the road. She could see no sign of the woman, and took the footpath across the fields away from the house to make sure she wasn't being followed. As she worked her way through the copse at the edge of the village, her years of experience stalking deer allowed her to surprise a fox and a number of rabbits before she climbed the last stile onto the main road. Slipping through a garden, she clambered over the fence onto the footpath that came out on the lane opposite the cottage. She still waited in the shadow, observing the hedges and trees, the thatch and tall chimneys just outlined against the starlit sky. She paused, her head thumping and her stomach contracting.

She tried the handle of the back door, the dog rushing over and pawing at the paintwork, but she was locked out. Maggie walked into the kitchen, turned the key and opened the door.

"What happened? You look terrible. Oh . . . you're hurt, sit down."

It was all Jack could do to fend off Ches, who was frantic, whining and butting her thighs for attention.

"Ches, get down. I'm OK, but I crashed the car." As she looked into the living room, Sadie's white face was leaning forward from one of the settees. When Jack lifted her arms to take her jacket off, the muscles ached with the effort, and she staggered.

Maggie maintained a flow of motherly comments as she ushered her to the other sofa. Jack had to clench her teeth to stop them from chattering. She slumped, shivering, onto the empty couch, and leaned against the worn cushions.

"Now, tell me what happened." Maggie moved as if to touch Jack's head, then grimaced and pulled away.

"There was a woman in the backseat, I don't know how she got in. She cast a hell of a mesmer spell. I had to crash the car to break it, before I drove her right here." She winced as Maggie's fingers brushed her hairline. "She's looking for Sadie."

"What?" Alarm creased Sadie's sharp features, making her blue eyes look even bigger.

Maggie ignored her. "Does she know about *you*? You said Pierce was very interested in another borrowed timer."

Jack shook her head. "She thinks *I'm* the witch."

Maggie took a blanket from the end of Sadie's sofa and draped it around Jack's shoulders. She touched her cheek with the back of one hand.

"You're freezing. And that's a terrible bump on your forehead. Let me clean up some of the blood."

"Blood?" Jack stood, her legs shaky under her, and looked in the mirror over the fireplace. It had poured down one side of her face from a split in her scalp along her hairline, and had dried. As she grimaced, she could feel it crack. "I must have banged my head on the steering wheel."

"You may need stitches. Let me do a healing spell . . ."

"Just put strips on it." Jack sat back on the settee with a sigh.

"Lie down and let me look after you, for a change." While Maggie helped get her boots off, Jack let herself relax.

"Why would someone want me?" Sadie pulled at a loose thread on the sleeve of her jumper. "You said before, I'm valuable, you could sell me. But what would they want me *for*?"

Jack rolled her head on the cushion, looking at Sadie, who was curled up on the end of the sofa, hugging her legs.

"Borrowed timers have some kind of special magic in their blood, I don't understand it myself. But healers use it to treat terminally ill people."

Sadie recoiled, hunching herself up tight. "So that's the real reason you rescued me?" She glared at Jack, her hair sweeping across one eye in a flat curtain. "You're going to keep me like . . . a blood bank?"

"No, it's not why—well, it's not the only reason." Jack sighed, her head throbbing.

Maggie came back in, carrying a tray. "What happened?"

"A man was watching the professor in the pub."

Maggie set the tray on the box in the middle of the room,

and Jack noticed a large bottle of antiseptic and a bag of cotton wool, with some reservations.

Maggie parted Jack's hair with gentle fingers. "Ouch. That looks deep."

Jack looked across at Sadie. "I know how hard this is. I asked all the same questions, and I was a lot younger than you."

Maggie spoke with an edge in her voice. "I think Sadie would be safer downstairs, in the priest hole."

Jack looked over at the girl, whose mouth was set in a hard line, her eyes glaring but filled with tears. "I think this concerns Sadie as much as any of us."

"Jack—"

"No, Maggie. I hated it when you kept me in the dark, and you had to tell me eventually, right? If we had told Carla more, explained—" She choked up for a moment. "Sadie, I'm going to tell you things and you won't believe them. But at least hear me out." Jack looked at the thin arms folded over the blankets.

"Listen to my kidnappers." Sadie's voice was thin. "Right."

"If I meant to hurt you, I could just have left you to die, couldn't I?"

Sadie opened her mouth, then seemed to think better of it. The girl's eyes seemed huge in the dim light. "So you claim."

"Twenty-one years ago, I was supposed to die of a broken neck, a riding accident. I was ten years old, competing in a local gymkhana." Jack spoke distantly, shivering under the blankets. "I had just competed, and my pony threw me at a jump." She could remember the fall, it wasn't even a bad one, she had landed on her feet. "My arm hurt, so my parents sent me to the trailer to sit down. I started to feel dizzy and breathless, and my neck hurt. Maggie grabbed me, put me in a hard collar and locked me in her van. My neck was broken . . . I would have died, no matter what doctors would have done. She saved my life, became my family." She watched Sadie open her eyes, look at her. "It takes a long time to come back from the moment you were destined to die. It took a year for my neck to heal—nothing works as fast when you're half dead."

Sadie's gaze flickered over Maggie, who was frozen, one hand holding a bloodstained swab. "Why? Why would you do that for someone you don't even know?"

"Charley." Maggie choked on the word. "My daughter, Charley. She was only two, she was dying. Acute myeloblastic leukemia." She started dabbing at dried blood on Jack's forehead. "It was her last chance."

"Maggie is a healer." Jack watched the tension drain from the girl's body. "But she couldn't save her own baby."

"I was told of the spell," Maggie said. "A ritual my grandmother knew about. I needed to try it. I would have tried anything."

Sadie snorted as if in disbelief, but her face looked uncertain. "Magic spells."

Maggie peeled the backing off a dressing. "It needed blood from someone who had died, but not died." She carefully applied the dressing to Jack's hairline. "I knew John Dee had written a book about necromancy; my grandmother left me some old papers of his. She studied his books; my family has a long tradition of folk medicine and healing. I started researching her diaries, and the papers and medals, and found these symbols." She rounded up the detritus of the first aid. "I knew a seer; Roisin was the midwife who had delivered Charley. I asked her to find someone destined to die whom we could try to save. Jack was the third one we found."

"Third?" Sadie looked at Jack. "What happened to the other two?"

Jack winced at the gentle pulling on her scalp. "Ask Maggie."

Maggie drew a deep breath beside Jack. "They died, despite my efforts. They couldn't be saved. It was awful."

Jack closed her eyes for a moment. "But I survived and then, because of me, Charley made it. Not just Charley . . . my blood has saved a dozen people." She glanced at Sadie.

Sadie pressed one hand to her chest, over her heart. She looked back, eyes wide.

Jack dabbed at her forehead with a cloth as disinfectant trickled into an eyebrow. "You can feel your heart wavering, can't you? You can feel the cold coming. That's death, actual death." Jack let the words flow over Sadie, watched their meaning sink in. "That's what Dee's symbols do, keep death at bay."

"Who is this . . . Dee?"

Jack pulled her sleeves over her cold fingers. "Dee was an Elizabethan magician, looking for the secrets of life and death. He's supposed to have raised the dead several times. He wrote his research down, and people have been using it to keep borrowed timers like you and me alive ever since."

Sadie huddled into her blanket. "So this is it, I'm stuck like this?"

Jack nodded. "For the moment. As time goes on, you will get better, be able to manage away from the circle for longer."

"So I'll be stronger?" The appeal was in the voice of a child. "Then you'll let me go home?"

Jack shook her head. "You will always be dependent on the magic." She sighed, and let her head fall back on the cushions. "You can never go home."

Chapter 18

JACK WOKE UP, FINDING ACHES THE MOMENT SHE MOVED. She dressed slowly, and followed the smell of food downstairs. Maggie must have gone before breakfast, but had left a casserole in the range. Sadie was still asleep in the priest hole, but Jack unlocked the chain anyway and replaced the bucket.

She went back to the kitchen, stirred the stew and put it back in the top oven. The radio in the kitchen played something classical, which suited the old house. She hardly noticed the break for the news as she turned baked potatoes over on the bottom shelf.

" . . . and local news. The mother of missing teenager Sadie Williams has appealed on national television for local police forces to consider all missing children abducted rather than runaways. Fourteen-year-old Sadie disappeared one week ago—"

Jack switched the radio off. *Shit. No one even noticed Carla; they just wrote her off as a runaway.* Jack looked through the open door in the paneling to find Sadie sitting up in bed, her face tense.

"I heard that. The police are looking for me." Sadie climbed out of bed and clung to the wall.

"I know."

Sadie climbed the steps, wobbling at the top between the sigiled stones in the priest hole and the edge of the living-room circle. Before she could throw up, Jack half pulled, half lifted her into the room, and onto the sofa.

"If they do find me, they'll arrest you. For kidnapping." Sadie pushed Jack away, and pulled the folded throw over herself. The dog greeted her with a wag.

Jack shrugged. "Then they would try to take you to hospital. You would die before you reached the ambulance." Jack took a deep breath, and locked the chain onto the ring in the floor. "I didn't take it as well as you. I cried and screamed a lot."

Sadie shifted her weight and turned her bright blue eyes on Jack. Her thin fingers clutched the edge of the blanket. "I miss my mum."

"I know." Silence built up in unseen layers in the room. The clock on the mantelpiece, left from the days when the cottage belonged to Maggie's mother, ticked off the seconds. *I still miss my mum.* "What about your dad?"

Sadie shrugged one shoulder. "It's just me and Mum." She ran her hands over Ches's head. "So, you really believe in this . . . this magic stuff?"

Jack could almost see the thoughts racing in Sadie's mind, as expressions chased across her features. Jack knelt in front of the wood burner, which sat, surrounded by logs, in the inglenook by the fireplace. She opened the door and threw on more fuel. Sparks shot toward the flue before yellow flames started curling around the bark.

"I don't know what I believe. I tested it, I challenged it—and fought Maggie. But I understand now, the symbols keep me well and alive. I just don't know how they work."

Jack jumped when someone rapped on the kitchen door. The dog started whining and trotted to the frosted glass panel. Jack turned back to Sadie.

"It's Maggie's daughter, you'll like her. Charley! Come in, don't mind the dog."

Charley shouted through the glass. "I would come in, if he wasn't leaning on the bloody door!"

Jack walked into the kitchen and pulled Ches away.

Charley dropped her coat onto the rocking chair, and set a box on the table.

"Shit, it's cold out. Sunny, but freezing. Oh . . . ouch, your head's a mess. Mum said you've been in the wars." Jack tolerated a quick hug, then Charley leaned back to look at the dressing on Jack's hairline. "The police are doing house-to-house inquiries in the village." She bent, threw her arms around the dog, and hugged him. "Stupid beast!"

Jack glanced over her shoulder and lowered her voice. "It's all over the radio. They are calling it an abduction." The girl was huddled on the sofa, apparently oblivious.

"I know. It's Sadie's mother, she's on the telly every night," Charley whispered.

Jack put the kettle on as Charley walked away, and heard the exchange of voices. Maybe Sadie would talk to someone nearer her own age. Charley was twenty-two, red hair straggling down her back, and clad in her own eclectic, charity-shop style. Today she was wearing a pair of leggings, a leather jacket and a tulle skirt. And was the picture of health.

Charley put her head around the door. "Can we have some of that hot chocolate you make? You know, with the real chocolate and the whippy cream on top?"

Jack smiled at her. "What are you, twelve?"

Charley laughed. "Thanks, Grandma."

"I'm nine years older than you. Do you want it, or not?" Jack's pretended outrage made Charley laugh, and Jack thought she could hear a weak snort of laughter from Sadie as well.

She made three mugs of frothy hot chocolate, topped with Flake pieces as well as cream. The girl could use the calories, assuming she kept it down. She carried them in on a tray.

". . . and she's got this amazing tattoo. So she can go out, away from the house. The car's got all these charms as well." Charley's voice was animated. "When you get better you'll have a lot more freedom."

Sadie sat up when Jack came in, refolded her arms, and scowled.

"Hot chocolate." Jack offered it, and for a moment she wondered whether Sadie would take it. Then one thin hand reached out, and retreated with the cup. She watched Charley slurp hers before she bent her head for a small sip.

"She won't help me escape," Sadie said, while Charley was drinking.

"Charley understands borrowed time," Jack replied. "She knows what would happen to you if she did."

The dog padded over to Jack, who was perched on the arm of the other sofa, and leaned against her, resting his head on her knee. Jack couldn't resist his pleading eyes. She dipped her finger in the cream, and smeared it on his nose. "It's bad for you, you silly animal."

Sadie waved a hand. "She—Charley—says you have a tattoo. So you can go outside."

Jack put the mug on the bookcase and rolled up her sweater and T-shirt a few inches, turning her back on the girl. She assumed from the silence that they were both impressed by the circle of sigils, inscribed in four colors.

"There's more up here." Holding her hair aside, she showed them the symbols tracing up her neck onto her scalp. "They shaved part of my head to do it."

"And that means you can go out of the circle?" said Sadie. "Did it hurt?"

Jack straightened her clothes and turned back to Sadie.

"It was painful, and they had to go over it several times. But it does mean I can go anywhere I want, for a few hours anyway." She pulled down the neck of her shirt to show the beginning of the tattoo on her chest. "The one on the front is smaller."

Sadie leaned forward, cupping the hot drink as if she were still cold. "My mum would kill me if I got a tattoo."

"Well, now it might kill you if you don't. You can just draw them on all the time, that works as well. The sigils we drew on your back seemed to help when you were . . . at your worst."

Jack remembered the box on the kitchen table and brought it into the front room. It seemed very light. "This is the hedgehog?"

Charley drained her chocolate with vigorous slurping. She looked across at Sadie. "Jack's really good with sick animals. We've got two other hedgehogs, eating their heads off in the corner of our kitchen. But this one's bad."

Jack knelt by the fire and opened the box. The hedgehog was on its side, curved loosely, panting. It looked very thin. Jack grimaced. "It doesn't look hopeful."

"Can I see?" Sadie was standing, swaying but upright, the empty mug hanging from one hand.

Jack moved the box and showed Sadie. "Sometimes they are too small to hibernate, and too cold to find anything to eat. I'll put him on the floor by the fire, while we get him some warm food. You can help, if you like." The girl sank to her knees beside it.

She watched Sadie put her fingers in, brush the spines. They tightened a little as her hand passed over the skin.

"It's still alive. Can you save it?" asked Sadie.

"We'll do our best."

Jack filled a hot-water bottle from the kettle in the kitchen, and mixed some dog food into a sloppy paste. Returning to Sadie, she lifted the hedgehog with both hands, feeling its cold belly, the hard prickles slack against her fingers.

"Slide that bottle in the box. That's it, put a bit of that hay over the top."

The girl hesitated for a second. "Are those fleas?"

"They won't bite you." Jack watched the girl pad the box. "Now, get that teaspoon and dip the handle into the food. When I open his mouth, just put a tiny bit in, on his tongue. We don't want to choke him."

Jack stroked the dished snout, pulling back the skin toward

its half-closed eyes. The upper lip slid back, showing four sharp yellow teeth and a small pink tongue. Sadie slid the meaty spoon just inside. It slowly shut its mouth.

The creature felt limp in Jack's hands. "He's very cold."

As if in slow motion, the pink tongue swept around the paste on its lips.

"Try again," Jack said.

Sadie loaded up another spoon handle and dabbed it on the creature's teeth and tongue.

Jack laid the creature on its stomach in the warm hay. "On the other hand . . . young animals are resilient, like teenagers, apparently. You have a go, every mouthful helps."

She beckoned to Charley to join her in the kitchen.

"If the police are in the village, they'll come here," she said in a low voice. "I cleaned the car, but I'm worried they'll want to come into the house to look around. How do I keep Sadie quiet?"

"I wouldn't be surprised if she cooperates. She seems bright and I think she's coming round. Now, tell me about this woman in your car."

Jack wrapped her arms around herself. "A witch, I think, much more powerful than anyone I've met. She wants Sadie." She sighed, reached for her coat. "Everyone wants Sadie. Pierce offered me big bucks for a new borrowed timer."

"That's a bit of a coincidence, isn't it? Does he know anything?"

Jack considered the question for a moment. "I think it might be worth finding out. I'll arrange to meet him, somewhere neutral. In the meantime, I need to go and talk to the vicar, and get the garage to tow the car. Can you keep an eye on Sadie and the hedgehog for me?"

"Sure." Charley reached up for the cookie tin, rattled it. "I like her. She reminds me of you." She bit into a cookie, spilling crumbs down her top. "Grumpy, difficult, opinionated."

"Thanks." Jack wound a scarf around her neck and shrugged a warm jacket on. "I won't be long." She opened the door, looking out into the yard, gray under a blanket of cloud, and pressed her hand to the protective charm carved into the plaster. "Keep her safe."

Chapter 19

*Everyone knows that women are filled with original
sin, yet I have known virtuous ones. Doctor Dee's
wife, Jane, for example, is a pattern of purity and
womanly goodness. But there are other women,
who spread great wickedness in the world. Who are
witches, and demons in human form.*

—EDWARD KELLEY
  22 November 1585
  Niepolomice

LATE IN THE AFTERNOON, I HEARD THE RUMBLE OF HORSES'
hooves pounding over the drawbridge, then clattering
over the cobbles in the yard. Shouts, in the dialect I now
recognized as Magyar, were answered with what sounded like
abuse in Polish. Then the name Báthory, over and over, like a
battle cry.

As Dee was in consultation elsewhere, with the king's advisers, our guards were absent. I walked down the corridors,
through the small door at the end, which led to the minstrels'
gallery I had observed over the main feasting hall. The door
at the other end, I had discovered with smiles and a few Polish pennies, led directly to the outside stairs, to the vast stable-
yard. Here men were dismounting, dressed in bearskin jackets
over split riding cloaks, the dark fur silvered with dew. Officers
in jaunty hats and the ubiquitous red boots strutted around,

calling out jibes, which were met with laughter from the men. Many faces and hands were scarred, some men limped.

"They are Nádasdy's own elite troops." The female voice, in slow German, was unexpected and I jumped.

I turned to see the fox-haired woman from the yard. The voice was warm and low, and sounded as if it promised caresses to follow. I am not a carnal man, and my wife cannot complain that I intrude upon her rest, but the witch's voice stirred me. She was of my own height, strongly built, and I guessed of my own age.

"The soldiers are here to take my mistress home, when your Dee has cured her with your old books." Her voice was sharp with sarcasm, even in German. She was wrapped in a dark red cloak, fashioned from rich fabrics.

"You think he cannot do it?" I was genuinely surprised. I could scarcely compare the superstitions of a handful of heretics to Dee's theosophical investigations and research.

"This is women's work, the giving and . . . what word is it . . . the *preserving* of life." She allowed her cloak to fall open, revealing her close-fitting gown beneath. As she stepped nearer, looking on the men below, I caught the scent of a perfume that made my head spin. "We must call upon ancient wisdoms, known only to women. My mother had power drawn from the mountains themselves, from the forests that cradled my people."

"You are the witch."

"I am Zsófia Draskovich, the countess's healer. And you are the poor adventurer Eduárd Kelley, with his sorcerer master."

"Doctor Dee is a natural philosopher, and has been consulted on matters of state by kings. He even cast your emperor's horoscope on the occasion of his coronation."

She smiled, her teeth very even and white against her tanned skin. "Stars and charts? He thinks to reduce a man to numbers?"

I was entranced by the scent coming off her clothes and hair. Her eyes glowed, and I was filled with the wish to please her. As she turned toward me, I leaned, intoxicated, as if to kiss her. She divined it, and pulled away with a low laugh.

"You think to tumble me like a drab?"

I stepped back, my face heating up my fair complexion in a boyish blush. "No, of course not . . ."

She leaned forward again, and this time, put her lips to my ear. "Why would I want you, the sorcerer's assistant, when I could have *royalty*?"

I recoiled, and turned to leave the way I had come, my thoughts in disorder.

Zsófia called out to me before I reached the door back to the tower. "I am bidden to invite you to the countess's private rooms. Tonight, after sunset, with your master. She will show him the marks."

I walked away, trying not to let it seem like flight.

After the late meal, we were taken through the keep to the Nádasdys' private rooms, and to the countess's chamber.

The lady looked even thinner in her shift, like the pole in the center of a tent. Many yards of fine linen fell to the floor from her shoulders. She leaned heavily upon the arm of Zsófia, who was dressed in velvet. I nodded to the witch, my eyes on her heavy red hair twisted at the nape of her neck, then to her green eyes. Her lips curved into a smile, and warmth curled low in my belly.

The countess whispered something, then repeated it in Latin. "Show them."

A heavyset serving woman curtsied and started unlacing the neck of the countess's shift. Zsófia steadied her mistress, breathing such life into the scene that the countess looked even less vital.

"Zsófia . . ." The countess put out a hand to the taller woman, who took her fingers tenderly, and lifted them to kiss.

"Is this the witch?" Dee asked me in English. Zsófia narrowed her eyes for a moment, and a half smile curved her lips again.

"This is Zsófia Draskovich, who calls herself a healing woman," I replied, but I resisted the urge to cross myself nevertheless. "Some call her a witch."

Zsófia crooked a finger and we moved a little closer. As she eased the countess's linens from her throat and chest we began to see red marks, in patterns not unlike some of the angelic symbols we had been given. There were weeping sores on each thin shoulder, and as the shift was lowered more appeared. The fabric had to be peeled from many wounds. The young woman whimpered, and the pain must have been severe, but she spoke no words. The lacerations continued over her small breasts and onto her hollow belly. Zsófia snapped out a command and the shift was pulled up, giving the poor lady her modesty back.

"How are these patterns made?" Dee's voice was shaking. "They look like burns."

The countess was draped in a velvet gown, and helped to a chair by Zsófia.

"Some are made with a caustic powder," the countess said. "Is that how you say it? Lye, painted on the skin. Others have been incised with a knife and herbs rubbed in to create a scar. If they start to heal, I become weaker." She was shivering, and the women helped her into a chair by the fire. "Tell me, are these the same symbols the angels gave you?"

"They are very like them." Dee bowed low again. "If I might ask your lady-in-waiting to draw the shapes, I can make further comparisons. May I ask, where did you get the symbols from?"

The countess turned her head toward Zsófia and spoke in some local language. The woman stepped forward and answered in German.

"These signs have been used by my people for centuries, to heal the sick. They healed the Lady Anna, and her mother,

Lady Katalin." She reached into her kirtle and withdrew a folded package. "You have the parchment from the priest. This is my mother's own copy."

Dee spread the page upon the table.

"These are much finer than the notes drawn by the priest, Edward," he murmured.

"We call them dragon marks." The countess sighed again. Each breath seemed an effort for her. "The gypsies brought them, and inscribed them on stones and trees. Zsófia . . ."

The woman lifted a goblet and held it to the girl's lips.

"Take the parchment," she said, over her shoulder. "I must tend to my lady." She set the goblet down and turned. Then with a peculiar strength and ease, she lifted the countess in her arms like a child. The servant opened a door and then stood back, her face set in something that looked like mingled respect and fear. As the women vanished, I heard the witch hiss something, and the servant closed the door between us.

Dee was already lost in the analysis of the symbols, his lips moving as he made mental notes. I looked around the apartment, seeing nothing out of the ordinary. I picked up the countess's goblet and sniffed it cautiously. Not wine, but a bitter herbal brew perhaps. I detected the scents of wormwood, maybe valerian. I dipped my finger in it, and it glowed ruby dark and thick, sticky on my fingertip. A careful taste, which I expected to be sweet with honey or some other flavor, was salty.

I realized, with a surge of nausea, that it had been thickened with blood.

Chapter 20

"Professor." Soames clasped Felix's hand, and waved him to a chair. "This is Stephen McNamara, an investigator from the Art and Antiques unit. Professor Felix Guichard is an expert on the symbols we found . . . the ones on the dead girl."

Felix turned to see someone seated, a thin man who looked familiar, who nodded to him. "Professor."

"Mr. McNamara."

Soames sat down, and leaned back. "So, what can you tell us about these shapes?"

"As I said on the phone, I've found something very similar inscribed on two medals, presently in the British Museum." Felix spread prints of the images on the desk.

"These are almost identical to the ones on the body." Soames looked up. "Who else would know about this?"

"Well, I don't know that these figures are unique. I've been looking through the literature. A number of different circles of sigils appear in Dee's own books and pamphlets. Others are mentioned in books of his that no longer exist, but are quoted in books by his contemporaries."

"Exactly like the ones on the body?"

"No. Most of the symbols he used were either characters from medieval astrology or his own Enochian alphabet. The ones on the medal include many new figures, as far as I can tell."

McNamara leaned forward. "So it might be reasonable to

assume that someone must have seen these medals, and copied the symbols?"

Felix glanced at the gray man. *He was at the pub.* "These medals were in the attic of a woman in Devon, before they were put up for sale in an open auction. Where anyone could have seen them—they may even have been pictured in the catalogue."

Soames tapped the image. "Why? What are they for?"

Felix folded his arms. "They were prescribed for ailments, to bring good luck, that sort of thing. People drew them on vellum or scratched them on metal disks to make charms."

"And this was widespread?" asked Soames.

Felix shrugged. "In the absence of a systematic scientific explanation, people would try anything to heal or protect themselves. These were superstitious times."

"Have you ever heard of drawing the symbols on a person?" said Soames.

"No. That's new."

McNamara spoke. "So, this attic in Devon. Who owned the medals?" He had a notepad open on his knee. "And did you keep copies of the associated documents?"

Felix found himself reluctant to involve Jack. "The medals were sold more than two years ago. A woman, by the name of Slee, sold them at auction. She also put the bundle of papers and letters in the auction. She may not have realized how valuable the documents were, but the medals fetched very little money. And, no, I didn't keep copies," he lied, uncomfortable with the questioning.

"What do you know about these papers?" Felix watched McNamara write notes, record the name Slee.

"I'm afraid they went to a university in the States. Harvard, I believe." Felix shrugged, and looked at McNamara's bent head. "What's your interest, Mr. McNamara?"

"I am investigating a number of forged documents, ascribed to John Dee."

"I am certain none of the documents I examined were forgeries."

"You authenticated the Dee papers for the auction house," McNamara said. "A simple examination."

Felix kept his shoulders loose, his expression open. "I did. They were on display at the auction house for some weeks, then off to the States. I didn't know they were going to be significant, so I just confirmed the notes were by Dee."

McNamara leaned in. "And that some of the items described as letters were by Edward Kelley?"

"They appeared to be some sort of journal, but in a very poor state. They were written on paper, which doesn't do well in damp attics." Felix turned back to Soames. "So, have you concluded this was a suspicious death?"

The inspector grimaced. "No. In fact, we can't even confirm an actual cause. That's not the problem."

"Oh?"

"A fourteen-year-old disappeared last week. Her mother swears her kid would never run away and must have been abducted." He shrugged. "My instincts tell me these girls may have been targeted for something. Perhaps the sex trade, maybe some weird cult. I'd appreciate it if you could track those papers down. They might explain why a dead girl was covered with four-hundred-year-old designs. It might give us a starting point for finding this Sadie Williams." Soames sighed. "Let me know if you find anything new, but I'm not sure we'll be taking this forward if it proves to be a natural death."

McNamara held out a card. "I would like to speak to you further, Professor Guichard. We have found similar documents in private sales, and are looking into the case of the other letters attributed to Dee that appear to be clever fakes. They could only have been made by someone with a lot of knowledge about Dee."

"A Dee scholar?" Felix was intrigued, in spite of himself. "I'll be interested in his knowledge, if you find him. But I'm certain these letters and documents were authentic."

"Please keep me informed of any new developments. I'll be in touch." The man rose, nodded to Soames, and walked out of the room.

Back at his office, Felix hesitated before calling Jack's number. There was something about her that made him uncomfortable and attracted him at the same time.

She answered promptly. "Felix." Her voice was less hostile than the first time, at least, and he became aware of a warmth spreading through him. He could instantly conjure up her face, her watchful expression.

"I need to talk to you about the documents you sold. The police have a special investigator looking into their provenance, who claims they might be forgeries."

"They can't be, I'm certain of it. Anyway, why would someone forge the pages then virtually obliterate them, reducing their value? My whole childhood, they were stuck up in the attic."

Felix pulled up the image of the medals on his laptop. "And no one is disputing the authenticity of the medals."

"Exactly." Her voice changed. "Did you know you were followed by the man from the pub last night? He drove after your car."

"Well, I met that man at the police station this morning. His name is McNamara, he's an investigator with the Art and Antiques squad."

"He suspects you?"

"Well, maybe not me, but certainly the letters. And I am an expert on Dee."

She hesitated for a long moment: he could hear the hiss of her breathing. "After you drove off, I got into my car. There was someone on the backseat, a woman."

He rocked back in his chair, hearing a note of tension in the flatness of her voice. "Who was it? Are you all right?"

"I don't really know . . . I ended up hitting a wall."

He leaned forward. "Are you OK? What happened?"

"There was something strange about her. I just found myself doing exactly what she said. I could hardly resist—until I crashed."

"But you're all right?" He was concerned. Despite her attitude, there was something fragile about Jack.

"A few bruises. I'll mend, but the car's at the garage. Anyway, how can I help you with the letters?"

He pulled out the folder of images he had printed from the British Museum's e-mail. "I have copies of the documents you sold. One was a folded package of papers, written by Dee's assistant. Do you remember it?"

"If it was that scruffy story with long sections in other languages, yes, I remember it. I even tried to read bits of it when I was younger."

Her face was vivid in his mind. "I have good, magnified copies to work from. I would value your opinion, to see if the document is all there, for example." He traced her name on the page in front of him. "Maybe they will trigger other memories." He really did want to see her again.

"OK. I suppose we could meet once more." Her voice was guarded. "That man, why would he follow you from the pub?"

"Maybe I really am a forgery suspect," he joked weakly. "Only a Dee scholar could create really convincing fakes. Otherwise, I have no idea. Look, I'm free tomorrow evening, if we could meet up?"

She didn't answer for a moment, then sighed. "OK. At your place, though, I don't want to be seen in public with you, with all this interest in the symbols. I got the impression this woman was trying to find out where I live. Be careful, Felix."

"I will." He promised to text her his address, and rang off. His eyes settled on the notes he was making. A name caught his eye. Zsófia Draskovich, named as a witch.

Chapter 21

*The servants speak little to me, but I found a soldier
with passable German. He was from Lithuania, and
a farmer's son, and he knew much of these "forest
witches" and their sorceries. He told me no honest
folk prosper where these hags live, and in his country
they are outcast, living on refuse and carrion.*

—EDWARD KELLEY
  23 November 1585
  Niepolomice

I MADE NO MENTION OF BLOOD TO DEE, KNOWING IT WOULD
appall him, although we had heard of stranger cures. He
had spent the day closeted with the witch Zsófia in the main
hall, unmoved by her beauty, or the enchanting effect she had
on me.

I went down to the village, which leaned into the shelter of
the fortress. The walls were pockmarked with evidence of mis-
siles, and the hovels showed signs of previous conflagrations,
ancient battles of which we in England were ignorant.

The forest was like a blanket swaddling the castle. Paths and
roads disappeared into dark tunnels through the woods. I had
never seen trees so densely packed; it looked like a wall of bole
and leaf. Cries of jays and magpies mingled with strange sounds
of birds I hadn't heard before. A man, dressed in clean, neat
clothing, attracted my attention by tugging on my shirt. I rec-

ognized the mute Gábor from the consultation with the king. He pointed onward, then gestured for me to follow.

I walked along a line of rickety cottages, past a line of stone-built stables and a group of children playing with sticks, battling up and down the cobbled road between the fortress and the huts. I was led to a terrace overlooking the mountains and a river far below, which threaded its way like quicksilver between the hills. On a litter, covered with rich fabrics that draped onto the grass, the countess was half sitting, half lying. In the pale sunlight she looked even closer to death, gray shadows drawing into the hollows of her face. She opened her eyes.

"Master Kelley." I noticed the heaviness of her light brown hair, tumbled against her shoulders as if it burdened her neck. In England, I think doctors would have wanted to cut off the hair, lest it drain energy from the sick body, but here it was the only part of her that looked alive. That and the sapphire eyes, staring at me directly. Not like a child, more like a man. Or a queen.

I bowed low. "My lady."

"Are you free of your duties, then?"

"I am my master's assistant, not his body servant, my lady." True enough, though I served him any way I could from affection as well as obligation. I had learned more from Dee in two years than from a decade of study.

"Will you sit with me, and tell me stories of your land?"

"Of course, lady." I sat, and looked over the view. "Although, we have nothing as magnificent as these forests and mountains."

She uttered a small chuckle of laughter, the smile lighting her face, giving her lips the tiniest flush of color. "These are not mountains, Master Kelley. These are just a few hills. The forest, I grant you, is as good as anything we have in Transylvania."

I looked at the jagged horizon, the undulating landscape. A distant bellowing, like a distressed ox or bull, echoed over the trees.

"Bison," she said, smoothing her hand over the dense fur rug she was seated on. "Do you have bison in England?"

"Indeed, not, my lady. Nor bears, nor wolves of recent years. We are a country of much farmland and many orchards. And villages and towns, every few leagues."

She sighed, looking at me with those piercing eyes. "I long to visit it. Yet I miss my home at Csejte." She pronounced it "Chay-tay"; it was only later that I learned the outlandish spelling. "It was a wedding present from my husband. It is the favorite of our residences."

"Tell me about it, lady," I asked, politely.

She needed no encouragement. "It is in the Little Carpathians. It sits on the top of a hill with its back to the mountains. It is the one place in my life where we live as Hungarians, without my husband's allies and military commanders or the king's troops watching us."

"Does King Istvan visit?"

She shrugged. "He used to come, to hunt. We have excellent wolf chases in the autumn, and take wild boar and deer through the winter. Now that he is king in Poland, he does not have time for such leisure."

There seemed to be little warmth for her uncle. I ventured: "The king hopes for your recovery. We all pray for a happy outcome."

"The king, Master Kelley, wishes me to do my duty and give Count Nádasdy the heir he needs." Her voice weakened. "And you are here with your master, Doctor Dee, to help me. Perhaps I will be able to return to health, and hunting, and riding and dancing. And be a better wife to my husband and a useful niece to my uncle."

"If the good Lord wills it," I replied.

The tiniest grimace flitted across her face.

"If He wills it." She looked for a moment at her bloodless hands. "You have heard of my family's curse."

"I have, my lady."

She looked again at me, and something inside me felt cold, as if I had swallowed a goblet of ice.

"There are those," she said, "who say that my affliction is the death my grandmother should have suffered. That my existence is unnatural and cursed." Her eyes held mine, as I struggled to say something that would not offend.

"I shall pray for your deliverance," I offered.

"I appreciate your efforts, Master Kelley, but you may need the prayers for yourself," she said, in a dry voice. "The king has asked you, and your master, to join the state banquet tonight in honor of the inquisitor. He, as I'm sure you know, would make a bonfire of us all."

Chapter 22

FELIX FINISHED HIS ANCIENT CIVILIZATION LECTURE LATE, as usual, and crossed the quad to his office. There were assignments to mark, grant applications to complete, dissertation drafts to consider. The police file sat on the corner of his desk, reminding him of the dead young woman he couldn't quite get out of his mind. A tap on the door made him look up.

"Come in, Rose." She looked strange, as if she were shaky. "Are you OK?"

"Of course . . . I just wanted to tell you . . . someone visited. I didn't see any appointments in the diary, but she came anyway."

He stood up, concerned to see Rose looking so pale. "For God's sake, sit down. You look dreadful."

She smiled, but sat down anyway. "I do feel odd. I just thought I should tell you about this woman."

"Did she leave a name?"

"Oh, I forgot." Rose took a card out of her pocket and gave it to him.

He read the name on the card. "Bachmeier and Holtz Pharmaceuticals. I haven't heard of them."

"She . . . I remember now, she was interested in the Dee letters we authenticated. She said something about the Komáromy letters, as well. Apparently, they came down to her through her family."

Felix sat opposite her. Rose normally had a rather acid style of speaking, sharpness that hid warmth for the students and a kindness toward him. She was looking strange, almost as if she were sedated.

"What was she like?"

"I . . . I can't remember very much," she said. "This is crazy, she was only here a few minutes ago. She just left to go to her car."

He stood, looking into the car park. "Is she down there?"

Rose stood next to him, and pointed. "There."

At the back of the chemistry building, a silver car was attended by a man in uniform; the driver, he supposed. The woman walking toward the driver wore high heels and a long wool coat. He had an impression of glamor, of elegance. When she turned to look back at the building, he could see she wasn't young, although it was hard to tell her age, but a wave of calm washed over him.

It was a familiar feeling. On the windowsill were a number of carvings and tokens he had gathered from his research, all associated with witchcraft and sorcery in some way. When he moved his hand toward them one gave off a sense of cold, as if it had been refrigerated. He ran his hand over the carved figure, and looked back at the woman, now just bending to get into the car. For a second he thought he saw the movement of an older woman, then the door was closed and the driver vanished around the other side.

"What did she want?" he asked, watching the car reverse out of the narrow space.

"I . . . I . . ." Rose was gasping like a goldfish, and when he glanced at her, she seemed stunned.

"Rose!" He put his hands on her shoulders and turned her away from the window. "Rose, sit down, are you OK?" For a second he wondered if she was having a stroke. He guided her to a chair.

There was something familiar about the glazed expression. He'd seen it in West Africa when he was researching a rash of witchcraft killings. People had become almost catatonic, they had been so suggestible. The wooden figure was supposed to guard against it, and it pulled the heat from his hand as he held it.

"Take this." He had to pry her clenched fingers open before he put it in her palm, watched her hand curve around it.

"What?"

She sat down, staring at the talisman. He poured her a glass of water from the bottle on his desk, and offered it to her, wondering if it would be more useful to pour it over her. She took it, and smiled up at him.

"Thanks. I must be tired," she said.

"Tell me more about this woman, your visitor."

"She said she was hoping we had copies of the letters. I told her we did—oh, I shouldn't have, really. But she had already been to the British Museum to see the medals. She knew all about them."

"But you didn't show her anything?" No, he remembered, the printed copies were still in his case.

"Just the pictures of the medals. She wanted to know who sold them, but I didn't know that. I don't know your password on your desktop, you must have . . . Oh, Felix, I'm so sorry! She tried to get me to use your computer, and at the time, I just went along with it. I don't know what came over me."

Jack's words came back to him, of the woman in her car, the hypnotic spell she cast. "It's OK, Rose, I think she's very persuasive."

"She came to talk about grant money. She's offering funding for a couple of students to look at the Komáromy letters, in Bucharest."

"I'll investigate this woman. Do you feel any better?"

She frowned, looking down at the amulet. "This is the anti-witchcraft carving that con man in the Ivory Coast gave you."

"Amusaa. I challenged him to cast a spell on me. I ended

up giving him everything I owned, including my shoes. I don't know how he did it to this day. He gave me the anti-hex carving as a thank you for my father's watch. It's supposed to counteract the mesmerizing spell."

She put the carving back on the windowsill with a hand that still shook a little. "Well, I think we can establish that it works."

Chapter 23

*My dear wife, I hope your sickness has passed and
that you and Mistress Jane Dee are well. Our work
prospers and Doctor Dee and I have found many
clues about our mission to save one of the great ladies
of court from a dangerous affliction. Expect your
husband home within no more than one month, and, I
hope, with crowns to support us all until we return to
England. I have about me my charms for protection,
and the finger bone of Saint Anselm you gave me for
my safety, which I am glad of in this place of witches
and spirits. I shall send this by a messenger the king
is commanding to return to Krakow. Look after dear
Eliza and John, and bid them attend their studies.
May the Lord keep you, your husband, Edward Kelley.*

—Sent 25 November 1585 to Jane Kelley

THE BANQUET WAS HELD, NOT IN THE FEASTING HALL,
but in the state dining room of the king. For the first
time I saw noble ladies accompanied by their husbands.
The countess seemed stronger, and was seated with a group of
other young women as we waited for the king to arrive. Nobles
sat around the room on benches or stood in little groups. The
glances Dee and I attracted were more curious than hostile.

Dressed in his scarlet robes, Father Konrad was in the middle of a group of ladies, appearing to charm them all. When he caught my eye, he bowed to them and walked over to us. He was as tall as Dee, and smiled at us both.

"Our English visitors. I hope your scientific investigations prosper?"

Dee bowed politely. "Indeed, my research has been interesting to His Majesty. There are a number of natural scientists in this country. I find myself surrounded by fascinating texts."

"Science." Konrad gave the word emphasis. "Some of my colleagues at the Vatican are concerned that the explanation of God's creations, in terms of man's understanding, can only undermine faith."

"But you are less concerned?" I hazarded.

He shrugged. "The church is resisting an invasion of heresy and godlessness. That seems more important to me. It is good to visit a court where the king, at least, has not bowed to Protestantism."

I noticed the embroidered insignia of the Holy Roman Empire upon his breast. "We have recently traveled to Prague to visit your emperor."

He snorted with disdain. "Rudolf will not stir himself to fight Protestantism even in his own lands." He bowed his head. "Respectfully, I say he is consorting with occultists and sorcerers in the name of your 'science.'"

Dee interrupted in his deep, precise Latin. "We found him a learned and spiritual man."

"He is a pederast and a coward." This he said smiling, while dipping his head to a passing lady. "He defies nature even as he studies it." The sweeping judgment almost took my breath away. I must have let something of my surprise show, because his smile broadened. "Are you shocked that I judge my emperor so?"

Dee shook his head. "No, Reichsritter von Schönborn. My surprise is equating the sin of unnatural practices with the study of science. Surely, further enjoying the intricacy and wonder of God's handiwork cannot be seen in the same light as deviance?"

Konrad bowed, his mouth in a crooked smile. "If that was what science was doing—appreciating God's creations—I would support it. But you, Master Dee, and your fellow scientists, seek to interfere in nature. You meddle with incantations to change the natural course of God's design. That is the definition of sorcery."

Dee's face had reddened above his beard. "Man has been enlightened by angels throughout history. God does not intend us to ignore the messages He sends us."

"Is not the Bible sufficient?" asked Konrad, waving at a man carrying a tray of goblets. "Try this wine, my friends. It is a Hungarian wine, grown on the slopes of the Carpathians since the time of the Romans." He took a deep draft. "It reminds me of my youth, as a student in Vienna."

It was a heady, scented wine that smelled earthy, like the forest. We were ushered by servants toward the long table. Konrad was seated closer to the king and opposite Dee. I noticed, at Istvan's right hand, the black lion that was Nádasdy. The king's brother Lord Miklós sat to his left. The three conversed for the first part of the meal, while I struggled in German to speak to a flirty lady-in-waiting, and to eat my meats. I noticed a constant stream of interruptions for the king: a soldier in Polish uniform, a quiet man in a green suit, a servant carrying papers, one of his own guards. As the evening wore on, more lamps and candles were lit, filling the atmosphere with smoke that created a haze that softened my view of the table. But I noticed the slow increase in the king's guard. A half-dozen men leaning against the end wall of the dining chamber at the beginning of the meal had somehow become twenty, then thirty, breastplates picking up the flickering light under jerkins. Most had a hand on their swords. I scanned the other walls, lined with shields with the coats of arms of the many rulers of this disputed land. Above the shields, a narrow walkway was peopled with two, then four archers, each with a bolt loosely fitted in a crossbow, facing the double doors at the end of the chamber. I glanced around the company. Many such as Dee and the inquisitor could not have such a view of the gallery. I braced myself to dive under the table if needed, which ruined my appetite for a pastry full of pears.

Anxiety made my senses sharper. I noticed a black-clad form that walked in the side door, and bowed low to the king. Then he—a priest with a mud-flecked cloak and filthy boots— proceeded down the table toward Konrad. Conversations faded as he passed. He knelt and presented a leather pouch to the inquisitor, who drew out a vellum package with a huge red seal. With great ceremony, the priest, still bowed at his knee, slit the seal with a flourished knife, and a cracking sound echoed around the room. Konrad pushed aside his food, and spread the sheets onto the table. Finally, he nodded dismissal to the priest and stood.

"Your gracious Majesty." He bowed low. "I have but now received an urgent missive from His Holiness Xystus Quintus. He sends greetings and heartfelt blessings for your health, and your mission. He respectfully commands that you assist the Holy Inquisition in arresting a known and dangerous heretic." He bowed again, and I noticed the guards had moved forward to secure the doors. "His Holiness has sent a small escort to bring the accused heretic to Rome, so that he may argue his innocence or confess his guilt and receive the eternal forgiveness of the Lord."

I knew such a man would be tested by torture, and looked up and down the table for signs that the guards were coming to get the unfortunate accused.

The king did not speak for a full minute, and I think I was not the only person there who held his breath. Most of the nobles down the table were Protestant.

"The Holy Father does not have sovereignty in the court of an anointed king." Istvan's voice was stern.

Konrad nodded. "Indeed. Your sovereignty over your own peoples is sacrosanct." The truth started to grow inside me, a bubble of terror. "But Il Papa asks your support in returning to him a subject of a heretic queen of a godless land, whose people are denied the solace of Rome."

"Silence!" The roar of the king came in a huge wave of anger as he pushed back his chair and stood. The sound of thirty swords, hissing from their scabbards filled the room. Their steel gleamed in the lamplight. "You will remember that you are also an invited guest at my court."

Konrad bowed low. "I ask pardon for any offense caused. My duty is to pass on His Holiness's wishes. And this. A message in his own hand, for his beloved brother, His Majesty King Ist-van Báthory of Poland, King and Duke of Lithuania, King and Voivode of Transylvania, Prince of Hungary. I am to place it into your own hand."

I could see conflicting emotions chasing across the heavy features of the king. After a long pause, he waved his guards aside to allow the priest to approach.

Konrad knelt and presented the note, wrapped in scarlet ribbons and sealed with an ornate black seal.

Istvan accepted the missive, then waved him away. Konrad gracefully rose and stepped back, his head bowed, lips moving in prayer as Istvan broke the seal. The king read slowly, squinting a little, a servant holding a candle near to assist. He refolded the letter and handed it to one of his servants. Konrad continued his prayer, then crossed himself, so Istvan was forced to wait.

"I should throw you into the cells for this rudeness."

Konrad nodded. "If I have offended, I grieve for it. If I have overstepped my authority, place me in your dungeons. The Lord will be with me there. But I am a servant of the papacy, and His Holiness. My duty, and my conscience, is to him."

Istvan turned to the nobles, many of whom were standing beside their women, with hands on swords.

"I am commanded to place our visitors Dr. John Dee and Edward Kelley into the custody of the Vatican escort, and allow them to be taken to Rome for questioning. This contravenes every custom of hospitality my people hold in common: that a guest under our roof is to be treated like a brother. I will consider His Holiness's . . . request, and deliver my judgment in the morning."

I already knew what the answer would be. No Catholic king would defy the Pope, especially not one with as tenuous a claim as Istvan to the crowns of Lithuania and Poland. On the morrow, I would start the journey toward hell on earth. As an Englishman and a Protestant, only death could relieve me.

Chapter 24

JACK PEERED AT STREET NAMES AS SHE DROVE THROUGH THE town. She hated leaving Sadie chained up in the priest hole, but was worried someone might hear her shouting from the living room if they came to the door. She turned into the road Felix had directed her to, wondering why she had agreed to go to his house. Information, she told herself, knowing it was more than that.

"Jack." He was waiting at the door even as she locked the car, which she had parked on the long drive. A quick look up at three floors of Victorian prosperity in sand-colored brick, then she followed him into the hallway. "Thank you for coming." He reached his hands out, and she slid out of her coat. "I think your mysterious woman may have come to the university. She was trying to find out about the letters and medals."

"Why do you think that?" Jack looked around at the hall, which had an original tiled floor in patterned mosaic, overlaid by patches of color from stained glass in the door.

"Rose—my assistant—said she asked about them. You say a strange woman was in the back of your car?" He showed her into a room at the front of the house, lined with books and dominated by a large oak desk, and waved her to an armchair.

Jack looked at him more closely; he didn't look as if he were still under the effects of a mesmer spell. "Yes. If it's the same person. What did your visitor look like?" She scanned the books on his shelves.

He sat down in an office chair; its cracked and buttoned

leather looked as old as the house. "Well, there's a question. I'm not sure what she looked like. I just caught a glimpse of her in the car park."

"What did you see?" She turned to look at him, as his face tensed into a frown.

"To be honest, I'm not sure what I saw." He reached for a leather satchel and withdrew a stack of papers. He handed her one of the sheets. "But I think this is what she was really after. It's what this McNamara wants, as well."

"It's one of those ratty old papers Maggie sold." She could read more words now that they were magnified on the printout. "I could never decipher them completely, but they were a lot more interesting than Dee's lists and numbers." She reached for another. "They can't be forgeries. I remember looking at these when I was just a teenager. Maggie inherited them from her grandmother."

"Did you read any of them?"

Jack shrugged. "The bits that were in 'ye olde English.' I managed some, some of it read like an adventure story. Were they written by Dee himself?"

He tapped the pile of papers still in his hand. "They were written by his collaborator, Edward Kelley. Some say he became more of a sorcerer than Dee, certainly in his later years. This is a journal he wrote while traveling in Europe in 1585, when he was still Dee's assistant."

Jack sat in the armchair opposite Felix, and looked at him. "So, this is what everyone is after?"

He ran a finger along a line of text on the photocopy. "I think Dee and Kelley were in Poland looking for some ritual, some spell perhaps, to preserve life. These pages of Kelley's are notes on what they did. The medals record the final research, the circles of symbols." He leaned back in the chair. "Listen to this. 'We observed the lady, unclothed against her

modesty, adorned with divers burns and scratches such as
may have been made with a knife. The . . . something . . . sigils, burned with dressings of caustic lye.' Sigils, symbols, inscribed into her skin. He was trying to treat someone, who
must have been seriously ill." He looked up at her. "This case
I've been investigating had sigils drawn on the skin of a drug
addict."

"The girl who died on the train."

"Right. I've wondered whether they were somehow there
to keep her safe, maybe heal her in some way." He tapped the
paper with one finger. Jack watched his forehead crease with
concentration as he squinted at the pages. "These symbols were
associated with a ritual called binding."

Jack took the page he had read from. "What else does it
say?"

He looked up at her. "Up until the fifteen hundreds, people
explained everything they could see through religion. Dee and
Kelley were trying to use science to explain the world around
them instead of belief."

Jack turned the paper around, trying to follow a line of text.
"Why?"

"Their world was being torn apart by religious dissent, and
Dee thought that if he could find the true nature of God, people
could stop fighting wars over it."

"But you said this wasn't written by Dee." A line of Latin
caught her eye, and it reminded her of something the woman
had said. "Have you ever heard the words '*morturi masticantes*'?"

"Have you searched it on the Internet?" He looked at her,
his green eyes dark in the fading light.

She shrugged. "I haven't got around to it, no." She didn't
like to say that she had no idea how to do that, nor how to use
a computer. She had only mastered a mobile phone when it became necessary for business.

He opened the laptop on the desk and it whirred into life. "Why do you want to know? Is it in the Kelley paper?"

"No. No, it's something . . . that woman said, the one in my car. She used the words."

He tapped on the keyboard, his face lit up by the screen. "It's . . . Hungarian. No, Latin, used in Hungary. Something to do with—revenants."

She leaned forward, running her eyes over the unfamiliar words. She noticed Felix touching a finger to his lower lip and caught her breath. She sat back in the chair. "Look, this woman—"

"Middle-aged, slim, well dressed, very friendly, calls herself Bachmeier. That was my assistant's first impression. You?"

"Right. My *first* impression." She studied her hands, trying to describe the memory without sounding insane. "She was a lot less friendly when I didn't do what she wanted."

"But she was compelling, at first. You were compliant. How persuasive was she?" His voice was soft, and she looked up to find him leaning forward.

"It was as if I were hypnotized. I drove eighteen miles because she told me to. I felt like a rabbit, fascinated by a stoat. I was terrified, but I just wanted to do whatever she asked."

"She tried to make Rose show her my private files on my office computer. Rose would never do that, normally. No one can use hypnosis to influence people against their will, but there are techniques . . . methods connected with Dee's belief system." He hesitated, his lips curving into a smile that tugged at something in Jack.

Shadows gathered in the room, the light graying as the moments passed. "You're talking about Dee's sorcery?"

He hesitated for a moment, and his lips creased into a lopsided smile. "You're going to laugh at me, but hear me out. I spent a lot of time in Benin, Liberia, the Ivory Coast, while I was doing research for my PhD. Belief in witchcraft is common in large areas of rural Africa." He fumbled in one pocket, then another, drawing out a dark carving and putting it on the desk between them. "Sorcerers there have a way of making people . . . susceptible, obedient."

Jack took the carving, immediately sensing something dark and powerful in the wood that made it feel heavier and warmer than she expected. The figure, which she at first thought was a monkey, was in fact a big-headed, ugly caricature of a man. It had faces on both sides of its head, and massive genitals. She realized she had picked it up by its penis, and blushed faintly, putting it back gently.

"What is it?"

"An anti-witchcraft charm." He laughed awkwardly, picking up the unprepossessing carving and staring at it. "The things I saw out there—real power in ancient rituals, people dying from curses, people defying nature by *not* dying. I hardly believe it myself, but when she was looking at me, I felt this warm feeling." He shrugged. "It was familiar from working with *izinyanga*, local healers, sorcerers. One particular *inyanga*, named Amusaa, gave me this charm, after he persuaded me to give him practically everything I owned." He half smiled, turning the carving over in his hand. "It's embarrassing to admit it, but I can't explain everything I've seen."

She sat, watching expressions move over his face. "So, you're open-minded about this witchcraft thing. Magic, sorcery."

He hesitated, shaking his head even as he spoke.

"I have to be, through experience. I have seen . . . things that are hard to explain, in a strictly scientific way, anyway. And, to answer your question, revenants, or *morturi masticantes*, were believed to be created by witches throughout Eastern Europe right down to Venice and the Mediterranean islands. They were described as dead people who were somehow animated by magic. Many places still have those beliefs. In Chinese traditions of sorcery, they are *jiang shi*, in Angola, they are called *nzumbe*. That's where I came upon the tradition."

Jack tried to keep her expression neutral. "The living dead."

"Right. Revenants were taken seriously by cardinals right up to the level of the Pope. They believed certain people were turned into revenants by sorcery, and they survived by killing others."

She felt uncomfortable but interested at the same time. Maggie hadn't been able to answer many questions about the nature of borrowed time. "So, these revenants are . . . ?"

"The Church defined them as souls held back from heaven by sorcery. The Vatican created a branch of the Inquisition in the fifteen hundreds, to send them on to the afterlife, and punish those sorcerers who created them." He swiveled his chair around to face her, leaning back, his attention intense, raising the hairs on the back of her neck. "Take Adeliza de Borgomanero, born in the thirteen-fifties in Italy, for example. She was believed to have been saved from a fever by some magic potion, but afterward she murdered the young men she seduced and dropped their bodies into a lake. She was defined as a revenant and the Inquisition hunted her down in the fifteen-nineties. I found out about her because the inquisitor at the time, Konrad von Schönborn, also mentioned Dee in an earlier report to the Vatican."

"So, they got her."

"After more than two hundred years, yes. What I don't understand is, why would this woman, whether we saw the same one or not, mention a revenant . . . *morturi masticantes* . . . to you?"

Jack turned away. "Because Maggie and I sold the medals?"

"Maybe." He sighed, and she felt a soft, slow thudding in her chest. She felt an urge to confide in him, and wondered at it.

She glanced back at him. "So, what's the connection between these revenants and Dee?"

He paused for a moment, dropping his gaze from her to the text. "I think Dee worked out how to create one."

Chapter 25

*There is much muttering among the Poles about
their new king. It is said that his soldiers use dark
forces to keep the Sultan's armies at bay, though
they are outnumbered many times. Istvan's
generals are said to belong to a cadre of blood
brothers, who hunted wolves and bears, and some
say Jews and outlaws, and the rumor is that they
have sold their souls to the devil in exchange for
supremacy on the field of battle.*

—EDWARD KELLEY
   26 November 1585
   Niepolomice

OUR NEW PRISON WAS A CHAMBER CLOSE TO THE KING'S quarters, perhaps because it was easier to secure. We were escorted by a group of men in red uniforms, Swiss guards from the Vatican, each with a cross emblazoned on his tunic. I was cowed. Not one stood under two yards tall, and their hair was cropped short so it was hard to tell one from another, their chins bare. They were supplemented by men with the blue uniforms of the Polish guard, their steel breastplates covered with short cloaks.

"It seems we are dangerous, dear Edward." Dee looked tired but still managed a smile. "There must be a dozen sentries just for us."

Twenty, more like, I thought. "Master Dee, this is the Inquisition. We are lost." The words choked me.

The quarters were larger than we had been given before, a good fire crackling in the hearth, our belongings carefully unpacked. Dee spent some minutes looking through them. I took my prayer book and journal.

"Better burn the psalter my wife gave you." It was softly spoken, but Dee had authority in his deep voice. "It will be tangible proof of heresy in Rome."

"I cannot believe you are so calm! We are destined for the auto-da-fé and all you say is burn a holy book." Tears rose to my eyes, as much from anger as fear. Tales of torture, dismemberment and burning came unbidden into my head.

He smiled sadly. "You are so young. I have faced an Inquisition before, and lived. You must have faith, Edward."

"You have?"

"It was in the reign of Her Grace, Queen Mary." He bit his lip, perhaps recalling that time of terror for English Protestants. "I was younger than you, and indiscreet with my beliefs. I had cast horoscopes for both the royal princesses and was called to account for it." He stretched out his arms, cracking knuckles on his long fingers. "This was thirty years ago. I was quite as afraid as you are now. Queen Mary and her papal advisers from Rome sent Bishop Bonner to investigate and prosecute me for treason and heresy."

"The Burning Bishop?" I was amazed. History had demonized all of Bloody Mary's henchmen, and Bonner had died in the tower at the command of my queen.

"Indeed." Dee dropped onto a stool, rubbing his knees. "I am getting too old for these adventures. Perhaps I should retire to dote on my children back in Mortlake."

"What happened at your inquisition?" I was fascinated, and the tale gave me a little hope.

"I was called to account for my actions in the Star Chamber.

I was exonerated of treason, naturally, as my intention was entirely benign. But my religious proclivities were seen as heretical and I was turned over for further religious examination to Edmund Bonner."

I had grown up with tales of torture and imprisonment of the hundreds of Protestant martyrs who had suffered under Queen Mary's piety. It seemed impossible that this urbane old man could have survived unscarred by it. My disquiet must have shown on my face.

"I wasn't tortured. I was placed under house arrest, but my friends could come and go as they pleased. Then I was taken to see the bishop at his palace. I was vindicated." He shrugged, holding a hand out for the psalter. "Our intentions are pure, Edward, we are doing God's work. You must have faith."

He cast the treasured book, a gift from Jane Dee, into the fire, along with a handful of his own notes. "The rest, I think, we shall be able to explain. Do you have any of those pamphlets we picked up in Bohemia?"

I rummaged through my pack, and found them, dropping them into the yellow blaze as the psalms burst into flame. "I would find it easier to have my faith being questioned in England than in the heart of Rome."

He looked at me, his dark eyes filled with compassion. "And, of course, Edward, you can always tell them you are, at heart, a Catholic. If you agree to attend mass and confession . . ."

"Master Dee, I have never—" I was shocked.

"I know. I think of you as a fine Christian, Edward, but I suspected you had Catholic sympathies when I met you, and the last journey through Europe has confirmed my suspicions. It is nothing to be ashamed of, surely?"

"I have worshipped as a Protestant in good faith," I said. "I speak to the one God."

In my early years I had wanted to become a priest but my base nature betrayed me with some slattern who worked for my father. I had still found comfort in the Mass, but Elizabeth's coronation made celebrating it difficult, and my parents converted away from Rome.

"Indeed. The angels have blessed you, Edward, and me. They, at least, know our hearts are honest and true. They will protect us."

I turned away, shaking with the fear again. The angels, their bright faces and bell-like voices, half imagined, half heard. I shut my eyes as my doubts crowded me like the Swiss guards outside. It had seemed so harmless back in London, becoming Dee's scryer, allowing the images to spill into words. I prayed as never before.

I must have fallen asleep in the chair, still clothed in Dee's finery, because I was woken by a hand clamped onto my face, almost suffocating me.

"*Silens.*" The harsh whisper was hissed into my ear. I struggled like a madman, the image of the squad of Swiss guards still in the forefront of my mind. Another man swung around, bearing a lamp, and I saw maybe five or six shapes in black, muffled in cloaks up to their eyes, all with naked swords. Dee was being gagged in rough fashion, and two men restrained him.

"*Exsisto silens. Vel nex.*" Silence or death. I stopped struggling, and shut my eyes, holding on to the last of my dignity with my bladder.

My arms were pinned to my side by a rope, another binding my hands before me. A cloth gag was forced into my mouth and tied cruelly tight. It reeked of sweat and smoke. One man lifted me by the rope and set me on my feet, before pulling me to the door. I was grateful I was still in my boots. Dee's bare legs and feet were dragged into the corridor ahead of me. I stumbled over something, and realized it was one of the Polish guards. The remains of the food in my stomach rose, as I saw his head had been split by a single sword blow. I swallowed it back down, not wanting to suffocate in the gag. More bodies, some in the red of the Swiss, were slumped in doorways. As we passed into the inner curtain, the muffled thud of a crossbow sounded close to my left ear, and one of Istvan's Hungarian guards fell, gurgling, a bolt in his throat. I watched the life leave his eyes, as I staggered over his twitching body under the light of a torch set in the wall.

A scuffle ahead of us was resolved swiftly by our kidnappers, who went among the fallen and slit throats as if slaughtering pigs. We were taken to the outer courtyard and I was boosted into a saddle. I was trussed tight, but at least they placed my feet in the stirrups and tied my hands to the pommel. A tall man ahead, swathed in a cloak that covered his face, grabbed my reins, jerking the horse forward.

As the creature bounded ahead I was knocked sideways, this way and that, riding faster than I would have attempted in daylight. After a few minutes, my bonds tightened cruelly by my being tied to the pommel, I managed to catch the thing in my hands, and get a sense of the rhythm of the horse. The saddle pounded under me painfully, bruising me as we traversed half a league or more, past the remains of my slaughtered nag. Her scarlet wounds and thrusting bones suggested a corpse half-eaten in the glimpse afforded by our captors' torches, which streamed behind them as they galloped, the burnt tallow stench in their wake. My teeth rattled in my head until I clenched them, and I finally managed to look about myself. The world was dark and confusing as it jerked along. Dee, there, his bare head lighter in the orange glow of his leader's torch, as tossed about as I. My ears strained for the sound of a pursuit, but the hooves upon the hard-packed road deafened me. I did not know whether to pray for pursuit, for surely to return us to Niepolomice would be a certain deliverance to the Inquisition. Yet these bandits terrified me, occasionally whooping like a yelping animal, or crying out some command in their fluid, hissing tongue. Hungarian, I guessed, not German or any language I could understand.

A slash in the face from a branch of pine needles slapped me back in the saddle, and I tasted blood where my lip had been split. I cried out in terror, blinded for a moment, then leaned forward, low over the horse's neck against a more solid collision.

As I clung to the saddle, my thighs shaking with tiredness as they kept my body anchored to the horse, I started to think about the events of the night. If this was—God save us— Konrad, then the examination was going to be a private one, in some torture chamber. Then the Pope would not have to explain the killing of English gentlemen to our allies. If this was one of Báthory's allies . . . I could only speculate what they wanted, or what they would do if we did not provide it.

My childhood prayers rose, unbidden, into my mind, in snatches between stumbles and turns.

"O Lord," I sounded in my head, "from ill deliver us, the days and times . . . times are dangerous: from everlasting death deliver us. And in our last end"—I prayed that it was not so— "comfort us." I misremembered the rest, so melancholy was the thought of my end, that I was filled with misery and instead, my mind turned to the smile, the kind words and friendship of Mistress Jane Dee.

My nose was barely a foot from the neck of the horse, so low that the pommel brushed my chest upon its exertions. I prayed in snatches, clinging with fingers numbed as much by cold as by my cruel bonds. As the pain in my hams and arms grew, the rain started, needling into my face and down my neck, until I could do no more than hang on and wait for death.

Chapter 26

THE POLICE HAD GONE FROM THE VILLAGE, SO JACK LEFT Sadie chained up in the living room. She had arranged to meet Pierce in a public place, safely in daylight, and the girl had pleaded and begged to stay upstairs. Jack didn't have the heart to drag her down to the priest hole again. She left her with a few magazines and a tray of food and drink. She made extra, knowing Sadie would ignore her instruction not to feed the dog. She smiled to herself as she sat down, remembering the tricks Sadie was somehow persuading the half wolf to perform.

She looked around, her back against one of the benches in the cathedral green. Lichens, in shades of yellow, stained the silvered oak against a bronze plaque: "IN MEMORY OF PEGGY, FROM HER LOVING HUSBAND LARRY CLARKE. 1987." The late sunshine had little warmth in it, but it had taken the chill off the damp wood. A few dozen people wandered around the walls of the great church in the late afternoon. It gave her time to think about the man with the lazy smile who was uncomfortably creeping into her thoughts. She hardly knew him and yet . . . somehow she trusted him. He was here somewhere in the town, at the university, perhaps teaching. She checked her phone for texts yet again, then shook herself mentally. Focus. What relationship could she have with him? She had maybe five years left of her continued, unnatural existence. What had he said the Vatican called it? Souls held back from heaven by sorcery.

She scanned the road alongside the cathedral. Some tingle

in the air made her twitchy, and she turned to look at the stand of trees behind her. When she turned back, Pierce was staring at her, maybe a dozen feet away.

She jumped, and reached in her pocket for a weapon.

He grinned, his long teeth uneven and stained nicotine yellow like the rest of him. "Nice to see you, too, Jackdaw. Easy now, I won't hurt you."

She waved to the end of the bench, her bag a barrier in the middle. "Sit over there."

He did, stretching out cracked and split boots, and folding his hands over his stomach. "Nice spot."

She had never seen him in daylight before. His filthy raincoat hung open over a sweater full of holes, revealing another beneath it, bulking him up. His narrow face was dominated by a curved nose, and his pointed chin was covered with gray stubble. He folded one arm over the other, revealing overly long fingernails, tapered and nicotine yellow. He turned to look at her, his small eyes deep-set into his skull, and bloodshot. "You have a girl," he gloated. "A young girl. Perfect." His tongue snaked over his lips.

She tried to keep her expression blank.

"I got a buyer." He waved one hand at her. "We could make a killing, you and I. This woman, she's prepared to pay big money."

"What woman?"

He chuckled, his barks of laughter turning into a cough. "I could tell you that, but then you could sell to her direct and cut me out." He held both hands up, wafting the smell of mold at her.

"She has already approached me." She turned in the seat, to watch his hands. "Even if I had a girl, I wouldn't hand her over like . . . merchandise."

His eyes started looking her over, and she realized he had never seen her in daylight either. "You don't look so good, Jack. Pale."

"I wouldn't hand a child over like a mongrel. You don't know what this woman wants with her."

"You ain't got to worry. She told me she was doing medical research. Very exclusive, for this big magical clinic. Your girl would be well cared for, and helping people."

Jack couldn't keep the sarcasm out of her voice. "Like a cow, chained up and milked of her blood."

He shrugged. "That's what you want her for, ain't it? Easy money."

She clenched her fists with frustration, her breath misting out of her. It was getting colder, the sky darkening as the afternoon drew on. "I need to know more about this woman."

He cracked a smile. "And why would I do that? What you going to do, Jack, zap me again?"

"You think I won't?" She watched his smile contort into a sneer.

"You're so far out of your league, you're going to get burned," he hissed. "Once she finds where the girl is, she'll take her, and neither of us will see a penny." He fumbled in a pocket and brought out a half-smoked roll-up. "Very charming woman, and more important, she's loaded." He patted another pocket, and pulled out a box of matches.

She leaned away from him, pulling her coat around her neck, feeling the chill seeping up the sleeves of her jacket as she did. Damn it, she couldn't afford to get so cold, she could feel her heart rate dropping.

"This woman, she's not just easy money." She sat forward, brushing the leather bag where his foul raincoat might have touched it. "She's trouble. You and I might have had our differences—but this woman is really dangerous."

He looked up at her, his thin lips twisted into a parody of a smile. "I'm touched by your concern." He sucked in foul-smelling smoke and hacked a few times before spitting on the grass. "But it's not me who needs to worry, *Jackdaw*. We'll get the girl anyway; I'm just suggesting you might like to make it easier, for a sensible price. Then no one gets hurt."

"Fuck off." She stood up, brushing off the lichens. "You have no idea where she is."

"Oh, but you're going to tell me where she is. You won't get away this time . . ." He grinned, and leaned forward as if to stand. When he couldn't, he scowled, and curled his claws onto the arm of the bench. He tried to lurch forward, but the effort recoiled him back into his seat, his eyes widening.

"Wha . . . ?" He struggled, fighting to lean forward, move his arms, anything. His fingers twitched as if they were trying to make fists.

"I scratched a binding circle on the bench." Under the bench, actually, where he would be less likely to look. "You'll be fine once I've gone."

The more he struggled, the less his muscles worked, and he slumped back, relaxing his jaw until it softened enough to speak. "Your little tricks won't help you with this buyer. She's the real thing," he whispered. He was so angry spittle sprayed the air in front of him.

Jack watched his hand clench on the arm of the bench, the long claws digging in. The bench creaked, groaning under some internal pressure, and she could see parallel cracks inching along the bleached wood. *Shit, he's going to escape.*

She darted forward. "You're a spent force, Pierce, a little go-between. You don't know anything."

She turned her back on him, feeling rather than hearing his reaction, as his rage entrapped him, welding his muscles with his own anger. *That should last for a few seconds.* Nevertheless, she let the slight slope help her into a run, dodged under a huge rhododendron and vaulted over the wall of the green. She landed in the backyard of a shop. She paused for a second, crouching, and looked back in time to see the bench disintegrate. She raced through the shop—a florist's, redolent with lilies—and onto the high street. That was the moment the paralysis hit, a flash of cold erupting into her. Painful pins and needles cramped her midriff, forcing her to bend forward, staggering. She realized the paving slabs were coming to meet her, even as she tried to put weak hands out to break her fall.

Chapter 27

THE LIVING ROOM WAS THE WARMEST ROOM IN THE COTtage. Sadie was tired of inactivity but every time she stood up, the weakness flowed over her like a blanket of sleep. She tried standing a little closer to the edge of the circle, breathing through the wave of nausea as she moved, letting it recede. She found she could stand no closer than about two feet from the edge before she gagged. She started to explore by shuffling around on the thin carpet.

The room was squarish, with an old rug almost as big as the room. It probably had flowery patterns on it at some time, like Gran's. Gran wouldn't have put up with the dirty marks, dog hairs and bald patches, though. In the time Sadie had been at Jack's cottage, she couldn't recall the sound of a vacuum cleaner. The sofas were much the same, sagging cushions, greasy arms, like old people's furniture. But it was homely in its own way, two of the walls lined with rickety shelves covered with books. The other walls were covered with painted paneling, scuffs and scratches giving no clue to the secret door that led to the little cell that Jack called the priest hole and Sadie called the dungeon. She looked at the books.

The majority seemed old, as if no one had moved them for a while. There were several piles of envelopes that had been torn open, stacked along the top of the books, and a pile of old magazines. By standing on tiptoe, Sadie could just get her fingers out of the circle, although the air outside it felt thicker and colder, her movements causing invisible eddies. Her hands brushed the spines of the nearest books, pulling on one that stuck out a bit.

It was an old-fashioned book about the growing of herbs to make medicines. The pictures were line drawings of—well, weeds, really—and the instructions were in a strange form of English. She flipped the book over to look at the back, then rejected it, putting it on the sofa before stretching out for some more. She managed to reach a book of English birds, a more modern book on herbs, and then a story by Agatha Christie. As she pulled the novel out, a handful of old notebooks fell out with it, bouncing over the rug. The dog looked at her, and wagged his tail.

She crouched and lifted one of the booklets up, fighting nausea as she reached over the invisible barrier. It was filled with writing in blue biro, and the edges and corners were covered with sketches and doodles. There were recipes, jottings, phone numbers and the odd diary entry. Intrigued, Sadie pulled the rug toward her until she could reach the rest. The most battered one was written in faded childlike letters, sprawling over the lines.

"Maggie made me eat this wholewheat crap, it was horrible. I just want pizza." The thought of pizza filled Sadie's mouth with saliva. A few pages further on: "They came and took my blood today. I screamed and told Maggie I would bite her but she did it anyway. The baby is in the hospital again. Dad will come soon and put them in prison. Not the baby though I'm going to take her home with me as my new little sister. I'm going to teach her to ride, but not Tinker becuase he's too tempramental."

Sadie smiled at the spelling, and the sentiment, then looked at the cover of the book. The name was Melissa Harcourt, age ten, the numbers in big, slanted writing. *Was this Jack's*, she wondered, leafing through the later pages. "More blood, big bruise this time. I hate needles. Maggie brought some strawberries home and she made meringues. Charley is growing her hair back, she looks like a kiwi fruit." There was a little cartoon in the margin. "I'm teaching her to call me Mel but Maggie tells her my new name is Jack so she calls me Jock because she can't say Jack . . ."

The pages rambled on, while Sadie sat and thought about Jack, her occasional flashes of warmth and humor. She had been chained up, maybe on this same old carpet. She must have sat here, grieving for her mum like Sadie did.

Missing her mother oozed through Sadie, leaving her eyes stinging. She rubbed them with the back of her hand, and dried her nose on the sleeve of the old sweatshirt Jack had found for her to wear. Slim though Jack was, Sadie was several inches shorter, and had lost a lot of weight. The clothes hung off her. Sadie wrapped her arms around her newly incurved belly, crawled onto the sofa and huddled in the quilt.

She remembered home, the upstairs flat, the new curtains Mum liked so much, the high stools in the kitchen, watching telly together over a takeaway at the end of Mum's work. Hugs, little talks late at night on Mum's bed—it all hurt, as if strings had been yanked in her chest.

Something brushed the window, clattering like leaves. Sadie looked up at the same time that the dog did. The ivy that clambered around the window was silhouetted in black against the deep blue of the sky. Sadie's skin prickled, and she held her breath, listening. She could hear the sizzle of a log in the wood burner, the occasional crackle, the soft tick of the clock over the fireplace, and underneath that, her heart beating in her ears like someone tapping sticks together. Then she noticed the almost subsonic rumble coming from the dog.

Turning to Ches, she watched the dog lift his body off the ground as if pulled by strings, the hair along his back arching and his eyes widening until there was a rim of white around the gray irises. The air seemed heavy, as if it were flowing onto her and growing thicker, pinning her in place. She could just hear the trees outside, rustling. She realized the single lightbulb was dimmer, growing more yellow, before it started flickering. She stared up at it, willing it to keep glowing. After a few seconds, it exploded like a firework, showering her with hot glass and enfolding her in a layer of darkness.

Sadie screamed. She brought her hand to her mouth, frightened by her own sounds echoing around the still, black room. Her eyes began to adjust to the gloom. The branches of the ash tree in the garden reached into the cobalt sky, and the fire glowed red and orange beside her.

Sadie crept to her feet, over the shackle in the floor, into the middle of the circle, where she felt strongest. Glass crunched under her thick socks, and the dog whined. Before she could make him out among the deep shadows, he cannoned into her. She put out a hand to stop herself from falling, and it plunged into his fur.

"It's OK, it's OK," she whispered. "It's just the light." She felt along the dog's spine until she found his head, just a shape against the faint glow from the wood burner. "Good boy." She patted him, feeling him panting in distress, every breath out a faint whine. She kneeled beside him, and he leaned against her and yawned in her face, enveloping her in warm meaty breath. "Silly dog." A brief thump on the floor suggested he had wagged his tail.

The stink of smoke made her look at the fire, which had dimmed to red. A rattle against the window made them both jump.

A call came from the back garden, beyond the kitchen, maybe from the trees. Some sort of bird, calling as if in alarm, croaking; then other, lighter voices shrieking. The cawing and crowing rose until it was deafening. Sadie huddled beside the dog, hands over her head to reduce the noise. It still sounded loud, as if the terrified birds were in the room with her. She felt vulnerable, chained up like bait, so she scooted over toward the hearth. Stretching at the end of the chain, she could feel along the fireplace for the poker. The whole stand fell over with a clatter, and she fumbled along its length until she found the metal rod.

The birds stopped screaming, and she crouched, her breath wheezing in the silence. Cold air spread invisible fingers over her skin as she crawled back to the dog, putting her free arm around him. She could hear his paws pedaling on the floor as if he were losing his balance, and smelled the bitterness of dog urine.

A scream broke the quietness, and for a moment Sadie thought it was human. As she processed the sound and realized it was animal, something hit the window with a wet thud, sliding down like a handful of leaves. In the last of the light from the sky, she had the impression of black fingers spread against the smeared glass, then slipping onto the sill. Another shape smashed into the pane, making Ches howl, and more screeches rose from the birds outside. It sounded as if something was torturing the crows.

Sadie buried her face in Ches's fur, feeling him shake, her mind filled with the image of the thing, the broken bird on the windowsill. The sound of the wind had risen, wrapping itself around the house with a slow roar, like traffic noise. She waited, tears streaming down her face at the occasional agonized cry, cut short with each missile that splatted the glass.

Air in the room started to move, tugging her clothes and lifting her short hair. She slid her fingers down the chain through the hole in the carpet to the metal ring in the floorboards, tearing at it with her fingernails. The ring was attached to a square metal plate, screwed at each corner into the floorboards. It wouldn't budge. The sound and the drafts dropped almost as fast as they had started. The silence thickened. The tingling cold made her shiver, even as sweat started to prickle her skin.

"*Sadieeeeee.*"

The voice called, and sounded not quite human, as if the wind itself had found a voice. It seemed to come from all directions, and the air snatched at her again, like spiteful fingers. A few books fell from the shelves, their pages fluttering. She heard a tiny, sobbed whimper, and realized it had come from her own dry throat. The next time the voice came from the chimney, and a little soot fell with the smell of tar being spread on a hot road.

"*Sadieeeeee.*" The wind increased and made her stagger, pulling her in a spiral toward the corners of the room.

She crouched low, holding on to the cold shackle, its metal scent released by the sweat on her hands. Rising through the terror like a wave, she started to feel a growing rage at the senseless destruction of Jack's precious birds. Each wave of fear seemed to bring a little more anger, and she staggered upright. Papers flapped around her in the whirlwind. She wrapped the chain around the poker a few times, leaned her whole weight against it, and pulled until her feet slipped on the carpet. The ring in the floor creaked, but didn't move. The air buffeted her, thick with the stench of soot and smoke, and books and furniture skidded around the floor. The wind ran through her hair, whipping it into her eyes, pulling at her feet. She heaved on the chain again, feeling the tiniest shudder. Dropping to her knees, she touched the plate through the hole in the carpet, and found it was still solid. But her shaking fingers found a gap in the ring, as if she had opened it up. She forced the end of the poker into the ring and pulled back, the metal biting into her hands. It eased the circle open, and straining, she forced the last link of the chain through the gap.

The wind seemed to grow instantly until it almost lifted her up, and she crouched down, clinging to the ring as her feet were pulled off the floor for a few seconds. She screamed, and again as she felt the dog smash into her. He was dragged away, it was too dark to see where, but his claws scrunched up the carpet and he yowled.

"Ches!" She felt around in the direction of his cry. "Ches, boy!"

The wind seemed to blow the words straight back at her, and bits of paper and soot flew into her face. She could hear a banging, something intermittently thumping through the racket. The door. She tried crawling across the carpet, but within a couple of feet the coldness and nausea overwhelmed her, and she retreated to pant in a heap on the floor. *Jack, please, please come back.* Another scraping on her right made her fumble a hand in its direction, as a huge thump was followed by a howl from Ches, this time from behind her. *He's being blown around, he'll be killed.*

Gathering all her strength, she bellowed, "Ches!"

This time she could track the squeal of his claws as he was shunted around her, and was able to flail in his direction to grab something—a leg or a tail—before it was snatched away from her again. She shuffled closer to the scraping noise, hoping it was the priest-hole door. She held her breath against the rising nausea, and squinted into the flying debris whistling around the edges of the room. She caught a glimpse of light fur, lit perhaps from the starlight outside, as Ches careered around the walls, no longer howling. Reaching with both arms, she caught him as he slid past. Holding him in her arms like a crazy dancer, she staggered to her feet and launched herself into the cold toward the darker shadow of the doorway, and tripped over the step into the priest hole.

Chapter 28

The thud of hooves striking the road was deafening,
the heaving of the mare's breath no less so. The road
was so poorly lit, even with several lanterns held
aloft on short poles, that I expected every moment to
be dashed against a tree or thrown down a hillside.

—EDWARD KELLEY
  Believed 27 November 1585
  On the road

THE POUNDING AGAINST THE SADDLE, AND THE UTTER
cold, seeped into me as the journey progressed. It exhausted me, and I must have fallen into insensibility by
dawn. I woke with the clatter of iron shoes on cobbles as we
turned into a yard in the first light.

I was lifted down as if I were a child. I lurched on my feet,
the world seemed to heave more than the horse. The gag was
pulled down, and I vomited a mouthful of foul liquid onto my
captor's mud-splashed boots. The guard brought out a dagger
the length of my forearm, and in front of my horrified eyes,
waved it close to my throat. As I shrank back, he brought the
knife down and cut the knot holding my hands in front of me,
and turned away with a bellow of laughter.

As my hands came back to life, they burned with pain, and
I almost cried out. Another man gestured, and I was waved to a
wall where several of the guards were relieving themselves. Dee

was there, his face as white as chalk, a bruise obscuring one eye, which was purpled and swollen. He, at least, had put up a fight. I noticed he now wore crude boots.

"Master—"

"Who are these men? Have you heard them speak among themselves?" he asked in a low voice. "I can't believe they are from the Inquisition, they seemed to kill the Swiss guards and the Poles. Are they Istvan's Hungarians?"

I shrugged, glancing over my shoulder at the group of warriors. "They killed one of them on the way out."

"Magyars? Mercenaries? Who but the Pope would go to these lengths to take us?"

Who, indeed. An idea crossed my mind, but I dared not give it voice where it might be heard. My giant guard gestured to me to follow him to a doorway, and an old woman handed me a tankard. I drank deep, the ale made delicious by my privations, followed by a hunk of bread filled with some sort of sausage. It took away the acid in my mouth, and I realized I was ravenous. The small kindness filled me with hope, which faltered when another horse was brought forward. The man pulled the rope from a pocket, and I fell back, shaking my head. "I will ride. I can ride." I mimed holding reins.

He looked at one of his compatriots and held up the rope. Some signal passed between them, and he pointed at the horse. I was shivering with cold, but at least I was trusted to ride with them. I drew comfort from the fact that I was not chained in a carriage surrounded by the Vatican guards.

One side of the track was silvered in moonlight, the trees looked like metal bars making a prison of the road. We set out, heading southwest this time, the men riding in a close group around us. I estimated by its width that it was the highway between Poland and Hungary, but they soon veered onto a track through the forest. We were back into gallops where the road and the light were good. I don't know how many leagues we traversed, but we only stopped for another tankard and necessary relief, and my rump was so bruised I cried out when I sat back on my next horse, more pony than steed. My captors laughed aloud. In the first daylight they were clearly Magyars, and they were less discreet, hissing in their native language. There were eleven of them, two wounded with rude bandages around limbs.

A third bloodstained man, younger than the others, rode without complaint, but even with his bandages tightened by his comrades, a sheet of blood fell down his side and his face grew whiter in the early light. As we climbed up a steep path in single file, he toppled without warning off his horse, in front of my own pony, which shied. The injured man rolled off the path into the skeletons of brambles lining the track. The man I had thought of as the leader dismounted and pushed him with a boot. This raised a groan from the injured man, who rolled onto his back. The captain pulled the scarf from the injured man's face. The boy—for he was barely bearded—opened his eyes, almost black, surrounded by lashes as long and thick as a girl's. The captain did not hesitate, drawing a long knife, the one he had threatened me with, I think. He slid the blade under the boy's ear, slashing it across his neck. The young man died with a gurgle from the gaping throat, his eyes closing.

The big man bent his head for a moment, perhaps in prayer, then hefted the body onto his shoulder. He disappeared off the path into the bushes, followed by a stocky man, whose hair was grizzled like an old terrier. They returned a few minutes later, with everything the boy had been wearing, down to his linens. I was shaking, my eyes meeting Dee's for a moment. As we rode off, I reflected that perhaps our captors didn't want anyone to identify the boy, and the animals in the forest around us would soon deal with the naked corpse. The rain started falling again, and trickled down the back of my cloak and along my spine, adding to my miseries.

Chapter 29

ELIX WAS STANDING IN THE UNIVERSITY CAR PARK AFTER a long evening of tutorials when his phone rang.

"Yes?" He fumbled with his briefcase, trying to get the car keys out without dropping the phone.

"Felix?" He almost didn't recognize the voice.

"Jack? Is that you?"

"Felix . . ." There was a long pause and he could hear other sounds. "I need your help."

"What's happened?"

"I'm at St. David's Hospital." She sounded hoarse. "I need you to come and get me."

He unlocked his car and threw his case in. "What happened?"

The phone clicked and went dead. He looked at the screen. Jack, thirty-four seconds, and his heart was already hammering in his chest. He started the car and drove over a speed bump in the exit too fast, clunking his exhaust.

Felix turned into a side street, heading toward the hospital. It was already dark, the town center lit by hundreds of headlights and taillights, splashes of white and red illuminating shoppers filling up the town. Signs on lampposts and shop windows announced late-night Christmas shopping. He was forced to concentrate as he was boxed in by queues of traffic. In the end, it was twenty minutes before he got to the hospital.

At almost nine o'clock, main reception was closed. That left the emergency room. He looked around the waiting room, with its beige plastic chairs and a handful of huddled drunks, and turned to the emergency room receptionist. Before he could open his mouth, he heard Jack's voice.

"Felix."

One of the heaps of clothing turned out to be a muddy and disheveled Jack, a scrape down one side of her face bruised purple, and one eye shot with scarlet.

"Jack!" He reached out his hands for hers, and she clutched his arm as if she were going to fall. "What happened? Have you seen a doctor?"

"Let's go. Please." Her voice was hoarse.

A male nurse in blue scrubs walked up to them. "Are you sure I can't persuade you to stay? Just to warm you up."

Jack's fingers were shaking, and Felix covered them in his. "You're freezing."

"I'll be fine when I get home." Her words came out slowly.

The nurse looked at Felix. "She's hypothermic, and she may be in shock. We can't make her stay. At least make sure she goes to bed and stays there. Bring her back at once if she feels worse."

"I'll be fine." Jack waved the man off.

He ignored her, and handed Felix a sheet of paper.

"You need to stay with her, and bring her back if she shows any of the signs on the sheet. Seriously, she should be in the hospital. This is against all medical advice."

"I signed the papers, it's OK." Jack cast herself off from Felix's arm, and stood, swaying. "I need to go home." She started toward the doors, which swished open.

"Oh, wait." The receptionist fumbled under her desk. "The ambulance dropped this off for you." She held out a leather bag, muddy and wet, and Jack took it. "They couldn't find your purse, though."

Felix looked at the shaking Jack, now searching through the bag. "What happened?"

"I passed out. It's fine; some shoppers helped me. I had my phone in my pocket so I called you . . . can we just go?"

She walked through the doors, and Felix could do little but smile his thanks at the staff and follow her. The cold air outside knocked her into a wobble, and she grabbed Felix's arm.

"I need you to take me back to my car." She sounded distant, her voice rough. "I have to get home."

"You can't drive like this. Let me take you." He gripped her elbow, steering her toward the car park.

She stumbled along beside him as he took more of her weight, holding her around her waist. "I can't . . . I can't let you into the house."

"You can't stay on your own."

"I won't be. I don't live alone, I'll be fine."

The words rolled over him, stinging more than he would have expected. Boyfriend, husband?

"Why didn't you call . . . them instead?" He stopped at his car, and she put both hands out, leaning on it. He heard her groan, as if in pain.

"I'll call Maggie—my foster mother. She'll come over."

He opened the car door, and helped her into the passenger seat. The light made her look smaller in the bulky coat. "My bag," she said, "in the bottom, there should be a small bottle." Her hands burrowed into the layers of her coat.

He took the bag, shut the door and walked around to get in the driver's side. The bottle, brown and unmarked, was in a pocket right at the bottom. He held it up to the light but it was opaque, like ink. "This?"

He held it out to her, and she fumbled with the top, until he took it from her and loosened it. The smell of the liquid inside made him recoil, a putrescent sweetness. He winced when she lifted it to her lips and drank deep.

"What is that?" He leaned back from the stink of it.

She capped the bottle, then sat still for a moment, breathing deeply, eyes shut. "That's better." She sighed, a warm mist that smelled of compost reaching him. "It's an herbal medicine."

"The treatment seems worse than the disease."

"You get used to it." Jack rolled her head to face him, and opened her eyes. "Thank you for coming. I didn't know who to call, I couldn't reach Maggie."

Jack fumbled with the seat belt clasp and Felix reached over to help her with it. The light inside the car shone on a familiar symbol inked below Jack's throat, just under her scarf.

He sat back, and she stared at him, one hand pressed to her chest. Anger filled him up, choking him. She slowly pulled her fingers away, drawing back the layers of her clothes by a few inches, revealing three of the shapes.

"I *do* know what these are used for," she said, her voice calm. "I wanted to explain, but there are other lives at risk."

"One life has already been lost, Jack. A girl is dead in the mortuary, and you didn't tell me . . . this is all to do with the medals." He put both hands on the steering wheel, gripping the cold leather. He felt unreasonably hurt. He had thought the rapport between them was mutual trust. "You've been lying to me all along."

"No!" She breathed heavily for a moment, as if frustrated. "Yes, maybe by omission. I wanted to tell you, I really did. You were right. The sigils are healing symbols, that's all."

"So, you just wanted to find out what I knew." He turned the key in the ignition. "I'm taking you home. And then you are going to tell me everything you know. Or I'm calling the police, and this McNamara."

"No!" Her voice was fluttery, weak over the purr of the engine. "Just take me to my car."

"You aren't safe to drive." Her hand covered his, and the touch of her skin shocked him. "You're frozen." His anger started to fade.

"I have this medical condition, it leaves me prone to hypothermia." She gripped his hand, pulling at it. "Felix, if I tell you everything I can, will you help me get home—safely?"

He hesitated, still angry, but the touch of her fingers was burning him despite their extreme cold. They were vibrating, as if she were shivering, before she withdrew them.

"I'm tired of being mucked around, Jack. These symbols are somehow linked to a girl's death." A horrible thought hit Felix, as he drove around a traffic circle toward the main road. "You're involved in this girl's death, aren't you?" He gripped the wheel harder, thinking how he'd been taken for a fool.

"I . . ." She rubbed her face with her hands, as he glanced at her.

His voice was cold. "Tell me the truth, Jack. Did you . . . kill that girl?" He looked back to see her expression.

She looked straight into his eyes, a foot away. "I didn't kill her. I failed to save her."

Chapter 30

The forests of Poland are dense and wrap themselves around a traveler like a cloak. Within its folds are many hazards: wolves that the guards fought off several times; a bear that crossed the road and held us at bay for many minutes; dark forest men, carrying poached deer and hares. And the deep, killing cold that takes away a man's senses and burns his face and limbs.

—EDWARD KELLEY
30 November 1585
Carpathia

W E TRAVELED FOR MOST OF FIVE NIGHTS AND FOUR days, riding on worse roads than I have ever seen. I fell off an assortment of ponies and horses at a number of inns, castles and the odd peasant hovel. There I was fed ale and bread and allowed a few hours' rest when it was too dark to travel. I slept tied up in the squalid warmth of stables or cowsheds. Our kidnappers seemed to suffer no discomfort at this speed of travel, often by torchlight, but were constantly looking back for pursuit. Dee and I were able to exchange but a few whispers.

Around dawn after the fifth night, the party wound along a curving road that seemed to rise steeply, and I was jerked from a daydream by the shout of one of our guards.

"Báthory! Báthory!" The cry was taken up by our group, even the two injured men, who had survived, despite the lack of a surgeon. The men seemed as hardy as their mounts. I shook the hood from my head, and urged my pony onward to keep up with our escort. They were holding their weapons aloft and chanting in their own language. My mount slowed as it came to the top of the road.

Falling away below me, a deep valley was covered with a patchwork of fields and forest, which then rose to the slopes of a mountain. Perhaps the countess would have called it a hill, I do not know, but it was so steep it looked as if nothing could climb it without wings. Yet perched on the top, like a stone eagle, was a castle. It projected turrets and towers into the sky, the walls tinted in golds and pinks by the glow of dawn.

The leader of the men kicked his mount toward me. "Csejte. Báthory!" He added something in accented Latin and my muddled, exhausted mind ordered the words to make some sense. We were "home."

Dee sat tall in the stirrups to look at the vista. It was as if we faced a bowl made of mountains, which serrated the horizons all around.

"Look, Edward." His voice was dry and rough, as I suspected mine would have been, but his eyes were shining and his bruises yellowing. "We have been traveling south and west. This must be the Little Carpathians. We have traveled sixty leagues or more." He coughed, then spat onto the road. He shook with cold, and wrapped his wet cloak around his shoulders.

"I know, master . . ." I spat dust in an effort to make enough saliva to speak. "I know where we are. The captain said Csejte, it's one of the Báthory castles. The countess was talking about it."

"Clever. Istvan is a fox, Edward. He cannot refuse Rome, but he still wants us to cure his niece. So he allows Nádasdy to kidnap us, and he can avoid responsibility."

It hadn't taken me more than a night to work that out, but I hesitated on the path, looking down the shaggy flank of my stolid mount. Viewed occasionally as a bare ribbon, a road cut between the forest and fields lining the valley. A mountain goat, perhaps, could negotiate it, but I could not imagine . . .

I did not have to envisage it for long. A callous hand grasped my reins, and with my pony squealing like a pig, dragged us all over the edge into the valley. My poor nag half walked, half slid on its rump down the path, the man on the horse ahead of us calling out some heathen war cry, as others followed. In places the track cut along the edge of the cliffs, barely a yard wide, my patient horse slipping and tripping on boulders larger than my head, each lurch giving me a falcon's-eye view of the trees from above.

As we rode past farms and cottages, cries of recognition met the riders. The slope softened and we reached a village with a small, pointed church, much fortified. Here we paused, and were greeted with foaming tankards and handfuls of dumplings to be dipped in bowls of some meaty soup. I ate with the men and I filled my belly with the hot, greasy food. I wiped my mouth on my cloak, which, I am ashamed to say, had been used as a napkin and worse over the journey. Then I was led to a midden and allowed to relieve myself, while children peeped around the wall at me and giggled. They seemed well fed enough, and strong, unlike some of the thin, white faces we had seen along our ride. I sought about me for some hay or shavings, and a child, just a girl of maybe six or seven, shyly ventured forward with some leaves. I smiled at her, but she dropped them beside me and ran back, laughing. The encounter cheered me, and when I walked back to my pony under the eye of a captor, I looked up to the castle, which seemed to loom overhead.

The clatter of iron-shod ponies on the stone courtyard within the open doors of the citadel was muted with a foot of mud. The count and countess appeared to keep a garrison of many servants, as the ground was covered with the marks of traffic. Horse, hound and boot prints were criss-crossed with cart tracks. I was pulled off the saddle to sprawl upon the ground, a laugh rising from the men who had accompanied me. I was full of gratitude that at least I wouldn't have to ride again for a while. Seeing them standing by their horses, I realized only the captain and one of the injured men was actually taller than me, and neither was taller than my mentor. Dee was staggering across the yard to help me to my feet. We supported each other in the dull light, clouds racing across the sky, so close it felt like a broom would reach them. Dee was unable to stand upright, and his face was tight with pain. But his voice was warm and his smile wide.

"Safe from the Inquisition, Edward, at least. Though I'm afraid I am becoming too old for riding above a trot." He looked quite gray with exhaustion. "God grant us rest, at least."

"And dry clothes," I answered, brushing the mud on my jacket with an equally muddy hand. My courtly dress—or Dee's, as it happened—was ruined, torn under one arm, soaked in mud and stinking of horse sweat and urine from hours fettered in stables. "And food."

Our captain strode forward, buffeting my shoulder with one hand so I reeled again. "You are safe, safe, understand?" he said in his strange Latin. "Safe from the poxed Inquisition and their whoreson priest."

I attempted a grin, and nodded. "Safe, yes. Good."

He bowed his head a little to us, then reached inside his jacket for an inner pocket.

"My master bade me give you this, and grant you sanctuary in his castle."

Dee took the folded missive, and opened it, holding it so I could read.

*At your service Doctor Dee and Master Kelley, may God con-
tinue to grant you long life. At the bidding of the countess, my
wife, I have taken the liberty with your safety to remove you
from the court of His Highness Istvan Báthory, our esteemed
uncle, and place you in the castle at Csejte for your own protection. My men have your possessions with them, that you might
continue to work upon your studies, that the countess will, with
the grace of God, be healed of her afflictions.*

HIS LORDSHIP COUNT FERENC NÁDASDY, written at
Niepolomice, St. Matthew's eve, 1585, by his own hand

The whole was scribbled in untidy and misspelled Latin, as if
in a hurry, but the intention was clear. We had exchanged one
prison for another.

Chapter 31

FELIX DROVE IN SILENCE, PERHAPS SHOCKED BY THE REVelations of the night, Jack couldn't tell. She touched her face, feeling the smooth tightness of the swelling beside her eye. It hurt, more than expected, and she winced, the skin pulling. Felix glanced at her.

"You said you fell."

"Yes." She swallowed, her throat dry and her voice croaky. "I went to consult someone about this woman, this Bachmeier. He must have tripped me or something."

"Tripped you?" His voice was dry. "You aren't as good a liar as you think you are, Jack."

"Well, if I explained how he tripped me you wouldn't believe it."

"Try me."

He took the turn to the village.

"This guy, Pierce, hit me with a charm to knock the energy out of me." She reached for her bag and started looking through it. "I managed to get to the high street before it really hit me." She found it in the small pocket on the outside. It was a charred circle of thorns and plaited herbs, and greasy with some sort of animal fat. "It's called a hex grenade. He must have planted it in my bag."

He held out one hand for it, and she dropped it onto his palm. He started for a moment, then weighed it, glancing down. "It feels cold." He gave it back to her, replacing his hand on the wheel.

"That's how it works, it pulls the energy out from whoever's near it. It's spent now."

He drove for a few moments, staring ahead. "Dee wrote about something similar, but not to hurt people. To store up energy that could be released in magic spells."

"Well, Pierce uses them to debilitate."

"Did this man know anything useful?"

"Pierce? He's met her, the woman in the back of my car. She's offered him money. It's the only language he understands." She reached for the charm, and opened the window a few inches. "It's got to go, I don't want him tracing me through it."

He smiled crookedly at her. "So he's some sort of witch doctor, here in Devon?"

"No, he just knows a few people, a few tricks." She directed him through the crossroad. "Just take me to the village. I can walk from there."

"You don't trust me." Felix's voice was soft.

"This isn't just my secret to tell, there are other people involved."

"OK." He looked at her, one eyebrow raised. "Go on."

She watched his jaw tighten, his lips thin. He had nice lips, she thought. "This is half legend, half tradition. You probably know more about its origins than I do."

"This is something to do with the Dee medals, obviously."

"Some people believe that we are fated to die at a certain time."

"OK." He didn't sound like he was one of them, but she pressed on.

"So, for most people, that moment comes and they die. But for others, they will *probably* die. There's some uncertainty."

"And this is related to the symbols on your chest?"

"On my back, too, and in every room in my home. These keep me alive."

He frowned. "Are they drawn on?"

"I have tattoos, they last longer." She wrapped her coat tight around her neck, her fingers stiff with cold. "They are healing sigils, Felix, nothing more sinister than that. The dead girl, Carla, was dying of an overdose when we found her. She had seconds, a minute, no more. The magic kept her alive long enough to get her to safety. We call it borrowed time."

"You didn't call an ambulance, get expert medical care?"

"There isn't medical care for what was wrong with Carla, or with me." She caught his arm and shook it for a moment. "Her time was up, Felix, she was dying. A seer predicted her death."

"And these shapes saved her, somehow, where medicine wouldn't have?" He looked angry. "You don't know that, you can't be sure."

She was piqued by the cold tone. "I have a fair amount of evidence backing that belief. Carla was fine all the time she stuck to the rules. The second she stopped, she . . ." Her voice thickened, and she choked on the word *died*.

He looked at the darkness out of the window, his face reflected in the black glass.

"What do you mean by *seer*?"

"A seer predicted when she would die, where she would be. We—"

"We?" He jumped on the word.

"Maggie, my foster mother and I, we went there to find Carla. She was in an alley, dying, was all but dead, because it was her time to die. She was emaciated, covered with sores, septic. She'd taken a huge overdose, was barely breathing."

"So you . . . did what?"

She took a deep breath, nibbled a fingernail. She was exhausted, but somehow Felix radiated energy. "Maggie drew the sigils on her, there in the alley. Then we carried her to my car, which has the same symbols drawn in circles."

She could still feel the revulsion of seeing the girl's white skin revealed in the light of the torch, veins inching like a giant red spider from the abscess on her leg, pus oozing. She stank of drink. It looked as if Carla's last choice had been to put herself down like a sick dog.

"And you have these same symbols? The ones from the medals."

"Because I was going to die, yes. Take the next right."

Felix peered at the road ahead. "Maybe this is what Kelley was writing about. He was asked to help someone whose life might be saved by some magical means."

"I suppose." She had never been able to decipher much of Kelley's cryptic handwriting.

He frowned at her, but at least he didn't seem angry anymore. "Why? Why would you save someone you didn't even know existed?"

She smiled slightly at him, wondering how much disbelief he could suspend. "People believe that individuals living on borrowed time have magical healing powers." She shrugged. "Imagine chemo with no side effects, no baldness, no sickness."

"Is that why you were saved?"

"Maggie had a baby with leukemia. Who is now healthy and safe, thanks to me."

"I'm taking you home. And then I'm going to call this Maggie, just to make sure she will look after you."

She turned to face him, studying his dark silhouette as they passed the village streetlights. "There's more. Can I really trust you?"

"You can trust me to try to do the right thing." His voice was soft, and as he glanced across in the dim light she could see his eyes gleam. "Is this the right road?"

"It's up here." After a quarter of a mile Jack pointed at the long hedge. "The cottage is there, that's the gate."

"Nice. Right in the country," he murmured, as he slowly drove the car over the gravel, toward the cattle grid.

"Wait!" Jack put a hand over his, and he braked.

"What is it?" he asked, in a low voice.

"I don't know. It just seems . . . quiet." She looked through the brambles at the side of the house, in darkness, and tried to remember whether she'd left the kitchen light on. *Something's different . . .*

"Drive over the cattle grid."

As the headlights swung around the backyard, they picked up bunches of feathers, black shapes on the concrete . . . birds, scattered and torn. Jack pushed open the door and her boots rattled onto the yard. As her eyes adjusted to the brightness she realized it was strewn with dead rooks. She lifted a wing, a mouthful of bile rising in her throat.

Felix came up behind her. "What is it?"

"My birds . . . the rookery." She choked, and looked back at the trees, the silhouetted branches emptied of their mounds of sticks. "They're destroyed. What could do this?"

Felix took the wing from her fingers, and dropped it. "Let's get inside. Where are your keys?"

"Oh my God!" She leapt forward, feeling the door handle. At least it was still locked. She dragged her keys from her pocket and fumbled with them. Her breath was coming in little sobs, and she couldn't get enough air. Light from the car spilled into the kitchen as the door swung open. She reached in to flick the switch, but the bulb didn't come on.

"Stay here," he said, as he brushed past her. "The power must be out." He stumbled in, and swore as he hit something. "Where's the fuse box?"

"Cupboard . . ." She leaned against the doorjamb, trying to catch her breath. The wedge of light from the doorway showed an unfamiliar landscape. "Corner of the kitchen, under the stairs."

More swearing, then the fluorescent bulb flickered on, illuminating more of the yard beyond the doorway. More black feathers, spots of scarlet blood, gaping beaks. *Oh God, Sadie, Ches. Why can't I hear them?*

She turned toward the kitchen.

Everything lighter than the dresser had been overturned. The table and the chairs were tumbled, two of them broken. The elm rocker, at least, was intact, although it was upside down. Parts of the floor were calf-deep in shattered crockery, torn papers and the contents of smashed jars. The range stank of soot, as if it had been snuffed out. The ceiling was cracked, and there were holes in the plaster on the walls down to the cob.

"Let me help." Felix held a hand out as she slid across the floor, and they clung together in the rubble, skating toward the living-room door.

It took a few kicks from Felix's shoe to clear the floor enough to scrape it open.

Jack pushed ahead of him, into what remained of the front room. There was a breeze coming through the smashed panes in the window, but even so, it felt unnaturally cold and still. The furniture had been flung into the corners of the room, and covered in pages of books. The carpet was twisted up onto one side of the room, and the chain that had restrained the girl was gone. The wall showed through cracks in the plaster. The bulb was broken, and the only light had spilled in from the kitchen.

Jack stumbled toward the edge of the room, looking for Sadie under the debris, among the shadows. "Ches!" She could feel tears pouring down her face. "Felix, help me find them."

"Who?"

"My dog, and Sadie . . ." She started pulling at one of the tumbled sofas.

Felix was standing over by the paneling door, frowning. "Can you hear that?"

As she held her breath, halting the sobs that were suffocating her, she could hear the faint whining of the dog. She fell to her knees in front of the concealed door, dragging the wreckage away. After a moment, Felix pushed her aside, and cleared the floor in a few sweeps. Jack pressed the hidden catch, and it clicked open, the sound sharp in the dark room. The door swung out, and the lantern lit the white face of the girl, curled on the bed, clutching the dog around his neck. Ches whined and leapt, the momentum dragging the girl forward even as her eyes rolled back.

Chapter 32

It is said that the castle at Csejte, one of the smallest strongholds of the Nádasdy's estates, was given as a wedding gift to his countess, Elizabeth Báthory. Here, servants loyal to the couple will do their bidding, even to the point of mortal sin. They are, it seems, more afraid of the Báthory family than the fires of hell.

—EDWARD KELLEY
1 December 1585
Csejte Castle

D EE AND I WERE SHOWN TO SEPARATE ROOMS, AND A succession of solemn maids entered with tall cans of hot water. One elderly woman indicated that I should remove my ruined clothing and sit in a wooden tub she had carried in with the help of a guard. I was too tired to argue, although I did try to keep my linens. The woman prevailed.

I sat, shivering and naked, and the maid began to pour scented water over my head. I lifted heavy arms to soap myself, washing off the stink of the fear I had suffered as well as the dirt. I was then wrapped in a rough towel, and rubbed down like a horse. The old woman fussed and muttered. I fear they were not flattering comments, as the guard laughed several times. I was handed a length of cloth instead of good hose and a cod, and had to be dressed in the loincloth by the woman, much like the swaddling of a baby. Then I was given heavy trousers, such as a peasant in England might wear, and a fine shirt, with much embroidery about the neck and with silver points on the laces. Finally the woman presented me, on one knee, with a long robe such as the nobles wore.

"*Dolman.*" She said, smoothing the brown fabric. Then she stumbled in Latin. "Nádasdy. The *dolman* of Lord Nádasdy."

The garment almost swept the floor. I was then fed a hot stew, which I started to fall asleep over, and lay down upon the bed to rest.

When I awoke, it was evening already. Feeling somewhat restored, I slid off the high bed, put on thick woolen stockings and my own, cleaned boots. Somewhat guilty of the neglect of my master, I looked around for his quarters.

A small door beside the fire was open a crack, and I pushed it farther. Although dressed in a nightshirt and wrapped in a blanket, Dee was seated in a chair looking at a large map spread over the table.

"Edward!" He coughed into his hand, then shook his head. "Are you well?"

"I am, but are you?" I had never seen him ill before, but now there was a heavy-eyed, flushed look about him. "Shall I burn some pastilles? Do you need a physician to bleed you?"

He waved away the notion. "A quotidian fever, no doubt, from traveling in such wet conditions. I've been aware of it for several days, good food and rest will surely resolve it. Look, Edward, this map shows what I believe must have been our journey."

I had never met a man so casual about his health, yet I had known others to fall into a decline and die from less. "Master Dee—"

"Edward." There was a sharpness in his voice, which softened as he continued. "Your eyesight is better than mine. Can you see the name of the castle?"

I struggled with the unfamiliar lettering, very ornate and

tiny. I had heard the name as "Chay-tay" and struggled with the Hungarian spelling. "Here, I think. C-s-j-e is pronounced 'Chay,' is it not?" The castle overlooked the main road to the south, and the Turkish occupation. He leaned over, looking at the peak indicated by my finger.

"You would think the countess would be safer farther north," he said. "We can be no more than forty or so leagues from the Turkish occupation. A good place for Nádasdy to base his military forces, I suppose."

A knock on the main door was followed by two maidservants, one carrying a vast wooden tray of savory foods. The women bowed to us, and seemed anxious to go. I caught the door as they left, holding it open. There were no guards outside, so I left it ajar.

Dee looked at the food, and brushed his shaking hand over his brow. "Do you know, Edward, I think I will go to bed now."

"Let me get a doctor, please." I put a hand under his elbow and helped him limp to the bed.

"Nonsense." He sat on the side of the bed and swung his legs in. "I shall be better when I have rested. I am not a young man, you know. Mull me some ale, and I shall have a little bread."

I looked around and found a sturdy poker. Having wiped it on a napkin, I placed it in the fire to warm, and cut Dee a soft inner slice from the small, round loaf. It was dark, and smelled bitter but the crust tasted very good. I dusted the poker off, and plunged it into a tall flagon of ale.

"There. I shall be better in no time." He waved at the table. "And the big, leather-bound book next to the map, I think." He took a small bite of the bread. He placed the food and drink on a chair beside the bed, and took the volume I offered. Then, with as little attention to me as if I had already gone, he opened the pages and leaned back against the pillows. As I left, I could hear his rattling chest, wheezing like that of a dying man.

Chapter 33

JACK CLAMBERED DOWN INTO THE CELL AND GATHERED THE collapsed girl up in her arms. Sadie's skin was icy, and Jack wasn't sure she was breathing. Felix followed, and crouched beside them.

"Is she . . . ?" He touched the girl's neck. "Let's get her upstairs. Let me have her, Jack." He pried her fingers off the girl, his hands warm.

Jack followed them up the steps, and was relieved to hear Sadie start retching as she got to the gap between the circles.

"Bring her here, in the middle of the room." Jack slumped onto the debris in the middle of the circle, holding out her arms for Sadie, who sank against her without speaking. As Jack clung to her, she realized the girl stank, and pulled back a little, grimacing.

"It was Ches." Sadie's whisper barely reached Jack. "He got scared and shat himself."

Jack looked around the dark living room, seeing the dog's eyes gleaming from the corner, behind the tumbled sofa. She whistled for him, and he slunk forward on his belly, whining. He fitted into the two of them, licking both faces, until Jack told him to stop. She could hear Felix in the kitchen, opening things, banging around. He came back in, and stretched over their heads to replace the bulb. This time, when he flicked the switch, the room lit up.

He stared at them, and then at Sadie. He was shocked, Jack realized. He looked around the room with wild eyes.

"You're Sadie Williams. The girl the police are looking for."

Sadie looked at Felix, then back at Jack. "Who is he?" Her hand clutched Jack's sleeve. "Is he the police?"

"My name is Felix Guichard," he answered. "I was helping Jack. What happened here?"

Sadie's eyes widened as she looked at the devastation in the room. "There was this insane storm, inside the house."

"What?" Jack pushed off the floor, lifting Sadie to her feet.

Felix hefted one of the sofas up, and eyed the exposed boards of the floor, the circle of symbols inscribed in black.

"Put it right in the middle of the circle," Jack said. He set it down, and held out a hand to Sadie. After a moment's pause, she took it, and climbed onto the sofa. Jack had to restrain the dog, his feet covered in shit, from crawling after her.

"I'm going to clean up the dog. You," she pointed at Sadie, "stay put and keep an eye on Felix. If you think he's going to do anything stupid—like call the police—scream the place down."

She grabbed the dog by his collar and dragged him toward the stairs to the bedroom level. The carpet was hanging loose on the bottom few steps, pulled out from antique stair rods by whatever had trashed the house. She managed to half lift, half pull the dog into the old claw-footed bath, even though it made her reel with dizziness for a few moments. She ran a few inches of warm water into it and added a squeeze of dog shampoo. She sponged him down in the pine-scented steam, while he wagged his tail and tried to lick her face. She couldn't find any major injuries, but his mouth was cut and his tongue had purple marks on it, as if he'd bitten it. She roughly toweled him off and let him go. He shot downstairs in the puppyish euphoria that always took over him after he'd had a bath.

Jack paused to wash her hands, and looked into the mirror. She was shocked. Her eyes were red in a white face. Her skin seemed sucked back onto the bones of her skull, accentuating the swollen purple scrape down the side of her face. When was the last time she had eaten properly? The truth was, she had lost her appetite months ago. Her hands were still blue, despite being in the warm water.

The dog growled and Sadie shouted. Jack stumbled downstairs. Felix was standing with his back against the wall, the dog staring at him, in the "guard" position, hackles up, teeth bared, spine straight.

"I was trying to clear up," Felix said, inching toward the corner of the room.

"Ches!" Jack snapped, and after a moment, the dog backed off. She rubbed her wet hands on her jeans. "He's just spooked. Now, Sadie, tell me what happened here."

The teenager rubbed her neck, livid with parallel scratches. There was a bruise on her forehead, and she was filthy. She sniffed her shaking hand and pulled a face.

"I told you. It was like a storm. It started outside." She rubbed a sleeve over her face, then looked at Felix. "Who are you, again?"

"Felix. I'm a friend of Jack's." He met Jack's eyes, as she gazed back, and lifted the corners of her mouth in a reluctant smile.

Sadie went on. "It was like a whirlwind, like the one in *The Wizard of Oz*. It picked Ches up, I think, and threw him around the edges of the room. I could only just reach him." Sadie held up the cuff, the length of chain dangling. "It was horrible, I thought we were both going to die. I managed to get free. Ches was terrified."

The dog chose that moment to yawn, revealing two perfect Vs of ivory sharpness, and Sadie patted him. Felix's smile faded.

"Then, something called my name," continued Sadie. "I was scared—and I thought we would be safer in the dungeon. So I dragged him down the stairs. Then it was like a lorry crashed into the house, there was this huge bang and everything started hitting the floor."

Jack looked around. The room was carpeted with a thick layer of torn pages and dismembered books. "Then what?"

Sadie shrugged, and touched the scratches on her neck. "It went quiet. Really quiet and dark, I couldn't find the lamp at first. Then we waited for ages. Then you came."

Jack lifted a hand, hesitated, then took one of the girl's, pressing it for a moment.

"I'm so sorry. Thank you for saving Ches as well."

Sadie looked at her, surprised. "Of course." She showed Jack the raw circle of her wrist, under the shackle. "I had to use the poker to get free." She rubbed the dog's head with the other hand, and he leaned back to sweep her fingers with a pink tongue. "It picked him up like a leaf and threw him against the wall. I thought it was going to kill him." Sadie shuddered. "Did you see the birds?"

"The rookery?" Jack shut her eyes for a moment, a stab of grief cutting through her. "Yes, I saw."

Felix lifted the other sofa back onto its feet. He sat on it and leaned forward, his elbows on his knees. "I still don't understand. You think this was some sort of attack? It could have been a natural event. Tornadoes do happen, even in Devon."

"No." Sadie stretched forward. "It started when the light went out, and birds started hitting the window. That was before the wind started blowing. Then it called my name."

"Are you sure?" Jack was startled.

"Yeah, twice. Then it sort of came down the chimney. It put the fire out, and started blowing around the edge of the circle. That's when I carried Ches to the dungeon. The door blew shut."

"The priest hole is a sanctuary," Jack explained to Felix. She turned to Sadie. "If you hadn't got free . . ."

"I told you not to chain me up. I'm not stupid."

Jack nodded. "I'm sorry."

The silence stretched out. Then Sadie broke it, looking from Felix to Jack. "So. Someone's trying to take me?"

Jack sighed. "Someone's after you, and I have no idea why. I'm sorry, I didn't know any of this was going to happen."

Sadie looked back at Felix. "Are you going to help us?"

He turned to Jack. "You kidnapped her, and chained her up like a dog. Now she's in danger. What do you expect me to do?" He sounded angry again.

Jack opened her mouth, but it was Sadie who answered. "You can't call the police, I'll die."

"You believe that because Jack has told you—"

"I *know* that. You do, too, if you stop to think about it. Look at what happened to Carla." Sadie held out her hand to Jack. "You can unlock this now. You won't need to chain me up again."

Jack searched her pocket for her house keys. She tried to stand, the room rolling around her in a nauseating manner, and she sat down again. "Felix?"

"What do you need?" The anger had gone from his voice, and concern had replaced it.

"The bottle, it's in my bag. And my keys, they're still in the door." She leaned back until he returned.

The handcuff key was on the set. She unlocked the manacle from Sadie's wrist and opened the bottle.

"Oh, not that stuff! I don't need it."

"I do." Jack took a swig, wincing, then wiped off the top. "And so do you. I have an idea."

Sadie took the bottle, screwed up her face, and took a couple of sips. "I hate this stuff." She scowled at Jack. "I don't know why I need it now, I feel OK."

"Because with a bit of help, and half a bottle of potion, I may be able to get you upstairs to the bathroom." Jack started picking over the rubbish on the floor, looking for the contents of the shattered pen pot. "Aha." She picked up a marker pen, which seemed unharmed, then turned to Felix.

He was staring at Sadie, then his eyes met Jack's. For a long moment, she waited for him to speak, but he just gazed at her.

"Felix," she said. He jumped a little, as if shaken out of whatever he was thinking. "I couldn't tell you the whole truth," she continued, "because you would never have believed it. And I had to look after Sadie. If we make one mistake, she could die. Are you going to help us, or not?"

She waited for a long moment, before he stepped toward her. "If you do anything to put that child in danger, I will call the police." Ignoring a protest from Sadie he continued, stepping close to Jack, until she staggered back half a step. "And I don't think it's just Sadie who is in danger. You are being attacked by witches in your car, and in the street by this Pierce. Not to mention the police are already looking into Carla's death, and this art detective is looking for forgeries he thinks *you* sold. There's a big picture here, and I don't think any of us sees it yet. But somehow, it's all to do with Dee and those documents. That's the common link."

"And Sadie." Jack looked at the girl, seeing her wide eyes. "She isn't just a pawn in all this, she's central. So, you're in, are you, Professor?"

He looked at Sadie, then back at Jack, one corner of his mouth sliding up in a smile. "I suppose I am."

Felix followed Jack upstairs and held the stepladder as she drew symbols on the bathroom tiles in permanent marker.

"You do realize I could probably draw these better than you could?" he said. "I've been studying them from the medals as well as the girl . . . the one who died."

She paused, looking down at him. "Carla. That must be a

horrible job. I mean, looking at dead bodies." She inscribed another sigil on a tile by the ceiling. The upper floor was disturbed, but less wrecked than downstairs.

"How did she die?" he asked.

"She got out of the circle after four months. It was too early. I only went out to walk the dog. When I got back, the door was open, and money was gone from my purse. She must have run to the station. I tried to catch her, but was caught behind the level crossing. The train was already pulling out." She swallowed hard, and Felix stepped closer.

"I'm sorry." She could feel the warmth from his body.

"She was dead by the time I caught up with her at the last station. I thought, if I could just get her between the circles in the car . . . but it was too late." She looked down at him, her face tight with the effort of not crying. "I tried to explain it to her, but she wouldn't listen." She closed her eyes, the face against the window vivid in her mind. "She was just dead."

"I know." His baritone was soft, as if it rumbled straight into her brain. "She died a very gentle death, you know. Just fell asleep. If she was dying when you found her, she had four extra months, good months, off the streets."

She opened her eyes, looked at his face, and stepped down from the ladder, close to him. This time the emotion was unmistakeable, she could feel the attraction between them pulling him, as he glanced at her mouth.

"I'm going to run Sadie a bath." She felt uncertain, unsettled. She bent to turn the hot tap on. "Then I'll draw the sigils on the floor."

"Jack . . ."

She straightened up and he put one hand on her waist, as if to steady her. He bent slowly. She stood still as his lips brushed hers. She didn't respond, but felt every nerve ending come to life where he touched her.

"I'm sorry. I don't know . . ." He stepped back.

A clatter from downstairs broke the spell, and Jack stepped away, hands up.

"I can't . . ." She slid around him so she didn't touch him, and turned off the tap. "Could you carry Sadie upstairs? You'll have to be quick, although the stairs are sigiled."

"Of course." His voice was soft, and he stepped onto the landing, taking the stepladder with him.

Jack tipped in a good slug of bubble bath, before she knelt to inscribe each floor tile, enveloped in a fog of lavender. The imprint of his lips and fingers seemed to linger on her skin.

Chapter 34

*Within the citadel are many chambers and towers.
As I explored within the main wall, I saw women
and servants doing their work about the castle. They
seemed strangely fearful of me, crossing and blessing
themselves in mangled Latin and their own cursed
tongue. I can only think they fear my master, and his
reputation spills onto me.*

*The castle is filled with children, grave-faced,
going about their business. It seems the countess
prefers them as maid servants, and they drift
around the castle like ghosts, as pale-faced as owls
and almost as silent.*

—Edward Kelley
3 December 1585
Csejte Castle

THE CASTLE WAS BUILT ON GRAY ROCK, WITH A NUMBER OF
stone towers surrounding a central fortress. The servants
scurried past me without speaking or even looking at me,
as if I were dangerous in some way. I finally found a chamber
where the captain of our abduction was seated. He was in close
conversation with a small, twisted man, who had a scar that ran
from the corner of his eye down to his neck.

"Master Kelley." The captain bowed while grinning, his
white teeth flashing against his black beard like a hunting dog's.

"I trust you are . . . ?" I did not recognize the word, so he tried again. "Well? Without injury?"

"Indeed. Well. But Doctor Dee is ill. He has a fever and a cough. How may I address you, sir?"

The man frowned over my Latin, then his brow cleared again. "I am the Lord Asztalnokmester János Báthory of Somlyó." He nodded to the scarred man. "This is Tarnokmester László Báthory of Ecsed. Understand, yes?"

Lord László looked at me from dark eyes. "Sickness, you say?"

"He needs a physician."

Blackbeard—Lord János—launched into a flood of tongue-twisting dialect, the scarred man nodding, staring at me from his brown face. Then he turned back to me.

"We have a cure for this cough. It is common in the mountains, yes? We will get one of the . . ." I didn't catch the rest of his words, as his Latin was heavily accented and some words were unfamiliar. "I will send for help. Medicine, yes?"

"Thank you. Yes." I watched as the twisted man limped from the room.

"The count commanded that I show you the library," said Lord János. "From these books you will be able to help the lady, the Countess Báthory, yes?"

The "library" turned out to be a small room off the family quarters, lined with books. I was much impressed with the selection, many were botanicals and astrologies that would help us. The alcove opposite had a door with a carving of a cross on it, and when I was alone, I pushed the door open. Inside was a chapel, plainly appointed as appropriate for a Protestant family, but made with fine polished woods and blue velvet cushions. I returned to the volumes, selecting three that I thought might be useful. I summoned a passing servant, and with much gesturing, conveyed a message that he was to get someone who would unlock them. He disappeared, returning with a fat steward or chamberlain, much flustered, who unlocked the chains that secured the books to the shelves, and carried them back to our rooms himself.

Dee seemed much revived by the new tomes, and spent a few hours hunched in his bed turning pages and reading me passages. Toward evening, he started to doze, and I found his head very hot and his breathing labored.

"Jane?" he murmured, then opened his eyes. "Oh, Edward. Was I asleep?"

I took the papers away, and compelled him to lie down again. "It is late. Rest now." But I was worried. I had found nothing that might help the countess, and Dee seemed more feverish. I signaled that I needed help to a servant girl, and within a few minutes, the scarred Count László arrived.

"The healer is here," he told me, in a soft voice. "She will not treat him with a man in the room."

"What? I don't want some drab from the country . . ." I recalled that I was speaking in English and changed to Latin. "Dee needs a physician. A doctor of medicine."

He did not respond, but took my arm. "Come. She will help your master."

I would have resisted, but the strength in his fingers gripped painfully and carried me away into the corridor. The woman, dressed in a green dress and brown headscarf, was ushered into our rooms by a servant. I was swept toward the main hall.

I noticed, as I passed, the child standing behind her. I judged her to be perhaps eight or nine years old, and she was clad in a simple gray kirtle. She stared back at me, her face as pale as the countess's had been. A low word from the woman, and she took one step toward the door. When she turned to me, her face was creased with fear, her eyes so wide they looked black. Her lips trembled but a hand grasped hers, and pulled her out of sight into Dee's room. The heavy door swung shut.

"We shall dine." Lord László bowed to me and held out a

hand toward the keep staircase. "We shall entertain you with stories of the Báthorys. And you will tell us of your many battles and adventures."

The viands served at the castle were of high quality, and I was feasted like a king. It appeared that some of our abductors were a group of noble cousins, or brothers in arms, who had served the Báthorys and the Nádasdy family for generations. They drank toasts until my head spun and their speech was slurred, and laughter flew about the chamber. I kept my wits about me, and sipped my wine slowly, watching the strange men. They boasted incessantly. Then they settled down, as far as I understood, to tell the tallest tales.

Claims from each were greeted with jeers and groans of disbelief, but as I didn't speak Hungarian I was free to watch their faces and antics. They acted unsophisticated, but I discerned some learning about them, and most spoke reasonable bastardized Latin when they had to, as well as some German. One of them, a great fellow with a reddish beard, turned to me.

"Hey, you," he called in Latin. "Is it true your master is a sorcerer?"

"My master is a scholar." I shrugged. "To a peasant, gunpowder is sorcery. What we understand we call science, what we don't we call magic."

"The fire he threw around the wolves on the road." The scarred Lord László sat at the end of the table, running a finger around a goblet. I noticed he had lost two fingers, and part of his hand. "Was that science?"

"Indeed," I lied.

"A useful trick. I could have used it." He held up his arm for my inspection. "I was caught by a wolf pack in my youth, boar hunting with some of these ruffians. A single bitch did this."

"Then Pál ran it through with his spear." Another man raised his goblet once more. "Pál!"

Another round of drinking deep, though I noticed the hunched László sipped, as I did, his dark eyes less clouded than his companions'.

Redbeard thumped the table. "You are a noble, back in your England?" he asked.

I answered simply, shrugging to make the lie more convincing. "My father is a baron, but I am a younger son. May I have the honor of knowing your lordship's name?"

"I am Mihály Báthory of Ecsed, captain of guards of this castle."

This released a battle cry that almost deafened me, from half the men around the table. "Ecsed, Ecsed!"

I laughed nervously, as they thumped their fists upon the table. A roar came back at them: "Somlyó! Báthory Somlyó!" to be answered with a wall of bellowing and stamping that dissolved into raucous laughter.

I raised my goblet, and the men fell silent, watching my movements much as the wolves had done.

"Báthory!" I shouted, and a storm of repeated battle shouts came back. As I lifted the goblet to my lips, the sound died down, and they drank deep. Except László, who instead raised his drink to me, as if he understood what I was doing. I smacked my lips, calling to the manservant for more wine, though in truth my cup was almost full.

"Tell me, what is this division of the Báthorys?" I asked.

Lord László leaned back in his chair. "It is simple," he replied. "But you must go back to the very first Báthory. The story tells of a great dragon. No man could kill it, and it grew fat on the bodies of knights and heroes sent to slay it. Then a man, his name was Vitus, took up the quest. He offered to slay the dragon if the people gave him a swamp called Ecsed, at the heart of the dragon's domain. The people laughed at him, as no one wanted the swamp anyway, and the land around was barren and stony."

László ran his finger around his cup as before. "He went into the swamp, and fought the dragon for three days and three nights. At the end of it, the dragon's tail and wings had cut great dikes into the Ecsed swamp, and its breath had burned away all the rushes and trees. Then Vitus went into the lair of the foul worm itself, and the dragon took him by the leg, its teeth piercing his thigh through his chainmail. At that very moment, Vitus hacked off the dragon's head."

"A great hero, indeed," I said, nodding.

"But three teeth had lodged themselves in the bones of the man, and he was lame forever. The swamp, drained by the dragon's thrashing and enriched by its blood, became the most fertile land for many leagues. The peasants named Vitus, his sons and his grandsons 'Bator,' Hungarian for brave. Vitus married Orsolya, the heiress to the great estate of Somlyó." He drained his cup, and grimaced at the dregs. "That dragon left its teeth in all the Báthory descendants. They fight like a litter of wolf cubs, until a weaker prey comes along. Sometimes the Ecseds have been overlord, sometimes Somlyó, but always Báthory."

"And now?"

"She," he said, waving at the hall around him, "is Somlyó *and* Ecsed. She has two cups of the dragon's blood in her veins." He held up his mutilated hand. "Remember this when you approach her. Cross her, and she will bite. If you do not make her well enough to bear a child, the countess, her husband, and every Báthory in this castle will fight over your bones like the wolves we are."

Chapter 35

B Y THE TIME DAWN BLUED THE SKY, THE WORST OF THE wreckage in the cottage was either bagged up for the dump, or awaiting repair. Jack rubbed sore eyes that prickled with tears at all the destruction. The body of the hedgehog, its neck broken, was discovered under a three-legged chair in the kitchen.

Jack found herself staggering, as if she were dozing on her feet. Sadie was in Jack's bed, safe between two circles, and hopefully sleeping. Now and then, Felix would press another chipped mug of tea into Jack's hand, and stand over her until she drank it. She'd also finished the last of the decoction, and knew she should be brewing more. She leaned against the relit range as she measured out the herbs she could find. The ones in glass jars had been scattered but the most important ones were safe in battered biscuit tins. She rested in the rocking chair, and closed her eyes for a moment, soothed by the rhythmic sound of sweeping in the front room.

The noise of vigorous knocking woke her up. It seemed to be coming from the front of the house, from the barely used porch. She could hear Felix shifting boxes, and the tone of his deep voice. She called the growling Ches to her, and locked him in the kitchen with a handful of biscuits. Standing at the bottom of the steps, she couldn't hear any sound from upstairs, but couldn't believe Sadie hadn't heard the commotion. *Please be quiet, don't look out the front window.* Jack rubbed damp hands down her jeans, and tried to straighten her mop of hair. She walked through the front room and into the porch. Felix was speaking to a female police officer, in uniform.

"No, I'm just visiting a friend. Uh . . . yes, well, I'm helping her decorate."

Jack took a deep breath, and joined Felix in the porch. "Can I help?"

The officer looked past her into the wreckage beyond.

"Could we talk inside? It's cold out here." She smiled, but it didn't reach her eyes. When Felix fell back, the officer followed, brushing past Jack, followed by a young man with a clipboard.

Jack looked around the room. Felix had rolled the carpet back down, stacked boxes of presumably salvageable books against the wall, and restored the one intact bookcase to its usual place. It was half full with the books that had survived. There were a dozen black bags ready for the dump, but the furniture was upright and apart from a smell of disinfectant wafting from the priest hole, the door propped open, the room felt clean. The draft from the smashed window, despite cardboard wedged in the frame, made her shiver.

"How can we help you, Officers?" He sounded calm, as if there was nothing unusual going on.

"Well, Mr. . . . ?"

"Guichard. Professor Felix Guichard, and this is my friend Jack Hammond. It's her house, really." He smiled down at her, put an arm around her waist, and her mind went blank.

"Decorating?" The officer looked at Jack, huddled against Felix.

Jack eased her shoulders back, attempted a smile. She knew she must look terrible. "Well, if you take the wallpaper off, the plaster comes too. But it will be nice when it's done."

"We are doing house-to-house inquiries in the area, and we understand you have a Volvo station wagon?" She rattled off the registration number.

Jack slid an arm around Felix's waist, leaning on him as she started to shake. "Yes, but it's at the garage. The brakes failed, and I crashed it into a wall at the church. The vicar knows all about it."

The officer looked at Jack's face, with its huge bruise and black eye.

"Our inquiry is into a missing teenager, Sadie Williams. Perhaps you've seen her mentioned in the press?" Jack shook her head, but Felix spoke.

"I've been following the story, of course. I've been helping DI Soames with the investigation of another runaway girl, Carla Marshall. If there's anything I can do . . ."

The woman seemed to warm a little, and smiled at Jack. "If you could just tell me where you were on the evening of the twelfth of November, between ten and twelve?"

Jack's mind went blank. *They must have a record of the car, perhaps on CCTV, in the city.* She looked at Felix.

"That was the night you came to see me at the university, wasn't it?" he said, as if trying to remember. "No, that was the tenth . . . uh, we were supposed to meet at a pub somewhere . . ."

"The day you couldn't make it?" Jack improvised. "So I picked up some dog food and a bit of shopping, and drove home again."

The male officer was making notes and looking less interested. The female officer swept her gaze around the room once more, before turning back toward the door.

"Just for our records, would you have any objection to our lab techs examining your car?"

"Oh . . . well, no, of course not." Jack had to clench her teeth to stop them from chattering. She had cleaned the car, but had no idea how much of Sadie's DNA might still be in there. "But the people at the garage are working on it at the moment."

The officer smiled again. "Well, I can see you are busy and

we have more people to talk to. I'm sorry to bother you so early in the morning, but calling before nine means we catch more people in."

"Of course. I hope you find her soon," Felix said, and stepped away from Jack to shut the door behind them.

Jack staggered the moment he took his arm away. She reached down to steady herself on the sofa arm, and sank onto the cushions. She looked up to see Sadie standing at the foot of the stairs.

"I heard them, they were looking for me."

"I know. Thank you for not calling out, or coming down."

"I nearly did, for a moment, when I first woke up." Sadie was biting her lip, her eyes staring into Jack's. "But I felt sick when I got to the top of the steps."

Felix stood between them, looking from one to the other. "Now what?"

Jack waved at Sadie. "You can carry her into the circle, and I'll let Ches out. Then we need to work out what the *fuck* is going on."

Jack stopped by the back door, clutching a bag of shopping, looking at the devastation wreaked in the yard. The wire of the aviary, empty at the time, had been torn open down one side, and the yard was covered in black feathers. A white feather caught her eye, and she bent to pick it up. One of the magpies, probably one of the pair she had hand-reared a couple of years ago. She found a body lying under the hedge, perfect except for its broken neck.

She stood, cried and wiped her eyes on the sleeve of her coat, while Ches bumped his head against her and whimpered. It wasn't until she turned to go back in the house that she saw Felix standing by the door.

"They mate for life, you know." Jack's voice caught in her throat. "Crows, rooks, magpies. Those nests were almost as old as the oaks. There's been a rookery here for hundreds of years."

"Will they rebuild?" He walked up to her, holding a couple of full black bags.

She looked around the yard, littered with branches and sticks.

"I don't think there's a pair left."

"I thought I would clear up the . . ." He looked around. "Save you doing it."

"Felix, what could have done this?"

The gloomy look on Felix's long features lifted. "Ah, I've been thinking about that. I've got Sadie doing some research for me."

"You have?" The dog, who had been bristling at Felix, started sniffing him.

"Does he bite?" Felix froze, looking at her with a nervous smile.

"Yes." She snapped her fingers at Ches, who bounded toward the house, and judging by the squeals inside, straight into Sadie.

Felix followed her into the kitchen, their feet crunching over the fine dust from china and glass. "We need to have a look at your books and, ideally, I need to get my laptop."

"I didn't know much about the books . . . I mean, they're not mine, they came with the cottage. But a lot of them were wrecked."

"Well, I think you have a very comprehensive occult library. Had. Most could be restored."

"I haven't even looked at most of them. Maggie and I were going to sell them off, but the documents made enough money." She stopped, and looked at him.

"Money for what?" He started looking through the bag Jack had dumped on the table. "The hot chocolate is for Sadie, I presume?" He lined up the three least-chipped mugs and started spooning in the powder. "You were saying you needed money?"

"For Maggie and Charley, so they could move out, but leave me the cottage." She stepped closer to him.

"I see . . ." He looked down at her, into her eyes.

"Thank you," she whispered. "Thank you for helping us."

"It's OK." He shook himself a little, and smiled. "And you bought cookies. Sadie will be thrilled. Apparently you've been feeding her on 'hand-knitted organic crap.'"

She stood studying at his mobile features, watching him stir the drinks, and was amazed that she felt so at home with someone. Men were not something she had had much experience with. There had been a few little crushes in her teenage years, mostly on boys in the village, but her weakness had made relationships impossible. For the last decade she had ruled out any romantic entanglements, yet Felix showed up and within days she couldn't stop thinking about him.

Jack carried two of the drinks through to the front room, and gave one to Sadie, who had a speculative look in her eyes. Thankfully, she didn't say anything. She was looking better, her hair glossy and tousled, and a dozen old books in various stages of deterioration covered the sofa.

It seemed that during the time Jack had walked Ches to the village for some bread and a few other supplies, Felix and Sadie had gone from wary collaborators to friends.

"I've found something." Sadie reached for the packet of biscuits Felix was holding out and took a handful. She took a massive bite from one and, as Ches slumped against her legs, fed him the remaining sliver. "You said to look for conjurations, raising weather, that sort of thing," she mumbled through the crumbs. "Listen to this."

She paused for effect, appearing better than Jack had seen, with a little color in her heart-shaped face. "'In the raising of elementals, let the magician beware, that the element of air shall be so destructive as to rend from limb to limb unwary conjurers.' Isn't that the sort of thing we're searching for?"

"Exactly what we're looking for." Felix glanced around the room. "Do you have a computer?"

Jack opened her mouth to reply but Sadie spoke first. "No computer, no social networking, no e-mail. She hasn't even got a telly."

"I never needed one," Jack said, defending herself. Sadie exchanged glances with Felix. Both appeared baffled. "I never wanted one, either."

"You are a technological Luddite, you know that?" Felix leaned on the back of the sofa, reading over Sadie's shoulder. "My research assistant here can look through these amazing books. You do know that is an original *Hasquith's Demonology*, don't you?" He stood up, pressing his hand against the small of his back. "I need to go home, get some sleep and a shower. I've got some things to do this afternoon, but I'll be back by this evening with my laptop. You can get a mobile signal here, I presume?"

"Mostly." Jack sat down on the other sofa, and the dog padded over to lay his heavy head on her knee.

"And Sadie will learn everything she can about elementals and conjuring."

He walked toward the kitchen, but turned back. "The symbols you drew on Carla. Did you copy them from the medals directly?"

Jack shrugged. "They are carved and drawn all over the cottage. Maggie's grandmother is supposed to have used them. They are very similar to the ones on the medals."

"But not identical. The ones on the medals may not have even been the originals."

"So?"

"I was thinking. Suppose, over the years, the symbols had been copied. And copied from copies."

"Like Chinese whispers?"

"Exactly. Maybe Kelley described Dee's original research. If that was what he was doing, perhaps this Bachmeier woman is trying to find the *original* sigils." He beckoned to Jack. "You'd better direct me back to town."

Ignoring Sadie's knowing look, Jack walked past Felix with an attempt at dignity, and they went out into the yard. Felix had even washed the bloodstains off the concrete.

His breath warmed the back of her neck. "Jack—"

"You are a married man, aren't you? I mean, you wear a ring."

"I'm about to be divorced." His eyes were green, in nests of laughter lines. "I hadn't thought about taking it off."

She turned to look past him, feeling the warmth fade.

"How did a tornado come into my home and attack that poor kid? I'm fighting for Sadie's life here."

"*We* are fighting for Sadie's life. If someone had told me all this yesterday, I would have called the police. But now, you and I—and Sadie, for that matter—are in this together." His hands covered her shoulders, and gave her a little shake. "I like you, Jack. When this is over . . ."

She sighed. "I might be dead. Sadie might be dead."

He raised one eyebrow. "Or not." He laid his hand on her forehead. "You're still frozen."

She shrugged. "We're always cold. Barely alive, remember?"

He did his coat up. "I've stuck some cardboard over the broken windows, and brought in some logs. Just stay in, keep warm and I'll be back as soon as I can."

"OK." A cold tightness built up in her chest, as she struggled to say *Goodbye*, which had somehow got tangled up with *Don't go*.

He turned toward her and slid one hand behind the small of her back. He leaned forward and kissed her, his stubbly cheek rubbing hers for a moment. "Be careful," he murmured, his words misting the air.

She nodded, unable to speak, and as he turned away, exhaled all at once. She hadn't even noticed she was holding her breath.

It was a relief to see Maggie drive into the yard. She stared around the house, hands on hips. "I leave it for two days, and this is what you get up to," she quipped, but there was no laughter in her voice. She sniffed, as if she could smell the force that did all the damage. She passed a hand over the space where the protective charm had been carved into the plaster. Like all the others in the house it had been crushed, as if someone had gone around the place with a sledgehammer.

"I'm going into town," Jack said. "I have to pick up the rental car." Jack zipped up her warmest boots. Swathed in layers of wool and a ski jacket, it was hard to lean forward. "I've lit both fires, but the place is still cold. Hopefully they can cut glass for the windows while I wait."

"Windows?" Maggie's eyes were wide as she looked into the living room.

"Two have gone. Don't ask me how."

"The place stinks of elemental energy, that's how." Maggie touched the table, then brushed her hands clean. "I'll start a deep cleansing, see if we can clean up the atmosphere a bit." She hesitated, looking at Jack. "I'll get Sadie to help, and see if we can teach her a few tricks to protect herself in the future."

"She's a bit battered, but . . ." Jack couldn't find the word to describe the mood Sadie was in. "She's bounced back. I don't know how she survived."

Maggie rolled up her sleeves. "She's tough. Good job. Go on, we'll be fine."

Jack left Maggie explaining spell casting to Sadie. A gate, partly hidden in the hedge, led onto the field and the footpath.

It took a while to cross the quiet field, and she had the feeling she was being watched. Paranoia, she decided as she scanned the bushes and paths, from the events of the last day. A single rook cawed over and over, hopelessly calling its lost mate. Spiders' webs silvered with dew picked up the weak sunshine, and the last of the hawthorn berries shriveled in the cold. She wished she had brought the dog for company, but he was too shaken up.

She had warmed up a little, but whatever hex grenade Pierce had slipped into her bag, the effects were still lingering. She felt as if the wind were blowing straight through her as she clambered over each stile and gate on the footpath to the railway station.

She let her mind roam over what Felix had said, and how he had said it. Was this what women saw in men? Christ, she had only known him five minutes, but she couldn't stop thinking about him. Even Sadie seemed to know more about it than Jack, asking searching questions all morning, and causing Maggie to watch her and drop hints. She wasn't ready to talk about Felix, not before she understood it herself. She boarded the train for the three stops into town.

She had left the car less than a mile from the city station, and she felt warmer once she got walking. She had just reached the vehicle when the phone rang. She jumped, and fumbled to open the phone and press buttons with her thick gloves.

Maggie's voice was higher pitched than normal. "Jack, a car has stopped outside, and now they're looking at the house. I think it's the police."

"What? You need to hide Sadie."

Jack could hear Maggie's irregular breathing. Then a whisper. "The car's coming into the yard, with two men. What do I do? She can't leave the house yet. She'll die."

"Take Ches and Sadie into the priest hole. The panel at the end of Sadie's bed, it's a tunnel to the inspection bay in the garage. I found it years ago. It's just a crawl space, but you should be able to make it."

"But Sadie? She won't survive it."

"I scratched sigils, right through to the garage. I'll get there as soon as I can."

Jack broke off the call, and got into the rental car. She had scribed sigils in spit and salt under the seats and on the roof, but that was only just enough for her, let alone Sadie. She put it to the back of her mind. She knew that if Sadie left the circle, she would probably be dead by the time Jack got there.

Chapter 36

I tried, without success, to make my captors
understand the importance of medical science. I
wished to bleed Dee, as his color was high and his
pulse tumultuous, but was forcibly prevented by two
soldiers, who thought, perhaps, I threatened his life.

—EDWARD KELLEY
  From his own journal, 4 December 1585
  Csejte Castle

I WAS RELIEVED TO SEE DEE SLEEPING PEACEFULLY, AND A
servant woman watching over him. She was spinning from
a long spindle, and nodded to me as I shut the door to my
own chamber. I was shaken by the words of László Báthory. No
one knew we were at Csejte, although many would guess. If we
disappeared there would be disapproval, but no proof. Our bodies could be stripped and dumped in the forest and our bones
would lie naked on foreign soil. I undressed for bed in a melancholy mood, slipping my dagger under my pillow.

By dawn, I had slept poorly, and dreamed of dragons and
treachery when I did. I dressed and tried to find comfort in
prayer. I then decided to at least become familiar with our
prison, in case a chance for escape offered itself.

The main rooms were being swept by servants, and fires
laid, with food being put out on tables in the hall. I heard some

deep voice calling for someone in Hungarian, and ducked down the corridor toward the library.

I tried the door to the chapel, and it opened. Before the altar rested a small covered box, some servant's casket perhaps. It was surrounded by rush lights. I crossed myself from habit, offering a small prayer for the dead, as I looked around at the wall hangings. I lifted the edge of one, then another, working my way around the room. One, to the side of the altar, concealed a low door. I wondered if it led to the countess's quarters. It was locked.

The sound of footsteps made me jump, and in my fearful state, I ducked behind the altar as the door creaked open. Women's voices murmured at the coffin. I looked around the side, but could see nothing except the rough lid of the simple box, lifted off. One began to wail as if in pain, and the others offered soothing clucks. Finally, they prayed. When they left, I crouched for a minute to make sure I was alone, then crept out. As I passed the box, my curiosity afflicted me. I lifted the lid, just a crack, and saw a shrunken body lying on a folded shroud.

The body was that of a child, her face now the color of the linens she was laid upon. Livid on her neck and hands were symbols, shapes that reminded me of the scars on the countess. I looked at her white face, and recognized the fearful child who had walked behind the witch. A gash in her neck gaped open. She had been bled like a slaughtered pig.

There was no opportunity to speak to Dee upon the next day, as we were never left alone. Someone always seemed to be listening, and I dared not converse in English lest they get suspicious. Instead, Dee and I examined the documents given to us. There were letters from scholars, patrons, botanists and doctors whom the count himself had consulted for his wife. There were even papers from the emperor. Dee cast a number of horoscopes, inscribing them with care on fine vellum and worrying about exact calculations.

I worked on a number of herbals in Latin, and two fat treatises in German. But I could feel Dee watching me, as the cloud began to descend upon me.

"Edward."

I looked up, very conscious of the manservant trimming the lamps, as he lit them against the evening. "Master?"

"Are you being visited?"

It was our code for the voices that whispered in my head from time to time. "I . . . I am." I was reluctant to admit it, but the sound was growing more insistent.

"If you would consent, we could ask higher beings for assistance." His voice was gentle but there was a frown upon his brow. "I fear Lord Nádasdy will be . . . disappointed if we cannot help his lady. These books, though interesting, are unlikely to bear fruit."

I leaned back in my chair, easing my shoulders, which were cramped with leaning over spindly script from one of the King of Hungary's physicians. "Dr. Andrassy recommends spiders' webs collected at the full moon, in mead. He writes that it helps with barrenness. He used it with some success with Count Nádasdy's mother."

"I fear more for her life, Edward, than her womb. I have a recipe here for a remedy involving taking the patient's blood, and placing it inside a blown egg."

I must have looked skeptical. He smiled, adding: "Then we are to feed the egg to a black hunting dog, then kill it. This is believed to take away the choleric humors that may be affecting her ladyship." He took a deep breath, moderating his tone so he would not be overheard. "Of course, to consult the angels, we will need to be completely alone."

I nudged the door closed and sat beside the crackling fire, speaking in English.

"I am not certain, Master Dee."

"What concerns you, Edward?"

"I found a child within the countess's chapel." I dared not tell him the whole of my suspicions.

He frowned, as if puzzled. "Children die, Edward, their souls are much nearer to God. Why does this pain you so much?"

"I saw the same child yesterday, brought by a witch into the castle. She was mortally afraid, master." I stumbled over the words. "The witch, Zsófia, she made a potion to sustain the countess. It was spiced with herbs, but thickened with blood."

Dee's voice was reasonable. "Blood has been used as a tonic for centuries. Horse and cattle blood is a stimulant and strengthens the vital reactions."

"I don't think it was animal blood she was using." I stumbled over the words. "Master, since we have been here, I have been hearing the whispers of the *others* . . ."

Dee shook himself out of his melancholy. "What do they say?"

I couldn't say that the angels' voices filled me with such dread that I was revolted, and tried to shut them out. "I don't know what they are saying. But they seem voices of foreboding and warning."

"Edward, I am reminded of the story of Pope Innocent the Eighth. His final illness was so profound, and so unwelcome, that his advisers sought to save him by feeding him the blood of young boys."

"Did it work?"

"I'm afraid the story is that each child was drained of blood completely, but the Pope refused the libations, and died. They all died. Terrible."

"So blood, human blood, has been used in that way?"

Dee chose his words with care. "There is a belief, even within the educated, that many mysteries of life are contained within the blood of children. Jesus himself offered us his blood, his body. I cannot, myself, see that to use children in this way is anything but a heresy."

"But could it work?" I sat on a stool and watched him struggle with our problem.

"We must ask our angelic guides. You must let me speak to Saraquel."

"I can't . . ." Even as I spoke, the ringing started. "Please, blessed Lord—"

I was in the trance before I could complete the thought. The sensation of boiling water filled me up, bloating me, as if my tiny body could not hold the giant angel. It overwhelmed my senses. I was blinded by the brightness, as if my eyes could no longer stand the light from the tiny window, nor from the small fire. Somewhere inside, I cried out at the pain of it, or if not pain, the *wrongness* of it. Every limb stiffened, and I could feel myself stand upon my toes, held up as if from heaven itself. My shoulder blades cramped with an unfamiliar pulling, and I felt the weight of great wings, the feathers brushing the air around me with a sharp heat, like that of a blacksmith's forge.

Dee knelt in prayer, recognizing the change in my face and body, but I could no longer move.

"Lord Saraquel," he said. "Advise us, please."

The angel spoke. I couldn't understand it, although my lips and tongue moved and Dee answered. I was deafened by the ringing of a thousand bells in my head. My hands swept the air before me, and my body almost fell. He—Saraquel—put out his great wings, which at once felt as if my shoulder blades were ripping from my back, and my fingers were somehow brushing the walls on both sides of the chamber. Pain shrank me to a dream, and time flowed away from me. Then, with a snap, Saraquel was gone, and I was poured back into my body like ale into a bucket.

I collapsed, my muscles disobedient until I had located them all. Dee softened the drop, and laid me upon the floor until I regained my senses.

"What . . . what did he say?" I managed to ask.

"I'm not sure I understand. He showed me how to save the lady, but he also told me of the terrible consequence if we do." His face was ashen, the lines on it drawn tight like a man of eighty. "I cannot divine what he wants us to do. It seems as if he tempts us. He showed me some signs."

The room smelled of some flower, like violets or lilies, and it refreshed me.

"So, we can devise a cure for the lady and leave for Prague." I wiped my drenched brow on my sleeve, my hand shaking with exhaustion. "Master?"

"Edward, if you knew the horrors that will befall the countess and her people . . ." He stopped, shaking his head. "I must pray on this, Edward."

Pray, pray indeed, for our souls and our deliverance, thought I. For the message I received was plain—there was nothing but a terrible death for us if we failed.

Chapter 37

Before Maggie had turned her phone off, Sadie watched the kitchen door implode, the frame skewing in and the lock flying off. She slid to her feet and saw a tall man in a gray suit and tie brush his hands clean and advance toward Maggie. The older woman fell back before him, reaching a hand behind her for Sadie's. A heavier man brushed through the doorway into the front room, pausing to look around.

"Ah." He stretched his vowels like a pizza commercial on TV. He was dressed in a dark suit. "Sadie Williams. It seems we are only just in time. *She* is closing in." He gestured at the cracked walls, and stepped forward. Sadie pressed back as far as she could without stepping out of the circle.

"What . . . what do you want?" She grabbed Ches's collar as the dog lurched toward the man. Her voice was meant to be confident, defiant, anything but thin and childish. She cleared her throat. "Who are you?"

"I am a doctor who specializes in your . . . *malattia*. Condition." He glanced up at the ceiling, eyes focused on the sigils. "Medieval but, I suppose, effective."

Sadie had to kneel to use both arms to restrain the dog, who pulled against her weight. "If you don't get out of here, I'll let him go."

"I would hate to shoot him, he's quite a beauty."

Sadie looked at Maggie, who seemed frozen. "What do you want with me?"

He turned, and spoke to the younger man in a foreign language. Maggie slid along the wall and crouched, putting her arms around the girl and the dog.

"I'm so sorry, Sadie." She realized Maggie was shaking. "I can't imagine how they found us."

Sadie looked at the older man again, who smiled.

"She's wondering whether someone from her world has betrayed your location. A lot of people would like to meet you, Sadie."

"So, how did you find me, then?"

"Our forensic experts, of course, traced your energy signature to the rear of Ms. Hammond's car, and her address was located from her registration." He turned to Maggie. "Leave us, *strega*."

Maggie hugged tighter. "I'm staying."

He brushed the sofa with one hand, and sat.

"You will leave and live, or stay and die. *Preparare la vettura*."

Sadie saw the younger man standing just inside the kitchen. He nodded, and then looked at her with something strange in his eyes. Sadness? She stumbled to her feet, shaking off Maggie, and shouted at the older man.

"Don't hurt Maggie. She saved my life. She was trying to help me."

He gave a short bark of laughter. "By locking you up in this . . . hovel? My poor child, you were denied everlasting life by hags, and witches. This state you are in is unnatural, *un abominio*."

Sadie had no difficulty distrusting *my poor child*.

"So, you are here to rescue me?" She let her voice rise into a childish note and added uncertainty.

"Of course." He leaned forward and rested his elbows on his knees. He had very clean, very white hands. "Our car is equipped with the latest medical devices to keep you safe."

Leaning forward to spit the words at him, Maggie spoke. "Your kind don't show compassion to girls like Sadie."

He smiled without warmth, showing very white teeth. He spoke directly to Sadie. "My orders are to bring you safely into our care." He shrugged. "In your present condition, we have to make that decision for you. If you come quietly, we will spare the witch and her mongrel."

Sadie thought fast. "Can she help me get changed?"

"That is unnecessary. We have very generous donors who ensure the care of special cases like you."

"I just want my own clothes. My mum bought me the jeans." She let her voice rise to a whine. "And my dad gave me the necklace for Christmas," she lied.

A flicker of some expression crossed his face but Sadie couldn't decipher it.

"Two minutes, then."

Sadie paused. "But I can't get dressed by myself. I need Maggie." She made her voice as weak and breathless as she could. "I think I need to pee, as well. Five minutes. I don't want to wet myself in your car."

That expression again. Distaste. It was enough to get him to stand up. "Hurry."

As he walked into the kitchen, Sadie could hear him giving commands, but couldn't understand them.

"Maggie?" It came out more of a whimper than a whisper, but Maggie was shaking.

"He's an inquisitor." The older woman dragged Ches, now whining, over to the door to the priest hole. "He'll kill me and he'll burn the house down. We've got to get you out of here."

"What . . . ?" Sadie opened the door to the priest hole; stale air drifted out with more than a hint of dog crap and disinfectant. Without his lead, the dog was difficult to move. It took both of them to lift him over the threshold, and tip him down the steps.

"Go." Maggie pushed her. "I'll make them think we got away. I can lock the priest hole. There's some loose planks at the end of your old bed, the tunnel is safe, it comes out in the garage. Jack is coming."

"What about you?" Sadie grabbed a handful of Maggie's sleeve. "They'll kill you."

Maggie smiled; her mouth was tight but there was a gleam in her eyes. "They'll have to catch me first."

The panel snapped shut behind Sadie, followed by the clunk of the lock.

The priest hole was dark, just a crack of light around one edge of the secret door. Fumbling in the dark, Sadie found the wind-up lantern and gave the handle a few turns. The whirring seemed loud, but the light was welcome, illuminating the tiny cell. The walls were mostly stone, but behind the bed was a square of painted planks. A crack suggested some of the boards were loose. She got a finger into a knothole, and the panel moved. Tugging harder, it fell into her hands with a cloud of dust and the smell of decay. Shining the lamp into the hole, she could see a square hatch, lined with stones that gleamed with moisture. White growths, like cotton wool, hung down from the roof of the dark space in fungal garlands. She placed the light in the tunnel, trying to avoid the mold. The light revealed ancient stones, each one inscribed with a sigil. It was just high enough for someone lying flat.

Behind her, in the stone cell, Ches's eyes gleamed and he looked more wolf than dog in the low light. Hoping he would follow, she lifted her weight onto her hands and tipped headfirst into the passageway, trying not to touch the damp mounds of mildew.

"Ches. Ches!" she hissed. "Come on, boy."

It was bigger inside than the opening suggested, uneven across its width. She could hear the dog whine, as she wriggled on her elbows inside the gap, hands cold on the stones and her hair brushing the roof in places. The air was sour, and she started to shiver. She fought for another few feet on her elbows as the floor of the tunnel started to dip. Sliding downhill, she felt suffocated. The energy seemed to leach out of her muscles as a wave of exhaustion and nausea overtook her. Shit—the sigils. In front of her, a pile of stones and black soil suggested part of the wall had given way. The light flickered and went out. Sadie dropped her head on one arm, and swallowed acid spit . . .

The dog's snuffling on the leg of her jeans brought Sadie back to consciousness. One of his feet was scratching the back of her knee, the claws digging, pain creeping up her thigh.

"Ow . . . Ches, stop it." A huff from the dog filled the air with warm meatiness, but at least he stopped scrabbling at her calf. She forced one arm out in front of her, then leaned on it, dragging herself a few inches, feeling for the lantern. Both shoulders were tight against the sides of the tunnel, as she inched past the collapsed wall. *Don't fall down, don't bury me alive* . . . She squeezed her shoulders through, and pushed the lamp in front of her. It clattered away, and the light flickered and faded. Darkness, and the sound of her gasps, pressed in like a smothering blanket. She could hardly breathe now, and the air stank. *I'm going to get stuck.* Her heartbeat wavered.

The thought of the house being set on fire, the flames reaching into the tunnel, spurred her on. She pulled the rough floor with her arms until she was sliding forward. Banging her head on the roof sent stabs of light through the darkness, but her fingers found the lamp. Fumbling, her breath coming in sobs, she found the wind-up handle. The dim bulb wavered into life.

The roof was bulging down but under the dip she could see a wider passage running a short distance.

"Come on, Ches. Come on, boy." She commando-crawled under the dip, catching her socks on the rough stone. She stopped to wind the handle on the torch for another minute as she let the dog catch up. There was enough room now for him to slide alongside her, his head at her waist, and when she reached down his warm tongue curved around her fingers. The sigils were undisturbed here, her breathing easier. The tunnel reached around a corner, then abruptly stopped. When the torch went out again, a sliver of gray light glowed around the corner of a panel ahead. She could smell oil, car smells. The dog wriggled his way forward, his claws scratching with a metallic sound on the stones, until he could lick her chin.

"Shut up, they'll hear you," she hissed.

Someone was talking, clipped words ringing as if in the yard. The sound of an engine starting turned the voices into shouts, as a car revved up and crashed through something, rattling away from the house. As it roared away, Sadie could hear another car start. It screeched away after the first one. Sadie waited for a long, long moment. No sounds. She put her head on her hands and rested. Tears rose up, whether from the adrenaline that was making her heart thump slowly, like a drum, or from fear for Maggie, she couldn't tell. Her mouth filled with vomit. She could feel her chest tighten, and her breath felt bubbly, as she began to drown.

Chapter 38

JACK TORE OVER THE CATTLE GRID AND INTO THE YARD. The fence at the back of the garden was flattened, and tire tracks wound through the field gate, which hung from one hinge, the post and padlock ripped out of the ground.

The back door was open and the kitchen stank of gasoline. The sound of distant sirens suggested there was something going on in the village, and some emergency vehicle shot past the cottage. Jack raced through the house, straight to the locked panel. She wrenched it open and shouted into the dark cell for Sadie, and for Ches. Nothing, no one. She raced around to the garage, with its inspection pit in the floor. The wooden boarding that lined the pit was old and gave way in a shower of rotten splinters as she tore it first with her hands, then with a chisel from the toolbox. Slowly, a rectangular opening was revealed to the sound of whining. She reached in and grasped Ches by his collar, and heaved him toward her. He wriggled, shot out into her arms, and knocked her to her knees. He leapt around, whimpering with pleasure, and jumped to lick her face.

"Sadie!" Jack stood, pushed the dog down, and leaned into the dark to feel for the girl. She could just reach the dark shape that turned out to be Sadie's head. "Wake up!" When Sadie didn't move, Jack grabbed a clump of hair, and pulled.

The girl moved, and began to cough.

Jack felt a rush of relief. "Is Maggie in there?"

Sadie's white face lifted slowly toward Jack. "No." The girl began to reach forward with thin fingers, pulling on the stones to gain an inch or two at a time. Jack grasped her cold wrists and pulled. Slowly, Sadie emerged, and Jack lifted her down.

"The . . . sigils," panted the girl, looking around anxiously.

"Top and bottom. You're OK. I used to look after my birds in here."

"Cold . . ." The girl sank to her knees and wrapped her arms around herself. She gagged and coughed, spat onto the ground.

"It's too early for you to be out. I have to get you somewhere safe." Jack stood, undecided, looking out of the garage door toward the hole in the fence. They could come back at any moment. "Stay there."

Jack climbed out of the pit, then started the rental car and drove it right up to the garage doors. She jumped down. There was still a gap of eight or ten feet between the circles in the garage and the scribbled sigils in the car.

"Sadie. Sadie, wake up." The girl was crouched in the center of the circles, saliva threading down her front, half conscious. "Sadie, I'm sorry, but I need to put you in the car."

"No." The girl's teeth clicked together as she shuddered.

"I've drawn the sigils in the car. I'm sorry, but I have to carry you across that little bit of yard."

Sadie mumbled something in protest.

"I need you to try to help me, so we can be as quick as possible. OK? Before they come back." Jack boosted the dog up and turned to find Sadie wavering to her feet, face tight with the effort. She looked awful, her face going blue as she approached the edge of the circle. Jack started up the ramp, then reached her hands down for Sadie. "Come on. You can do it."

Sadie hesitated, as she looked at the gap to the car, and reached trembling arms up for Jack to grab her. She faded with the first step up the ramp. By the time they reached the car, Sadie was a deadweight, and Jack pulled her in one back door and slid out the other side, and fumbled for Sadie's pulse. Nothing.

Oh shit, oh shit. Jack leaned in awkwardly, holding Sadie's face and head, and squeezed in alongside to give her a hasty, panicked breath, then another. She shook the girl, screaming at her to wake up. Another breath, this one inflating her chest, then another. This time, Sadie moved a little, and Jack's shaky fingers felt the weak, irregular pulse. Jack curled her into the recovery position and tucked her legs in, covering her with the dog blanket. She dragged Ches into the trunk of the hatchback, too small for comfort but functional, and turned the car around in the yard. Driving toward town, away from whatever was going on in the village, Jack headed toward Ches's favorite woodland. It was away from the house and she knew it would have a signal for her mobile phone.

When she parked, she let the dog out and tried Maggie. No answer. But Felix answered on the third ring.

"Felix. Thank God."

"Jack? You sound terrible, what's wrong?"

"We're in trouble. We've had some people at the house, trying to take Sadie. I've got her in the car, but she's bad, really bad. It's too soon for her to leave the house."

"How can I help?" He sounded so sympathetic, she had to brush tears off her face with an impatient hand.

"Do you think you could draw those sigils in a circle in a room in your house? On the floor, and on the ceiling?"

"Of course. Do the sigils have to match up?"

"The one like the omega sign goes at the northernmost point, the rest go around. In as big a circle as you can do."

She squeezed Sadie's hands. She looked less gray, and was at least a bit warmer, but she barely responded. Jack rummaged in the glove compartment for a pen that worked, and came up with a blue ballpoint. She got out of the car, catching Ches as he launched himself at her. "Not now, silly beast." She threw a stick for him, and opened the back door of the car. A quick look around revealed just two empty vehicles some distance away, their owners presumably off in the woods. Lifting Sadie's T-shirt, she started redrawing the sigils. She managed to go over most of them before Sadie started to come around.

"What . . . ?" The teenager was groggy, batting Jack's hands away.

"I need to draw the sigils again. Just let me." She looked around, but Ches wasn't interested in the forest; he was just looking down one of the paths.

"We're outside. I remember." Sadie still acted dazed, and let Jack trace the circle in the middle of her chest.

"You remember what happened? We have to get to Felix's house. This will help you get between the car and the door." The dog launched himself away from the car, growling. "Oh, shit. Stay down. Your picture's on the front page of every news-paper in the county."

She watched Sadie slump back, and wrap herself in the dog blanket Jack had draped over her. The girl's eyelids were already sagging.

Jack called Ches to heel as a fat Labrador stormed up to him, tail high. His owner, a plump middle-aged woman, was puffing along behind him.

"Sorry, sorry. He's very friendly."

"No problem. We're just going." Jack opened the front pas-senger door and watched Ches hesitate before jumping in, con-fused by the change of seat. Maybe he would block the view of the girl. Jack tucked his tail in and shut the door.

"Lovely dog. Is he a husky?" The woman's eyes were focused on the backseat of the car.

"He's a Tamaskan sled dog. Like a husky, yes."

"Your daughter—is she all right?"

Jack managed a tight smile. "She's fine. I . . . she wasn't feel-ing well at school. They asked me to take her home." She low-ered her voice. "She's been sick, she's a bit embarrassed. I'll take her back now."

The woman smiled but had an odd expression. "Well, I hope she gets better soon. Here, Derry. Good boy." As the woman fussed over her dog, Jack got in, shut the door and started the engine. The woman didn't move. Jack realized there was nothing she could do. She was going to have to reverse the car, and Sadie, right by her.

Chapter 39

*My dreams were haunted by the child's body in
the chapel. As I leaned over the casket, her eyelids
opened, their orbs milky with death. I woke, sweating
and trembling, and remembered the tales we heard
about Venice, of the revenants, the undead, cursed
creatures of the canals, created by sorcerers as their
servants, even though the hearts beat no longer in
their breasts. These fearsome creatures will feed on
your children, and haunt you through your dreams.*

—EDWARD KELLEY
9 December 1585
Csejte Castle

THE DAYS DREW ON, AND THE RESPONSIBILITY SAT HEAVY
on Dee's brow, as we worked ever harder on the books.
He was engaged with his own copy of Weger's *De Praes-
tigiis Daemonum* when I left him to take one of my walks.

I went about the castle as I pleased, through the kitchens
and into the outer yard. It was kept ready, the stronghold of
a military man; the soldiers drilled every day; and the cavalry
rode out into the countryside to train most afternoons.

There were maybe thirty horsemen and as many as sixty in-
fantry, with their rough cloaks and blunt practice swords, and
their maneuvers were terrifying to see. I have never seen such
horsemanship before or since. The cavalry could, at full gal-

lop, swing under their horses' bellies, even touch the ground and bounce back onto their mounts, with much laughter and mocking from their fellows, who would try more daring trials until I feared one would be killed. But they seemed to be glued to their mounts, and I would watch them canter up to the castle. Often they would tease people walking to the gatehouse as they passed, either plucking their hats or cloaks from them or, on more than one occasion, taking a child or a young woman from the ground and passing them from horse to horse. None was injured, though much startled, and the japes seemed harmless.

On the tenth day since our arrival, the mood in the castle changed. The servants bustled everywhere, scrubbing and dusting, and the soldiers polished real weapons. They donned black uniforms and steel helmets, and rode and marched in strict formation. The chapel was filled to capacity by the officers and higher servants, and the priest held prayers in the yard for the poorer people. The church in the village tolled bells five times a day for services, instead of the usual two. It was as if the count's people wanted to be as spiritually ready as they were physically. Our borrowed clothes were taken away and brought back clean, smelling of rosemary and other herbs. Dee had to chase away women who tried to tidy his notes and charts.

Late in the afternoon, a fanfare at the gate called us all down to the inner court, where a large traveling carriage rattled over the stones, shedding great arcs of mud. Beside it rode the count, on a bay horse that struck sparks from its shoes upon the cobbles. He dismounted, and strode to us, standing alongside the entire staff and garrison of Csejte Castle.

"I thank you for coming to the castle to help my wife."

Ignoring the cruel and ignominious way we had been transported, Dee bowed. "We have worked on a number of treatments. I shall be happy to discuss them with your lordship. I hope the countess prospers?"

"She is weak. We will speak of it later." The count turned to watch his wife, wrapped in a fur cloak, being lifted from the coach in the arms of an impassive chamberlain. Servants flocked around them, taking up bags and items and following the lady as she was carried into the castle. "Do you have everything you need?"

"There is one thing, your lordship." Dee's voice had assumed an authority he used rarely. "We would like to know more about the practice of folk medicine in these parts. The gypsy tradition they call 'dragon marks.'"

"I shall send Zsófia to you." The count watched as the cavalcade passed beyond the great doors. "When she can be spared." I noticed Lord Miklós, the king's brother, among the throng of men.

Dee bowed, and I copied him, and the count marched into the castle keep, his tall boots with cruel spurs clinking on the ground.

"Folk medicine? More likely witchcraft, Master Dee." I had not dared to mention it to Dee after his own illness.

"There is some great evil here, Edward, I feel it. And I know you do too. I am prepared to listen to healing women and botanical doctors, but something here is darker."

Chapter 40

JACK DROVE CAREFULLY, SO SHE WOULDN'T ATTRACT ATTENtion. When addressed, Sadie would groan from the back of the car, and Ches would whine as if in sympathy, his head resting on the back of the passenger seat. When Jack stopped at traffic lights, he squeezed his body through to the girl, and settled down with Sadie's arms around him.

After half an hour, Jack drew into the tree-lined street of Victorian three-story semis. She read the numbers as she crawled along until she recognized Felix's. She saw his car parked in the street, leaving the drive free for her to maneuver right up to the porch. He met the car. Jack opened the back door, grabbed the dog by his collar and led him out first.

Felix bent to speak to her. "I drew the sigils in my study—it's closest to the front of the house."

"Otherwise I'll just have to stay in the car." Sadie's sleepy voice was at odds with the fear tightening her face, her eyes wide. "Will I faint again, when I get out?"

"I hope not." Jack exchanged concerned glances with Felix. "She . . . how's your first aid?" She dropped her voice. "She needed CPR before."

"Oh." Felix looked startled. "Well, let's make this *really* quick, then." He reached his arms for Sadie, and Jack stood back with the dog. He swept the girl, still in the blanket, into his arms and loped up the drive and through the open door. Jack shut the car doors and followed, as fast as she could, shaky with adrenaline. She felt like she was wading in treacle until she reached the study, where the feeling eased.

She found Sadie sitting up, weakly, in the middle of a wooden floor inscribed with the sigils.

Jack was so grateful, she dropped to her knee and hugged the girl, who hugged back. She looked up at Felix, who was pulling his shirt away from his body, soaked in vomit.

"Well, that could have been worse, I suppose." He wrinkled his nose up at the stink. "Will you be all right there, Sadie? Jack and I need to talk. And I need to change my shirt."

Sadie was preoccupied with the dog, who was reduced to a wagging puppy by the scratching of his spine, which got his hind leg pedaling in the air. "Just don't talk about me behind my back."

"Of course not." Jack followed Felix into the rear of the house, away from the healing warmth of the sigils in the study. He opened the door to a cloakroom, undid his shirt and stripped it off, filling Jack with confusion. Living in seclusion meant a limited exposure to men. Felix's skin was smooth, a sprinkling of hair on his lanky chest, hardly a figure of beauty, but she was strangely affected by the sight of him as he washed in the sink and dried himself with a towel. He reached inside a dryer tucked under the stairs, and pulled out a worn T-shirt.

"Do you know what happened at the house?"

Jack was startled out of her thoughts and looked away. "No. I went to get my car from the cathedral car park. Maggie phoned. She said two men had driven into the yard, she thought they might be the police. I got there as fast as I could, and found Sadie. She managed to hide with Ches. The back door had been kicked in, the place stank of gas, and someone had crashed through the fence into the field—I think that might have been Maggie, her car is missing."

"Damn it, Jack, you have to tell me the truth. All of it." He rested his big hands on her shoulders.

Close to him, the scent of fresh laundry was intoxicating. Warmth seemed to spread from his fingers. "I don't know all of it, I don't know any more than you do." She breathed out, releasing tension in her neck. "We should ask Sadie."

He was quiet for a moment and rested his hands a little longer.

"These were men, not this Bachmeier woman." He looked into her eyes. "Any idea who? Maybe this Pierce, he sounds as if he's serious about getting Sadie."

"Ask her."

He frowned. "She is a sick child. I don't want to frighten her."

Jack shrugged his hands off and stepped back. "Sadie's got this far. I didn't save her, she made it through the tunnel all by herself, and she rescued my dog as well. *Again*."

"OK. We'll ask Sadie." He followed her back into the study, and Jack stood, with relief, in the comfort of the circle, feeling energy creep back into her.

Sadie was sitting against the desk, the dog slumped over her legs. "There were these men. Maggie said they were inquirers, no, inquisitors or something."

"Inquisitors?" Jack slid down to the center of the circle, leaning against a worn old armchair. There was ragged carpet around the edges of the room, where Felix must have cut it away before drawing the sigils. Jack touched one of the shapes, infusing it with a little energy, although she could feel she had little to spare. "You mean, like the Spanish Inquisition? From history?"

The chair she was resting against sagged, as Felix squeezed into it beside her, and she leaned against his warm leg.

"Actually," he said, "the Inquisition is alive and well. They investigate heresies and magical phenomena."

Sadie nudged Jack's ankle with her foot. "He said I'd been denied everlasting life."

"He didn't say he was with the police, though?" Felix said.

"No. He said he was going to take me to some hospital." Sadie's forehead was wrinkled as she spoke. "He did say he wouldn't hurt me, he was there to rescue me."

Felix stood up and walked over to his briefcase. "Look, Sadie, how about you do an Internet search for Bachmeier and Holtz? That might be a place to start; these men might have been working for them. I'll make a few calls, see what I can find out about the modern Inquisition." Felix handed the laptop down to Sadie. "You know you can't check e-mails, or go on networking sites. They may be monitored."

Sadie scowled at him. "I know!" She started tapping on the keys as Jack watched. "Elizabeth . . . Bachmeyer . . ." She snorted. "Only about one million hits."

"Try Bach-M-E-I-E-R," Felix suggested, and sat back down.

A lightning sequence of taps later, Sadie searched the screen again. "OK . . . a pharmaceutical company . . . is that how you say it? Bachmeier and Holtz."

Felix leaned forward. "Maybe the research Bachmeier and Holtz does is into this 'borrowed time' phenomenon."

Jack thought about it. "Well, our blood is used for healing spells. I mean, I'm not sure how it works—or even if it does— but I know my blood has been used to help people."

Felix rested his fingers on Jack's shoulder. "Let's make the leap, and assume that some people believe it can save seriously ill people. Rich people get cancer, you know. They would pay a lot for a magical cure. What was the name of that actor last year, the one they said was going home to die, the one that ended up in a miraculous remission?"

He stood up, leaving Jack aware of the drift of cold air down her side.

"Felix . . . could you put your heating on?"

"It's on full already." His eyes met hers. "You feel frozen to me."

"I am." She smiled up at him, hugging her knees. "Can I borrow a sweater, then? Maybe one for Sadie, too? We weren't expecting to go out of the house."

"Sadie can research this woman, and you can come and choose from my extensive range of knitwear." He managed a lopsided smile. The dog walked over to him, and sniffed his hand. "At least he's not growling at me anymore."

"He'd like you more if you fed him." Jack hesitated, seeing Sadie's enthusiasm for the computer. "Sadie—you have to be careful. You can't contact your family."

Sadie tossed her hair back, and scowled. "I'm not stupid. They would want to take me outside and I'd last—what—three seconds?" She tapped more keys on the laptop.

Jack followed Felix down a dark hall, the dog's claws clicking on old tiles, and into a large, modern kitchen at the back.

"Wow. Glass doors. You must be able to open them right out onto the garden." But not very secure, she thought. There were no blinds or curtains, and windows from other houses looked down into the kitchen, as the lights flickered on.

"It was Marianne's idea. My wife . . . well, ex-wife." He turned at the sound of a click from what Jack could now see was a cat flap through the wall. "Oh, shit. Tycho."

A second click was followed by the head of a large tabby cat, which slid into the kitchen and froze for a second when it saw the dog. In what felt like slow motion, Jack reached out her hand to connect with Ches's collar and the cat inflated into a spitting missile, which launched itself at the middle of the kitchen, just stopping short of Ches. Its arched body was sideways to them, to make itself look even bigger.

Felix dived toward the cat as Jack grabbed Ches's neck but there was a muffled yowl, a bellow from Felix as the cat leapt from his hands toward an island unit, and a yelp from the dog, as a scratch opened up along his snout.

"I'm sorry. He's not very good with dogs." Felix examined his hands, spotted with puncture wounds that oozed with scarlet beads.

Jack knelt and comforted the dog. She looked at the cat, which sat peering down at them from the top of a kitchen cupboard, only its flattened ears showing any disquiet. A slow growl started from the feline, and Ches whined back.

Felix pulled down a large box, and showed Jack the contents. "I know they're cat treats, but they should be all right for him."

"Oh, he'll love them." The cat sniffed the air and stopped growling. By the time Felix had turned a large tin of cat food and a big handful of treats onto a plate, the cat had deigned to investigate. Ches, wolfing half the meat off the plate before it even rested on the kitchen floor, retreated as the cat advanced. Tycho delicately pawed a portion onto the floor.

Jack nudged the plate closer to the dog so he could eat. "I suppose they will work out some sort of truce."

"He's supposed to be at Marianne's, but he keeps coming back."

"So she didn't move out long ago?"

Felix stroked the cat, who arched his back in response, then hooked another pawful off the dog's plate. "Five months. She'd been in a relationship with Heinrich for quite a while, but they didn't make it official for some time. I thought if I was patient she would get over it, but it seems not."

"That must have been hard. And that's what you wanted . . . her to get over it and come back?" She had to ask the questions, even as she braced herself for the answers.

He sat back on his haunches, eyes level with the kneeling Jack's, separated by their respective animals. "At the time."

She pushed the plate over for the cat to swipe a few stray treats. "You loved her."

"For a long time. Then . . . I didn't anymore. But I didn't know anything better would come along." He paused. "I hadn't met you."

She found she couldn't meet his eyes, and fussed the dog, now chasing the empty plate around the floor. The cat leapt out of his way onto a stool, and started washing its paws.

"Jack—" Before he could finish, Sadie shouted his name, her voice high with excitement or alarm.

Jack followed him into the study. Sadie was hunched over the laptop, her face white in the glow from the screen.

"I looked up elementals and tornadoes. Look at this."

She angled the screen toward them, a lurid purple page with the title "Freak Weather," with a photograph of shattered head-stones and a damaged tree.

"Listen to this," she read. "'In July 1978, in Norwich, England, a woman named Mary Kinley, twenty, was found dead in a funeral chapel in St. Mark's cemetery. Police said unusual weather conditions had caused extensive damage around the churchyard. Local meteor . . . meteorologist James Bettson said the circular pattern of debris suggested a tornado.' It looks a bit like the cottage." She clicked on a button at the side of the page, and Jack leaned in closer to read it.

"The woman apparently died of blood loss, but none was found at the scene," Jack said.

Sadie moved the arrow on the screen to an underlined area. "Look, more 'vampire tornadoes.'"

Felix interrupted. "You do know ninety-nine percent of the stuff on the Internet is either fraud or pure imagination."

Another picture loaded, this time of grainy men carrying a coffin. Sadie squinted at the screen. "Helen McNamara. Found dead after a storm wrecked a car park in Leicester. 'Police dismissed an account from an eyewitness who claimed a tornado had picked Helen up and taken her from three streets away. The inquest has been adjourned.' That was 1996. Look, there's a comment here saying police found she had been exsanguinated. That's drained of blood, isn't it?"

"Look up the inquest," said Jack.

"No, wait." Felix leaned forward to stare at the screen, and Sadie pulled it around so he could see better. "Look at the pall-bearer. He looks familiar." He dug in his pocket for the card he'd been given at the police station.

A young man, maybe in his early twenties, was staring into the camera, his face tense and set. He was tall and thin, his face sculpted by his grief, perhaps.

"He looks like the man from the Arts and Antiquities squad," Felix said.

Sadie pushed the laptop toward him. "That man," she pointed, "was at the cottage. He was the one that kicked the door in, I'm sure."

Jack chewed her lower lip for a moment. "He does look like the man in the pub. So who is he?"

Felix enlarged the news-clipping image, the face becoming less clear as it devolved into dots. The words under it came into focus. "'Helen's coffin was carried by her father, uncles, and brother Stephen.' That's McNamara." He waved the card at them. "I met him when I went to talk about the photographs with the police."

New pictures came up of Helen on the beach, Helen graduating from university. Sadie bowed her head over the screen. "There's something funny about these pictures . . ." She scrolled through the images, enlarging them. "Look at this dress she's wearing."

Jack looked. "I can't see anything odd."

Sadie brought up another one. "Try this blue one, it's clearer. Look at her top. Look at the pattern."

Jack stared at the screen, unable to breathe out for a moment as she recognized the symbols printed on the fabric. Then the air escaped in a whoosh. "Oh, my God. Helen McNamara was a borrowed timer." It was a young face, a blond girl in her early twenties, laughing at the photographer. Jack caught her breath. It looked like a younger version of the woman who had been in her car.

Chapter 41

*Our studies took us to the lower realms: that is, not
the higher angelic kingdom of heaven, not the earthly
demesne of men. The lower realms are peopled with
goblins and spirits, of the most elemental nature, and
forces that run through our lives. They are powerful
and dangerous, like hurricanes and infernos.*

—EDWARD KELLEY
10 December 1585
Csejte Castle

THE COUNT'S HOSPITALITY EXTENDED TO THE EVENING
meal, where his captains and brothers in arms feasted
loudly. But their eyes were often upon Dee, as if they expected him to leap to his feet and ensorcell them at any moment. Lord Miklós ignored us, and was much fêted as guest of
honor as befitted the king's brother.

When our bellies were full, and the shouting had receded a
little in the warmth of the wine, Count Nádasdy turned to me.
"Master Kelley. I had reason to speak to Count Laski. He has
great faith in your alchemical experiments."

"Indeed, my lord?" I was wary about speaking of Albert
Laski, whose adventuring sometimes crossed the line of honesty, although I had been accused of that myself.

"He told me he was present when you raised a dead man
from a crypt in London."

I glanced at Dee, whose downcast eyes gleamed with awareness even though he looked half asleep. "Doctor Dee will tell
the tale better—"

In truth, Laski can't have seen much, scrabbling at the door
as he did for a way out.

"I would rather hear your version, at this moment." The
count waved at Dee. "Your colleague is older, and my servants
tell me he has been ill. Perhaps you would entertain us with the
story instead."

"Sir?" I was unsure, but Dee smiled through his beard.

"Please do, Edward." He settled back in his chair. I caught a
movement out of the corner of my eye and, as I walked around
the table to address the company, was able to get a better view.
The witch Zsófia was standing half concealed behind one of
the door curtains, just the flash of fox hair making her known
to me.

"My lords." I bowed, as one is wont to do in royal courts,
when one entertains the gathering. "This event took place more
than two years since, in the churchyard of Greyfriars Church
in London town. It had been a bad year for miasmas and agues,
and there were many deaths. In the height of summer there
came a fever that took Doctor Dee's old friend and fellow natural scientist Sir Gregory Whichall." I looked around to make
sure the captains could follow my Latin, but they seemed flat-
teringly attentive. "Doctor Dee and Sir Gregory had a pact, my
lords, that when one of them died he would come back to report
to the other on events after death."

There was a ripple of reaction. A few men murmured to
their friends, and I allowed my eyes to range across the back of
the hall and saw the flash of a skirt still in the doorway.

I stood tall. "Lord Laski, Doctor Dee and I walked, at midnight, to the chapel where Sir Gregory's body lay. This is our
custom, to stand vigil until the morning. Once there, we dismissed his servant, who kept watch in that place. Truly, he was

grateful to be relieved of his morbid and lonely duty. My master and I prayed for the blessing of the Lord upon our work, then Master Dee drew a restraining circle beyond the funeral bier, and Laski and I removed the lid."

In honesty, my knees had been knocking together, and Sir Gregory's shrunken features were most horrid. It had been a very hot and humid week, and his stomach was bloated and stinking, blood dribbling down his cheeks from the putrefaction. I went to the door for fresh air, more than inclined to leave, but the graveyard was filled with mists. They swept around the walls like wraiths trying to seize the living.

"Master Dee spoke the summoning words, but nothing happened," I intoned. I waited, for a long moment, watching the nobles, letting the suspense build. I raised my voice to a cry.

"'Speak, speak, shade!' said my master in a great voice." A few of the men laughed nervously, as I had intended them to do. I lowered my voice, and the men fell silent, the better to hear me. "At first I thought I heard the wind rising, or that an animal was caught somewhere, but then I realized it was a voice calling, wailing."

At the time, I had almost fled, but the thought of traversing that foggy churchyard at midnight alone had kept me close to Dee, newly my master and mentor. He had held his ground, calling upon the spirit to show itself, even as I prayed it would not.

"As Dee conjured the spirit of his friend, I anticipated we would see the specter of the man in the circle we had drawn. But no, the strangest of lights, like the glimmer of marsh gas, lit up the room with a glow." As luck provided, a draft from the doorway made the candles flicker, and my eye was drawn to the figure behind the tapestry. The count's black eyes looked around the room, but I fancied I had everyone else's attention, even Dee's.

"To my horror, the corpse began to seethe and move. The spirit made it heave with unnatural breath that filled the crypt with a stench of death." I paused for effect. "And Doctor Dee spoke with it."

Heads turned toward Dee, who leaned back in his chair. "Indeed," he said, then stood and joined me. "And my dear old friend answered. He spoke of the pain and grief of being an earthbound spirit. He had left tasks undone, left sins unshriven."

"What happened when you had finished speaking?" The count leaned back in his chair, toying with the reddest of apples. Dee caught my eye, then proceeded with a version—not an entirely accurate one—of the story.

"Upon being called to pray, he set up a wailing and crying. He submitted under coercion to kneel in his casket, and pray for the mercy of the Heavenly Father. Then, as he said the word 'Amen,' he fell into his coffin, at peace."

The count murmured something to his neighbor, the one I called Redbeard, Lord Mihály, whose lips twisted into a grim smile. He rose to his feet and pointed at me.

"Thus speaks the wizard. But what of his assistant? What did you see?"

I looked at Dee, and back at the count, and shrugged.

"I was too afraid to stop praying and look, my lords." I hung my head as if in shame, but the scars on my forearm itched to be revealed.

A shout of laughter deflected the attention of the nobles, and I sighed. I sneaked a glance under my lowered eyelids to the doorway, but it was empty.

"So, what really happened?" The voice came from a dark corner of my chamber, which was lit by the single candle I was carrying. I flinched, and I almost dropped the light, but I fumbled it over my head to illuminate the room. I knew it was Zsófia from her voice.

"What?" I said, in stern accents.

"The dead man you raised, the revenant. I can't believe it said its prayers like a child, then lay down."

I put the candle on the table, and circled around the witch. My books and papers were, as far as I could tell, in order. I carried precious items in a secret pocket in my jacket, and my most important items in the sole of my specially adapted boots. "There was . . . some resistance."

The memory, of the corpse throwing itself at Dee and knocking me to the ground, erupted into my mind. I rubbed the scar on my arm.

"We subdued it. We called upon heaven to take the man's spirit and it did." I tried to sound as assured as I could.

She walked to me, immodest in a dress with a low bodice, her hair loose upon her white shoulders as if she were a courtesan. She reached out one slender hand—not roughened by work, but fine—and took my arm, pulling back the sleeve of my shirt. The ugly marks were purple in the low light. If Dee had not stanched the blood that night, I fear I would have died.

"It bit you?" Her touch was gentle, yet it burned me. She smelled of apples. Her eyes were uncertain, and she took her fingers away. "It bit you, yet you live?"

"Of course. The angels keep us safe."

It had been Dee who struck the thing, for it was no longer a man, with his staff. He drove it with abjurations into the magic enclosure. When he closed the circle with a single sweep of his chalk, the thing had succumbed to the natural course of putrefaction, and exploded in a shower of limbs and entrails. I couldn't keep food down for weeks, every morsel brought back the horrible wet sound and the wall of foulness that swept over me as I lay bleeding upon the ground. My wound mortified, and only the most vigilant care from Lady Jane kept me anchored to this plane, God protect and bless her. Thus we passed from master and servant to teacher and student, and the experience bound Dee and me together.

Zsófia walked around me, as if looking over a horse, inspecting my face and limbs. Then she stood before me, and sniffed the air, as if trying to detect my nature. I stared back, looking at her eyes, the darkest of greens in the low light.

"You have power. Dee has much knowledge, true, but you have power. You must help my mistress."

"You have much affection for her."

"I love her." She spoke as if she were talking about a sister or a daughter. "She is my life." She approached, now so close that I could feel her breath upon my cheek when she sighed. I looked at her eyes, and my hands reached around her waist as if under their own power. All objections that a God-fearing man might raise were dissolved in the touch of her lips on mine, and I found my fingers pulling at her laces, which fell away. As she stood before me in a fine shift that barely covered her breasts, that sense of danger that has kept me alive screamed at me to retreat. I stepped back, shaking with lust and shame, and tried to summon my wife's face to my mind. Jane Dee's sweet face drifted up, instead, insubstantial as a cloud, but I held on to it as I pushed the witch away. I dropped my voice, lest Dee hear me in the adjoining room.

"I thought . . . I thought you would not lie with a sorcerer's assistant, when you could have royalty."

"I take anyone I want," she boasted.

"Not me." I was shaking with emotion, which was in truth a mixture of fear and desire. "I do not lie with witches. I am a married man."

I closed my eyes and spoke the words of warding against succubi and other demons.

When I opened them, she was there, the only woman I have loved, her pale oval face in the flicker of the single candle. Flaxen hair, not wound tight around her head, as was her custom, but loose over her shoulders. Her cornflower eyes picked up glints from the single flame. My mind should have said, "How, why?," but instead, I was enchanted completely as she let her shift fall to her feet. Her skin was flat and supple, as if she had not borne Dee several children but was somehow a girl again.

"Edward," she breathed. "My dearest Edward."

I opened my lips to whisper her name. "Jane, Jane." Then she covered my mouth with her own.

Thus was I conquered by the witch.

Chapter 42

EARLY NEXT MORNING, FELIX STOOD IN THE CITY'S MAIN police station, smiling at the sergeant, hoping to soften her up.

"I was just doing some research into the symbols found in the Carla Marshall case."

"The coroner ruled that as natural causes. There's no case." She wasn't uncooperative, just uninterested.

"Ah, but I may be able to link those specific symbols to another suspicious death."

There was a flicker of interest in the eyes of the sergeant for a moment. "And is that an open case?"

"Well, no, the coroner found it to be misadventure. But it would be an unusual coincidence, two cases with sixteenth-century symbolism."

The glimmer of interest had died. "Coincidences are not a police matter. We don't have the resources."

"I just need a copy of the investigations made into their deaths, one from Leicester in 1996, and one from Norwich, 1978, for my official report." He pushed a sheet of paper with all the details across the desk. "I don't get paid until the investigation is complete, and I can't finish it until I have all the details. The more time it takes, the more it costs . . . I was hoping to wrap it all up by the weekend."

She sighed, turned to a passing officer and spoke to him. She handed him the note. "PC Travers here will get you the details. Just wait over there, please."

He sat in a row of chairs provided for visitors, and could just see Soames's office if he leaned back. The door was shut, but he could see through the glass panel that Soames was talking to someone. By leaning back farther, he could just see it was Stephen McNamara.

His heart beat uncomfortably loud in his ears as he approached the desk.

"Look, I have an urgent appointment somewhere else. I'll come back for the files, if you don't mind. Thanks."

Even as he stepped back, he heard a door open, and Soames's voice drifted down the corridor. He left the police station with as much dignity as he could while semi-jogging, and realized his car was parked in plain view across the street. He ducked down the side of the building and watched as the man walked out of the double doors. McNamara checked as he did so, and looked up and down the road. Felix ducked behind an industrial bin that, from the stink of it, needed emptying. When he looked out, McNamara was standing a few feet away, staring straight at him.

"Professor Guichard?"

Feeling foolish, Felix emerged from the corner of the building. "Mr. McNamara, I presume. Posing as a police officer."

The man's face changed from impassive to wary. "I have been forced into certain subterfuges. I have to find Sadie Williams."

"You almost had her yesterday." Felix's animosity bubbled over. "She's a child, for God's sake! Whatever was done to her, she is innocent in this."

"I know. But she is a danger to others in ways you cannot imagine." He looked up at the sky, and Felix realized the first drops were already spotting his coat. "I don't want to hurt her. Please, hear me out."

Felix hesitated, then looked down the road. "I have a season ticket to the cathedral. Would you object to talking there?"

The two men walked in silence across the road and down the narrow alley that led to the cathedral green. A few students were sitting on benches and the broad white steps. One recognized Felix and raised a hand in greeting. He managed a half smile in response, but his palms were sweating at the thought that, even now, he was putting Sadie in more danger. He already regretted speaking to McNamara.

The limestone arches soared from pillars all around them, dwarfing the two men under the ornate vaulted ceiling. Felix looked around, distrusting the man. The Lady Chapel, seven hundred years old, was quiet but in plain view of the guides and visitors. McNamara followed, his face as blank as the carvings of saints all around. He sat on a bench, a few feet away from Felix.

He closed his eyes and bent his head a little, and Felix realized he was praying. It gave him time to study the man. He was nondescript, dark suit, speckled hair cut very short, lighter plain tie. His blue eyes gleamed in the low light, the only color against the grays of his suit and hair.

"Are you surprised that I pray in an Anglican cathedral?"

"I'm surprised that you pray at all." Speculation ran through Felix's mind.

McNamara's face was grim, his mouth thin-lipped and downturned. "I am an inquisitor. I work for His Holiness."

Felix's surprise must have shown on his face, because McNamara managed the smallest lift of one corner of his mouth.

"The Inquisition is a legitimate office of the Holy See. We come under the department of the Congregation for the Doctrine of the Faith. I am a lay investigator for a special project within that department."

"Oh, I know all about the CDF. It's the special project I haven't heard about."

"It is necessarily secret." McNamara sighed, stretching his feet out in front of him and looking down at them. "I am breaking my oath just speaking with you."

Despite himself, Felix was impressed by the man's quiet sincerity. "So, why are you talking to me?"

"Because I find I have a conflict of interests."

Felix waited for him to explain, as a small party of visitors passed by with a guide. Words drifted over him. *The Lady Chapel was built between 1272 and 1298, and was the first part of the new gothic cathedral to be completed . . .*

Felix ran through all the crazy ideas Jack had fed him, each one building upon another like a house of cards. Here was a chance to either confirm or deny Jack and Sadie's world, and he couldn't think of a single question.

McNamara explained. "My duties include identifying revenants, and helping to eliminate them. They are unnatural, and contrary to God's will."

"By revenants, you mean people like Sadie. And by eliminate, you mean kill them."

"My colleagues, after time to reconcile her to her fate with prayer and confession, intended to release her to heaven by stopping the sorcery. But an opportunity has arisen to right a greater wrong. I am here as a free agent."

"Did they kill your sister?"

That straightened McNamara's back. "No!" He bit his lip for a moment. "I was just a student when she was killed. I didn't understand what she was until after her death. The Inquisition recruited me years later."

"But someone made her, extended her life."

McNamara grimaced. "My mother knew how to. She was part of an occult circle." He studied his long hands. "My sister was born with a fatal genetic disorder, and my mother knew she would die in childhood. The circle came up with an old ritual and found her death was not inevitable, not certain."

"You mean, she was treatable?"

"No, no." He chopped the air with one hand. "You don't understand. For most of us, our moment of death is set, it is

God's will. But in a few cases, that moment can be extended by unnatural magics."

"But surely, that would also be God's will?" Despite himself, Felix warmed to the man, whose face was twisted in anguish.

"I cannot believe that God wishes the soul of a child to be harnessed to a body that is trapped forever in the moment of dying."

"So, brought up in a household that used magic, you ended up persecuting similar families. How can you reconcile that?"

"I never questioned it until Helen was killed in that barbaric manner. My primary aim has always been to find the creature that killed my sister, and destroy it."

Felix looked around the arches, up to the carved and painted ceiling. "A woman came to visit my office at the university. She looked somewhat like an older version of your sister. She called herself Bachmeier."

"That's what they do. These fiends take on the appearance of their victims." He rubbed his hand over his face. "It has been the hardest thing for me to hunt her, because she looks like Helen. But I will catch her, and kill her."

Felix frowned, confused. "But what does this woman want with Sadie?"

McNamara locked eyes with him. "You have no idea what Bachmeier is, do you?"

"I know she has the power to mesmerize people." He pulled out the dark carving Amusaa had given him. "She tried to persuade my assistant to hand over some documents I have about the original symbols. This reduced her power over us."

McNamara brought out an ornamented crucifix from a pocket, about as long as his hand. "This is my defense against her."

"Have you met her?"

"Once." McNamara shuddered. "She let me live. I think she likes the idea of her victims suffering. But she will kill the child."

"Why?"

McNamara took a deep breath, as if trying to decide how much to say to Felix. "If I tell you, I break my sacred vow and give you information my enemies can use. Do you understand?"

"I am not your enemy. I want to know why you, and this woman, want to get hold of a fourteen-year-old girl."

McNamara leaned forward, hissing the answer at him. "Because this woman can only prolong her unnatural existence in one way. She must drain the blood of another revenant, until she drinks in her last moments of life."

Chapter 43

*That demons possess men I have no doubt; also angels,
who first communicated to me when I was a student
at Cambridge. Here one spoke through me whenever
I was cup-shotten, which made me eschew becoming
intoxicated by liquors forthwith. They bade me seek
out John Dee, and through me, he was able to speak
directly with divine beings. I never doubted that they
were angels, and that they would not lead us astray.*

—EDWARD KELLEY
From his own journal, 13 December 1585
Csejte Castle

I HAD LITTLE TIME TO WALLOW IN THE SHAME OF MY AC-
tions because Dee woke me in my bed at dawn. Mercifully,
I was alone, but his eyes were so wild and his demeanor so
upset I was distracted from my own concerns.

"Edward, you must get up now," he whispered. He raised
his hand to his lips. "Not a word, dear friend, just come and see
what I have been working on."

I slipped into the robe I had been lent, and my boots, and
joined Dee within a few minutes. A splash of cold water upon
my face had brought me awake, and I stood wiping my face on
a square of linen, looking down at a table covered in pieces of
vellum and open books.

"These symbols are described by this Batthyány as being

involved with healing." His hand swept over the open pages. "And these are from the Soyga notes I brought from London."

I recognized the elaborate diagrams in Dee's hand. But the figures sketched out on squares of vellum were different. "And these?"

"These are the symbols inscribed into the countess's skin. Here"—he pointed to a star-shaped one—"and here are shapes I believe have been wrongly transcribed from another tradition. Take these . . ."

He swept aside the notes to reveal a pattern he had drawn upon the dark wood of the table, in chalk. I recognized the ring of letters immediately. It was the circle of necromancy.

"These symbols do not bolster a failing life energy or heal sickness. They are to bind a soul to a dying—or dead—body. This is not the work of God, Edward, this is not strengthening the weak. This poor lady isn't ill, but living beyond her natural span."

I could see how upset he was, his eyes looking over the scattered notes, as if searching for something to refute his conclusions.

"Master Dee," I ventured, lifting the oddments one by one. "We need to be careful. It would not be politic to say such things to the count."

"I have no doubt, Edward, that we are in as much danger as we have ever been. I cannot see how we might satisfy the count and travel back to Krakow."

I straightened a few books. "The evil is done, surely? Having been created by such unnatural magics, our work is simply to strengthen the poor lady."

He looked at me, as a disappointed father might, with a frown. "To sustain evil is as bad as creating evil. We cannot help the countess."

"Master Dee. We are prisoners in this castle, among these savage people. You will condemn yourself to die by refusing to help."

"If necessary."

I took a deep breath, to confront my master. "And you condemn me, also."

Here his distress showed on his features. "I am sorry for that, truly—"

"Not to mention Mistress Jane and Mrs. Kelley, and your children, whom I love as my own. What will happen to them, alone in Krakow?"

His mouth opened but he could find no words.

I added my next argument to the pile. "Saraquel did not tell you to foreswear helping the lady; you know he did not. Indeed, he described for you the very symbols you seek."

Dee nodded slowly. "He did."

"Dear sir, if we save this poor lady, who is as much a victim as anyone, we can ask for an escort back to Krakow and get out of the country."

Dee looked shocked. "Edward, this is sorcery, and you know I have foresworn all magics."

"Yet you used foxfire on the road against the wolves."

A faint flush darkened his cheeks above the flowing beard. "In a moment of intense danger, Edward. My affection for you made me incautious. But this must be my decision, as your preceptor and master."

"Look at the danger we are in now!" I moderated my tone. "Sir, sometimes the worst, most vile things have good consequences." I took a deep breath. "The child that died, the one that came to the castle."

"Yes?" His tone was cooler than I was used to, but courteous.

"I fear that her life, her blood, was taken for sorcery."

"In what way?" he scoffed. "For what purpose?"

"It was used by witches, forest women." I took a deep breath, for I knew the words must hurt my old friend. "It was done to save you."

Chapter 44

Jack was astonished at how much Sadie could discover with the computer in one evening. After breakfast, they sat down again on the floor of the study and turned on the laptop Felix had left them. First, Jack called Charley, and found that Maggie had been taken to hospital but her injuries were not life-threatening. Having lured the intruders to follow her, she had clipped a reversing tractor and overturned the car. Charley had confirmed that apart from a mild concussion and a sprained wrist, Maggie would be fine.

Sadie also spent an emotional few minutes showing Jack the good wishes that had been set up on a webpage for missing teens. Messages from family, friends, schoolmates and neighbors had been left every day. "Come home . . . We miss you . . . We're not angry, just let us know you are OK . . ."

Jack wanted to distract her. "Sadie, could you look for any mention of Melissa Harcourt?"

Sadie tapped the keyboard. She scrolled down a list of results. "That's your name, isn't it? I found your notebook." She clicked on one line. "This might be you."

Jack was transported back to the dining hall at school, the smell of cabbage and custard, the polished bench. One chance to smile, and then the next child was sent along. The girl in the picture had a puzzled half smirk, as if the photographer had just missed the real grin. She could remember her hair band pulling her scalp, her mother's insistence that she have everything smart for the school portrait. Mum and Dad always bought several copies for her grandparents. She snatched a deep breath, as something tugged in her chest. Grandma Lydia, was she still alive? She would be over eighty now.

"That's you, isn't it?" Sadie sounded uncertain, looking at Jack.

The headline above the photograph was "Yorkshire's Child Abduction Mystery—Finally Solved?"

"What does it say?" Jack looked away from the screen, after a quick glance at a picture of her parents in front of their old house.

Sadie read off the screen, in a subdued voice. "'The body of a girl has been found . . . between ten and thirteen . . . examination of the remains, including DNA tests, are ongoing.'" She looked up. "But they know it wasn't you. There's a link to a later article, saying it's someone else."

"What does it say?" Jack stood up, and looked out of the window.

"Your mum was upset it wasn't you. Maybe she needed closure." Sadie hesitated for a moment. "Why didn't you ever contact them once you grew up? You didn't, did you?" She closed the lid on the laptop with a soft click.

"They would have called the police. They would have wanted to know what happened, and at that age, how could I have explained? Besides, I wasn't as strong as you; I couldn't have coped away from the circle for very long. They would never have understood the potions, the tattoos . . ."

When Jack looked back at Sadie the girl was crying into her hands. "I miss my mum so badly," she said, her voice muffled.

"I know." Jack crossed the hall to the bathroom to pull off a length of tissue for Sadie, but when she handed it over she found her own eyes were stinging. "Here. We've got to keep our focus, so we'll be ready for whatever Felix will tell us."

Sadie sniffed, warded off the dog who had wandered over when she started crying, and opened the laptop again.

Jack handed her a sheaf of notes. "Here are a few ideas Felix had last night, he jotted them on the back."

"Did you sleep with him?" The question dangled in the air, and Jack couldn't breathe for a moment. She didn't know how to answer, there was no frame of reference for it. Sadie carried on, still typing. "It's obvious you fancy each other. I just wondered."

Jack's voice sounded prim and high-pitched when she answered. "I slept downstairs, on the sofa. Alone, of course. I don't . . ." She ran out of words.

"I just wondered. I don't really care." Sadie looked at Jack from under long eyelashes, her blue eyes inquisitive. "He's pretty old, anyway."

Jack opened her mouth to protest, then shut it when she saw the mischief on Sadie's face. "There are more important things to think about. Like keeping us all safe."

The key squeaking in the lock alerted her to Felix's return. She brushed by him in the hall, unable to meet his eye. "I'm putting the kettle on," she threw over her shoulder.

"Great." Felix hung his coat on a hook by the kitchen door and followed her in. "I've ordered the police reports, I can pick them up later. Jack . . ."

He looked awkward, as if he didn't know what to say. She turned back to the cups and clattered a spoon into one with unnecessary force. "What?"

"I met with Stephen McNamara." His voice was low, as if he was trying to prevent Sadie from overhearing. "Helen McNamara's brother. He is an inquisitor, as Sadie said."

"What?" She turned to face him. "You might have led him straight here!"

"No. No, I haven't. He's not after Sadie."

"He came to my house, soaked it in gasoline and tried to kidnap Sadie! You can't trust him." Words piled up in her throat. "How could you, Felix?" The betrayal choked her.

"Look, I didn't seek him out, he found me. He was at the

police station." He stepped toward her as she pulled away, then reached out to catch her by the shoulders. "Listen to me, Jack. Trust me."

Why should I trust you? She looked into his eyes, dark green, and watched his expression change from frustration to something else, something that made his breath come faster and eyes wander to her mouth.

"Because I like you, Jack. I like Sadie." He shook her lightly for emphasis. "And the reason I trust what he's saying is because he told me why everyone is after Sadie."

"Go on." Somehow her anger had transmuted itself into something softer.

"He thinks this Bachmeier woman needs Sadie's blood to stay alive. He thinks Bachmeier is some sort of creature, not human anymore."

Jack remembered the woman's face, stripped of its glamor. "So she really could be older?"

"He believes that she takes on some characteristics of the person she kills. That's why she reminds us of the picture of his sister." He dropped his voice. "She wants to feed on Sadie. The Inquisition want to stop her. They were going to use Sadie . . . for bait. To catch this woman."

Jack pulled away from Felix's hands and led the way into the study. "We've discovered things, too. Sadie?"

The girl had moved to the desk, her eyes looking huge in the light from the screen.

"We've found out more about Edward Kelley," she said, without looking up. "Have you got those old papers Jack was talking about?"

Felix pulled out a folder, and leafed through the papers. "I assumed they were by Edward Kelley from the content."

Sadie spread some of the photocopies over the desk, a dozen or so of them, then Felix's transcripts. She frowned. "Your notes are as badly written as the original."

"Well, I've left the Latin bits, as I can read those."

As she bent her head over the papers, she started reading aloud. "'That whych . . . sustayns the countess shall be the detrimente of every chylde in the castle . . .'"

"I'm not sure," began Felix, "but I think Dee was trying to help a noblewoman in Hungary. I think he working on creating someone like you, or at least refining her treatment."

"Making a borrowed timer?" Sadie turned back to her notes, her mouth moving as she continued reading.

Jack sipped her tea, watching Felix as he read his own notes.

"Here. Something about using symbols of necromancy, not healing," Felix said. "I got that far."

He was interrupted by a thunderous banging on the door. The dog jumped up, and Jack caught him.

"Police! Open up."

"Oh, shit." Jack felt as if the floor was shuddering under her feet.

Sadie was standing, looking around the room, her eyes wide. She stuffed the papers into a pile, and hugged them against her chest. "There's nowhere to hide."

"Under the desk." Felix pulled the bulky leather chair out. "Scoot under there, there's a gap behind the drawers. I used to squeeze in there when I was little. It's just inside the edge of the circle."

Jack pulled the dog back, as the pounding started again.

Felix jogged into the hall. "I'm coming, I'm coming," he called.

Jack pushed the chair in front of the desk, and hauled the dog toward the living room, his hissing whine as close as he would normally come to a bark. She just had time to restrain him before several uniformed officers clattered down the tiled hallway, shouting to one another.

"Are you the owner of the car in the driveway?" The first

officer in the room was wearing a padded jacket, like he was expecting a fight.

"No. I mean, it belongs to the garage, they have my car in for repair. Why?"

"We have reason to believe . . ." *Oh God, it was that dog walker, she must have reported the registration to the police.* ". . . Sadie Williams . . ."

Jack could feel her whole life unraveling. Sadie would die within seconds of being "rescued," and Jack would fade within a day or two, away from the circle and the herbs. One part of her was so tired that it didn't care, it just wanted to let go and sleep. The other part of her wanted to follow the feelings to Felix and lose herself in his touch, his warmth . . . The dog heaved against his collar in an effort to reach the new threat.

"Jack."

Felix's voice reached her, and touched the part of Jack that wanted to live. He was standing in the doorway, looking as pale as she felt. She let the dog go, the collar slipping through her fingers, and stood up, even as the policeman seemed to stiffen. The dog ignored him and Jack locked eyes with Felix. It seemed it was all she could do, paralyzed somehow between breaths. She could see confusion then effort in Felix's eyes, but all he seemed to be able to move was his face. Then, darkness swept in like icy sleep, and her knees buckled as if they were boneless. The last thing she saw was Felix, crumpling toward the ground.

Chapter 45

*I was undecided as to the nature of my angelic
adviser—or my demonic possession, whichever it was—
and whether to tell Dee. Since Saraquel, whatever
his nature, was showing us a way to satisfy our
kidnappers and leave the castle, I could hardly go
against his wisdoms but held my tongue against my
fears.*

—EDWARD KELLEY
14 December 1585
Csejte Castle

DEE SPENT THE REST OF THE DAY, AND SOME OF THE night, in prayer. I could hear him, and sometimes I wondered if there were a few tears, also. Dee had great love for children. The thought that one was sacrificed to save an old man was sickening to him. By the next morning he was pale but resolute.

"We must be guided by Saraquel, Edward. Look here." He led me to the table, with the remains of the smudged necromancy circle. "These letters will never work, not sufficiently. We would need to use the witch's symbols as well. I imagine they should be centered about the lady's heart, and supported with herbs and ritual. She should lie within a circle cast with the correct ceremony, this will bind her soul . . . but to what, Edward? A dying body?"

"It is the only body she has, master."

Eventually he nodded. "And should angels speak, you must hear them, Edward. They must be our guides in this. Indeed, they may be our only friends in this accursed place." He shuddered, pulling his jacket around his shoulders.

"Master," I said, fearing to distress him more. "The blood potion—"

"It is done, Edward. I shall strive to make that child's sacrifice a reason to work harder in the Lord's work." He hesitated for a moment, then said, in a soft voice, "For she is surely better in heaven than in this serpent's den."

We worked in silence. I transcribed all the necromancy figures onto pieces of parchment, as Dee directed, and he researched more books he had taken from the library. The entrance of a young woman with a pitcher of warm water and a woven basket of kindling to restart the fire surprised us both.

My eye was drawn to her pale face, so like many of the other servant girls. I understood it was like trefoil leaves; you might search a meadow for many minutes, and see none, yet once your eye has fallen upon one, you see them all. I realized that I had accepted that the people here were fair of skin, sallow at best, but now I suspected that this wench was sickly. Their elders were so ruddy and dark of feature that their young were in shameful contrast. I could not deny the possibility that these children were being used to sustain the dying countess. She was not just a victim of her strange malady, but the cause of great weakness in others.

We worked through the next day, and the servants must have reported our diligence to their masters, as we noticed more visits and more covert looks at our notes. Dee began encoding the shapes into the Enochian letters we had developed, just to prevent observers from reading our work. Finally, we sat around the table, the symbols arranged in a rough circle.

"This must be nearest the head. This one should be nearest the organs of generation," Dee said, pointing to the main sigil. Then he hesitated. "What do you think, Edward?"

I considered the symbols he had designed. "I think it should do well. Master," I asked in English, "if we are able to help the countess, do you think the count will ever release us?"

"I do not know." Dee bent to the final symbol, adding a precise line. "But this will not help the poor lady recover, as we know it, just prolong an unnatural life."

"And bear a child?"

He shook his head. "I can't believe that is possible. I heard the story the king told us, but it must be that the woman Katalin was merely wounded, and weakened by it. How could a living child grow within a dead womb?"

I hesitated. "The witch believes it and her mother was present."

He stared at me over his long nose. "And you believe that ungodly harlot? You have allowed yourself to be contaminated."

I huddled miserably upon the stool, shamed and mortified that Dee should know of my lapse. He must have heard us through the connecting door, when I had thought him asleep.

"I believe that she believes it," I said. "She has many more years' experience of this phenomenon than we do. Her own mother attended Lady Báthory's grandmother." I drained the dregs of the watered wine we had been fortifying ourselves with. "Master, Zsófia . . ."

Dee waved me away. "I don't wish to speak of it, Edward. I was surprised at your lewd behavior, you have always struck me as a decent and faithful man." He sounded more sad than angry.

"I am! I have never before . . ." I shook my head. "She bewitched me."

"She bewitched you? I don't believe she could have done so unless you wanted that same event." He turned back to his work. "But we waste time talking of distasteful subjects. I wonder that angels find you a suitable mouthpiece."

I was hurt by his coldness, and angered. "I believe the angels will be more understanding than my own master." When I said the words, I remembered the form the witch had seduced me in, and was filled again with shame. That was one story I could not tell Dee. I moderated my tone. "But I am sorry for my mistake. I truly regret that behavior, which was far from my normal nature."

He sighed and shrugged. "My dear Edward, I do forgive you." Dee half smiled through his beard. "In truth, if I were much younger, and more to the witch's taste, perhaps I too would have been bewitched." He ran his hands over the table and smoothed a piece of paper torn from my journal. "Come, my friend. Your eyes and hands are steadier than mine own. Copy these figures down onto one sheet, and we will see if we can effect an improvement in the countess."

The whispers in my ears had become as ringing bells. I was distracted and my head began to ache. I noticed Dee watching me more as the afternoon went on. I excused myself to go to the close stool, but instead, I went to the chapel, which was empty between services. Here I tried to still the voices with prayer, but, with a surge like water rushing through a pipe, the words gushed into me.

"*Audite, audite nos narro verum,*" they sang, "*quod sono of misericordia quod diligo of Deo.*"

Listen to the mercy of God, I thought bitterly. That mercy had led me to a citadel filled with rich tapestries and good food, and the company of harlots and witches. It had brought me to do the work of the devil.

I managed to still my anger enough to let the voices spill into my mind, although it was as if my soul was forced open and ravished. The voices became muted as they compelled my tongue to speak their words. I don't know the language they spoke, but I could understand it, so I shall recall it in my own.

"Save the woman." I must have said it dozens of times, maybe a hundred, my mouth spewing out the strange words. Then a single voice came into my ears, and I was dazzled by a great glow. It was unlike sunlight—it was as if the sun was at the same time all the colors and glittering, even with my eyes shut.

"Eduardus."

I prostrated myself on the floor, shaking with fear at the strange voice, praying that it would not demand that I perform some great feat of bravery. Instead, the light grew nearer, with great heat, and I covered my eyes with my hands. I decided to scramble to my feet, and stand against it. I shook in my great fear, my head bowed, my lips mumbling snatches of prayers. I could barely breathe. The last moment before my senses left me, I felt the touch of a burning like ice pressed upon my forehead, and I knew I had been kissed by an angel.

Chapter 46

SADIE CURLED UP TIGHT IN THE MUSTY SPACE BEHIND ONE of the pillars of the desk. It smelled like old wood, like her grandfather's house, and the dust on the floor made her face itch. So close to the edge of the circle she felt cold, and tasted acid as her stomach lurched. She heard shouting, as the door was pushed open, and the thump of hard shoes. After a moment, before anyone could find her, there was a series of loud bangs, then silence. It was broken by the patter of dog's claws on the floorboards. Ches whined, as if he was frustrated not to be able to find her. She ventured a look out, to see a mop of brown hair, which she realized was someone lying on the floor. A radio was attached to his shoulder. It hummed.

"Ches! Go away!" she hissed, as loud as she dared.

Almost deafened by the painful thudding of her own heart, she froze at the sound of light steps in the hallway. The dog pulled away as well, lifting his head. He growled, a deep rumble, and backed away. Sadie could see beige, high-heeled shoes, crossing the threshold. She shrank back, out of sight.

"It's all right, Sadie."

The voice was soft, with an accent, and she relaxed. Then the escalation of the growling interrupted her, and Sadie shook off the warm feeling. *It must be the witch with her mind control.*

"You'd better call off your dog. And come out from under there."

Sadie's limbs pulled her out from the cramped space, even as she decided to stay put. Flushed with the effort of resisting, she ended up crouching in the kneehole of the desk, glaring up at the woman. She caught the dog by the collar as he tried to lick her face.

"No, Ches!" He squatted down, panting, his eyes on the woman. "What's happened to everyone?" she asked, looking around at the collapsed police officer.

"They will be well"—the woman's accent was strange— "when you come with me."

A bubble of rage popped in Sadie. "I'm not going anywhere with you, and you can't make me."

She staggered to her feet, clutching the dog's collar in both hands.

"But your friends?" The woman spread her hands out in a gesture of questioning. The fingers re-curled in theatrical emphasis. She was wearing several rings and necklaces, and looked like she had a lot of money. A sweet scent began to make Sadie drowsy again. She gripped the heavy collar, balancing her weight against Ches's.

"What about them?"

"Well, they are asleep now. I wouldn't want them to pass into death."

"What?" She looked at the policeman sprawled at her feet. His face was blue.

"I'm afraid they aren't breathing. They won't take a breath until we leave the house."

"I don't believe you." Even as panic surged through Sadie, she stumbled forward a step.

"Or I could just touch them . . ." The woman stretched out her fingers and dropped them onto Ches's head. He fell, as if electrocuted, thumping to the wooden floor. Sadie couldn't hold his dead weight, and the collar was wrenched through her fingers.

"No!" She wanted to try to help him, but couldn't move. Tears poured down her face as she looked at the dog's open eyes and his tongue, which had slid over his teeth to touch the floor.

"Shall we go?" The woman's face was implacable, cool, simply certain Sadie would obey. "Or should I make another demonstration?"

Sadie could feel her muscles pulling her feet into one step, then another, even as her mouth shaped a howl of grief. It never left her throat. The woman smiled, and turned to leave the room.

Sadie finally found her voice. "I'll die if I go out there."

"Not under my protection. Shall we go? They are starting to look like fish left on a riverbank."

Sadie's feet stepped over the collapsed Jack, folded against the wall. Unlike everyone else, her face was white. Felix had landed by her feet, one hand extended as if to try and save her. Tears poured down Sadie's face. *I'm so sorry* . . .

As Sadie left the house into pale sunshine, she could hear a wheezing gasp from someone in the house. She fought the weakness and sickness that surged into her, as she reached the back door of a car. A man, dressed in a suit, opened it for her, and she slid inside. She couldn't see a circle, but could feel the relief of one.

The woman sat beside her as the driver got in. *"A templom, legyen szíves."* The words hissed out of her, and Sadie wondered what language it was.

"You're not German, are you?"

"No. I am speaking Hungarian. I have a number of servants from there."

The woman reached over and patted Sadie's hand. Her fingers were dry, like old twigs, and cooler than Sadie's, who was powerless even to flinch away.

"You didn't have to kill the dog." She choked on her tears, and wiped her sleeve across her face. "Or hurt my friends."

"Your friends were—overprotective." She rolled her tongue over the words. "I had to stop the police. And the dog? What do you say? Collateral damage. I needed to get your attention before time ran out for all those people."

"What do you want with me? Are you going to take some of my blood?" She spat the words out, folding her arms.

"My dear child, *Sárika*." The woman leaned back in the car, and smiled at Sadie. "I'm going to take all of it."

Chapter 47

*There are symbols of such power that they are a danger
to those that make them, and others, conversely, so
powerfully protective that God himself will send angels
to defend us. To know the difference in these sigils is
wonderful, but not given easily to us mortals.*

—EDWARD KELLEY
  Date not recorded, believed to be mid-December 1585
  Csejte Castle

WE STARTED EXPLORING THE CASTLE, TO LOOK FOR A
suitable arena for the ritual. Dee liked the large
feasting hall for its planetary alignments, but my
whispers led me higher and higher in the castle, until we found
ourselves at the foot of the tower stairs. The servant who was
acting as our guide shook his head, and in garbled German and
Latin indicated that going up to the tower was not permitted.

"I am hesitant to try a ritual, essentially of necromancy,
upon a floor suspended in the air, Edward. My feeling is that
contact with the earth will be crucial to act upon the clay that
is the body."

I turned away from the stairs but the chiming rose in my
mind until I was holding my head with the deafening pain of it.
"Master, I think . . ." I managed to choke out. Dee reached out
a strong hand to steady me, and must have divined my meaning.

"You, my man," he snapped out to the servant. "We must speak to the count. Count Nádasdy, do you understand?"

The man backed away, bowing, but I could see the fear on his face. We waited by the door to the main hall, but I was caught between the agony of each step away from the stairs and the wish to retreat to safety. I closed my eyes, and in my agony, felt something brush my face. The pain eased, and I lurched to my feet.

"I am better, Master Dee." I swallowed, the last of the pealing receding. "But I think our 'friends' wish us to go up into the tower."

The count gave us permission with, I felt, some reluctance. The tower room, when it was reached, proved to be my lady's solar. A spacious and pleasant chamber, it had a large curtained bed in one corner, two high-back chairs and some stools by the window. A lute was laid upon a side table. Here my lady's writing box was topped with what I took to be a prayer book. The windows faced due east, south and west, the bed being located against the long wall, to the north. Very practical, perhaps, but not auspicious for the conception of a child.

The floor was of close-fitted wooden planks, heavy and well polished.

"These could be marked with charcoal, Edward, then we could refine the best arrangement of symbols before we draw them with ink. Help me move these chairs."

We started clearing the smaller pieces of furniture. Using Dee's compass, a beautiful gilded instrument given to him by the Earl of Leicester, we lined up the first symbol on its scrap of vellum. Gradually, we divided the circle into cardinal points, then spread out the sigils between them. They made two complete circles.

"See," he said, gesturing to the marks, "these spell out the earth qualities, and these the air." He indicated which was which. "I hope to balance these symbols with some of the witch's, if they are truly healing marks."

He walked to the smoldering fire, and poked about for a moment, bringing out a half-charred piece of kindling. "Try this, Edward, your hand is more skillful than mine."

The reward of my youthful follies as a forger, thought I, but I started to draw the bold imprint of the shapes, with a little assistance from Dee on alignment and size. Then I lay down, in the center of the circle, and crossed my feet. I couldn't feel any of the cold drafts or shivers that I had come to associate with the calling up of the dead.

"It seems quite comfortable, master . . . ," I started to say, then caught sight of the ceiling above me. Twelve panels with a central motif, which was carved into a twelve-pointed star. "Look. What would be the effect of also drawing the sigils above the lady?"

Dee picked up the pages bearing the sigils. "But then, these ones would be reversed, and . . ." His voice trailed away as he started mumbling calculations under his breath. "And we would need more of the witch's symbols to complete the circle, and perhaps angelic names. What do you think of the archangels' marks as well, in the inner circle?"

"I think so, master."

He turned one sigil so it sat more perfectly in the circle. "I have come to appreciate your scholarship more and more, Edward." He smiled down at me. "I could not be trapped within a foreign castle with a better companion."

I was touched. I had started our acquaintance with venal, mercenary aims, but I had grown to value the man as a friend and teacher, as well as a great thinker. It made my coveting his wife even more repulsive, and I lowered my eyes in shame.

I heard the scuff of a heel, and saw the high red shoes that elevated the count. I scrambled to my feet, avoiding the charcoal marks. His stature was emphasized by his embroidered dolman and a tall black hat.

"My lord," I said, in Latin, and bowed.

Dee conversed in Latin about the possibility of drawing on the ceiling and moving the bed into the middle of the circle. I watched the count and his escorts. Two of his lords, Mihály and László, walked around looking at the circle, avoiding the symbols, discussing them in Hungarian. But it was the king's brother who caught my eye. He stared at me, and I got the impression that he was uncomfortable with our work. I walked over to him.

"Lord Miklós," I said, bowing low.

He nodded to me, and turned his face toward the circle. "Your master is certain of a cure through this sorcery?" he asked in German.

"My lord," I replied, in a low voice, shielding my lips from view behind a hand. "The countess has been saved, until now, through witchcraft, the devil's work. I believe we have been guided here by angels."

"Nádasdy has his own reasons for going to these extraordinary, and ungodly, lengths." His gaze flicked over his fellows. "They are children, amused by tricks. But what they ask is sorcery."

"Without them the countess will die."

"She is already dead." He murmured the words so low, I could barely hear them. "Did my brother not tell you that when Erzsébet was a child, even her parents believed her dead? She fell into a paroxysm, at her aunt's house, and could not be wakened. She lay in a coffin in the chapel for three days, as is our custom. When she did not begin to stiffen, or mortify, the witch was called to examine her. I escorted Zsuzsanna to the coffin myself."

I looked around the hall, and fancied Dee was watching me, though he was nodding to the count.

"I have known soldiers knocked insensible, and then recover," I said. "Also a child, fallen under the ice."

"Zsuzsanna breathed into her mouth thrice, then drew her sharpened nail across the child's chest. She bled, and cried out, a mew like a newborn kitten."

I shivered a little at his tale. "Go on."

"From that day, the witch started feeding the girl the potions to strengthen her. Slowly she woke, like a bear from hibernation. The local people called it a miracle. But then they would visit friends in distant villages whenever the Lady Erzsébet visited the castle."

I became aware that there were glances from the other lords now, and to my surprise, Lord Miklós smiled at me, and pressed my arm above my elbow. "And soon the lady will be well, and will give the castle hearty sons," he said loudly.

His fingers dug in more than I liked. I turned my face so that the count and his captains could see my smile. "Yes, many sons."

He held back as the count and his escort left, talking loudly down the stairs.

"And then," he whispered to me, "it would be better if the dead are banished to the grave."

Chapter 48

JACK'S FIRST THOUGHT WAS THAT SHE WAS BEING SUFFO-cated by something pressed against her face. She swatted at it, and dragged a breath into her lungs. Her hand seemed heavy, and fell back.

"Jack!" The voice sounded familiar, but strained. She opened her eyes a little, seeing Felix's face through her lashes.

She tried to speak but her tongue rolled in her mouth, and she only managed a faint sound.

He lifted her head and shoulders off the ground, and someone took her legs. She was carried to a sofa in the living room by the two men.

Sadie! her mind tried to scream, but all she could manage was a moan.

"It's all OK. Hear me, Jack? Everything is OK." His eyes warned her to be quiet.

"Need help in here!" The shout came from the study, with urgency in it. The paramedic—she registered that's what he was—climbed to his feet, and went to look. He returned, shaking his head to Felix.

Oh God, Sadie. Jack shut her eyes and shivered. She felt two large, warm hands enclose hers. *Please, please be alive.*

Shouts from the police announced the arrival of "Mike," whoever he was, and a lot of activity seemed to be centered on the study.

"Please . . ." she managed to whisper. "See what's . . ."

He nodded, exchanged a glance with the paramedic, and

walked from the room. She felt as if she was counting while he was away, one breath, two breaths. The paramedic put an oxygen mask over her face, a plastic smell. Three breaths, four.

"You're a bit shocked. Do you remember anything?" The man pressed a stethoscope to her chest.

She shook her head, one hand clutching the mask.

Felix's face was softer, more relaxed when he returned. "It's the dog. They are doing their best, he's taken a few breaths. The other paramedic just jump-started his heart."

"Ches?" she mumbled through the plastic.

He squeezed her hand. "He seems to be the worst off. Everyone else seems fine. Except you." He gazed into her eyes for a moment. "Everyone." He looked toward the paramedic. "How's she doing?"

Jack felt strong enough to push the mask away. "I'm OK."

"So, what happened?" The paramedic looked into her eyes with a light, one side, then the other.

"I don't know." It seemed the easiest answer. "I just passed out. Felix, you too?"

Felix shrugged, then sat beside her on the sofa, and put his arm around her. "The police burst in, looking for that missing girl. The next thing I knew, I was waking up on the floor."

She leaned her head against him for a moment. "I can't think why anyone would believe we could be involved in anything illegal."

Felix looked across her and she turned to the doorway, to see a police officer with a bruise on his face.

"We're off to the vet's, sir, Mike thinks he's looking better. He's an ex–dog handler, you can trust his judgment. We were thinking, maybe there was some sort of electrical event, and it hit the dog harder because he is smaller."

Jack stumbled over her words for a moment. "Why . . . why would anyone think we would be involved in this missing-child case?"

"A member of the public reported your car, miss. They said a girl matching Sadie Williams's description was on the back-seat."

Jack made an effort to sit up, but Felix's arm was heavy around her shoulders, pressing her against his side. "But Felix is working for the police on a similar case," she managed.

"So Professor Guichard told me, but we have to follow up all the tips, even the strange ones. I have to get my team checked out. One of them fell down some stairs when he passed out, and one of my female officers had to be resuscitated, like yourself."

"I did?" Jack was surprised, and glanced up at Felix.

"I thought you were dead," he said. "You wouldn't breathe by yourself for ages. If it wasn't for the sergeant here . . ." His voice failed.

"I didn't realize. Thank you." She managed a smile at the officer, who touched a finger to the bruised side of his head.

"Glad we could help. But I will be requesting a full electrical survey of your property. You haven't had anything like this happen before, Professor?"

"No, nothing. Could it have been some sort of lightning strike?"

"Possibly. Anyway, since the ambulance is already here we'll get Ms. Hammond down to the hospital for a check-up."

"No. I'm feeling better, and I really hate hospitals." She injected as much firmness into her wavering voice as she could. Wherever Sadie was, she needed Jack on her trail as quickly as possible.

"It looks like you hit your head."

"That was before—I crashed my car a few days ago." She managed a smile, though it was crooked. "I'm having a terrible week." The smile faded. "And Ches, my dog, I need to talk to the vet."

. . .

Every minute wasted, until they could start looking for Sadie, was agony for Jack. She needed to convince the police that they were mistaken about her abducting a child. She needed to see her dog, which had been placed on a drip and sedated at the vet's. More than anything, she needed to stop shaking inside from the cold. She could see Felix staring at her, feel the strength of his hand under her elbow steadying her at the veterinary surgery. She couldn't shake the feeling that the encounter with the witch had moved her closer to death.

She curled up in the front seat of his car, and let herself slump back. He leaned over to strap her into the seat, and then she was asleep.

She woke into a cocoon of warmth, and the smell of beeswax. For a moment, she thought she was still dreaming, but when she opened her eyes, the familiar face of Charley was hovering over her, smiling.

"Good morning."

"Morning? Where am I?" Her eyes took in the newly drawn symbols on the ceiling, the candles burning in holders around the bed.

"Felix's house, upstairs. It's great, he's been working on the sigils. He's also cooked up a bucket of the decoction, and come up with a magical formula to make it work better. I like him."

"You do?" Jack tried moving her limbs; some of the stiffness had melted away in the warmth. The events of the last days filtered into her brain. "How did you get here?"

"My number was on your phone. He called me."

Jack relaxed back into the pillow. "How's Maggie?"

Charley's smile faltered a little. "She's staying in the hospital. She wasn't badly hurt in the crash. She's still concussed, and she's got spectacular bruises from her seat belt. It's nothing too serious, but they are keeping an eye on her. She's sixty-one, you know."

Jack pushed herself up onto her elbows, one of which buckled. "Ow."

Charley managed a small smile. "Maggie's nosy about Felix, I can tell you."

Jack looked around the room, realizing she was in her underwear. "Where are my clothes?"

"I think Felix put them in the wash. I brought you some clothes from the cottage—the place stinks of gas. I left the windows open at the back. But I was upset at the state of it. I mean, it was my childhood home, too." She handed Jack some clothes from a bag on the floor. "So, tell me so I can tell Mum, because you know she'll interrogate me. How did you end up in Felix's bed. I mean, are you . . . ?"

"No! I hardly know him." At Charley's raised eyebrow, Jack winced. "Oh God. He put me to bed, didn't he?"

"I bet you wish you weren't wearing your oldest underwear."

It was strange, but the thought had occurred to her, among fears that she had appeared pathetic. She could feel her face heat up, even as she dressed. "I only have old underwear," she muttered to herself. "Where is he, anyway?"

"Ah. That's the other thing he thought you wouldn't like." Charley held out a mug of the foul-smelling decoction.

"What?" She sipped it, grimacing. It was weaker than she was used to, but the proportions were about right. She could feel the energy creeping back.

"He's downstairs talking to the Inquisition."

Jack brushed past Felix in the hallway, where he was waiting for her, and walked straight up to the inquisitor. "Where is Sadie?"

"I don't know." The man stared back with calm indifference. "But she is a captive of the woman I intend to destroy."

"Jack . . ." Felix tried to get her attention, but she waved him away.

"If we help you locate Sadie you'll kill her."

"I swear I will not."

She looked from one blue eye to the other, trying to read him. But he seemed icily sincere.

"But you don't care much, either way," she said.

His face softened a tiny bit, around the eyes. "I do not blame the child for what she was forced to become."

"Which is?"

His gaze on her face became more intense, as he studied her. "A revenant. A corpse that has clung to its soul, by sorcery." She stared back. *He has no idea I'm a "revenant" too.*

"Right. Great. Don't tell him anything, Felix, just chuck him out."

Felix walked up behind her. "Just listen to him. Then, if you want to send him packing, we will."

She sat on the end of the leather sofa. "I want Charley to hear this."

"The less people we involve—" the inquisitor started, but Charley sat next to Jack, leaning on her.

"Well?" Charley's voice was as calm and cool as Maggie's would have been. "Let's hear it."

McNamara walked to the fireplace, and stood staring into it for a moment. "You understand what Dee was trying to accomplish when he traveled to Hungary?"

Felix leaned against a sideboard, and answered. "I have been translating a journal that Edward Kelley kept in 1585. He was trying to assist King Istvan Báthory's niece."

"And you understand that she was the person we know as Elizabeth Báthory, in the West?"

"So?" ventured Jack. A memory of some lurid old vampire legend trickled down the back wall of her memory. "Wasn't she a myth?"

"She was tried and convicted of the torture and killing of up to eighty girls." McNamara spoke the uncompromising facts as if they were a weather report. "She was then walled up in a tower in her own castle because they could not execute a member of the royal family."

Jack risked a glance at Felix, who was standing with his head bowed. "What has this got to do with us?"

"The sigils that Dee created did extend her natural life. But they affected her behavior and she became aggressive. Dangerous."

"But she was . . . a borrowed timer?" Charley's voice was incredulous. She squeezed Jack's hand.

"Revenants cling to life, but they die within a few years, a couple of decades at most," McNamara said. "But she found a way to extend her life through the ingestion of human blood. Over the years, it became like a drug to her. The Vatican followed the case through an inquisitor named Father Konrad von Schönborn. He hunted the abomination until his death."

"Why is blood like a drug?" asked Jack.

McNamara's gaze flicked over her for a second. "It fills these creatures with the energy of the living donor. Báthory employed sorcerers to do more research. She found that exsanguinating other revenants and consuming their enchanted blood would extend her existence even further."

Felix looked at Jack. "That's what Bachmeier did to McNamara's sister. She consumed her blood. All of it. That's why he's here."

The realization trickled into Jack. "Oh my God, she's going to kill Sadie, like Elizabeth Báthory."

"Not exactly," McNamara spoke quietly. "She's going to kill Sadie because she *is* Elizabeth Báthory."

Chapter 49

*One spell witches use to confound mortal men is the
charm of appearing more alluring and irresistible
than any human woman. Her voice is that of a
siren, her body that of a courtesan, and she will
seduce innocent men. She is to be feared, and I pray
for freedom from such abominations and succubi.*

—EDWARD KELLEY
Handwritten epigraph in John Dee, *Propaedeumata
Aphoristica* (1558–68)
Ashmolean Museum

D EE BENT OVER HIS CONJURATIONS, WRITTEN IN FAIR
Latin upon squares of vellum that the count had provided. The room was fugged with smoke and incense,
and my master was experimenting with different combinations of
rare gums and woods. I coughed a few times before he looked up.

"I think I will get some air," I said, anxious to get away from
the atmosphere the constant guards provided—a reminder that
if we failed, our lives were forfeit. "If you can spare me."

"Go, go." He waved a hand toward me. "While you do so,
think of the angelic exhortations, will you, Edward? We need
to complete those . . ." He bent back over his books.

I walked past the guards to the corridor and out into the great
hall, already being set up for the evening meal. A shouting from
without, a female voice, called my curious nature to the door.

A woman, heavyset but still young, was pleading with one of the captains of the guard. I couldn't understand a word, but the way she cradled one arm in the other suggested a child. She pointed at the castle, tears running down her face, and shouted to men passing by.

Beside the main doors, I saw one of the men who had kidnapped us, a young noble. I approached him, keeping my head high.

"You, sirrah," I called in Latin, perhaps a little arrogantly, for he turned and scowled at me. Then his face cleared as he saw who it was. I pointed at the door, where the wailing was still audible. "Why does the woman cry so?"

He shrugged, but his feet shuffled, giving away his disquiet. "She seeks her daughter, a girl working in the kitchens."

I bethought myself of the child in the coffin. "Where is the maid?"

He half turned, his shoulders hunched away from me. "Who knows or cares? The vassals serve in any way they are commanded. Perhaps she is working." He shot another sly look around, maybe to see if we were overheard. "I ask no questions. It is safer."

"The children here seem so weak," I ventured, and we listened to more shouted voices outside. Some were women's, but a few were angry men's.

"This is a cursed land," the young man whispered to me. "I come from the north, at Szatmár, and there we value our villeins, our vassals, as the source of our wealth and our armies. If they prosper, we prosper; if they starve, we starve."

"But here?" I prompted.

"Here hags are ennobled and we, who have the blood of kings in our veins, are reduced to the service of women." He spat the last word at me, and I saw his distaste for serving the countess.

"Mayhap when the lady is healed . . ."

He regarded me with a look of wisdom beyond his years. "Here, the common people speak of monsters who live beyond the grave, feasting on the flesh of children, banishing God and his angels to the north. Evil spirits that take the form of wolves and hares and succubi."

I shuddered, having some experience of these demons in human—female—form. "Let God keep you and guide you," I said, "and grant that we both are able to go north."

He smiled without mirth. "God may direct me there, and I pray that he does. But you, sir, are guided by Satan himself, if you create an undead queen for these lands."

Chapter 50

SADIE CROUCHED ON A TILED FLOOR, GAGGING AND CHOK-
ing. The woman had drawn a few sigils around her, but
it wasn't enough, and the taste of regurgitated cider and
burger kept rising into her mouth.

Her kidnapper was bent over the center of the building,
which was lined with scaffolding draped in plastic sheeting.

"Where are we?" Sadie asked, straining her head up. She
tugged at plastic cable ties on her wrists, which were locked to
more ties restraining her ankles. She had spoken before, but the
woman paid no attention to her, just carried on working. It was
a painful position to be hunched in for hours, and Sadie tried to
keep her voice level. "I said, where are we?"

"St. Francis's hospital." She sounded foreign, and uninterested in Sadie. "They are developing it into apartments."

"Oh." Sadie pulled her head up to see over the back of a
wooden seat—a pew, she realized. There were stained-glass
windows at the far end of the building, but it was too dark to see
the design. "But this looks like a church."

"Yes, the hospital chapel. It is hallowed ground."

Sadie hunched back down, shaking with cold. She could see,
under the few rows of pews that remained, that the center of the
building had been cleared, and the woman was drawing on the
floor.

"I could help draw the sigils," she offered. Anything to get
out of this position, she thought. "I've got a steady hand."

For many seconds, she thought the woman wasn't going to answer, but then she replied, "These are different symbols."

"Really?" She tried to keep her voice level, even as she tugged at her bonds. The skin gave way at the back of her wrist and started to bleed.

The click of heels on the terra-cotta tiles meant the woman was moving—and getting closer.

"Don't struggle. I will make you more comfortable." The woman brought out a small blade, cutting the connection between the ties. She released all but the ones tying her wrists together. She half carried Sadie from behind the pews, while the blood throbbed its way back into her ankles. "Here. Sit down."

In the middle of an area that had been swept clear was a small office chair, in a circle of familiar sigils. Sadie sat in it, the nausea and weakness fading, and sneaked a glance around the walls. The woman's face twitched into a smile.

"You would die outside the building," she said. "Here. Drink." She twisted the top off a plastic bottle of water, and placed it in the teenager's linked hands. Sadie gulped at the cool water, realizing she hadn't drunk anything since breakfast, and the light was waning outside. She looked around at the floor. The chair sat within a bigger circle, made up of unfamiliar symbols. Outside that were four more circles, each about five or six feet across, filled with shapes and letters. The woman was sorting through a bag, pulling out what looked like sticks. She was pushing them into round bases before Sadie realized what they were.

"Black candles?"

"The dried roots make them look black." The woman started twisting bunches of dried twigs together. "The candles will summon. They are all different."

Sadie looked down at the trickle on the side of her hand. Blood was seeping from under the cable tie. She raised her wrist to lick it off, but the woman snapped at her.

"Don't!" She stood up, and walked toward Sadie. It was difficult to work out how old she was, because aspects of her kept shifting in appearance. One part of Sadie's brain put her at around Felix's age but another part was registering something grotesque and deformed about her. Her shoulders were at unequal heights, her neck projected forward from a hump on her back, her hair was so wispy Sadie could see—or imagine—brown spots on her scalp. Yet the moment she spoke, Sadie could only see a kind of beauty. Her eyes were the one thing that remained the same, so light blue they were almost white orbs.

The woman reached out long hands—twisted, bulbous claws one second, then manicured pianist's fingers the next—and took Sadie's wrist. Her skin was as cold as the ground had been. She inspected Sadie with care, lifting her arms with cold fingertips to look all around the restraints. She took the small blade from her pocket again and snipped the last of the cable ties. Then she licked her top lip, smiled slightly and bent her head. She fastened her mouth over the oozing skin, and bit deep into the bleeding wound.

Chapter 51

*As the countess grows weaker, so the witch works
harder to keep her alive. Zsófia spoke nothing to me
after her wicked enchantment, but secretly smiles in
a mocking way when she sees me. She did come to us
to identify an herb that soldiers had brought from
Araby, hoping it will sustain her mistress, but it was
common red root, and of no assistance. I thought her
love for the countess was that of a sister, or even a
mother, but when I saw them together by the fire,
awaiting his lordship's return from hunting, I saw
such caresses and kisses that a man might give a maid.
I long for the simplicity of home, and civilization.*

—EDWARD KELLEY
  16 December 1585
  Csejte Castle

THAT EVENING, DEE AND I HAD DRAWN THE LAST OF THE
sigils on the ceiling and floor of the solar, and Dee was
writing the ritual. A great banging on the locked main
doors brought torches and soldiers to the outer wall. There was
a party of men on horses, traveling south.

We left the room under guard to keep people out. We didn't
trust anyone, least of all the witch, or Lord Miklós, who seemed
to be working against us. The chiming of the angel in my head

had diminshed to a soft hum, like distant singing. We looked out from the hall doorway, across the inner yard.

The count, in his less formal dolman and with his head uncovered, walked to the doorway to speak with the newcomers.

"Father Konrad." His voice was hard with suspicion. "You take many risks riding in these hills."

"God keeps us safe," Konrad answered. "I must ask, however, if you can give us a place to rest, and to water and bait our horses. We head for Rome."

It was an unspoken rule, perhaps one that preceded Christianity, that no traveler be denied succor. Yet, for a long moment, I thought Nádasdy would refuse.

"Perhaps for one night," he conceded. "But I have troops arriving at any hour, and you must be away at daybreak." He beckoned to grooms, who took the bridles of some of the horses.

"You are very kind." Konrad dismounted, and bowed deep to Lord Miklós, who had followed Nádasdy. "I would also speak with the king's brother, if he has time."

Miklós strode forward.

"In private, my lord?" Konrad asked.

"There is little privacy in a garrison." Nádasdy's voice was harsh.

"Then I shall deliver your brother's message before witnesses, Lord Miklós Báthory of Somlyó. His Majesty King Istvan hopes you are filled with your customary good health. He hopes and prays you recall your last conversation with your king, and begs you to offer my Lord Nádasdy all assistance. He bids me give you this note." He turned to us, standing apart, and bowed his head. "I must greet you also, Doctor Dee and Master Kelley. I am surprised to see you here, and hope you are well?"

"Well, indeed, Reichsritter von Schönborn." Dee was calm. "We are also guests at Csejte."

"Perhaps, if your visit is ending, we can offer you an escort from the castle."

Dee shook his head. "Our families await us in Krakow, and we wish only to return there."

Konrad looked at me, and I fancied he knew something of what we were trying to do.

The count beckoned to his captains. "Secure the priest's men and lock the main gates." He turned to us. "You have much to do tomorrow. No doubt you will wish to rest."

Dismissed, we returned to our quarters.

We heard no more until the morning, when a guard came to get us.

"The priest wishes to speak with you," he barked at us, in execrable German.

Unlike previous audiences on the ground floor, he escorted us through the chapel and unlocked the door I had found in my explorations. Far from leading to a chamber, it came out onto steep stairs, spiraling down under the fortress. Torches lit the steps, stinking the air with burning tallow, and it was with relief that we arrived in a cavern hacked out of the bedrock beneath the castle.

As my eyes took in rough stone, with iron bars and chains bolted to the walls, I realized we were in some sort of dungeon. My throat contracted, choking back any words to Dee. He looked at me, then around the cave.

It was part man-made, with some mortared walls. Along one side were a number of small cages, with several prisoners in each. Clean-shaven men, they bore the marks of battle upon them, and I recognized their uniforms as those of Konrad's guards. Some were wounded, it appeared, bloodstained and lying in filthy straw. At one end, as assured as if he stood before the king, was the tall figure of Konrad, crammed into a space barely two yards wide. His robes were torn, a bruise darkened one side of his face and a scrap of linen was tied around one hand.

"Doctor Dee," he said, "and Master Kelley. I am glad to see you are well. We—the king and I—were concerned for your safety. As you see, Lord Nádasdy has concerns about the security of his citadel and has confined us. Some of my men resisted."

"Father Konrad." Dee bowed, equally polite. "I am sorry to see you in this condition. May we petition his lordship for your release?"

"The Lord that I petition watches over me, even here. But I would be grateful for anything that will ease the suffering of my men, who are guilty of nothing more than loyalty to me and to the office I represent."

A clattering of boots on the stairs was followed by Lord Nádasdy and his personal guards.

"Father Konrad," he said. "I'm afraid you must be detained until my wife's treatment is complete." He turned to Dee and me. "Father Konrad, who is driven by allegiance to the Pope, attempted to intervene in your work."

"And the Pope will be disappointed that his representative was attacked in such a fashion while asking for hospitality." Konrad's voice was calm.

Nádasdy's lips thinned in a smile. "In these lands, a party of men demanding ingress to my stronghold, with weapons drawn, is not considered worthy of hospitality." He shrugged. "We are a small castle with a modest garrison, not forty leagues from the Sultan's occupancy. We have to be cautious."

Konrad bowed. "Then I beg your forgiveness for rousing your people into such misguided loyalty. We are here on a mission of peace, so perhaps my men may be more comfortable? I ask as one commander to another."

Nádasdy looked at Dee. "Well, Doctor? He is your enemy, not mine."

Dee shook his head. "He is no enemy of mine, he is doing his duty as he sees it."

"Very well. Your men will remain confined, but I will send down food and healers. We can make them more comfortable."

"May we stay and consult with Father Konrad? He may have insights that can assist us." Dee smiled at Nádasdy, who glared back.

"If you wish. But he stays caged."

Chapter 52

JACK CALLED THE VET, BUT THE DOG STILL HADN'T REGAINED consciousness. She held her coffee in both hands, trying to capture some of the warmth, but could feel the cold starting to slow her down. She felt helpless, not a comfortable feeling. She jumped when Charley touched her shoulder.

"I'm going to have to go. Mum's ready to go home. She's got to rest, got to take it easy."

"Don't tell her what's going on. Say we're both at Felix's—"

"She's not stupid, Jack. She'll work out I'm lying." She lifted a package in a large shopping bag onto the table. "I brought this, you might need it."

"What is it?"

"The sword. You know . . ."

Jack did know. It was one of the items Maggie had inherited from her grandmother, along with the medals and papers. She unrolled the plastic, revealing the heavy scabbard, wound around with a cloth that started to crumble as she touched it.

"I can hardly lift it."

Charley boosted herself on her hands to sit on the end of the table. "Do you remember looking at this when we were kids? Mum went mad, said it was worth a fortune. She said it was inscribed with defensive charms."

Jack slid the first few inches of the blade out of its sheath. It was protected by a layer of grease, the spine heavy and gray, each side of the blade engraved with ornate letters. "Do you think this is Dee's or Kelley's too?"

Charley shrugged, and finished unwinding the cloth. "Even if it isn't, it's heavy enough to hurt someone. It probably needs polishing up."

"Sharpening, more like." The edge was dull, and there were patches of rust creeping along despite the grease. "So now we have to fight." A small part of her was angry enough to relish the thought. She pulled the sword right out and held it in both hands. It thrummed with some strange energy. "Maggie could have told us about the Inquisition."

"Yes, she could. But when did you ever want to know about our world?"

"I think I would have wanted to know that a branch of the Vatican had been formed to exterminate all borrowed timers."

"Maybe she didn't know that." Charley crossed her feet. "You know she loves you like a daughter. She's just a bit over-protective."

"But that's just it. She's not my mother. She took me because she could use me to save you. The rest . . ." The words crowded up in her throat, and caught. "I lost my family, everything." She swung the sword gently from side to side.

Charley shrugged. "You know you're being unreasonable, don't you? You would have been dead. Is that how you feel about Sadie? Just good for spare parts?"

"No, I . . ." She thought about it for a long moment. "She was going to choke to death because of a stupid, pointless mistake. I couldn't just leave her there to die."

Charley bit her lip, as if trying to stop herself saying something. "They are trying to work out where Sadie is. Mac and Felix. They've come up with some ideas."

Jack put the sword down on the table, drank her coffee and turned her back on Charley. The last leaves of a Virginia creeper clung in the lee of the window, in shades of scarlet and flame.

"Mac? We're on nickname terms with McNamara now?"

"He's OK, if you like that buttoned up, starched sort." Charley slid off the table. "Anyway, he's got a lot more contacts than we have; he has records of these rituals going back *centuries*. He thinks they would be looking for a church or graveyard on consecrated ground."

"So you believe that the original Countess Elizabeth Báthory is on the loose?"

"I've seen some pretty convincing evidence. You need to find this church."

"People believe all that hallowed-ground stuff, even now?" Jack swiveled to face her.

Charley smiled. "Well, they think she does. The previous exsanguinations all took place in derelict or unused churches."

"So Sadie could already be dead." Jack let the thought that had been chilling her hang in the air.

"It takes time to set up the ritual. Felix thinks she will wait until tonight. We need you on board."

Charley walked over and hugged her. She smelled like some sort of exotic flower, and looked like a fifteen-year-old, but she could be as forceful as her mother.

Jack held her, shutting her eyes for a moment. "I'm there. I'm just worried sick."

"Well, let Felix and Mac help you." Charley grabbed her coat and waved as she walked out into the hall. "See you later."

Jack took a deep breath before finding the men.

"What have you found out?" She addressed herself to Felix, still suspicious of McNamara and his crazy claims.

"I've got the police files of the last two women who died in this blood ritual," he answered, "and details of the ceremonial sites. Both old churches, one almost derelict, one used for occasional funerals." He waved at the other man, who hadn't looked up. "Mac is looking at similar unused churches and chapels in our area."

The man tapped a piece of paper and looked at her. "These are the sigils drawn at my sister's death site. I thought, as a witch, you could offer us your thoughts."

She took the paper, but looked at Felix. "I'm not really a witch."

McNamara frowned at her. "But you created a revenant, one of the hardest magics to perform."

"Yes, but I had Maggie's help."

Jack and Felix bent their heads over the paper.

"What are these?" Jack felt uneasy at the sight of the circles of figures, but couldn't work out why. They weren't familiar.

Felix clicked a button on his laptop. "I've studied ritual symbols and arrangements," he said, then added, "especially by Dee." He opened one file after another, stacking them up on the screen. "These are summoning circles. You can see the similarity."

"Summoning what?"

"Angels, demons, spirits."

She sat back, looking at the bent head of the inquisitor, but he appeared absorbed in his laptop. "Do you believe all this religious stuff?" she murmured to Felix.

"How about thinking of it in a slightly different way? All matter is made of atoms, in turn made of subatomic particles, right?"

She shrugged. "I suppose so. Electrons and so on."

"Well, electrons and protons are all made of energy. The whole universe boils down to energy fields all reacting to one another."

"O . . . K." Jack felt a bit out of her depth, but was prepared to go a little further.

"And your actions are all composed of energy transferred and moved around. So are your thoughts."

She stretched back in the seat, looking at his profile as he lectured. "Go on."

"Well, suppose a million people all think the same thing at the same time. Don't you feel on some level that that's going to leave an impression on an energy field?"

She hadn't thought of it before, but it seemed reasonable. "So . . . the belief of millions of people can, what . . . create God?"

"That's one way of looking at it. And if millions of people have created that kind of construct, maybe it's possible for someone to summon that up, or at least a tiny part of it."

She thought about it. "So, what you are saying is, since millions of people have believed in angels and demons for thousands of years, they must exist somewhere?"

"*Might* exist somewhere. Dee thought they did, but not because people believed. Because God believed. I suspect that's how magic works, if it does."

"I've always thought of it as math."

He lifted an eyebrow and smiled. "Math?"

"Well, how likely is it that a draft will sneak in and shut that door?"

He considered the still door, partly open. "I don't know, unlikely but possible?"

Jack concentrated, running through the intention in her mind, building, building, then . . . there, the right mind-set. A shiver ran down her spine and something snapped in her head.

The door slammed with enough force to lift the edges of papers on the desk.

"How . . . ?" Felix looked around at the room. "When we have Sadie back, you are going to have to explain that to me."

Jack smiled at his confusion, and widened the smile at the inquisitor's frown. "Easier than angels and demons, anyway."

Jack turned back to the laptop and tapped the screen with

one finger. "And these circles were used to try to summon them."

"So, what do our circles summon?" She rubbed her aching chest.

He tightened his lips, flicking a glance at McNamara. "They seem to be similar to the ones Dee used in necromancy, to bind the soul back to its body."

"That's what Maggie said. She used that booklet of Dee's."

"Except that it was really a diary, by Kelley. He was much more willing to share the darker aspects of sorcery than Dee."

"Sorcery." She looked at her hands, sadness settling on her like dust. "Something murky and unnatural." *My whole existence.* "What did McNamara call it?" She glanced over at the inquisitor and dropped her voice. "An abomination."

Felix put his hand over hers, warming her fingers. "I'm not religious, Jack. But I believe there's something out there. Maybe God is the totality of all human belief. And I'm sure borrowed timers' souls are as valid as anyone else's."

"And you're going along with his belief that this is Elizabeth Báthory—the actual four-hundred-year-old serial killer?"

"He's told me things about these people, plural, Jack. Women who drink the blood of dozens, maybe hundreds, of young girls to stay healthy, and every few years create a borrowed timer so they can exsanguinate them."

"So, how come we haven't heard of them before?"

Felix rubbed her hand between his. "You're still cold."

Her eyes warned him that McNamara was in earshot. "How many of these things are there?"

The inquisitor answered from behind her. "We know of sixteen. Most are less than a hundred years old, but several are much older."

"Name one," Jack scoffed.

"Catalina de los Ríos y Lisperguer." McNamara drew a line

in his notes. "Born at the beginning of the seventeenth century. She was turned into a revenant as a child. She was last heard of running a children's orphanage in Romania in 1989. She got away, that time, but we have a team tracking her."

"What?" Jack looked at Felix. "Really?"

Felix smiled sadly. "Mac showed me some of the files, some of the photographs. They called her La Quintrala; she murdered her tenants, as much from her sadistic sexual needs as the blood."

McNamara spoke in his quiet voice. "There was also de Borgomanero, back in the thirteen hundreds, in Italy. She was finally killed by the leader of my order, Father Konrad von Schönborn, two hundred years later. There was a Russian who tortured young servant girls, like Báthory. They called her Saltychikha. Another, a male, was created during the Second World War in Algeria—"

"OK, I get it." She turned to Felix. "And you believe all this, just because he told you? He's the enemy, the fucking Inquisition!"

McNamara coughed to get their attention and Felix dropped her hand.

"I've found two churches that stand out," the inquisitor said. "One is being restored and is vacant on weekends. The other is part of an old mental hospital called St. Francis's, which is being converted into flats. It, too, will be vacant today. I think it is the more likely of the two."

Jack turned, trying not to stagger, her whole body heavy with cold. "Let's go, then."

McNamara also stood, and stepped close enough for her to have to tilt her head back to look up at him. "You should stay here. You will slow us down." He turned to Felix. "Your knowledge of Dee may be helpful. But the fiend is powerful and deadly, so we cannot be distracted."

Jack looked at Felix, seeing uncertainty there.

"You *are* tired," he said. "You could leave us to check them out. She may not be at either location." Then he half smiled, as if he knew what she was going to say.

She took a deep breath. "You need me because I know more about borrowed time than either of you. I may not be a witch, but I'm your secret weapon."

Chapter 53

Being sound of body and mind, I bequeath all my
English goods to my sister-in-law for the sustenance
of her sons, my nephews. I leave my best doublet to
her eldest son, Rychard Kelley, and the French boots
in my luggage to her son Robert Kelley. Any monies
and belongings I hold in foreign lands, I leave to
my wife, Jane Kelley, that she might educate and
care for her children, Eliza and John. My personal
jewelery I leave to Mistress Jane Dee in brotherly
love, and if he should survive, my books and journals
to Doctor John Dee, my friend and master. If he
does not, I pray that his end, as mine, is swift and
that God smiles upon us with forgiveness.

—THE WILL OF EDWARD KELLEY
   Dated 16 or 17 December 1585
   Csejte Castle, Transylvania

WE WAITED UNTIL THE COUNT HAD LEFT THE DUNgeon, then Konrad spoke.

"Tell me you have not done it," he asked urgently. "The sorcery."

"We have not, yet," I answered. "But we have little choice but to help the countess, unless we seek our own deaths."

"You condemn her soul, and yours, to endless damnation if you help her."

Dee looked at me, speaking fast before anyone came within earshot. "We believe that we have been brought here to save the countess, for some reason we cannot divine but believe to be innocent. We have been visited by angels, indeed, they brought us here."

Konrad turned to me. "I beg you, Master Kelley, as one I know in his heart to be a good Catholic. Stop your master from being persuaded by these delusions. This is the work of demons."

I stared at him. He had the authority of a prince, as well as that of a papal emissary. "My lord, I am sure we are guided by creatures of God." Even as I said the word, my doubts must have shaped my brow.

"Angels?" He did not mock, or scoff, but a look of grief came over his features. "I should have told you before, I know . . ." He paused, as if gathering his authority around himself, and beckoned us closer.

Dee leaned in, and dropped his voice. "We are gravely afflicted by doubts and concerns, my lord. If you can advise us, without prejudice or agenda . . ."

"Have you ever heard of the Contessa de Borgomanero?" He hunched his shoulders against the cold and looked at the guards, who were straining to listen.

We looked at each other, as he spoke again. "She, Lady Adeliza, was born sickly, but she was her mother's only child, and they coddled her. They tried every remedy they knew to strengthen her."

Konrad stared into my eyes, his own almost black in the low light, as if trying to divine my response. "What did they do, Father?" I whispered.

"They owned a villa in Velletri, near Rome, where an old stone tablet was carved over the entrance to the atrium. This described a ritual, which was used to save a dying landowner who was struck by falling masonry during an earthquake." He looked at the guards, who were muttering to one another. "The ritual included symbols, and these were inscribed within each room. They realized the child prospered within these chambers, but sickened when she left them. They had jewelery made that covered the child in the sigils, and she began to thrive and grow."

"Do we have any record of these shapes?" I said.

"We do not, as the villa was destroyed by the local people. The plaques were crushed to rubble, and thrown in the river."

"Why?" I noticed the guards' arguments growing stronger, and saw hands caressing sword hilts.

"When she grew to womanhood, she inherited her parents' lands, and young men went to court her. She welcomed in the youngest lovers and took them to her bed, and they were never seen again."

We looked at each other. "What happened to them?" Dee asked.

"For years, no one knew. After dozens of young men had disappeared, the body of a youth washed up on the shore of the lake. His body was completely white, drained of blood, and his arms and neck were cut, as if he'd been bled by a butcher. That is when the locals raised a force against the *strega*, the witch, as they called her. They stormed her lakeside retreat, but she was already gone."

"How is this relevant to us?" asked Dee, his mouth tight with impatience.

"I have seen her." Konrad sighed, his hands resting on the bars. "I was a young man, traveling with my father and elder brother to Venice, when we stopped at an inn for wine, and to shelter from the heat of the afternoon. My companions paused to talk to other travelers, but I was curious about the sound of singing from the back of the inn. A beautiful woman was resting in a courtyard with a young minstrel. The woman spoke to me, and plied me with wine. After a while, I realized we were no longer attended by her servants, and after that, we were in her room, although I had no memory of how we came there. We passed the afternoon in the tryst, and I found myself growing languid and weak after my labors. When she caressed me with a dagger, I found I could not resist, or stop her from cutting into my arm and lapping at the blood like a cat. Indeed," he said, looking away for a moment, "never have I felt such erotic pleasure." He shook himself, as if throwing off the spell his words were weaving. "My father and brother beat down the door, and found me dazed and bleeding. They stanched my wound." He pulled up his wide, velvet sleeve, to show a linen bandage around his forearm, the marks of old blood brown upon it. "It has never healed."

"What happened to her?"

"We questioned the innkeeper, but he knew her only as Lady Adeliza and said she visited the place once or twice a year on her way from Venice. He said some of the servants who were at the inn before he was recalled her visiting for many years, as long as they could remember, although she remained youthful-looking." He pulled his sleeve down, wincing a little. "The wound festers. It has been touched by death."

Dee nudged me, and I looked to see Lord Miklós stepping off the lowest stair and barking an order that rang through the dungeon.

"It is time," he snapped at us.

Dee turned to Konrad, his voice urgent. "My lord, what was the nature of this fiend, this witch?"

"The sorcery had turned her into a *morturi masticantes*. She is no longer subject to mortal death through age, but sustains her life with the blood of others." He grasped Dee's coat through the iron bars that confined him. "Master Dee, you must not perform this sorcery. You do not know what you will create, a monster that cannot die but will prey upon children. Her dying body will be animated by a demonic being."

A guard pulled me away, and I staggered. Konrad called after us, as we were manhandled onto the stairs. "You will create a creature without a soul, without remorse. I have hunted the contessa all my adult life, and still she lives."

Dee called back to Konrad, even as he was bundled up the stairs. "No one is immortal."

Only I caught Konrad's shouted response. "When I met her, Adeliza de Borgomanero was more than two hundred years old."

Chapter 54

SADIE WOKE FEELING COLD AND WEAK, CRAMPED INTO A huddle on the floor. The chapel was now lit by candles, the windows black. The woman looked younger.

"Can I have some more of that water?" Sadie's voice was croaky.

The woman lifted her head from the trance she was in, and carried a bottle over. Sadie took it in her good hand, cradling the purpled bite against her. It took some fumbling to get the top off, but a long drink refreshed her a little.

"Who are you?" She looked at the woman, now walking between the various circles.

"I am a countess. In this century there is no respect for that. But once I had a name of great honor and antiquity."

"Why did you bring me here?" She tried to keep her voice level.

"You are here to rejuvenate me. And you are here to be released."

Sadie stood, dizziness making her sway. She inched to the edge of the circle, but even half a foot over the edge started the retching. She spat a mouthful of watery bile onto the floor.

"People will come and stop you," she managed to say, choking. "Jack will come for me."

"The witch?" The countess laughed, her voice warmer than it had been. "Zsuzsanna, Zsófia, all that tribe can do is serve us, they cannot destroy us."

"And the Inquisition? Can't they kill you?" Sadie perched on the edge of her chair and wrapped her arms around herself for warmth.

"They are just human, weak." She turned to Sadie. "It is time. We must begin the ritual."

She reached into her bag, unzipped a pocket, and brought out a long shape wrapped in what looked like a silk scarf. Unrolling it reverently, she placed it on a folding table she had set up. When she moved aside, Sadie could see the outline of a handle, maybe the length of her palm, and what looked like a shiny blade twice as long. The countess then brought out a gleaming gold cup, and set it down with a clink. She lifted the dagger from the scarf and kissed the blade, for a moment lost in her thoughts, then turned to Sadie with a smile. The upward twitch of her lips wasn't reassuring, and as she advanced toward Sadie she held out her other hand.

"This will be painful. But it will all be over in an hour or two."

She stepped close enough to reach the girl, who lurched to her feet and clutched the chair for protection.

The woman's smile stretched her cheeks with amusement. "I can taste your energy from here. Your death is recent, the magic strong."

"I'm warning you." Sadie swung the chair in the direction of the woman, pain stabbing through the bite on her hand. She caught her breath with the effort, already too close to the edge of the circle to do more than flap weakly in the countess's direction.

"Does the mouse threaten the cat?" The countess waved the knife, and to Sadie's horror, her own fingers unclenched and the metal chair clattered to the floor. "Come and be eaten, little mouse. It is over. You are alone."

Sadie's resistance evaporated, even as her mind raged, and

her mouth slackened, wordless. She sagged as the woman approached, lifted Sadie's limp arm and reached down with the silver blade. "You can't fight me. You don't even want to fight me."

Jack's voice sounded like a bell around the echoing church. "Then *I* will fight you."

Chapter 55

And I pray: For this cause, take ye the armoure of
God, that ye maye be able to resiste in the evil day,
and stande perfecte in all thinges. Stande firm
therfore, and gyrde yr loines aboute with the trueth,
havinge on the breast plate of righteousnes, and shod
yor feet with the gospell of peace, that ye maye be
prepared: Above all thinges take holde of the shielde of
faith, wherewith ye maye quenche all the fierye darts
of the wicked. And take the helmet of salvation, & the
sworde of the spirite, which is the worde of God.

—EDWARD KELLEY
  Quoting Epistle to the Ephesians 6:13–17
  Myles Coverdale Bible (1535)

WE WERE DRAGGED, AT SWORD POINT, TO THE SOLAR at midday.

Dee stood resolute before the Black Bear. "My Lord Nádasdy, our research has led us to a most unhappy conclusion."

The man was cracking hazelnuts between strong fingers, throwing the shells onto the fire, where they crackled. "What wisdoms did the priest impart?" He seemed calm, his black eyes sliding toward me before returning to Dee. He tossed back his head and crunched the meat of the nut.

"What you ask us to do is not to save the Lady Erzsébet, but to transform her into a creature of such miserable existence that you will come to regret it."

Nádasdy beckoned to one of his attendants and spoke into his ear, then turned back to us. "I ask again. Can you do it? Can you restore her to health?"

Dee hesitated, and again the count stared at me. I grew hot and fearful under his gaze.

Dee spoke as calmly as if he were talking of the weather. "What she would become is a creature of darkness and death. You would regret the day we tied her soul to her dying body."

Nádasdy jabbed a finger in my chest, making me stagger back. "You, sorcerer. Can you do it?"

I looked at Dee, who gazed back. "I . . . I don't . . ." I stammered.

Nádasdy nodded to the attendant and spoke a few words in the hissing and spitting language of the Magyars. The man slithered a yard of bright steel from his scabbard, which gleamed in the candlelight. He raised it above his head, and turned toward Dee.

"Then your master will die and you will do it," Nádasdy said to me.

"No! I need—I need Master Dee's wisdom, his knowledge. I don't know how to do it by myself."

"He would let my wife die."

"No, he won't, I mean . . ." I stammered, looking beseechingly at Dee, who stared at me.

Nádasdy nodded to the attendant, who twisted on one foot toward me, the sword cutting the air close to my neck. "Then we will sacrifice you, if your master will not oblige. Perhaps then, he will act to save his own life. Mayhap he does not take me seriously."

I stared at Dee, who looked sad. "Edward, you heard Konrad," he said in English. "Perhaps it would be better if we die, in God's grace." He sounded uncertain.

I was speechless, my mouth flapping open like a landed carp. I could not drag my eyes from the wicked blade, drawing back like a bowstring, the man's eyes narrowing as he aligned the edge with my throat.

"Master!" I reached up with one puny arm, as if to ward off my death.

"Wait!" Dee seemed to struggle with himself. "We will help, but I want your word that you will let both of us and also Father Konrad and his men go, as soon as the lady's life is secured."

The man with the sword stood like a statue, the very end of the blade quivering. Finally, he lowered it, and my breath escaped in a whoosh.

Dee turned to me and held out a steadying hand. As we clung together like children, the Black Bear snapped orders to his guards and we were left alone for a moment.

"Edward, we are misguided." Dee had tears rolling down his face into his beard. "I know not what to do."

I was quite certain. "What we do," I stopped to swallow a lump, the size of a loaf, in my throat, "is what has to be done. And then we shall help Konrad undo it."

He looked around the room, and wiped his face on the back of his sleeve. "Very well. Then let us set out the candles, Edward."

By the time we asked the countess to attend, the room was lit by dozens of candles and a fire blazed in the hearth. The bed had been placed in the center of the circle as Dee had commanded. Incense burned in small bowls at the cardinal points, adding their smoke to the haziness. Servants had shuttered the windows against the dusk.

A dog, somewhere within the castle yards, began to howl with a sound that ran cold fingers up my spine. Its fellows, wolfhounds and other dogs within the castle, began to add their voices, not in the song that the wolves created, but a screaming, as if they were terrified. Then I heard the horses.

When horses suffer great fear, they shriek with an almost human sound. Outside, we could hear men shouting, boots thudding along corridors and over the cobbles. It sounded as if every horse in the castle was being tortured, until I heard the great grinding of the latches and hinges that supported the main gates, after which the screaming, yelping, barking and wailing animals thundered in a great company over the yard and into the forest.

We stood like statues, looking at each other, when all the bats roosting in the roof of the solar dropped into the room. They poured from niches and corners, dozens of them, and we ducked, as they flew around looking for an exit. Some flew in desperation toward the fireplace, only to catch ablaze and fall to the floor. Dee threw open a wooden shutter, and after a few moments they found their retreat. I longed to follow them.

"Edward." Dee was looking out of the narrow window, and I followed him to it, and leaned out.

The yard was moving, a teeming sea of rats and mice, movement of all sort. Cats ran over the rats without attacking them, intent on reaching the forest and, I suppose, what they imagined was comparative safety. All living things but the people were fleeing the building. Then the door was thrown open and Zsófia carried her lady into the chamber, followed by Nádasdy and two servants.

The countess was wrapped in a long robe, her feet bare. The witch lifted the lady over the symbols, making sure she didn't touch them, and sat her upon the thick mattress. The countess slumped onto the bed, cradled in the arms of the witch, her face turning a shade of iron gray. Her mouth and eyes sagged open, as if life was extinct.

"She dies!" Zsófia wailed, looking around the room for us.

"Doctor Dee, Edward, please save her!" Her words shook themselves into sobs, as she bent her head over her mistress.

Nádasdy strode forward. "Perform the ritual. Now."

Dee pulled back his heavy sleeves. "I can only try, you understand?" His voice was severe, and the count took one step away. "Clear the room."

I harried the servants out, but the count would not go. The witch had ignored us, and was clutching the body of the countess like a lover, her whole body jerking with her sobs. I couldn't understand her words, but she was distraught. In the end, it took Nádasdy's strength to haul her away, and Dee was able to examine the countess. He pressed a finger to her throat, and listened to her breath.

"Life is not yet extinguished," he announced, flexing his arms. "Hurry, Edward, the circle."

I brought out a glass vessel of sea salt culled from the kitchens. The smell took me back to my childhood, cockling as a boy in the sands in Kent. I breathed the scent in for a moment, trying to stop the shaking in my hands.

"Edward." The reminder woke me from the past and I scattered a thin line of salt around the circle we had drawn earlier. I left a gap for Dee to cross.

"Ready, master."

Dee took up the dagger I had lent him to use as a substitute wand.

His voice took on the timbre of command, which sent shivers down my spine. We usually worked in Latin, but we knew Nádasdy understood that language, so we had agreed to try the ritual in English. Spirits understand all languages.

"Erzsébet, awake." He pulled out the bottle of hagweed and earthstar tincture we had made. "*Erzsébet.*"

She sighed. Dee lifted her head a little, and tipped the bottle against her lips. She swallowed some, I could only hope it was enough. He stepped back, out of the circle, and I sprinkled salt across the gap. With a loud breath, the countess pulled herself up to sit on the bed, head back, gasps filling the room as she labored for air.

"Zsófia!" she cried.

"Raphael!" Dee intoned, inscribing the first symbol over the eastern corner. "Bind this child to the clay of her creation!" He lit the candle that stood there.

He moved to the south, and I was impelled by a force behind my head to a kneeling position. I found my mouth chanting in a strange language, and the sense of something filling up my body, until I felt I would burst.

Dee continued, this time calling to Uriel. The words my mouth was mumbling became clear to me. "Bless the children of the dead, bless the undead, bless the dead . . ." I struggled to control my tongue but still the words flowed out of me in a mocking tone, and poured into the room. Then my lips formed the shapes of names. I grew cold with terror as I heard them gushing from my mouth. "Bael, Bathan, Morax, Asmodeus . . ."

"Gabriel!" shouted Dee, who must have been in the west at this point, but I had little time to think about it.

I breathed again, feeling the squeeze of my chest as the demons' names were forced out, as if I were a pair of bellows. "Stolas, Aguarès, Astaroth . . ."

"Michael!" Dee roared. I was released, in time to raise my head and see Dee draw the sigil of Michael in the air. Looking past him I could see Nádasdy. He had restrained the writhing witch, and drawn something gleaming over her bare arm. Blood was gushing into a wooden cup, and I sprang to my feet, taking the first step to her aid before I realized what they were doing.

Zsófia was not unwilling. She writhed in the man's arms as she had writhed in mine, as a lover. Her eyes were open, but not seeing, and her moans were of pleasure, not pain. Nádasdy kissed her with such savagery that her lips were reddened and bleeding, even as the blood flowed down her arm; it seemed as if he meant to devour her.

I glanced, horrified, toward the countess, Erzsébet. She was alive, and watching, with such a lustful expression on her face that I was ashamed to see it. Her skin was pale, but had lost the grayness of death.

Nádasdy dropped the witch, who fell to the floor almost insensible, and kicked through the salt barrier. Erzsébet was kneeling, hands outstretched to take the goblet. She drank the blood greedily, and threw the cup to the ground. Newly filled with energy, she clawed at her lord's clothes with such strength that she ripped his dolman almost in two, the remains falling to the floor. The count's heavy body emerged from his shirt, and he pulled her against him.

Dee gathered himself, and turned to me, his face as shocked as mine.

"Master," I mumbled, now that my voice was my own again. I took his arm, and led him toward the stairs. "Come. You have saved her. The ritual worked."

"This cannot be what the angels wanted," he said, distraught. "Stop them."

I looked back to Zsófia, who had dragged herself to her feet, and was cradling her bleeding arm. I called to her. "Zsófia, come with us, for God's sake."

"What do I care for God?" she called, watching the pair on the bed, who were now coupling like animals. "She is my life." She was swaying, grasping her injured arm.

She staggered to the bed, and I watched as she was gathered into the countess's embrace. Erzsébet kissed Zsófia on the mouth, smeared with her own blood, and threw her down between them.

Chapter 56

J ACK CHANNELED ALL THE RAGE SHE HAD BEEN BUILDING from looking at Sadie's bruised, shaking form. Distracted by the ritual to come, and her bloodlust, the woman hadn't seen her enter the church. Jack had crept under scaffolding and over rubble, carrying the sword.

She harvested all her feelings from remembering her dog's unconscious body, Maggie's injuries, the fury that consumed her when she looked at the injured teenager, and spat the binding spell at the woman.

The ritual words, enough to enervate a normal person, were devastating to a borrowed timer, as Jack had previously learned in an encounter with Pierce. They hit the countess with a force that knocked her to her knees. Caught by the nimbus, even in her protective circle, Sadie folded like a rag doll. Jack forced the rage into the words as she strode forward. She held her weapon—Maggie's sword—in front of her, but could feel the air thickening as she moved closer to the huddled old woman.

Jack raised the sword above her head with both hands, calling out the ritual words again. The woman turned her head, and Jack's mouth was frozen in the icy-blue stare.

"You don't think your tiny spells can stop *me*?" the woman hissed, before an energy bolt hit Jack and knocked her onto her back. The sword clattered away and she scuttled after it.

Jack climbed to her feet and swung the weapon. It hissed through the air and she could feel the words inscribed along its length whisper in their own musical sibilance.

"All I have to do is delay you," she shouted. "The Inquisition has stopped you from completing your ritual for too many years. This is your last chance. You are dying, old woman."

"The only way you can stop me is to run that toy through the child's heart." The woman dusted off her clothes, and Jack could see Sadie struggling to all fours. "Assuming you can get past me."

For one moment, Jack contemplated the arc of the sword spinning through the air and into the countess. She knew the chance of success was too low to risk it, so she walked around the side of the woman, step by careful step, avoiding the many shapes drawn on the floor.

"Sadie. Are you OK?" The girl looked up, blinked, and nodded. The countess grabbed Sadie's wrist and tugged her to her feet, and before Jack could react, drew the silver blade across the girl's forearm.

Sadie wailed in pain, still weaving from the effects of Jack's spell. Blood welled up and before it could run onto the ground, the woman dropped the knife and snatched the chalice off the table.

Jack tried to step nearer and found she couldn't. There was some sort of protective inner circle, unseen, but cold to the touch. She recoiled, feeling delicately with the sword to find its boundaries.

The invisible circle included Sadie, in her own small sanctuary, the table and the witch's tools. It excluded four separate circles at each of the cardinal points. Jack recognized a few symbols from Felix's laptop.

"These are summoning circles," she said, hazarding a guess.

The woman squeezed Sadie's arm to catch the last drops as the bleeding slowed. Then she held up the cup, calling out some words Jack didn't recognize, and lifted the chalice to her lips.

"No!" Jack shouted, but the woman started drinking. When she lowered the chalice, her mouth was scarlet, and she looked dazed. Sadie fell to her knees, her face even whiter than usual.

The witch took a long taper and lit it from one of her white candles, then turned to the long, black candle to the east, inside her circle. She ignited it, and began chanting.

The air inside the church started to move, the dust rising like mist, tumbling around Jack's feet. It seemed to be winding itself like a veil, catching on objects, streaming around the chapel, until it reached the easternmost summoning circle, where it arched itself around the edges and spun into a cylinder. Inside her shell, the witch's candles were unmoved, lighting the shape as it revolved faster. Jack watched as it started to creep inside the summoning circle, forming a roughly human shape.

The air started to stir, lifting her hair, exploring vulnerable skin at neck and cuffs, touching her ankles above her boots. It built, sighing around her, tugging at the edges of her jacket, which billowed around her like a windsock. A keening sound was threaded through it, which developed into a moan.

"*Jaaackkkk,*" it mourned.

"Jack!" Sadie's voice was wobbly but sharp. "It's the tornado! The air elemental." Jack staggered in the force buffeting her from different sides, trying to throw her. She dragged one foot back, then the other, pace on pace, trying to reach the shelter of the pews. She could see the nearest bench tremble, lift off the floor and tumble toward her. She ducked, rolling onto her shoulder as it smashed into the tiles a foot from her head, the dark oak splintering into long shards. Jack was already moving behind another unstable pew, running, slipping and scrambling behind the seats, away from the epicenter. She caught a glimpse of the thing—the elemental—trapped inside the circle, writhing as if trying to get out. As she rounded the back of the pews, which shattered beside her, she dived for the back of the stone altar. Wood slivers hit it like shrapnel, and she curled into a defensive ball. *Shit, Felix, where are you?*

Risking a glance around herself, she caught sight of a heavy carved door to the right of the altar and saw Mac. The inquisitor was kneeling, holding a book in one hand. He seemed to be chanting something, but Jack couldn't hear him over the thunderous gale. Felix peered past him, and at Mac's nod, half ran, half crawled to Jack's position behind the altar.

He pulled Jack close enough so he could bellow in her ear, the words barely audible over the storm. "We have to banish it!"

She could hear the words, but had no idea what he was talking about until he grabbed her sword arm and started dragging her toward the door, now slamming shut and wrenching itself open, the frame quivering with each impact.

Timing their scuttle through the door, they avoided being crushed, and huddled out of the extremes of the tornado behind Mac. Felix started sketching a few Latin words on the wall with a piece of displaced plaster. "Banishing!" he bellowed, pointing at the first of the words, and speaking them. Jack mumbled along until she got the hang of the first phrases, then as Felix raised his hands, she started shouting them back at the wind. Doing something, even as ineffectual as screaming into a storm, was satisfying.

Decibel by decibel, the roaring softened, the debris smashing into the door started sliding into it, and the howling inside the whirlwind lessened. Before it had gone entirely, Jack tightened her grip around the hilt of the sword and went back.

She forced her way into the nave, scraping the floor clear of wreckage. The interior of the church was trashed, but swept clear in the middle. Shattered pews made a pile of kindling several feet deep at the walls; the door was only passable because it had been sheltered by the stone altar. The protective circle had shielded Sadie and the witch.

"Sadie!" Jack held the sword in front of her, now truly pissed off. Sadie was curled on the floor, both arms now dribbling blood.

The woman was standing tall, looking exhilarated, her arms outstretched. "You think you can stop me? You think many others, far more powerful, have not tried to defeat me?" She lifted the chalice again, her eyes rolling back in her head in ecstasy. "Oh, the energy," she sighed, as she lowered the cup. "She is young, and strong."

Jack studied the markings on the floor. The circle enclosing the witch appeared to be reinforced with small symbols at intervals in red. The summoning circles outside were drawn in black ink, and she walked over to the nearest one, which had enclosed the air elemental. It was blackened and charred, and she could pass a hand through it. Sidling to the next one, she could only get within a few feet of it.

From the side, Jack could see Sadie curled around her injured arms. The teenager's eyes flickered open, and she looked at Jack. Their gazes locked, and Sadie seemed to gather some energy. She struggled to sit up. "Jack . . ."

"You see the power of my friends? You think you can cope with water, or fire?" The countess seemed to enjoy the taunting, so Jack tried to distract her.

"You can say that because you think you are safe in your little haven. But you don't dare tackle me yourself."

"What are you, really?" The countess tilted her head on one side, a strangely Sadie gesture. "I know you are not a witch, and you are too ignorant to be a sorcerer." The woman licked her blood-crusted lips with every appearance of enjoyment. "I could kill you in an instant. You should be running for your life, but you are still here. A fly buzzing around a giant."

She lit a taper, and touched the flame to the candle in the west.

Jack noticed a movement out of the corner of her eyes, and

realized it was a rivulet of water dribbling from the ceiling, illuminated by the witch's candles. The silver threads striated the wall, finding their way down the shattered plaster. As Jack watched, they joined into blobs, like mercury.

Felix and Mac slid out of the doorway, and made their way to her side. The witch smiled at them all, her teeth stained scarlet.

"Dear, dear Stephen. Your sister has served me well, but now I need to move on." She turned to Felix. "And Professor Guichard. Yours will be a great loss to the academic community. There is much still to learn of Dee and Kelley. But we shall study the original journals, and refine Dee's treatments."

McNamara drew Jack aside. "We need to summon a counter-elemental," he breathed into her ear. "I can call upon the angels to help me, but we need to get out of here when it's released."

Jack turned her face away from the countess. "I'm not going without the girl." She turned to see Sadie, her hands flat against the floor, pushing up as if holding the world at bay.

Felix joined them, stepping over rivulets running around their feet. "I hope you can swim."

"I'm going to raise an earth elemental." McNamara sounded strangely calm. "You should both leave. No mortal can survive this."

"I am the only immortal here." The countess laughed from her sanctuary, the sound mocking, as water started dribbling from the roof. Jack could see the droplets running together in the bottom of the summoning circle.

Jack got a wild idea. "That's not strictly true, is it?" she whispered to Felix. "If I . . ."

"If you . . . ?" The idea formed in Felix's mind, as Mac looked from one to the other. "Oh, God. Jack, no."

"If I drink blood, that will make me like her. I would have more power, at least for a short time."

The inquisitor stepped back, his hand going to his crucifix.

"You are a revenant?" he whispered. He studied her face. "Yes. I should have seen it earlier."

"So, if I drink blood—"

"—you will become like her. A fiend, a parasitical monster, feeding on the blood of others." McNamara's face was rigid, and he stepped farther back. "I would rather let the beast live than create a second. Go. I must raise the elemental." He placed his bag on the dais. He brought out a candle similar to the countess's, but smaller. When he fitted it into a stand and lit the wick, it started to stink of burnt meat and sulphur.

Jack realized she was now standing in several inches of water, and turned to Felix. "Listen, I'm talking about our only chance. We would only have an advantage for a moment."

"I don't want to lose you. If he's right—"

"He's not. I'm me, Felix, not that psychopathic bitch over there. It's Sadie's last hope."

He put big hands on her shoulders. "Can you even do it? It would have to be my blood, Jack."

She reached up and kissed him, some sort of desperation in the embrace, and after a moment he hugged her against him. Jack felt as if both of them were trying to put a whole relationship into a moment. The water was up to the laces of her boots, and starting to roil. With a shocking blast of cold, it flowed onto the skin of her feet, and liquid fingers began to crawl up her legs. Mac was standing on the dais, holding the candlestick above the water, chanting in Latin.

Felix dragged her into the cover of the altar.

"Have you got something sharp, maybe smaller than the sword?" he whispered.

Jack peered around the stone, watching the countess swaying in some sort of ecstatic trance. As she moved her hands the water writhed inside the summoning circle. It was filled to waist height, water rushing out of the base across the tiled floor.

The dagger was inside the poacher's pocket of her jacket.

She offered it to Felix. He bit his lip, then drew the edge over his skin, scoring a thin line in his flesh. "Ouch." Dark blood welled up. "Go," he said. She bent over his arm.

As she touched her tongue to his skin, she could feel him flinch. The first drops tasted like salt, and little more. She couldn't feel any difference, so she put her lips against his skin and sucked gently. A small surge of hot liquid in her mouth made her gag for a second, then involuntarily swallow.

The change was immediate. Jack could feel her heart race, and she filled with heat. She sucked again, tugging at the edges of the split skin against her tongue, and the energy gushed into her with a fresh spurt of blood. For a moment she was lost in the almost forgotten sense of vitality that she had taken for granted in her childhood. She was greedily sucking and swallowing when she realized the bleeding was slowing, so she bit his arm to make more. Felix's groan of pain brought her back to her senses.

"I'm sorry," she whispered, but brought up the sword with both hands. She stepped around the altar, stepping off the dais into thigh-deep water. She could hear McNamara chanting strange rolling words above her. *Gabriel, Michael, Raphael . . .*

"Elizabeth Báthory."

The woman turned to face her, and opened her pale eyes.

Jack raised her arms above her head and brought the sword down into the protective bubble enclosing the center of the building.

Jack had imagined it shattering, but in reality it felt like she'd hit a wall of toffee. The blade stuck fast, halfway up, but the woman reeled back inside the bubble as if she'd been hit. Jack tugged at the sword, dragging it free as the countess's face changed. She stormed to the other side of the barrier, her mouth open, and her claws reached for Jack, trying to grab her. Outside the protective circle, the water accumulating at her waist caught Jack, and dragged her away, and under.

She was swept along, mostly below the water, but with her new strength managed to force her head out of the top of what proved to be a wave traveling around the building. It was going so fast Felix couldn't get out of the way, and it swallowed him whole.

Some small part of Jack panicked, but she shook the fear off. She had to focus on the countess. Mac and his pitiful candle were absorbed by the surge breaking over the altar. The darkness and cold seemed to be her element; she felt as if she could surf on the wave, stand on it, play in its strength. It took her head smacking against a timber to realize she needed to concentrate. It was one of the rafters of the roof. The waters had risen and filled the building.

She plunged into the wave, looking for the inquisitor, dragging him into an air pocket between the rollers. She reached to hold Mac's head out of the water. After a moment of coughing, he began his chanting again. *Uriel, Raguel, Sariel, Jaramiel* . . .

A rumble, as if the sea itself had invaded the waters, reverberated through Jack. McNamara was swept away from her as the waters reached the roof again. She plunged into the darkness, reaching for the air pocket inside the magical bell jar that the countess had conjured. A boom thundered through Jack's world of dark and silence and pressure, and exploded it.

Chapter 57

When you will summon any spirit, you must know
his name and office; you must also fast, and be clean
from all pollution three or four days before; so will
the spirit be more obedient unto you. Then make a
circle, and call up the spirit with great intention, and
holding a wand in your hand, rehearse in your own
name, and your companions (for one must always
be with you) this prayer following, and so no spirit
shall annoy you, and your purpose shall take effect.
(And note how this agrees with popish charms and
conjurations.)

—JOHANN WEYER
Pseudomonarchia Daemonum (1563)
British Library, handwritten bookplate with the
name J. Dee inscribed

IN OUR CHAMBERS, WE SPOKE LITTLE ABOUT THE EVENTS IN
the solar. I was shocked, and I think I have seen more of the
world than Dee. He seemed downcast as he packed his most
important possessions. Books, maps, journals were randomly
tipped into bags, and I had to finish the task as he sat for some
time with his head in his hands.

"What have we done?" The whisper reached me across the
chamber, through the gloom of a single candle. "She is possessed by a demon."

"We have to leave." My mind ran from idea to idea, none of which seemed possible. I couldn't believe we would be released. Guards stood outside our doors, swords in hands.

"I do not deserve to be saved." He was shaking.

"We did what was asked of us, by angels." I prayed that it was so, and that we had not been led astray by demons.

"But, the blood . . . that wasn't in the ritual. They debased the angels we called upon, and contaminated them with their animal rutting."

I had no argument. How could this be the work of angels? We waited for our captors.

They came for us before dawn. Lord László led them, with half a dozen Magyars and two hooded men.

"It is time," he said, through clenched teeth, as if biting each word off. "The count has ordered your immediate executions."

My throat made a sound that I have to admit was a whimper. My knees softened until only the guards gripping me under my arms held me up.

They bound our hands behind our backs and dragged us to the chapel. I was surprised to see the hooded men carrying our bags, perhaps they feared our belongings were contaminated. László nodded to one of our guards, who opened the door to the top of the stairs that led down to the dungeon.

He shrugged, catching my eye. "I am sorry. But we cannot allow that which you have done to be undone. It will be swift." He turned to one of the guards. "Bring me their heads." He turned to go, leaving us as if we had been calves led to slaughter.

I wanted to scream at him, anyone, to spare me. I would like to think courage stopped me from pleading for my life, but I couldn't form a word. The guard to my left took my weight and started to pull me toward the stairs. Then I found my strength, and started resisting. I was overpowered, and half dragged, half thrown down the steps.

I fell upon the floor of the dungeon, crying out as my shoulder struck the stone. One of the hooded men snapped an order to the guards, who departed, leaving just four of us. We listened to the departing guards' boots on the steps and I struggled to my feet.

The hooded soldier fastened an iron gate across the bottom of the stairs. He drew back his cowl to show himself as the stern Lord Miklós. The other, grinning as he revealed himself, proved to be Lord János.

He reached out a hand and grasped my forearm in a soldier's greeting. I clung to his arm.

"You did it! I doubted you, but there will be sons now," he said, in his poor Latin.

Miklós threw a key at him. "We have little time for congratulations. Let the priest and his men out."

Konrad, squinting into the sudden light of a few torches, stepped out of his cell. He stood, looking back at Dee and myself with a hard expression.

"You did it, despite my warnings. Better you were dead, than damned eternally."

Miklós interrupted. "We will show your men the way out of the castle and assist your escape, if you will take the Englishmen with you."

"To Rome." Konrad stared into my very soul, with those black eyes.

"If you choose. But you will not spill English blood on Istvan's soil."

"The Inquisition?" The words stumbled out of me.

Konrad's voice softened a little. "I cannot help that. It is my duty to God and the Pope. Indeed, it offers your one hope for redemption."

"My family are in Krakow." Dee's voice was as calm as if he were making polite conversation. "Master Kelley's wife, also."

Miklós turned to him. "They will receive five thousand crowns in gratitude from the king for your help in saving the countess." He drew out his sword, the metal screeching from its scabbard. "If Erzsébet lives, Nádasdy does not demand monies of the king in repayment of loans. She will bear sons, and the Black Bear will revert to being utterly loyal to the Báthorys."

I stared at Dee. "But how will we get out of the castle? It is a fortress."

Dee spoke to János. "I thought you were with Nádasdy's men?"

"My first allegiance is to my voivode, Istvan."

Konrad's soldiers were arming themselves from the pile of discarded swords by the wall of the dungeon. János pulled one of them toward a shadowed recess on the wall. "Here. A tunnel to the outer courtyard. We have arranged weapons and horses there. You will have to fight, but some are my men, and under orders to be lenient, and to let you escape. Nádasdy's troops will be taken by surprise, but be warned, they are battle-hardened and dangerous. If I think you are losing, I will dispatch you myself, to avert suspicion."

"Why let us go?" I realized what a stupid question it was as it left my lips.

He grinned, white teeth shining against his black beard. "It serves our line, our king, our voivode. Because *we* are Somlyó."

Chapter 58

JACK WAS PULLED INTO A FIERCE SPIRAL, AS THE WATER DRAINED down cracks that opened up in the floor. She, Mac and Felix were dropped onto fissures in the concrete. She lifted her head and looked around. The floor was split in half a dozen places, one of them breaching the countess's protective barrier. She was hunched on the ground, squeezing a deep cut inside Sadie's elbow, as if she were milking the last drops out of her. The girl was either insensible or dead.

Jack staggered to her feet, and raced over the edge of the circle, now useless. Rage surged through her, threaded with exhilaration. She was filled with the desire to tear into the old woman like the bag of rags she appeared to be, but a last moment of caution made her veer toward Sadie. She ignored the huddled monster, and swept Sadie into her arms. She caught sight of Felix, kneeling over the prostrate McNamara, and carried the girl over to him.

"Here. Look after her."

Her fading compassion for the girl was swept away as she turned to see the woman drain the last of the harvested blood from the cup. She looked different, younger, her arms stretched out as if she'd been energized. Jack could feel something of the same energy, and wondered what a whole cup of blood would do, if one mouthful made her feel eight feet tall. There was something subtle about the face . . . the features. With horror, she realized the woman now looked a lot like Sadie.

The woman started to chant, slowing Jack's progress as the

protective wall was built back up. Jack looked around the building. Three of the four summoning circles were charred and useless, but the remaining one was beginning to glow with a soft orange light. *What's left, flood, tornado, earthquake . . .*

She looked for the sword. She saw a gleam of metal and vaulted over flood-dumped wreckage to reach for the blade. As she touched its cold flatness, the inscribed words started to glimmer with her new energy. She turned to confront the woman and held the sword high, preparing to charge.

"Stay." The woman held up a single finger and Jack's arm weakened, the sword dropping to the floor. "You are young, powerful. Don't you see what I can give you?"

"You can die." Jack's thoughts seemed strangely single-minded, with just a whisper of concern left to wonder if the others were dead.

"You can live. Live as long as you wish."

"By feeding off people like a fucking vampire?"

"By the use of careful transfusions. I don't kill people. I only take an occasional revenant, who would die anyway."

"They call you a monster." She pushed forward a step, and another, before a gesture from the woman stuck her like a fly in amber.

"Look at yourself, Jack. You are beautiful now, not that withered, cooling corpse you were. I can show you more. I can show you the whole world. No more circles, no more potions. Riches and freedom. Immortality."

"You killed all those girls."

The woman shrugged, her hands still weaving the spell that was binding Jack in its mesh. "Personal pleasure. I was experimenting."

Even as Jack's limbs became heavier, she was aware of the glow building in the circle. She could hear Felix's voice, shouting.

"Jack, listen to me!" He seemed very far away, but something made her turn her head. She could see him kneeling, holding Sadie, the inquisitor crawling on the ground in front of him.

She looked back, feeling her own body sway a little with the movement of the countess's now youthful hands—Sadie's hands. She stared at the undulating fingers, while Felix's words sank into her mind like wine into a napkin.

"You aren't like her . . . she was always a sadistic serial killer. You have a choice."

"I was dying, Felix." The words drifted out of her. She clenched her fingers on the sword, feeling the hilt cut into her palm. "I've been slowing down for years."

"We'll work it out. Mac will help." His voice became roughened. "Sadie's dying, Jack. We need to get out of here, get help. I can't move them both by myself. I need you to help me."

She could feel the heat through her damp clothes. She glanced at the summoning circle, seeing the flame filling the cylinder. It reached blazing fingers along cracks in the circle, perhaps looking for a way to get out.

"Jack." The voice of the witch cut through her thoughts and gave her a moment of clarity. "Join me and leave the mortals."

"Let them go." She found the words mumbling through her slack lips. "I'll come with you. I have nothing here to keep me, except coldness and death. Take me instead. But let them go. They are nothing to you."

Over her words, Jack could hear the wail of sirens.

The countess waved one hand and Felix hoisted Sadie into his arms. McNamara staggered, and fell. Felix disappeared into the doorway, then returned for the inquisitor.

"Jack. Come on." He had one hand stretched out to her.

The witch was triumphant. "She is mine, now." The light from the flames was almost blinding, white hot, and Jack realized her clothes were steaming, and smoke was rising from the floor around the elemental. "The fire devas will burn away the evidence and we will have a new life."

"Run, Felix." Jack stared at his hand: broad, square-fingered, brown. She had known him only a few days, but she knew exactly how it would feel, if she reached over for it. "Run *now*."

She let every corner of her being infuse with the cruelty of what the witch had done to Sadie, the rage of losing her childhood, her anger at not being told about the power of blood. She could waver the sword to chest height but no more. As she focused, another feeling crept in, warming her frozen muscles. Love for Maggie and Charley, for the animals who had shared her life for so many years, for the man who would not be banished by the threat of the monster. Summoning everything she had, she pulled her arms up like drawing a bowstring, and with one explosive hack, let the sword fly.

It hit the fiery being with a boom, breaching the circle, and tendrils smashed through the confinement. The thing grew as Jack started running, and the heat and sound chased her as she leapt over the altar. The witch turned to face her own creation.

Felix had taken cover in the lee of the entryway, supporting the inquisitor, sheltering from the searing heat. The witch's chanting grew into a screech as she tried to control the elemental she had raised, but her shrill voice was lost in the roar of the fire. Jack stumbled into the anteroom, and Felix slammed the heavy door behind her. The fire elemental in the church withdrew the air along the floor so fiercely that Jack could feel it racing around her feet; it felt as if it would suck her under the door. A moment's pause in the complete darkness, then the whoomph of an explosion deafened her. The whole room was lit in orange light from every crack around the door, and the heat sent them scuttling around the corner of the wall. Jack saw the inquisitor holding Sadie's body, her eyes half open. Before she could go over to the girl, Felix reached out his long arms and crushed her against him.

Chapter 59

THE FIRST RAPID-RESPONSE OFFICERS ROUNDED THE COR-
ner into the open doorway of the porch. At the same
time, the fireball exploded down the nave, carrying
with it the splayed body of a woman as if she were dancing on
tiptoe, fingers stretching for the arches of the roof. It plunged
greedy fingers toward the two men as they stared, frozen momentarily in the act of turning away, as it burned away her
floating hair in an instant, tentacles of flame exploring the
hollows of her face. Clothing wrapped her nakedness for a
second or two in coiling, oily smoke, then was incinerated.
She sucked in one glowing breath as her eyes shriveled into
her skull, her skin blackened and crazed over her scarlet body.
Her shriek mingled with the roar of the flame as it drew the
oxygen back from the porch, the searing vacuum plucking at
the men's uniforms as they staggered back, dropping close to
the still-cool flagstones. As they scuttled back like beetles,
one saw her body turn and drop, falling in a wave of sparks
that sent one pseudopod of heat toward him, scorching off his
eyebrows and burning his face before he buried it under his
jacket. The men ran, crawled and fell, holding their breath
against the skin-searing heat, until they turned the corner
onto the grass outside. More screeches, these mechanical,
rose as something inside the church started to fall. The crash
lit every window and for a moment, the churchyard glowed
orange, before smoke obscured everything.

Chapter 60

FELIX GAVE HIMSELF A FEW SECONDS OF HOLDING JACK, hiding his face against her hair, before he looked around. The door was on fire, the heat becoming unbearable. Mac was crouched over Sadie, silhouettes against the red flicker of flame. There was an entrance, probably to a sacristy, opposite the one to the nave. Another crash was followed by a finger of flame, reaching in around the solid door.

"Bring Sadie!" he shouted to McNamara, gasping in a lungful of smoke before he raced for the haven of the dark archway, dragging Jack by the arm.

He had no idea whether McNamara had heard, but as he slid into the cool darkness, stumbling over things on the floor, he heard someone coughing behind him. Smoke had followed them into the sacristy, exploring the ceiling and obscuring the top of a window lit by a streetlight nearby. The door behind them slammed shut.

Felix fumbled along the window wall, and his hand found the recess of the exit, the studded planks . . . on one side, a hinge . . . he trailed fingers to the other side, found the key-hole. He coughed, spat soot. He rattled the handle but it didn't budge. Felix could hear McNamara beside him, his breathing labored. Then, the light of a small torch illuminated the man's face. Jack had fallen to her knees beside Sadie, and was crouched on the floor, coughing.

"The child is dead." The man's voice was as scratchy as his

own. "We have to get out, the church is burning down. Let me see the lock."

Felix knelt beside the two women, and looked at Sadie, lying among what looked like builders' tools and old chairs. Her face was paper-white in the thin glow of the torch, her eyes closed, her elfin features softening to gray as the light moved. He lifted the girl's shoulders up, her head heavy on his arm. He thought, but couldn't be sure, that she sighed.

The light disappeared into the hollow of the inquisitor's body as he bent over the lock. Scratching, grinding noises were followed by another explosion in the nave behind them, bringing a tornado of hot smoke into the room. When Felix could see again, a yellow flicker outlined the sacristy door.

The lock mechanism clunked and ground, then a slap of cold air revived Felix. He lifted the girl, staggering toward the door, the teenager's head knocking against his collarbone with each step.

"Jack! Come on!" He followed McNamara into the grave-yard beyond.

"Is she really dead?" Jack's voice sounded rough, and taking another gasp made her cough. He could hear her dragging her feet behind him on the gravel behind the church.

Felix eased his burden onto the slight rise of a grave mound, below the shadow of the churchyard wall. The faint light of the torch illuminated the girl's face again. Felix felt for a pulse, but wasn't sure he could feel one, his own hands were shaking so much.

McNamara tapped an object in his hand. "My phone's dead. We need to get out of here before the police arrive and I need to call for backup."

"What for?" Alarm sharpened Felix's voice.

"You saw. You saw what *she* has become." The man's voice was low. "Jack is no better than the demon she destroyed."

Felix looked at Jack, slumped on the grass.

"She did what she had to, to save our lives. She was prepared to die for us."

"It would have been better if she had. You don't know the consequences of a revenant taking blood . . ." But his voice sounded less certain.

"Please." Felix swallowed more words. This strange hard man seemed driven more by duty than feeling, yet he had disobeyed orders. Emotional appeals might not work, but reason seemed to influence him. "Give her the benefit of the doubt. If she turns out like . . . that, then do your worst. With my blessing. But at least give her time to prove herself." He looked at Jack in the pale light available. She was huddled on the ground, head on the grass. "Is she out?"

"She appears to be. If she wakes up possessed by blood craving, we may not be able to control her." Still he waited. Finally, he turned the silhouette of his head. "I thought the child was dead."

Felix couldn't find a pulse on the collapsed girl's neck. He fumbled at her wrist, wincing at the torn flesh there. One bump, maybe imagined, brushed his fingers. A long moment, then another tiny pulsation.

"Not dead, no. We need Maggie's knowledge. She's the witch who created them. She knows more than I do about borrowed time."

The inquisitor bent his head, and over the crashing and crackling of the flames Felix could hear the screeching of wheels and sirens at the front of the church. Then Felix caught the murmur of prayer, the Latin words soft, pleading with an unseen authority. Felix held his breath. Finally the man lifted his head, his eyes glittering in the distant light.

"I will help you. But, if at any moment, she turns—"

"If she turns into what that woman was, I'll kill her myself." Felix gathered Sadie into his arms and lifted her up, staggering a little onto the gravel path. "Come on, the fire department will be here any minute."

Chapter 61

In my own country, the German school of
swordsmanship is the technique of our grandfathers.
I was taught Italian styles, and holding a bastard
weapon, a hand-and-a-half sword like a bladed
crucifix, was foreign to me. I recalled what I could of
Thomas Kelley when he chided me upon my earliest
battles with my cousin John. Attack at two lengths,
cut up against a blow, plant feet apart. Rather a
bastard sword than no sword, I say.

—Edward Kelley
   Date not recorded, believed to be mid-December 1585
   Csejte Castle

JÁNOS LED THE WAY ACROSS THE DUNGEON INTO THE CAVE, while Miklós handed me a sword. I am not completely ignorant of the art of swordsmanship—I was considered a nimble fighter in my youth—but I have never carried arms in earnest. I am certain Dee would have been even less useful, and they must have agreed as they burdened the old man with several of the leather bags.

The hilt was rough in my hand, the blade too long and heavy for comfort, and I resolved to use it only in defense. I followed Miklós's handful of grim-faced, hooded warriors ahead of Dee, and a group of Konrad's guards, one already injured. This man spoke to another in German. Perhaps he thought I would not understand.

"We go to our deaths," he said, his voice shaking.

He was a young man, less than twenty, I thought.

"To everlasting life, then," replied an older companion, clapping a fatherly hand upon the first's shoulder. This inspired no confidence in me as I struggled through the cave under the weight of the massive sword. In a far corner, the alcove that seemed to be used for storage was already being cleared out, and bundles of rusting armor were flung to the floor. Behind was a wooden panel, which, with the hammering of János's sword hilt, yielded to reveal a small doorway, barely wide enough for a man to squeeze through.

Miklós turned to address us in Latin.

"We go stealthily. No rattles, no stamping. We have surprise to aid us. Lord János's men are within the yard, to the left, they will smite only with the flat of the blade. Do not harm them. Nádasdy's troops are far more dangerous; they wear the bearskins. We have fed them much ale and wine, so we may have a small advantage." He paused for a moment, looking at the dark shapes before him. "Do not let them get to their horses. Once they are mounted we can never defeat them. I have arranged a diversion. Remember: stay left, head for the postern gate and kill anyone in a bearskin."

Shudders spread through me and I was filled with a sense of cold. The first group slid through the dark entryway, lit by a stinking tallow candle. Dee was handed another to light our way. I saw his face then, not the gentle scholar I knew so well, but the face of a determined and strong man, rich with experience.

"Onward, Edward," he said in English, with the light of battle in his eyes. "Onward, for God and St. George!" Then he smiled, and despite the uselessness of his words, I felt cheered.

The floor of the tunnel was roughly stepped, and I staggered and tripped at first. It led into the back of a stable, the horses gone, the mire stinking. The main gates were open, and men shouted outside as they attempted to recapture the horses, I suppose, that they released before the ritual. Miklós beckoned to Konrad, visible because of his height, and they crept to the stable doors. Miklós waved us on, and we ran forward. I followed my escort, emboldened by Dee's words, and raised my sword for protection.

The battle was confusing, and fast. Men grunted and heaved, sword against sword, and pushed shoulders into their opponents. Many buckled easily under the strain—János's troops, I presumed. For me, it was one blow after another. A buffet from a cudgel knocked me to my knees, a sword flashed in the light of a brazier toward my face. It was slashed away by Konrad's blade, his cloak swinging back from a polished breastplate over his robes. As I staggered to my feet my hood fell into my eyes, and when I raised my left hand, the flat of a sword caught my wrist with a blow I feared had cracked it. I howled in pain, and much by instinct, managed to parry another blow from one of the bearskinned Magyars, now pouring into the yard. The next strike would have sliced me in two if one of Konrad's men hadn't cannoned into me, and taken a cut that hacked his arm almost from his body. He did not hesitate, but threw himself into his attacker, his dying energy knocking the Magyar to the ground. Konrad, my guardian, dispatched him.

I followed the inquisitor, hoping that Dee was behind me, as we slipped past the mêlée to a small gate hidden beside the guard tower. A roar of shouts seemed to be chasing us, yet when I turned to see my fellow fighters, they seemed to have detached themselves from the battle outside.

János's voice reached me, still filled with some wry laughter. "The peasants have come to reclaim their daughters. We sent spies to tell them the countess will drain their blood."

I saw that we were down to Dee and me, Lord János, a

hooded man of János's, three of Konrad's soldiers and the inquisitor himself. János looked out of the gate, watching the riot outside.

"Come," he said, and slid out of the gate into the shadow of the wall. I followed, with Konrad's sword hand in the small of my back, urging me on.

The scene was hellish, the peasants armed with tools and sticks, the Magyars with swords and pikes, the scene lit by long torches carried by the invaders. As I watched, a screaming woman, her anguished face contorted with hate, reached a soldier with a flail and whipped it cruelly about his head. His sword ran under the tool and pierced her in what, with horror, I realized was a pregnant belly. He fell to the pitchfork of another woman, and I saw a soldier stabbed by a man with long white hair. Another bearskin screamed as a torch was thrust into his face, setting his cloak and beard ablaze. The peasants outnumbered the soldiers, and at a snapped order, the troops fell back into the main gateway.

I watched no more, dragged along with the group, away from the peasants. They would no doubt have killed us, had they seen us. János led us into a shallow moat filled with a foot of mud but at least no water, and we crept through the shadows, out of sight of the main gates. I staggered up the slope out of the ditch, finding support from Konrad's strong hand.

"Well done," he said, and I heard the smile in his voice.

As we stepped through the trees, a crack of a twig to my right made me swing around, my mouth open to cry an alarm. A hand clamped upon my face and swung me off my feet. A dagger's bite crept along my throat, but a murmur from János stilled the blade. A few dark shapes materialized out of the trees, the faintest hint of dawn tinting the sky. Horses, maybe a dozen, were tethered under the trees, and their warm breath surrounded me as I was shoved toward them.

Konrad threw his leg over one, as if he had flown onto its

back. I leaned on the nearest mount, fumbling for stirrups, then climbed into one of the high saddles. A strong hand grasped my bridle, and dragged my animal into a canter. No longer able to disguise the sound of the hooves, we came upon the mob at the main gates, and they turned for a moment toward us. Then a roar of words were thrown at us, one of which I'm sure was *czarownica*, the local word for witch. As we rode them down, slashing and smashing our swords against the peasants, I saw the faces of servants, people who had served me food, brought me clean linens, even the old woman who had bathed me. Their faces were twisted with hate and madness. In a few hoof beats, they were behind us and we were on the road, our horses toiling beneath us.

Chapter 62

A S THE INQUISITOR OPENED THE CAR DOOR, THE LIGHT showed the full extent of his injuries. His face was a mass of bruises, he favored one shoulder and dragged one foot. The front of his chest was soaked in blood. He helped Felix place Sadie on the backseat and they returned for Jack.

She hadn't moved, and Felix realized she had passed out. Her pulse was strong—maybe too strong, leaping under his fingers. McNamara helped Felix lift Jack, and directed him to lay her in the trunk. As he placed her in the car, Felix realized it was decorated with the sigils, top and bottom. It was also filled with chains and cuffs anchored to the metal of the floor.

"You aren't going to . . ." Felix watched as Jack groaned, rolled her head to one side, as if she were waking up.

"It's a precaution. See to the child."

Felix left Jack reluctantly, leaving McNamara to secure her. Sadie sighed when he touched her, and he covered her with a coat he found on the backseat.

He shut the door, and came around to look at Jack, shackled in the trunk like a wild animal. She was still out.

"Is that really necessary?"

"Yes." The man's voice was cool, convincing. Nevertheless, he reached around Jack to pull out a tarpaulin and cover her body. He added a jacket, wrapping it around her. "She is very cold, and in shock."

"She's resilient." Felix brushed his hand through his hair

and was surprised to find it was still wet. It was raining gently around them.

McNamara shook his head as he shut the trunk with a heavy click. "She was dying. They slow down, they run out of vital force as the years pass. She probably had a couple of years left at best. Twenty years is about the maximum most of them last, some much less."

"And now?" The man wouldn't meet his gaze.

"Now—she is something else. Something I have pledged my life to eliminate."

Felix held out his hand. "Give me the keys. You're in no condition to drive."

For a moment, McNamara looked down at him, then handed them over. He limped around the car, and slumped in the passenger seat. He collapsed against the seat and groaned.

"Was that really *the* Elizabeth Báthory?" The car purred into life, and Felix eased through the northern gate and onto the road as a police car, lights blazing, tore past in a shower of gravel toward the chapel.

McNamara rolled his head toward Felix and sighed. "That is what she became. We've been following her progress for more than four hundred years. She's killed hundreds of girls and left thousands half dead."

"We. You mean, the Inquisition." It still sounded strange to Felix.

"Yes, the Inquisition. I know you are emotionally involved with these women, but surely, seeing what they are must make you realize we can't perpetuate their unnatural existence."

"Or what?" Felix braked a little hard, hearing McNamara groan as he was thrown forward in the seat. "Sorry. Maybe you are right, and neither should have been saved. But here they are. They have feelings, and memories, and I can't just put them down like rabid dogs."

"I can't work . . . with witches and revenants." McNamara's voice was weaker. Felix looked at him. His face was pale, his eyes closed.

"Maybe I should drop you at a hospital."

"No! No, I will be fine." He winced. "I've been worse. And this time, we won."

Felix drove toward his house, listening for the sound that one of them was waking. McNamara leaned back several times to feel Sadie's pulse, but apart from confirming she was alive, said nothing else.

A car was in the drive already, and as he parked behind it, Charley ran out of the porch.

"Where's Jack?" She raced past him to wrench open the back door, and uncovered the unconscious girl. "Sadie!"

"Jack's in the trunk." Felix struggled out of his seat, feeling pulled muscles and bruises.

Charley stared at him, her face paled. "What—?"

"She's still alive," he added, then stalled as he tried to explain what had happened.

"Mum!" Charley called.

Felix looked back at the porch, to see the older woman, arm in a sling, watching him. "They're alive," he said.

"Bring them in, then." Maggie's eyes were on the inquisitor, silent and still in the passenger seat. "What about him? Is he dead?"

"He's injured. I hoped you would be able to help him." Felix reached into the car to lift the girl in his arms. She moaned, and he carried her into the house to lay her on the blanket someone had placed in the center of the circle.

When he returned, McNamara was standing, leaning against the porch, Maggie beside him. She turned to Felix, her face angry.

"He won't unlock the trunk."

"You won't like what's in there." McNamara was swaying against the wall. "That's not your friend anymore. I have to go."

Felix slid an arm around his waist and a shoulder under his good arm. "Come in, man, before you collapse. Maggie. Maggie!"

She turned her face toward Felix. "But Jack . . ."

"She'll be fine for another minute. Help me with McNamara, and then I'll bring Jack in."

Reluctantly, she stepped over to McNamara, and then her face changed as the light from the porch fell on him.

"Good God, what happened to you?" As they half dragged the injured man through the doorway, the light shone on an expanse of blood drenching his shirt, and soaking through his jacket. They propped him in a kitchen chair and Maggie grabbed a tea towel, pressing it to his chest. "Get Jack. I'll look after him."

Felix patted McNamara's pockets, coming up with a small set of keys. The man made one weak effort to speak, but Felix ignored him, and walked back down the drive, the muscles in his legs shaking with tiredness. Despite his show of confidence, he hesitated when he laid his hand on the trunk of the car.

The memory of Elizabeth Báthory—or the monster that inhabited her mortal remains, anyway—rose in his mind. He turned the key in the lock, to find Jack much as he'd left her, collapsed and shackled. As he bent forward to unlock the first handcuff, around her arm, she didn't move. He leaned across her to do the other one, and as his face came within a foot of hers, he glanced down. Her eyes were open, gazing at him steadily. He froze.

"Kill me." She breathed, so soft he wondered if he had imagined it. "Kill me," she repeated, louder, then cleared her throat and licked her lips. She grimaced.

"No." He unshackled her ankles, and reached for her. She put a hand against his chest, holding him at bay.

"You saw . . . you saw it. What I will become."

"You are nothing like her. You never were."

"I felt it. I felt the power of it. I don't know if I can handle that." Her hand wavered, and he put his arms under her shoulders and knees to lift her out, wondering if he had the strength left. "Felix, please . . ."

The tears in her eyes almost undid him, and for a moment he felt the weight of her in his arms before leaning back, pulling her out of the car. She cried out with pain from one of what must, he thought, be many injuries. One hand clutched the front of his jacket as he set her on her feet. He stood for a moment in the predawn cold, holding her as she shuddered against him.

"Listen to me," he said urgently, while he held her. "We've survived this far, we've defeated something that people have been trying to kill for four hundred years. I know who you are, Jack. I know your compassion, your courage . . ."

"I'm all right. You can let me go." She pushed against his chest, and after a moment, he let her stagger back half a pace. She'd lost a boot in the battle, and he winced in sympathy as she set her shoeless foot on the cold concrete of the path. Then she reached up for him, and he leaned down, and they kissed. Her lips were icy, but warmed under his. He imagined she still tasted of the coppery rust of his blood. They supported each other as they limped toward the house.

Charley seemed to have used stable tactics on the chilled Sadie, rubbing her down with the blanket and towel like a wet pony, and wrapping her in duvets to keep warm. The teenager was as silent and pale as the very first night, her sporadic breaths hissing.

Felix bent over the girl. "Will she survive?"

Charley shrugged. "I don't know. We've never seen anything like this. It's as if she's hibernating."

Jack knelt beside her, and took Sadie's hand. "She tried to fight the witch." Her hands were shaking as she looked up at Felix. "She lost so much blood. I can't believe what that woman did to her."

Charley crouched down beside Jack and wrapped her arms around Sadie. "She's still alive, just about. We have to warm her up." She looked up at Felix, then back at Jack, her eyes wide with curiosity. "Mum's brewing some potion now."

Felix left them together. He entered the kitchen, which was steamed up with aromatic herbs, to find Maggie working fast and efficiently on the injured man. She had his shirt off, revealing cuts and bruises that were developing in purple blotches. A piece of bloodied wood, the size and sharpness of a knife blade, lay on the table.

"I took that out of his chest," she said. "He's nicked a vein rather than an artery or he'd be long dead." She eyed Felix. "But he's lost a lot of blood. I think he has fractured ribs, a collapsed lung, maybe a concussion. He needs to be in a hospital."

McNamara opened his eyes. "We have our own doctors." He leaned back in the chair, fighting for breath.

"Can the Inquisition do anything for Sadie?" Felix met Maggie's eyes for a moment, then looked back at the other man. "Do they have any knowledge of this?"

"Even if they do, it's policy to release all the undead."

Maggie snorted. "Release." She peeled the paper off a large white dressing and stuck it to the ragged wound in the man's side. "The right spell from me and we could release you." She relented. "That's stopped bleeding, for now, but it needs proper cleaning and stitching. There's only so much a healing spell can do."

The man was silent for a long time. "If they thought I had helped Sadie I would be impeached. Maybe executed."

Felix could feel his fingernails cutting into his palms. "Even if she helped destroy a monster who has been preying on people for hundreds of years?"

"Creating another such as Báthory will never be condoned." McNamara sighed, coughed, then bent over, hugging his side with one bandaged arm. "If I make a full report, the whole department will come after Sadie and Jack."

"You don't know that Elizabeth Báthory was a borrowed timer." Felix reached his hands out for emphasis. "I read the account Edward Kelley wrote. Báthory was a third-generation survivor of this ritual, and she used all sorts of sorcery and necromancy to stay alive. One part of which was draining the blood of innocent girls. Jack and Sadie have never done anything like that."

"Until now." McNamara looked up at Maggie. "Surely you understand? Your friend is on the same path as the countess. She took blood."

Maggie frowned. "What?"

McNamara reached up one hand, touched her wrist for a moment. "Your friend Jack drank his blood. It gave her great energy, but it turned her. She's already infected." He twisted his mouth into a grimace, something between sympathy and contempt. "This isn't a harmless bit of spellcraft, witch. This is an abomination against God."

Maggie's hands trembled as she pulled away from McNamara. She glanced up at Felix, her eyes hard. He nodded back.

"Whatever your beliefs, you were there. Jack released the elemental. Jack killed her." Felix kept his voice calm.

The inquisitor shut his eyes, lying back in the chair. "Báthory's own pride killed her. She was arrogant enough to think she could control the heat of life itself." He looked at Felix. "I need to go somewhere safe, where my colleagues can collect me."

"Now you've killed Báthory, what will you do?"

"I've learned a lot," the man said, wincing as he moved in the chair. "There are others, some almost as old and just as dangerous. My work is just beginning."

"Others?" Felix met Maggie's eyes. "Will they come after Jack or Sadie?"

Finally the man smiled with genuine warmth. "I will do everything I can to make certain they don't."

Chapter 63

The Transylvanian nobles pride themselves upon their hunts, when they ride out upon sure-footed horses barely larger than the giant wolfhounds they breed, and sport in the great forests for days, sometimes feasting upon the animals they slay, and sleeping under shelters formed of cut pine branches. And servants follow with furs and wines, that all may be as comfortable as in their own castles.

—Sir Jerome Bowes
  *Travels in Russia, Poland, Hungary
  and the East* (1584)
  British Library

WE RACED, IN SINGLE FILE, THROUGH TREES AND BRUSH, disturbing the shapes of bison and deer as we traversed the forest in the palest of dawn light. Under the shadow of thickets, my horse breasted mounds of pine needles, stumbled on tree roots and slipped on muddy tracks. I watched as one of the guards was flung off as his mount crashed forward, its leg twisted under itself as it landed on its nose. The guard limped over toward us, swung his leg over the spare horse Konrad was dragging along by its bridle, and carried on. On we raced, away from the pink of dawn, from one shadowy copse to another, forcing our wretched horses through chest-high ferns and thorns. When we pulled up, they were panting, and the men bent over their withers to rest.

Konrad spurred his horse, shocking it into a trot in my direction. "Can you hear anything?"

I sat, listening to the forest, the jingling of bridles and bits, the creaking of leather, the breath whistling in my own throat . . . and the beat of hooves on the ground, several, sweeping around us.

"We are followed," I wheezed, then smothered a cough.

"Then onward! We stand little chance in battle." Konrad waved us on, and Lord János, the side of his gray steed stained with blood, took the lead. We journeyed on, the ground falling away gently at first, then steeper, until the horses were struggling to keep their footing. At the bottom of the slope a muddy river, quite shallow, had to be forded. Then up the bank, slipping again, two riders dismounted but no one hurt, my own pony as agile as a cat. Dee, who had fallen into the river, looked white-faced and exhausted as he clambered back into the saddle.

The sound, when it came to us from the pursuers, was that of a hunt, the laughter of men and women floating down to us. We fought with tired horses, onward, pulling them up when their heads fell to their knees. We goaded them over the next rise, through the boughs of a fallen tree and between great rocks. Past my shoulder, I glimpsed a flash of crimson, and renewed my flailing of my poor mount. Another figure, this one a deeper red, caught sight of through branches, then the baying of questing hounds. The dogs were dark shapes sliding through trees, clearing obstacles, their scarlet tongues lolling.

Lord János rounded the next outcrop of trees, and pulled his gray back onto its haunches. Other mounts crashed into his, the riders panting and shouting, as I dragged my own animal up. I saw dogs between the horses' legs, and arrows hissing through the air, thudding into the men. I saw one, two men fall, then János, an arrow in his throat, his eyes bulging and the blood pumping from him, even as he slid from his saddle.

I turned to see a way behind us, but already there were three Magyar riders in furs holding short bows, their sights upon us. Konrad had his sword upraised, an arrow protruding from his other shoulder, buried almost up to the flights in his body.

"Hold!" he called, and stood in his stirrups to bellow with all the authority a knight of the Holy Roman Empire can muster. "Who attacks the Pope's own soldiers?"

The first thing I saw of their leader was the scarlet cloak, then the ornate riding boots on slim, boyish legs, and finally the mass of hair rolling down her—for it was a woman's—shoulders. She ignored Konrad and looked at me. "Don't you recognize me, Master Kelley?"

Her voice was filled with warmth and strength, ringing across the forest like a bell. I had not at first, her cheeks rounded and pink with the ride and the cold air, her lips reddened with exercise.

"My lady?" I was astonished, as she urged her horse nearer to me.

"It worked, I am restored." She lifted her face up to the pinking dawn light, her eyes shut with greedy pleasure. "Ah, to be strong again, to be young."

She looked at me, her eyes intense, and her mouth curved in a smile. Her horse sidled, tossing his head and fidgeting as if he were nervous because of the Diana upon his back. "Stay, Edward. Together we may find much more about sorcery, and your alchemy."

"I cannot, my lady," I stammered.

"Then you will go with Konrad to face the Inquisition? An Englishman in Rome?" Her voice was full of laughter. "Better damned with us in luxury than redeemed by the torments of the Church."

I stared, anguished, at Konrad, then at Dee, both grave-faced. I gathered my courage. "I must live my conscience, my lady Erzsébet."

"Then go, for you cannot harm us now." She smiled, and her beauty was indeed wondrous, despite the evil that had formed her. Then, in a voice meant only for me, she leaned forward and murmured: "Go, Edward. But remember me as *Saraquel*."

Chapter 64

FELIX RECEIVED A CALL FROM THE POLICE, JUST AFTER dawn. Having cleaned up his own bruises, he went down to the chapel to meet Soames. Fire engines were parked all over the building site, one still playing a jet of water into the ruins. Police were everywhere. In daylight, Felix could see the extent of the place, a three-winged Victorian gothic hospital with the name of "Asylum of St. Francis" inset in terra-cotta tiles over the main door.

"Sorry to get you out so early, Professor. But we seem to have strange markings all over this scene."

Felix tried to look as if he had never been in the area before, but a feeling of evil and death made him shiver inside his jacket. "Was it arson?"

"We're not sure. There's no immediate evidence of accelerants, but the damage to the body was severe. Extreme, really, almost a complete cremation, like a gas leak or an industrial accident."

"There was a death?"

Soames took his arm and pulled him to one side. Felix could see a small crowd of people watching, being kept back by crime-scene tape and a couple of officers. One woman was sobbing in the arms of a female officer.

"The mother's turned up. We have been looking for a girl, Sadie Williams. The remains may be hers."

Felix wrapped his arms around himself. "So, how can I help?"

Soames pulled out his mobile phone. "I'll get you clearer pictures, but we found these on the floor of the chapel."

Squinting at the small screen, Felix could see charred and incomplete sigils, but recognized the fire elemental's summoning circle.

Soames looked at the phone himself. "It's a hell of a co-incidence that two girls have ended up dead around these drawings."

Felix squinted at them, then shook his head. "I'll need to examine them more closely, of course, but these are quite different from the Dee symbols found on the girl on the train." He shrugged, handing back the phone. "It's possible they are just a craze, maybe something to do with a band or a social-networking phenomenon. If this girl ran away from home, maybe she was squatting here."

"Maybe. Forensics is looking into a gas explosion, or some sort of fire following an attempt to heat the chapel or cook food. We'll know better when the building is safe. Most of the roof has already come down, but the rooms at the back are still smoldering, and unstable." He met Felix's eyes. "I was hoping you could slip a quick report regarding these markings in with your other report, keep department costs down."

"Well, I don't see why not. Tragic case, sad. I'll get a couple of my students on it. There may be a whole world of occult-like markings raging over the Internet that no one over the age of twenty would even think to look into."

He turned to go, then looked back to the police officer. Soames was watching the sobbing mother with a grimace on his face.

Felix lowered his voice. "I was wondering. How do you know it was the Williams girl?"

"We don't, but we have DNA," answered Soames. "Blood and tissue were retrieved at the scene. A preliminary blood-group match, and height and weight estimates, say it's likely to be the girl. It'll take days to confirm it, of course, the remains are badly degraded by heat. There's very little left of the body, even the teeth." He sighed. "Poor kid. She wasn't even fifteen."

Felix walked through the small crowd to his car, parked behind ranks of police vehicles. As he opened the door, he heard a voice behind him.

"Wait!"

"Excuse me?"

He turned, to see a short woman with red hair and Sadie's heart-shaped face. Her eyes were bloodshot and her face puffy with crying. "Have you seen—did you see the body?"

"No, I'm sorry."

"I just need to know, if it's her. My daughter, Sadie."

"I'm really sorry," he said. "I can't comment. You'll have to talk to DI Soames."

"They won't tell me anything." She gulped, sniffing back more tears. "I just want to know if she suffered."

"I'm sure whoever that is in there didn't suffer." It was the best he could do. "They think it must have been instant, as far as I can tell. Please, go with the officer."

She wrenched herself out of the hold of the policewoman, and grasped his arm. "And the other girl, the one on the train. Was she hurt, was she abused?"

He laid his fingers over her small hand, so like Sadie's. "I can assure you that the other girl was well cared for, and had a very gentle death. I have no reason to think that she was abused in any way." This had the virtue of being true, he thought, but seeing the woman dissolve into wrenching sobs in the arms of the policewoman was still painful.

As he drove away, he could feel the sting of guilt at keeping her child's survival from her. Although, as Sadie had not improved overnight, survival did seem a relative term.

Chapter 65

JACK BRUSHED THE HAIR OFF HER FACE AS SHE SIPPED THE coffee and ate a biscuit. The organic, fair-trade café had a few customers lost in their morning papers or taking advantage of the Wi-Fi. Pierce looked less scruffy than usual, but the waitress still had a pained look on her face as she took his order. He sat opposite Jack, his jaw moving, as if he were practicing what to say.

"Have a cookie, Pierce," Jack said, pushing the plate over. She was too tired, too emotionally numb, to worry about his games.

He took one, frowned at it as if it might be a trap.

"Just eat it." She sighed, sipped more of her coffee and looked out of the window at the Christmas shoppers bustling by.

"The kid in the chapel, that was the girl they wanted?"

She shrugged. "That's all over now."

"I lost money, big time. This better not be hexed." He bit into the cookie anyway.

"I don't think you would have lived to collect, honestly." She waved at the waitress to top her up, smiled thanks at her. "She was out of your league. Out of both our leagues. Old-style sorcery."

"So you said before." He nodded as the waitress brought his pot of tea. "This is all very civilized, Jackdaw. What do you want?"

"I want to know if we're still doing business." She shrugged. "I have other clients, but it's handy working with you because you're local."

He stared at her. "You don't trust me."

She started to laugh. "Trust you? I thought we had an arrangement that you would try to get my merchandise for free, as often as possible."

He grinned, baring his teeth like a terrier. "I do like our little . . . games."

Her smile faded. There was something odd about his features, as if they had been exaggerated somehow, the nose too sharp, the eyes too small, the cheekbones high and heavy under projecting brow ridges. His hands, on the cup, seemed too large for his wrists.

"What are you, really?" she breathed, and for a long moment she thought he hadn't heard her over the slurping of his tea. "Part goblin or something?" She was only half joking.

"I could ask you the same question." He flashed a look at her under bushy eyebrows. " 'Cus you ain't exactly human."

"I'm the dealer who keeps you in legitimate profit." She leaned back in her chair, watching him.

"I'm your loyal customer, buying products for my clients, all legal and aboveboard." He put his hand into his pocket and withdrew a piece of folded paper. "And they do have a bit of a shopping list."

She took the greasy note, and spread it out on the table with just her fingertips. "God, Pierce, why does it stink? Have you got a couple of ferrets in there?"

He shrugged. "Best price for a good local customer?"

Most of the items were rare herbs, easily sourced from the cottage garden, and a few animal products like bone and hair. A couple of potions devised by Maggie, one for healing and one for protection. "I don't know, a thousand?"

"A thousand?" His voice cracked with indignation. "Four hundred . . ."

It was good to be bartering with Pierce, away from the complications at the house. She let him ramble on, arguing the case item by item. She'd take six hundred, and he would pay it. She swung an amber pendulum gently under the table to check for spells, curses, hexes or traps, but for once, he seemed undefended. Here, away from the mundane world it was fun to have one foot in the magical, even as she mentally chanted the activation spell for the "speechless" cookie. His words trailed away, and he glared at her. She smiled, finished her coffee, and nodded. "Six hundred it is, then. See you, Pierce. Enjoy the other cookies, they're all fine."

She paid the bill on the way out.

Jack stretched her shoulders before tackling the stile into the copse. After a month of work, the cottage was being re-plastered and the windows restored before she and Ches could move back into it. Visiting it every day, and walking in the countryside, gave her a necessary relief from nursing Sadie. She was taking the opportunity to update the cottage's Victorian lead plumbing and the prewar wiring, so the events of the past were being exorcised by radios playing, men whistling and the smell of drying plaster and paint.

In the oak trees, a few sticks were being retrieved and re-modeled into nests. Jack put out food every day for the half dozen or so rooks that remained, and a handful of jackdaws that seemed to be keeping them company.

She delayed driving back to Felix's house each afternoon, watching Ches delight in the smells of the winter animals crisscrossing the grass. McNamara had disappeared back into his organization, and the only text from him had said he had been recalled to Rome. Báthory's remaining ashes and bones had been interred in Sadie's grave, in a ceremony attended by hundreds of well-wishers. Maggie was slower than usual but fighting for recovery. She helped nurse Sadie during each day, with Charley and Felix, if he wasn't teaching. But in the evening, when she went back to town, and Felix returned from work, there was no escaping the consequences of what they had done.

Jack whistled for Ches, and he lumbered toward her, tongue lolling from his mouth. Being so close to death seemed to have slowed him down a little. He was often found lying on the thick rug in front of Felix's open fireplace, whining until someone lit the coals. The cat had been picked up by Marianne but had returned the same day, apparently unwilling to leave the territory to the dog.

Marianne.

Jack had opened the door, a few days after the battle, still punch-drunk. She had a black eye, a yellowing bruise on the other side of her face, her short hair wet from a shower, and she was wearing old clothes of Felix's. The woman—still Felix's wife, she remembered—was taller than Jack, dark-blond hair running down onto her tailored suit. She was beautiful, and had a warm smile.

Jack had felt like a ragamuffin child, even though Marianne was far too polite to say anything, other than to inquire after the cat. She, Marianne, had kissed Felix warmly on the cheek and exclaimed at his bruises and the scratches across his neck and face. Their explanation of a car accident seemed to satisfy her, but then Felix had led her into the kitchen and closed the door on Jack. She had seen the way he looked at his wife, as if no one else existed, and it made her feel hollow inside.

So she had retired upstairs to the bedroom where the co-matose teenager lay, both arms swathed in dressings. The cuts didn't bleed, but they didn't heal either, the ugly tears in the flesh gray against red muscle underneath.

Every evening, Felix brought Jack food, failed to start a conversation, then retired to his study to work. She had become embarrassed by his presence, and by the mute unconsciousness of the girl. Finally, he had gone to the States for two weeks to teach. When he came back, it was as if they had lost the ability to talk to each other altogether.

As the weeks went on, Sadie's face was retreating, her skull advancing, as she shriveled from lack of food and drink. Roisin the seer was also a midwife and she helped them place a tube up Sadie's nose into her stomach. For a while, they infused a little water into the child, but hours later Maggie could draw it back with a syringe, so they withdrew the tube and went back to researching her condition. Jack could remember, as a child, reading about some saintly nun who fell into a trance and didn't eat or drink for years. She couldn't recall how the story ended.

As she walked up the slope into the tree line, she could feel new energy flowing through her. Sadie's sacrifice had been Jack's gain, and she had argued that perhaps her own blood could help the child, if that energy was somehow transmissible. But Felix was adamant: if Jack was infected with some dangerous contagion, at least she could fight it. His research had taken him to websites and groups all over the world. Maggie was involved in that side of it, but Jack wouldn't discuss it.

She called the dog to her side, and clipped the lead onto his harness. The walk back to the cottage was wintry, and a misting of fine rain blew into her face, but she no longer slowed down in the cold.

A beep alerted her to a message on her phone. She didn't recognize the number.

"Expert at Vatican suggests the blood that gave life could save girl. M."

Blood that gave life. Jack, for a moment, felt vindicated, maybe her own blood could be used . . . then it dawned on her. Blood that gave Sadie life. She ran back to the car.

"Mrs. Williams?" Jack didn't have to ask, the woman was the image of Sadie.

The woman pushed the door closed again without a word, but then paused. She opened it a few inches, staring past Jack at Felix.

"You're not press." Her voice was flat, as if all emotion had been burned away.

"I'm Professor Guichard, we met—"

"I remember. You were helping the police." Her eyes looked like they'd been scoured; they were swollen and raw, filling up with tears. "You know something. You know who killed my daughter. The police say it was an accident, but I know she wouldn't . . ."

Felix hesitated, looking at Jack.

She reached out a hand, caught one of the woman's. "Mrs. Williams, we need to show you something. We think it will make you feel better. But we can't let the press catch even a hint of this." *Or the police.* "Can you come with us? Would anyone be surprised or worried if you went out for a while?"

"I can leave a note." Mrs. Williams looked at them, clearly desperate for answers. "Come in. I'll just say I needed to spend some time on my own. Let me get my coat."

While she went off, Jack and Felix followed her in. The second-floor flat was a mess, a bottle of vodka open in the living room, papers all over the floor. Photographs of Sadie covered every inch of the windowsill, with vases that scented the room with the bitterness of decaying flowers.

"Tell me. Just tell me." The woman stared at Jack, clutching a coat in fuchsia pink, making her complexion seem more sallow.

"You need to meet someone."

"Someone who knows what happened to my Sadie?"

Felix's voice rumbled over Jack's shoulder. "Please, Mrs. Williams—"

"Angela."

"Angela. Can you trust us for a little while? I promise what we have to tell you won't make you feel worse, and may help."

They preceded her from the flat onto the landing, and Jack led the way down two flights of stairs. She could hear Felix talking to Angela, about Sadie's childhood, gentle, comforting questions. He was a gentle, comforting man, and Jack wanted . . . what? She was afraid to think about it.

Angela sat in the back while Jack drove, but she was aware of the eyes staring around the inside of the car as she turned into the main road for Felix's house. Driving the repaired Volvo, she had forgotten about the sigils on the underside of the roof, recently reapplied. The woman's eyes were wide, darting everywhere.

"What is this? Who are you?" The woman's voice was panicked, and Jack could see her hand fumbling for the door lock.

"Please, Angela, it isn't far. I promise you are safe." Felix rummaged in his pocket, and opened his wallet. "Here. This is my ID from the university. I promise that however strange this seems, we mean you no harm."

Angela sat back in her seat, staring out of the window. After a long moment she studied the card, then handed it back. "Here. I don't care anyway. No one can make me feel worse than I do now." She sighed. "God, I need a drink."

They pulled up in the drive behind Felix's car. Maggie's was parked farther down the road. The neighbors had put a Christmas tree in their bay window; the lights flickered in incongruous gaiety.

Maggie met them at the door in a soft pink sweater, a smile on her lips that widened when she saw Angela.

"Mrs. Williams. Thank you so much for coming." She stood back. "Please come inside. You must be wondering why we asked you here."

Angela looked around the street one more time, before following Maggie into the kitchen, which smelled of something baking and hot coffee. She sat on a chair, knees together. Her knuckles paled as she clenched her hands on her bag.

Maggie offered her a hot drink and she asked for tea.

Jack sat down in a chair opposite her. "Angela." She took a deep breath, looking up at Felix for a moment. "I met your daughter, after she went missing."

"You saw her?"

"She didn't run away, you know that? She was ill, she was drunk."

"My Sadie didn't drink—she wasn't that kind of girl." Her words were more certain than her voice.

"I'm afraid her friends had vodka and cider. She went to the bus stop to go home, but she was so intoxicated, she was vomiting and choking. That's when I found her."

"You found her? Why didn't you get an ambulance?"

Jack adjusted the truth. "I'm afraid I was too late. Sadie couldn't be saved. Not by medicine."

"She was dead? But . . . why didn't you call the police?"

Jack sighed. "Angela, this is going to sound impossible, but I want you to come upstairs with me. We have to show you something."

Angela stood. "I want to go home now." She was shaking, her hands trembling on the cheap leather of the bag. "Let me out."

"We need you to save Sadie."

The words floated around Angela, binding her with their impossible conundrum. Finally, she managed to spit out a few words.

"My daughter is dead, she was burned up."

"No. That wasn't Sadie. That was a woman named Elizabeth Bachmeier."

Hope flared in Angela's eyes, and her body shook as if she had taken a blow. "You said she died."

"Not quite. I said Sadie couldn't be saved by medicine. She was helped by something else." She paused, watched hope and fear battle across Angela's face. "Sadie is hovering between life and death. We can't save her without your help."

Angela stumbled back in the room, toward the garden doors. "You're insane."

"She's upstairs. Sadie is in the back bedroom upstairs." Jack watched Angela heave a breath as if she were in a race.

Maggie stretched out a hand. "Please, Angela. We're so sorry to frighten you, and this must all sound insane. But your daughter is upstairs and you are the only hope she has."

No one was close enough to catch Angela as she folded onto the floor.

Chapter 66

THE DEEP NIGHT WAS A TIME JACK HAD ALWAYS ENJOYED. Needing less sleep than a normal person, she had often walked through the local woods with Ches or wandered over the heath until a summer dawn. Now, with more energy, she took the night shift in nursing Sadie, turning her, checking on her. It became a simple ritual, and as her hands smoothed the hair away from the girl's face she wished she could infuse Sadie with some of her own new vitality. It had been more than a month since the fire.

The cat had made the bed a dog-free zone, and stretched out under Jack's hand. A noise on the landing made her look up, to see Felix, in T-shirt and pajama trousers, looking in the door.

"I thought I heard something . . ." he mumbled, his voice still rough with sleep. "Are you OK?"

She turned back to Sadie, and straightened the sheet folded under her chin. *No sleeping person lies this still.*

She felt, rather than heard, the movement of air as Felix came in and settled in the chair behind her.

"Do you need anything?" He yawned, making the cat stop purring for a moment.

Jack opened her mouth, but then shut it again. *What do you say? Where are we, you and I?* Instead, she leaned back in her chair, crossing her arms over her chest as if to keep the feelings in.

"Jack . . ." His voice was soft.

"What did Marianne want? When she came, last month?"

"The decree nisi. The last bit of the divorce. She just wanted to give me the paperwork."

"She was crying when she left." Jack's words echoed in the room, clear and hard.

"She was. I was. It's a sad thing, when love goes. She will always be an old friend, and my first love." The word hung in the air.

Sadie sighed, a small breath that didn't change her face. She breathed so slowly now it was easy to think her cooling body was already dead.

"Has there been any more change since we gave her Angela's blood?" asked Felix.

"She moves in her sleep, sometimes. But she seems to be slipping back again, getting weaker."

"Jack . . . we need time to—"

She cut him short with a slash of her hand. "Go back to bed."

"Jack." There was a note of yearning in his voice that made her turn toward him. His face, in the glow of the night light, looked twisted with all the things he needed to say. "I know things have been difficult with Sadie."

"I may not even be human, do you know that?" She looked at him, his uneven features, his bright eyes. "You saw what Báthory became. I drank your blood, Felix, and I liked it. It's the most alive I've ever felt. That blood pouring into me, the feeling of it—I want that, all the time. I crave it."

He moved closer. "Then take it. Take me."

His eyes trailed down her face to her lips, and to the open neck of her shirt. She leaned forward.

Kissing him was like drinking after a dry day. She leaned into him, hungry for the contact, his warmth. His hands pulled her toward him and out of the chair until they were locked together.

"Jack . . ." His voice made her shiver. This was what she wanted, this is what she craved. She kissed him again.

Another sigh whispered through the room, from the sleeping girl. She turned her head to listen, and now she could feel something underneath her body's need. Blood. His skin so close, so warm, smelling of soap and sleep and filled with warm, salty energy . . . she bared her teeth.

He stepped back, his hand pushing her away. "Jack, I spoke to Stephen McNamara. He thinks blood is like an addiction, like a drug." His breathing was ragged, and the roaring in her ears half drowned him out. "You can fight it."

She couldn't speak for the need to rip open a vein: his, Sadie's, anyone's.

She shook her head, trying to clear it. "He's right," she managed to whisper. "It is an addiction. You're like heroin to me. I need to stay away from you."

"Over time, it will get easier."

"Go. Go away, now." She turned back to the sleeping girl, and heard his footsteps across the hall. *Damn it.*

She could smell something sour, and lifted the covers. One consequence of Sadie's mother's blood, transfused into Sadie's veins a week ago, was that her kidneys had started to operate again. She put on the nearest lamp, and started to pull the sheet and quilt down the bed. Sadie exhaled, and opened her eyes.

Jack froze, looking at her, meeting her gaze. "Well, there you are."

Sadie's blue eyes wavered around the room, and she licked her lips with a dry-looking tongue. "D . . . drink?" she rasped.

Jack poured a little water, and lifted her up. Sadie's weak hand wobbled to the cup and tipped it back.

"More."

Jack obliged, giving her as much as she wanted. When the hand fell back, she lowered the teenager onto the pillows.

"The countess?"

"Dead."

Sadie nodded, her eyelids drooping as if exhausted. Then

she opened her eyes wide. "I dreamt my mum was here. With Felix and you."

Jack lifted her hand and held it. It was warmer now, as if waking had revived her body as well. "You were very ill. You remember what happened with the countess?"

Sadie didn't answer, but the horror in her eyes said that she did. She pulled her fingers from Jack's, and touched one of the bandages on her own arm.

Jack was filling up with emotion that somehow brought tears along with a smile. "McNamara did some research. He found out that you needed a transfusion from the person who gave you life."

"You?"

"No, your mother. She's been here for the last few days. She's asleep downstairs. I'll go and get her."

"Wait." Sadie's face was tight, Jack couldn't read her. She struggled to sit up. "Does she know what I am . . . what we are?"

"I'm not sure she entirely understands, but, yes, I think she does."

"But I can't go home. My nan, my friends . . ." Her face was anguished.

Jack reached out her hands, and Sadie hugged her with trembling arms. "We'll work something out. I promise," Jack whispered into her ear, cradling the girl, feeling the weak sobs. "I won't let you lose your family again."

Chapter 67

JACK DROVE UP THE LONG HILL, HER HEART HAMMERING IN her chest with unfamiliar energy, and a degree of nerves. The house was at the top, gray stone, four windows and a central door like an archetypal kid's drawing. It even had a chimney. It was smaller than the house Jack had grown up in, but had a good-sized garden around it, and a small red hatchback in the drive.

She pulled up opposite the sign for FURZEHILL, and wound the window down a few inches. She didn't see the woman at first. She was kneeling on the ground, dressed in jeans and a pink sweatshirt, her short hair flicked back behind her ears. She was weeding, her concentration on the small patch of ground between the path and the lawn, lost in her task.

Jack drank the sight in. Her hair was more gray than chestnut now, quite white at the front. She was trim, lighter than she remembered her, ready to hug after school and fuss over her daughter's hair before a gymkhana. She looked shorter too, though that could be because Jack was taller. Jack felt sick, her muscles froze, she couldn't breathe.

The woman suddenly noticed the stranger sitting in the car. She stood, as if to come over, but her feet stalled and she stared at Jack.

"Can I help . . . ?" Her voice drifted away as the air squeezed out of her. She stared at Jack, the color fading from her face, starting to frown.

Jack put the car into gear, and drove up the hill. She looked back in the mirror, but the view was obscured by tears.

EPILOGUE

The countess let us go, and Konrad, in his mercy, said we were worth more to the battle against evil alive than dead, and escorted us most of the way to Krakow. Upon the journey, he and Doctor Dee conferred frequently about the nature of the revenant we had created, and how Konrad could undo the sorcery.

Mistress Dee welcomed us with embraces and kisses that filled me with shame, so sisterly was her love. My stepchildren were also much relieved to see me, and I was pleased to see little Eliza presenting me with her first writings in Latin. Dee was taken with a sickness, but is now recovered, and already researching the mystery of the revenant. To our great surprise, money arrived at the house, not the many thousands we had been promised, but enough to support our future studies for a year or so.

I, though physically hearty, am jumping at shadows and racked with nightmares. I scan every court circular and handbill, lest the creature and her consort follow us to Poland.

The Countess Erzsébet Báthory, I hear, is fat with child, and her husband is back at the Turkish front. Of Zsófia, there are just rumors. Her body was left in the forest, covered in bites, drained of blood. Or she lives as a pale shadow, opening her veins for her mistress to suckle.

—EDWARD KELLEY
20 April 1586
Krakow
Private Archives of Professor Felix Guichard

HISTORICAL NOTE

WRITING A STORY rooted in the past is always a balancing act between being as grounded in the evidence as we can be, and telling an engaging and believable fiction. Dr. John Dee and Edward Kelley were extraordinary thinkers and travelers, and were in central Europe in the autumn of 1585. They did meet King Istvan Báthory (at least once, in April 1585) and his niece was really Elizabeth Báthory, the infamous murderer of young girls.

After she was found guilty of multiple murders her closest servants were executed. As a noblewoman and a Báthory, she was condemned to be imprisoned at Csejte (also called Čachtice, now in Slovakia) in 1611, where she was found dead in 1614. Her body, after local protests, was removed from the crypt of the church and has never been found. Her real story is more extraordinary than I could have imagined, and as much of the historical documents were suppressed, there is room for speculation.

With all this uncertainty about such interesting and sometimes infamous characters, I have stretched history to suit the story. If this causes any offense, I apologize.

ACKNOWLEDGMENTS

I HAVE MANY reasons to be grateful, because without the help of the people below, this book would never have been published.

Gerry Ryan of the Open College of the Arts, who taught me to trust my storytelling but to work on the craft of writing.

Diana Gittins and Morgaine Merch Lleuad were both inspiring and encouraging Open University tutors. They taught me to concentrate on the good, not the bad.

Carole Burns and my other lecturers at the University of Winchester, with special thanks to Judith Heneghan, who showed me the joy of writing fantasy.

My patient beta readers: Gilly Goldsworthy, Jenny Kline and Rachel Carter from the Open University, and Bethany Coombs and Downith Monaghan from my MA, who have been confident enough to tell me what doesn't work, as well as what does!

Debbie Taylor and the team at Mslexia, for running the novel writing competition that got the book noticed.

Charlotte Robertson, my agent, has been amazing, making the scary world of publishing seem easier. She showed the book to Michael Rowley, who polished it up with his team at Ebury and Del Rey UK. Charlotte and Michael have pushed the book into a better shape than I could have imagined.

My family, who have cajoled, read, argued and encouraged,

especially my eldest son, Carey. Without his enthusiasm and ideas this book might never have been written.

Finally, my husband, Russell, who has spent endless hours in the car listening to plot twists, characters, ideas. He has never, even once, told me to shut up. Another reason to say in public, he is the love of my life.

I thank you all.

A Reader's Guide

Introduction

When Professor Felix Guichard is called in to identify occult symbols found on the corpse of a young girl, his investigation brings him in contact with a mysterious woman, Jackdaw "Jack" Hammond. Jack guards a monumental secret—she's dead. Or she would be, were it not for magic that has artificially extended her life. But someone else knows her secret. Someone very old and very powerful, who won't rest until they've taken the magic keeping her alive. Her only hope lies in unraveling the truth of the diary of Edward Kelley, assistant to the Elizabethan alchemist John Dee, who once travelled to Krakow to investigate a dark sorcery related to the infamous Elizabeth Báthory. Together, Jack and Felix must solve a mystery centuries in the making, or die trying.

The Secrets of Life and Death blends historical fact and real human drama with elements of fantasy and horror. It will bewitch your reading group, and we hope this guide enriches your experience.

Questions and Topics for Discussion

1. Edward Kelley is a man of strong religious convictions. Do you think his faith was more of a help or a hindrance in dealing with Báthory?

2. Magic is a central focus of many of the characters' lives, yet in many cases it is a destructive force. Even when it keeps someone alive, it often does so in a way that severely restricts and weakens them. Do you think those who see magic as evil are correct?

3. In the real world, the Inquisition is often seen as emblematic of tyranny and fanaticism. Does the fact that the Inquisition in this story opposes real supernatural forces change your perception of them?

4. Characters often debate whether the life of a revenant is worth it, despite the heavy restrictions, or whether it is better to die a natural death. Which do you think is preferable? Is Maggie doing the right thing by magically extending people's lives?

5. Sadie's mother is repeatedly brought up as being desperate to find her daughter. Do you think keeping Sadie's existence a secret was the right thing to do, or should her mother have been told of her daughter's survival?

6. Jack eventually embraces forbidden magic to defeat Báthory, leading McNamara to think she herself must be corrupted. Felix argues they should give Jack the benefit of the doubt. Do you think that's a wise decision?

7. Kelley eventually learns that the angel Saraquel is, in fact, a means for Erzsébet to manipulate him. Do you think his actions were part of her plan all along?

8. Jack thinks that Pierce may not be entirely human. What do you think he really is, and do you think it's wise for Jack to continue to deal with him?

9. Kelley looks up to Dee as a wise man and valuable mentor, but in some ways Dee seems no more aware of Báthory's true nature and plans than anyone else. Do you think Kelley's trust in Dee is justified?

10. What do you think the future holds for Jack and Felix?

ABOUT THE AUTHOR

REBECCA ALEXANDER fell in love with all things sorcery and witchcraft at a young age and has enjoyed reading and writing fantasy ever since. She has worked in psychology and education, and she has an MA in creative writing. She lives with her husband and an assortment of cats and birds on the coast of England.

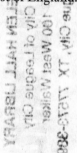